BLUE
HOURS

BLUE HOURS

HOURS

ACHESON

 ALISON

Freehand Books gratefully acknowledges
the financial support for its publishing
program provided by the Canada Council
for the Arts and the Alberta Media Fund,
and by the Government of Canada
through the Canada Book Fund.

This book is available in print and Global
Certified Accessible™ EPUB formats.

Freehand Books is located in Moh'kinsstis,
Calgary, Alberta, within Treaty 7 territory,
and on the traditional territories of the
Siksika, the Kainai, and the Piikani, as well
as the Iyarhe Nakoda and Tsuut'ina nations.

FREEHAND BOOKS
freehand-books.com

LIBRARY AND ARCHIVES CANADA
CATALOGUING IN PUBLICATION

Title: Blue hours : a novel /
  Alison Acheson.
Names: Acheson, Alison, author.
Identifiers:
  Canadiana (print) 20240519558
  Canadiana (ebook) 20240519566
  ISBN 9781990601897 (softcover)
  ISBN 9781990601903 (EPUB)
  ISBN 9781990601910 (PDF)
Subjects: LCGFT: Novels.
Classification: LCC PS8551.C32 B58
  2025 | DDC C813/.54—DC23

Edited by Naomi K. Lewis
Design by Natalie Olsen
Cover photo © kkgas/Stocksy.com
Author photo by Rex Logan
Printed and bound in Canada

FIRST PRINTING

For Bob, with love

"Three Little Birds" / *Elizabeth Mitchell*

"Casual Viewin'" / *54-40*

"Ooh La La" / *Rod Stewart*

Some days are a photograph in hand, coloured or black and white,
an image of a loved one cast in relief to a cloudy background.
Or every leaf on a tree clear, and the someone you know is cloudy.
Though even smudged, you are certain you know who it is.
Maybe they wouldn't, or couldn't, stop moving
as the shutter
clicked.

Pale early sun warmed the surface sand. Underneath was damp and grainy to Keith's bare feet. He stretched his toes, digging in to the cool. The air was clear for thought, and his mind dipped with the swallows. The earliest hours and the latest were the best of this season. The blue hour, according to Raziel. Golden, he would have said. But she was the photographer.

Morning shadows stretched to the left, and Keith's son, Charlie, turned and ran along the beach trying to catch the shadow that kept pace. His arms waved, and shadow arms waved, too. He'd understood the correlation for several years, but so long as no one laughed at him, he took pleasure in testing the hypothesis. His father wouldn't laugh, he knew. The boy finally stopped and bounced on the spot. Today the world was clean slated.

Father and son turned toward the tide pools, crossing sand patterned like child-drawn waves, pocked with air holes of creatures surviving, waiting for water to return. Did they know it would? Or hope? Or live without thought?

Charlie dug his heels deeply into his steps and turned to watch the soft spots fill with water. He tiptoed into a shallow pool, trying not to disturb, but his shadow moved in, and sparkling water shifted with ripple. He broke up the silver in the sand underwater.

The silver was fish.

Keith and Charlie bent over, looking into the pool, the water, the shimmer, the sand, the tiny tiniest fish, moving bits, broken mirror doing the butterfly. Glass fishes. Though, geographically, that couldn't be. Keith had one in an aquarium as a kid, marvelled at how he could see the guts, showed it to friends. He shared the story with Charlie, but the boy moved on, either not listening or absorbing in his child and kinetic way.

Under each fish, a shadow, darting. Keith looked to see the fish rather than the flitting shadows that drew his eyes first. He took off his sunglasses to feel the intensity of the sun. He squinted, and the fish still eluded him. He would have liked to feel one squiggle between his toes, to catch and hold. The sun played over the tops of his feet under the water.

"Spangles," he said.

"Spangles," Charlie repeated, and Keith knew he liked the sound of it.

"Spangles." They shared the single word and a smile.

Charlie picked up a piece of thin driftwood, an elaborately shaped Y with extra branching and knotted joints. "This is . . ." He tried to find the word. Keith expected the word *magic* to follow. But after a moment, loathe to give up a new find so soon, yet wanting to share, Charlie said, "You hold it," and Keith took the arthritic piece. He knew not to hand it back quickly, so he took his time, made some pretense at scrutinizing the scratchy bark that clung to parts of it. Then he did look closely at the greyed wood splitting through missing bark, and his pretense fell away. Fragility and bone and sinew were in the map-like grain. He handed it back, unsettled.

"You felt it?" Charlie's eyes sharpened in their deep blue. Or grey. They could change. "Did you?"

"It's an amazing specimen." Keith wished he felt exactly what Charlie did, but he'd have to be young again for that. "A magic wand," he offered.

Charlie's eyes shifted. "It's a stick."

"A stick," Keith repeated.

Charlie frowned. "A truth stick."

"Right," said Keith. For almost six years he'd been putting together the pieces of how his son thought.

Charlie narrowed his eyes, and Keith felt as if he'd had a mouthful of rich chocolate cake and tried to convince his son it was something else.

"You should show it to your momma when we get home." Maybe Raziel would be up now, awake, sitting on her stool in the kitchen or out on the balcony, coffee in hand. She had to start slowly, she said, to coax the day to reveal itself.

Charlie held up his stick and stared at it. "Maybe," he said. He sounded doubtful, and the hesitation made Keith wonder for a moment, and look away.

How far they'd come, so far it seemed the mountains across the water were closer than the sands of Spanish Banks.

"We should turn back."

It wasn't often he lost track of time. But this could've been an hour, or more than two. He wished the thought hadn't even come to mind.

Charlie had taken off again, this time with intent to overtake the shadow, not so long now. Maybe it seemed possible. He set off at a terrific and unsustainable pace weaving through pools and waving. Still the shadow got away. At noon it would be caught under his feet, and if he turned around, ran the other way, it would be behind him.

Still he ran.

Some days are so ordinary that it's easy to forget
they're not

I

•

Summer,
One Year Later

1

"In My Life" / *The Beatles*

"My Way" / *Shirley Bassey*

"Three Little Birds" / *Bob Marley & the Wailers*

This August day should have been on the beach, with glimpses of other summer days remembered, maybe an image of creating a shelter of driftwood, or of blinding sun in eyes. It could have been a day of hiding in the apartment with a book, wishing for air conditioning, or spent under a beech tree in the park. Instead it was the day to commemorate Raziel, a *celebration* some called it, in stark contrast to the February day Keith and Raz took vows to cherish, honour, and respect.

Keith hadn't wanted February as an anniversary month. Valentine's Day was enough. But that month, seventeen years ago, worked best with Raziel's work and travel. Then it snowed unexpectedly and filled the church parking lot with Vancouver slush. The maid of honour borrowed rubber boots to squelch through. There were no bridesmaids. "Too many dresses and to-do," said Raziel. Keith appreciated that dismissal of the fussing madness, as he saw it. Buggering off to elope would be just fine.

But in the end, the day was about acknowledging their love, having friends share food, music, dance. Raziel was centre.

For Raz, the day had to be about visuals. As must be for her soul. Everything processed through her photographer's heart, and though she'd hired a friend to shoot the day, more than once she'd taken the camera out of his hands to capture some piece that Keith knew he'd appreciate someday. If nothing else, he'd remember the sight of her, elfin and contorting to get that perfect shot. He loved her angles.

He'd hired a local band, one of his contributions to the day, who he'd reviewed for his first published work ever. He had an attachment to their unfolding — the quirky lyrics, evolving lineup, snags of sweet madness. Even then he knew the days of reviewing music were becoming historical. Really, the end had already passed, but he'd been ignoring. He'd struggled with that. Maybe he was always so behind.

Now this August day was hot, hotter than in hospice even. And held a sense of not grasping or facing reality.

The word *celebration* had puzzled Charlie. The night before he'd questioned: should they decorate? Keith started a quick *no*, but paused. "Like what?" he asked. "How would you decorate?" His son waved at the walls. "Pictures," he said. "Mommy's pictures."

Beside the shelf of family albums that Raz had insisted on sat a basket of loose photos. Family photos, and practice shots, themes of her work and interests. The decade of tree shots, bark, branches, roots, always oddly sensual. Then shots of human bodies, elbows, and other joints, Charlie's chubby toes and turns, and others' unexpected gnarls. Keith had always connected these photos with those of the trees.

His favourites were her winter images, and Charlie loved them, too. His fingerprints were on the shiny surfaces, once so heavily that Raz had taken a photograph of the prints. "What it looks like to be loved," she'd said. As a toddler, Charlie had picked up the photos and stared one by one. He would make patterns of them on the floor and walk through.

"Of course," Keith said now. "We'll decorate with the photos." He found a box of push-pins in the junk drawer, and pulled the four-rung household ladder into its climbing pyramid so Charlie could pin the images to the wall. First Charlie had to tie a pink kerchief around Old Daisy's neck to celebrate. Then the task appropriated the afternoon in a most unexpected way. After, they sat to dinner on their stools at the eating bar, the first real meal in days. They chewed, lustily at points, and talked memories and laughed.

"I wish we had cheesecake," said Charlie. Raz's favourite.

"We'll get one at the bakery next time," promised Keith.

Somehow that bit of day-before ritual eased this August day, hot and terrible for black. On the invite and posted information, Keith suggested that all should wear whatever colour came to mind with thoughts of Raziel. So as he and Charlie walked hand in hand down the aisle, their eyes were fed fuchsia and crimson, deep sunset orange, emerald green, indigo, lilac. Charlie had on most of these colours. He chose his clothes with wax-crayon thought. Keith wore the pinstriped suit Raz had picked out for him before Charlie showed up, deep blue with threads of purple. He remembered her voice: "You've got to see this," and then her eyes on him when he came out of the store changeroom, desiring, proud, possessive. In this suit she might be with him in the way he needed today. Yesterday the photos, today the suit. Each day would need some piece to find, to wrap up in.

The sensation of walking down the long sloped aisle, of being surrounded and held up by people, so many faces, every long pew filled over, hands reaching out to them, was overwhelming, but in the best way. He squeezed his son's hand, and Charlie squeezed back. He couldn't start crying, not yet, in spite of the curious physical quality to resisting tears; he'd become too familiar with that pressure, sternum and jawbones pressing.

He wished that Catalina and Eryk could walk with them. Raziel's sister and her spouse would bring more comfort than the footsteps of Miriam behind him, her mother. His own mother, gone for a decade, had come to mind through the weeks of illness. Having Miriam in the flesh, metres away, made him miss his mother more than he had in years. She'd died several years after he'd married Raziel, and several years before Charlie's birth. He regretted Charlie not knowing her.

On this day, with so many around them, there was the twoness of him and his son. Family had been small in his life as an only child. How small could it be? They were about to test.

14

But Cat, in Manitoba, had been ordered by her doctor not to travel. Already Miriam had complained that her daughters weren't there for her. Yet vulnerably pregnant seemed a solid reason for absence, and dead should be irrefutable. Not for Miriam, though, descending from London, in a pearl-grey suit probably new for the occasion. And she would see it as an occasion. She did look as if she'd gotten lost in a wedding-wear shop and wandered over.

They reached the front of the church pews, and he motioned to Charlie to slide in to the bench first, then took the space beside and wrapped an arm around those small shoulders, relieved to be in that row, where he couldn't see the eyes on him beyond the minister's and those who stepped up to the platform to speak, to share memories. Later, he would remember little of it, and forget that he'd put together the program.

His cousin Norah gave the eulogy. She spoke of how in life you can have three things: fulfilling work, a loving and lovable partner, a comfortable and welcoming home. The catch and common thought is that you can have only two of those three at any given time. But Raz, Norah said, had had all three, always, a woman who had it all.

Keith looked at Norah on the dais, and couldn't remember seeing any colour other than black on her in years. He'd always thought of her as their own-generation Patti Smith. But she must have made a trip to a vintage store to buy that red top, a deep nod indeed to Raziel.

He and Raz would have talked about it at home, after the service. "Did you see the red? So unlike her." Raz would have said, "Yes, I'm surprised." She might not have said that it truly touched her, but she would have said, "Norah looks quite seductive in red." And, "It's probably the only time we'll see that." *Would he ever stop having conversations with Raziel?*

Somebody sang. He couldn't remember asking. These long weeks had been spent getting through, followed by stretched out hours of nothingness, and now he was left with a gappiness of mind and duality of being. The singing was oddly grounding.

Keith had pulled his trousers on early in the day. In less than a month he'd shed pounds he didn't really have. He didn't expect to fill the skeletal hollowness any time soon. In the oddest way the hollow was reassuring; he'd been on Raziel's path, his body said to him, even if she'd veered off and left him on his own.

There was recorded music, too, the riffs lodging into his joints, a loosening piece. Someone from Raz's studio had added a video of her work. Next to him, Charlie sat up, suddenly attentive as her images bloomed on screen. Gratitude washed through Keith.

After, he and Charlie followed the minister back up the aisle, and he could hear the footfalls behind him, the sniffles and throat clearings. He'd never been a leader; he was the observer, the writer. Leading was Raziel's role. To have these followers placed him in a strange space.

People lined up to speak with him, to hug, to say words, with Charlie beside him. Didn't kids get sore necks, always having to look up? The line moving past was becoming the sensation of backing up the car next to a lane of traffic moving forward. Disequilibrium. At one point he wanted for everyone to go, quickly; for some giant blast of hot wind to carry away the lot, like the Mary Poppins nannies in Cherry Tree Lane, would be practically perfect.

How had that visual come to him? And the words? But these days, weeks of illness and care and crazy and dying, had worked strangely with his memories. Early days with Raz had flowed through his mind, memories not thought of for years. Of meeting. A certain dress. A look. A time of sexual connection, a first glimpse of breast, an orgasm that ended in tears. A shared joke. Snippets of misplaced conversations. Words. All pieces, nothing whole. Jolts. Hands reaching out of the dark to grab at him. What had been behind those tears? He wondered now.

All too fast. One June day spitting red from bleeding gums in Fosshotel Lind in Reykjavik on the holiday they'd planned for so long.

Next day flying home.

Next, doctors' appointments.

Diagnosis. They could be so quick when it was bad.

Telling Charlie.

Short weeks at home.

Explaining to Charlie.

Days in hospice.

Watching Charlie.

Then over. Like that.

Celebration of life.

He'd been blindfolded, turned around, turned again, spun. Thrust in a direction. Walked off an edge. When could he pull off the blindfold? Voices came to him now, leaving him blindsided too. Old friends' and cousins', turned up from hours' drives away.

Relief to see Norah with Trev beside her. Trev had shed the Billy Bragg T-shirt from the morning when he'd come over with a plate of waffles he claimed they couldn't eat. Now he had on a plain black tee, faded. He put out his hands to grasp Keith's, the first time in weeks that Keith had seen him without armfuls of dishes and food, showing up at the door as if he always wandered down the hall with dinner. "Hope you're up for blue cheese veggie burgers, just made them on the balcony." "Hey, some decent spag bol here."

Keith was grateful his cousin and her spouse lived in the building. It had created another level to community for Charlie growing up. Now Norah's mom, Auntie Nele, stood with her daughter, looking lost, as some do when people die, people the age of their children.

Trev said words about coming by later, words Keith promptly forgot. Later, he'd remember Norah's eyes as she reached out to give him a hug. Sorrowful, and something he never saw in easygoing Norah. Raz used to say Norah had all her edges untucked, she left pieces trailing, but she wouldn't have said that on this day. For once, everything was tucked away, no raw showing. The change jarred momentarily.

Along came the next in the lineup, Felicity and Ron, their grown daughter Lucy between them. When had Felicity become so shadowy? And there was Ron, sloppy drunk, with those grey-blue eyes of his, bleary in mid-afternoon, wrapping thick arms around Keith, wetting his neck with his tears. "What are we doing here, man?" he kept saying. "We shouldn't be here." Like someone in a first-year poetry class trying to find the rhythm in ordinary English. He must have had a flask in a pocket. He began to ramble a story of a barbecue or holiday meal, some time that Keith couldn't piece together in his head. "She was so beautiful," he said forlornly. As if beautiful people should escape death. Felicity, looking backwards-underwear uncomfortable, wrapped her arms around her husband and gently pulled him along. But behind Ron, the lineup was still there.

Keith caught a glimpse of Ruby, Charlie's boy-sitter, as his son had called her for the past few years. "Ruby!" Charlie burst.

The girl, holding her mother's hand, gave Keith an anguished look. Her mother put her other hand on his arm. "We'll talk soon," she whispered. "I'm so sorry. Sometimes it's hard to believe that everything happens for a reason."

"Yes, it is," Keith muttered. "It is hard to believe." He shook his head to clear those words. He couldn't look directly at her.

"Charlie!" Ruby said, hugged him tightly. "I'm sorry."

"It's okay, Ruby, honey," Keith whispered, and gave her mom a look to let her know he understood why a thirteen-year-old might feel she couldn't take care of a six-year-old whose mother had just died. He hoped she could reassure Ruby at home, too. Or would she tell her that things happen for a reason?

Keith suspected Charlie didn't understood why he'd been seeing nothing of his beloved Ruby. He'd asked about her. Ruby gulped sobbily, her mom turned her away, and they disappeared into the crowd. Keith kept his arm around Charlie's shoulders as the next group came through: the people who worked with Raz, in her studio. Could he name them? Names slipped away from him these days. Words slipped away, too. How long would this last? He hadn't written anything in so long. Could he still call himself a writer?

One after another, hugs and words, words and hugs. Some woman threw her arms around him. He couldn't recall ever meeting this person, but she behaved as if she knew him well. "I didn't know anything about this until this morning!" Her arms tightened. In an involuntary motion, he pulled on the sleeves that hung from her arms, trying to extricate himself.

"She was something, wasn't she. Our butterfly, our star, our Raziel, our . . ." she gasped, tears coming. "There is . . . was . . . magic about her. You know?" she said plaintively. "I always wanted to reach into that part. But I never could. You know what I mean?" she repeated.

That was the artist. No one could have that part. A thought closely followed by, *Now go away.* Did someone pull off her tentacle arms? He felt lightened as she disappeared into the crowd, doused by her own mauve, legs so tattooed they couldn't be naked. Walls of brighter colours closed in, and he had to catch his breath.

He recognized the next woman, though he hadn't seen her for almost two decades. Raz had called her *The Woman Before.* Serena. He'd left Serena shortly after he met Raz. That moment of Serena saying, "I knew this would happen when we met her. I could feel you beside me, I could feel you leave me." He remembered her acceptance.

She held out her arms. "I'm so sorry." She patted his back as one would a child's. "So sorry. Tobias let me know." More back patting, and Keith attempted to resurrect Tobias from his brain fog. The man beside Serena — not Tobias, Keith knew that much — nodded sadly, shook hands with Keith, and wrapped an arm around Serena to lead her away.

Strange to see someone from long ago, to touch yet not be connected. Layers on layers of human beings in our lives, time zones, emotional backroads. And times when what lay between the layers broke down to nothing, and blended. Polar bears and flamingoes, trying to talk. But he was numbed. Later he would wring it through his mind, try to process, and give up. Just let it in and out.

More lineup. He couldn't recall ever being to a memorial service with such a lineup. But then, he'd never been the one receiving the hugs and words. Charlie hadn't moved. His eyes were wider. Keith stroked his hand over his son's head, and Charlie leaned in to him.

Miriam had found her way to his side. Their eyes connected, and then her gaze wandered, for a brief moment. She would be noting who was watching her. She could do that. "Why am I still here?" she said, with an accent he'd never heard from her before, film actress of the 1940s. How could he have such a thought? But many of his thoughts today startled him. Like the sudden urge to send her off to find Ron, so they could wail together about why *they* were still *here*. Truth: he'd never liked nor trusted Raziel's mother.

An aspect of this time he would never have known was how raw life could feel, as if all the protectives that people wrapped around their selves had fallen away, and there was too much to take in, not even necessarily good and ugly, but just there, in front of him.

Maybe Miriam's presence caused others to disperse; for whatever reason the line came to an end. They were released, they could go home, the day so blurred it bled into all the other days of these past four weeks that were supposed to have been six, according to the doctor who had diagnosed. He looked for Charlie. Right behind him, reaching up like a toddler.

•

"We brought a picnic," Norah said when Keith opened the door, minutes after he and Charlie had returned to the apartment. Norah was back in her black — such vintage punks they were — her soft smile in place, too. She'd lost whatever tightness she had earlier. Though her cardigan had more buttons done up than was usual for her, in the right holes even. Auntie Nele was a step behind, still looking lost, maybe even more than she had at the service. Keith could see her trying to focus on Charlie as her eyes connected with him, trying to change the expression on her face. He was astonished how he could actually see this, as if she were trying to push away the sad, the grim, but failing miserably.

"Mom." Norah elbowed her. This must be connected to some earlier conversation, Keith guessed. Norah had her six-years-older over him. She liked to remind him she was his big cousin. Her protectiveness had circled him all his life. Now that his aunt was ageing and shrinking, Norah did the same with her.

"Auntie," he said and wrapped his arms around Nele. He couldn't remember when he'd last seen his aunt. She let out a sob. He could feel her convulse in his arms, and he shook with her, some stuck bit in him loosened, too, and he had to put his face into the hammocky spots in her bony shoulder and hold on tight. When he did look up, both Norah and Trev had left them together and alone in the doorway.

In his aunt's eyes, he saw a shadow of his mother, hard to see. But who knew what his aunt saw in him. He had to look back over her shoulder and hug her again, and straighten up, snug her head into his chest, feel tall and able. "We're going to eat dinner now," he told her, as he would Charlie. "We are." He led her to where the others had landed, on the balcony, a space that only barely held the four grownups, and Charlie took his place with Old Daisy, queen and golden retriever, on her pillow in the corner.

Charlie's eyes lit up when he saw the bag of pepper kettle-chips that Norah dangled in front of him. Trev handed around a basket of substantial sandwiches, his go-to as a baker, and cloth napkins. He cracked open a can of lager for Keith without asking. Keith bit into half a cheese and tomato sandwich. He'd forgotten to eat. Though after a few bites, his hunger might disappear. Hunger and appetite hit him then disappeared these days.

Norah plugged in the string of patio lights, and Charlie snuggled deeper into Old Daisy. Trev's oversized heart could pop with the best words at the worst time. Like now. He pulled a folded and scrunched envelope from his pocket and opened it. "Felicity handed me a card. She didn't want to leave it in the basket. It's about loaning you two their camper van. She thought we'd be seeing you, and to let you know so you can use it before the summer's gone."

Charlie's eyes cartooned. Trev saw, and his voice trailed off. "I should have told you when it was just the two of us."

"Can we, Daddy? Can we?" Charlie stood and wiggled, and not for the first time, Keith questioned an element of regression in him. "A camper van!"

"Maybe Felicity should have told you herself," Trev said.

Keith managed to say, "It's okay." Too much to think about. He felt regression in his own self. The jittery feeling under his surface was seeping out.

"You can think about it later," said Norah, mildly irritated with Trev. She struggled to be angry with those she loved. "You can talk with Felicity or Ron. He must be in on this, too."

A summer evening breeze came up to talk about. The banal has its place and worth. But Auntie Nele had to ask: "Ron is that poor fellow who was rather drunk. You boys used to play hockey with him, no?"

You boys. Trev and Keith shared a glance, and, for the briefest moment, life felt normal.

"Still do sometimes," said Trev. "Though he doesn't show up as much as he used to. We play late at night, and will again once the season starts. Right, Keith?"

Pause. "Yes, right." How was this going to work? With just him and Charlie?

"I'll be hanging out with Charlie, then," said Norah, as if she'd heard the thought.

Auntie Nele appeared to be regretting her question. All things circled back to Raziel in spite of her efforts. She looked at Charlie, with his Old Daisy, and after a long moment, she whispered — as if she didn't realize they could all hear her — "Poor boy, poor boy. Oh my."

Norah blanched and looked to Keith. He gazed steadily back at her as if to say, *let's let it go.*

"It's late." Trev stood up. Work came early for Trev at his bicycle-bakery, Rise Up. *Bicycle* because tricycles delivered all product. Days off, he'd give Charlie rides in the back cart, and told him he'd hire him for his first job.

On the way out they had to stop at the photograph wall. "Charlie thought that if we're going to have a celebration, we should be decorating."

"I love how he thinks," said Norah. She pointed to a series of Charlie's feet with tree roots, toddler feet at the time. Then to one of the *Vancouver Sun* building capped in white. "Raz used to go crazy when it snowed or was frosty. That one time, the only time when we had anything close to hoar frost, she had her camera all morning until it melted. Do you think it reminded her of the prairies?"

"Could be," Keith said. Raziel had so little connection with her birth province. He'd always thought the urge to photograph real winter was about variety. Vancouver was rarely white.

Auntie Nele hiccupped, and Keith realized she was working hard not to cry. He gave his weepy aunt a hug. Then, "Get her out of here," he murmured to Norah. They left, and he returned to the balcony, where he sat and watched the last light of the day and his boy and dog curled together. From some other balcony, voices drifted, a Saturday singalong that made him think about being twenty again, or twenty-two. Was he recalling it as it had been?

He picked up the folded card that Trev had left, full of scribbled words his eyes skimmed over, the usual condolences. But at the end, a P.S. *Ron and I would like for you and Charlie to enjoy our camper van for a road trip. It's one thing we can do.* Signed with an old-fashioned curvy F.

Felicity. His thoughts stopped. It was true: he and Trev and Ron had played hockey together since the end of high school. Rec hockey, in cold, acrid-smelling arenas. Felicity had been one of the girls who hung round for those late-night games, and up for the bar afterwards. They were the first, and for a long time the only, people in their group to have a child, Lucy, an adult now. Felicity had always been a part of Ron.

Maybe that was how people saw him: a part of Raziel. That had never been their intention. Their intention was to be two wholes. He liked to think they'd been successful. But if ever there was a day to feel like a half, this was it.

He breathed deeper than he had in days. Only when the night sky was black did he carry his son to bed, Old Daisy pulling herself up to stumble after.

He'd planned to leave his own bedroom door ajar after tucking in Charlie. Neither wanted closed doors these days. But for a long moment, he stood in his son's doorway, then lay on the bed beside him. Charlie snugged into his stomach, and Keith wrapped an arm around, grateful his son could sleep, and envious, too. Every time he closed his eyes, he saw Raziel. Laughing. He'd worked to bring this image to mind over the past few weeks. The image had helped ease the pain he saw in her face. He'd never known anyone who could set free a laugh as she did, as if she couldn't give a half-thought to whether it would come back to her.

"Sweet Caroline" | Neil Diamond

"Daphne" | Biréli Lagrène

"Peg" | Steely Dan

2

"Did Grandmother go?" Charlie asked.

"She did, yes." It wasn't unusual for Miriam to leave without a goodbye.

Aunt Nele would see them once more before she left. Her sadness was almost unbearable. How did Norah stand it? Norah had been unable to share her last two miscarriages with her mother, and she swore Keith and Raz to secrecy. Sometimes people who did love you couldn't support you.

But Miriam was a different story. She'd asked if Keith could drive her to the cruise-ship dock, and he said no. Only Miriam could see a memorial service as a starting point for a vacation. His no was a first. He stopped shy of reminding her that there were a few taxicabs in this city. He was unable to drive her, and offered no excuse, reason, or alternative.

How often had Raz said, "Just because she's my mother, doesn't mean you have to. She'll ask for more and more, always has." Raz would have approved of his no, and that pleased him.

Miriam sent money at Christmas, and that was the connection between her and her grandson. Last year, to make it meaningful, Keith and Charlie had gone to cash the cheque, spent it at the toy store, and wrapped the puzzle and book that Charlie chose to give to the family shelter down on Homer Street. Charlie coloured cards to go with the packages.

He'd never seemed upset that his grandmother would leave without a word, but this morning he stood wobbily in the doorway in his mismatched flannel pajamas, rubbing sleep out of his eyes. "She always does that. She just goes."

Keith held out his arms, and Charlie dived in for a hug.

"And she never remembers Old Daisy's name." He mumbled into his dad's stomach. "She called her something else." Charlie had a short but not negotiable list of unforgiveables.

Keith rubbed his shoulders.

Now, service done and day after, and all those lilies in the apartment, over bloomed. Under the sweet smell was rot. Keith recut ends, plucked dead blooms, and salvaged. He was brittle today, barely keeping together. He couldn't throw away pieces connected with Raziel. Not yet.

Cards covered every surface. He hadn't read most of them, only opened and lined them up for protection. How he would go about taking them down, he didn't know. No one told you how to do these things. He'd found Charlie looking through, not that he could read the handwritten messages. But some of the images were beautiful. Two or three were even funny. One had words about punching anyone who said a word about *being out of pain now* or *in a better place*. Yes, he'd had that thought, and found his hands clenching. He'd opened the card, read, had a laugh. Whoever had the courage to put together this, no Hallmark garbage, knew all about it.

He'd pointed out Ms. Duffy's card, and read it aloud. Charlie listened, mystified that his last year's teacher would do such a thing. He took his time looking at the card, an abstract with flecks of gold that he poked a finger at. Grade 1 was forever ago. Later, Keith found Charlie sitting in the curl of Old Daisy on the floor, the card again in his hands. "That's my name." Charlie copied over the letters in blocky teacher-hand. He got to his feet and circled the room. "There're so many cards."

"A lot of people loved your momma," Keith said.

"Mommy was shiny."

"She was." Keith's throat tightened.

"Like a mirror," said Charlie. Keith wanted to say, "Like a light." But left it at that for Charlie.

He could almost see Raz move across the room, in that purposefully drifting way of hers. The more people in a room, the brighter she shone. Once some long timer had asked if she was pregnant. "That old wives' tale!" Raz had said. "No, I glow all on my own!" She'd given the old man a kiss, danced away, left him shaking his head. "You her husband?" he'd asked Keith. When Keith said, "I am," he hadn't stopped the head shaking, but a curious look came over his face, maybe a question of how you pin down a butterfly without damaging its wings.

Strange how that memory of more than a decade ago came to him. But she'd never lost the glow. Even caregivers at the hospice remarked. "We don't see that here," one had whispered.

Hard to let a memory like that linger, and hard to chase it away. Speaking aloud could break the threads. "All these cards," he said, with Charlie listening.

"Don't take them down. Don't put them away."

Keith shook his head. He couldn't speak.

"Maybe we could take one down every day." Charlie stared at his dad. "Like the Christmas calendar thing, where we put one ornament on the fabric tree each day. Except we put one card away."

It would take months. But that might be right. This was going to be day by day. He'd started to learn that in those weeks, those hospice hours. Don't think ahead.

Charlie went into his room and returned with an empty shoebox. He carried it around the room, eyeballing the cards, finally reaching in to extract some hideous floral thing with *Sincere Condolences* written across. Good choice, thought Keith, but kept the thought to himself. Charlie put the lid on, and set it under the coffee table.

The muddled morning redefined itself as afternoon.

Charlie was playing chess-solitaire, practicing the moves Keith had shown him those hospice afternoons, when he remembered. "That camper van. When are we going?"

"Just like that, eh? Do you think we can leave today?"

Charlie leapt up from the chess game and ran out of the room. Curious, Keith followed, to find him emptying his sock and underwear drawer into a box. On top, he put his favourite pajamas and books.

"Whoa," said Keith. This wasn't what he'd had in mind for the remainder of the summer. "I don't know about this, buddy," he said slowly. He hadn't had anything in mind, really.

Charlie focused on the next drawer, thick winter sweaters, and added them to the pile. Keith tried to make light of it. "Okay, we don't need those. We can't take all that in a van." Charlie didn't look at his father as he stared into the last drawer. He reached in. T-shirts and shorts started to fly.

Keith stepped back. Clothes flew faster until Charlie collapsed to the floor, shouting about wanting to go, somewhere, away. "I want the camper van!" Tears came. Keith moved closer. His son's pain was palpable, and he had the urge to back out of the room. Instead, he took a breath, let it out, forced himself to stay put and close. Charlie scrambled over the heap of clothing and curled over his dad's legs. Keith held him. He wished he could absorb some of this anguish. But they were both too full.

"We'll talk with Felicity," he promised. "Soon."

Later, for dinner, Keith started to make oatmeal. He couldn't think what else. Then turned it into pancakes. As they sizzled in the frying pan, bubbled surface popping, he threw in the sweet blueberries languishing in the fridge. Charlie sprinkled cinnamon as he liked, tapping it out of the dispenser, some in clumps. They smeared butter, poured syrup, and ate in quiet. Keith was spent. For certain Charlie was, too. But they kicked each other's feet under their stools, and the contact made them smile.

They read together, salve and slow-down, and Charlie went to sleep, Old Daisy at his toes. Keith sat out on the balcony until deep into the night, until the wind cooled as it does late summer nights, and he could feel it over his shoulders, the back of his neck. A light breeze even felt like a hand on his shoulder for a moment, the gentlest weight. But no, that wasn't possible, as much as he would have liked to feel a hand. He was surprised that the thought of such a thing, a ghostly caress, would even come to him. He'd never been able to bring himself to believe in such.

Music wafted up from the street again, voices singing, summer Sunday night sounds. The wind picked up. Voices lessened as the hour deepened. Keith reached for the blanket folded over the back of the other chair.

He must have drifted off. Late in the night he started awake, pulling himself to come to, wondering why was he out here with cold air blowing over his face, and not in bed? *Where was Raziel?* Why did even asking that feel wrong? He knew all the answers even as the questions came. He knew. He struggled to stand, to extricate himself from the blanket, wrapped too tightly around him, and stumbled inside to bed.

Another life-crushing airbag of a day.

A week passed, flowers gone, and Charlie had put away seven more cards into that shoebox.

They went to the park, trying for one trip outside the apartment. A trip to the grocery store, or to the bookstore, or the waterpark. One each day was enough.

Keith suggested the beach, but Charlie said the park, and Keith knew he meant their beloved wild place off Marine Drive, south of the city, near the river. In the spring they'd spot eagles. It was marshy, and Charlie was always pleased with a reason for gumboots. Keith packed sandwiches and they'd travel back in time to when Charlie was about three, and they spent days walking and talking and sharing books. That mental space of their olden days seemed appropriate now.

They locked the car and set out for the riverbank. Mid-path, Keith's jaw loosened suddenly. He'd been holding his breath, hadn't been conscious of the tightness. When had he come to think jaw ache was a part of him?

An enormous stump kept watch at the end of the walk, and they sat on it, too rot-pocked to count its rounds. The temperature of the sun was more forgiving than on the day of the service. Keith could feel warmth through his shirt, healing warmth, not mindless heat. The small clouds gave them things to name. He would have liked to take off his shirt and let sun soak into him. He opened the sandwiches instead. Charlie could be any other kid out for a walk, and that heartened Keith. "Here's a dark maroon, a kalamata!" He pulled out a small container of their favourite olives. The smile from Charlie was good.

The boy went rigid.

"What?" Keith knew to whisper.

"There." Charlie directed his dad with his eyes.

For a long moment, Keith saw nothing beyond the golden coloured dried grasses. Then movement, more golden, a coyote, hungry, thin, looking right at them.

Usually Charlie was excited to see wildlife, any wildlife. But Keith saw him shiver.

"What?" His own arms and neck prickled.

"It's her," Charlie said.

Keith didn't want to ask. The coyote took a step toward them, Keith could see its eyes, keen, then it turned and was gone.

"Mommy." Charlie's voice was flat.

Keith's ribs ached. He looked to where the animal had been, back to his son, and at the ground to feel balanced. Everywhere, that stiff grass, golden in summer heat, straw-like. Whir of insects. Diving of birds. River movement. He wasn't ready for any of this.

Topic change: "The camper van. We should go. Soon."

The look on Charlie's face. "Really?"

"Really." Anything but this.

A child could be so easily distracted if he wanted to be. Then he'd drive it home: "When?"

Keith had to laugh aloud, to hear himself, to break the sound of insects whirring, and the other sound, of absolutely nothing.

To let the coyote know they were there.

He'd been thinking. "We need to see your Auntie Cat and Uncle Eryk." Catalina still lived in the town where she and Raz had grown up. He'd been pondering taking Raziel's ashes to her birth province, though Raz had been silent about such instruction. When Charlie was born, they'd drawn up wills and named Cat and Eryk as guardians, but Raz had shaken her head about any further planning. Twice Keith had brought up *after* in those weeks. He'd decided not to bring it up again, though, through the days. Not if she didn't.

"Tomorrow," said Charlie.

"Okay. Tomorrow we'll hammer down a time with Felicity and Ron."

"Tomorrow," repeated Charlie. "Hammer." He mime-hammered that old stump.

They packed up the waxed paper sandwich wraps, he handed Charlie another olive, which he popped in his mouth, and they set off.

How are we going to do this?

"When are you going to work again? When is Ruby coming to look after me?" Charlie trotted along beside him, gumboots snapping his sock-free heels.

Was this how Charlie asked about normal? Whether it might ever be?

"When you go back to school, I'll start to write again."

What would it be like to return to *The House-Band Plays On*, his blog, his offering to the world, all so in the past? He'd left a post sitting half-written. But what was there to say about fathers and playdates for children? He'd been writing about fathering for Charlie's lifetime, but he wasn't ready to write about what was right in front of him. Not yet.

Then again, returning to questions about fathers and play-dates might be just right.

"When will Ruby come again?" Charlie persisted.

"You miss her." How did you tell a kid that his sitter was scared of all the grief in him? "I was thinking maybe we'd all get together, you and me, and Ruby and her folks, and have dinner or hang out." Or he'd been thinking that before Anne, Ruby's mother, had dropped the platitude on him.

"Okay!" Charlie was happy with that. For now.

They walked the blocks east to Ron and Felicity's. "Come take a look," Ron had said on the phone, sounding distracted.

When they arrived, he said, "I didn't know Felicity offered it to you."

"I hope that's okay," Keith said. "Is it?"

The briefest hesitation. "Of course." Ron plucked a set of keys off the wall. "Come and see." This was directed at Charlie, whose energy was high, about-to-explode emanating from him as he trotted directly behind Ron, imitating his gait almost perfectly, laughably.

Felicity showed up, after some phone call that had kept her from answering the door. A whiff of alcohol came to Keith's nostrils as she gave him the quickest hug. "I'm so glad you're going to do this," she said. "I think you'll enjoy our old van. It's ugly on the outside but has inner beauty. Like all us old ones."

"We're not old," he had to say. But he never liked feeling pushed to reassure. Maybe that's not what she wanted, maybe she was just saying. "Once Charlie heard the plan, there was no talking him out of it. And we need to see Cat and Eryk."

"Yes, you do," she said. All four of them were outside by the parking spot off the back alley. The van was an odd shade of dark grey, painted by hand. At least the raised roof was white, or it'd be screaming hot inside. "What's that say?" Charlie pointed to a word graffitied on the side. He started to sound out the bulging letters.

"Hopper," said Ron. "The name was there when we bought it. I keep meaning to paint over." He bark-laughed. "It's a Trev-thing, eh? A black van named Hopper?"

In spite of knowing Ron for almost as long as Keith had known Trev, in spite of holiday times together, even memorable times, this was another moment when Keith knew why they'd never quite clicked. "Trev knows how not to take things so seriously."

"I don't take anything seriously," was Ron's quick response.

"There are things," said Keith, "and there are other things. Trev knows what's important." He couldn't remember ever being this blunt with Ron, and couldn't think why he'd choose this time. "Charlie's so excited about this," he had to add, a peace offering of sorts.

Ron didn't look at him as he dropped the keys into Felicity's hand. "Show them the works," he said shortly. "Let me know the dates you'll be away. Enjoy the old thing!" He hurried off, Felicity looking after him.

There'd been no eye contact between them. Keith suspected he wasn't supposed to pick up on that. "You're sure this is all okay? Had you guys planned a vacation?"

"Ron has a fishing trip, or some excursion. But I told him he can work around. I think you need this more than he does." She slid the side door open. Charlie hopped up inside and, first thing, turned on and off the sink tap. He opened the small fridge and a cupboard, pulled out a knife and spoon as if they were unknowns, studied them.

Keith made a conscious decision to ignore the thought that there was some subtext going on here. If Ron and Felicity were having problems, he didn't want to know. He couldn't back out of this now. He wouldn't do anything to take the smile off his son's face.

"I think we're going to leave on Labour Day," he said. "I'm honestly not sure when we'll return. If that's okay."

"That's fine," said Felicity. "Take your time."

Charlie stood in the doorway. "Wow! This is the best!"

Felicity spoke to Charlie, eye to eye. "Your dad probably won't believe me, but this old van is magic. She can help you find what you need, and take you right there. Sometimes, if you lose your way, she'll find a new one."

Charlie's eyes shone.

"I believe you," said Keith, maybe to stop her words. The kindness in this offer took off all his carefully wrapped duct tape. It was too much like the question that some were asking him these days, peering into his eyes and asking, "Are you okay?" and actually meaning it, wanting a real answer. Sometimes he couldn't take it.

He listened to her instructions about how to light the stove, how to use the composting toilet, how to refill water. Charlie wanted to know where they would sleep and how the windows opened. He tested the handles of each, and he used his body, getting onto the floor, to measure out how Old Daisy would fit between the seats.

II

●

Into the Fall

3

"Miles from Our Home" / *Cowboy Junkies*
"Everything Reminds Me of My Dog" / *Jane Siberry*
"The Tracks of My Tears" / *Billy Bragg*

They would leave in the early morning on Labour Day. Others would be coming home from vacation, and they'd be going. The decision gave Keith a deadline, not the minutes of a flight time or the hour of a ferry, but a day. The school year would be starting but it could wait. There was no point in rushing back into that routine.

He wrote a list: banking, closing joint account, paperwork for life insurance policy. The policy was enough to keep them going for a while. Charlie spent time with Trev, who wanted to teach him to throw a frisbee, while Keith went to the government services office with Raziel's passport and social insurance number. He worked his way through the list. If there was a time to make use of the male capacity for compartmentalization, if such existed, this was the time. Back home, and they filled a basket with provincial maps from the automobile association, and even a few states south of the border. Keith began to hear the call of Hopper.

The only determined goal was to get to Cat and Eryk's place in Gimli, Manitoba, on the shores of the lake. They could make their way home, or go beyond. Keith took Felicity at her word and ignored the thought of Ron's face, soured, as he dropped the keys into her hand. In the fall he'd get Ron back on the ice, stick in hand, and all would be good.

The night before they left, they went around to fetch the van, and found a spot where they could leave it overnight in front of their building. Charlie insisted that they begin to pack, making trips up and down the elevator. "I need to pack Old Daisy's stuff, too," he said, after clothing was stowed in compartments.

36

"Old Daisy's going to stay home. Trev and Norah will take care of her." Charlie's end-of-world face rolled down like a window blind. "Old Daisy *has* to come with us. We can't leave her."

Keith had been hearing only Raziel's word: *don't*. Old Daisy wouldn't be happy in a vehicle all those hours, she'd say. Remember the time she threw up in the car, made a mess, stained the seat? The smell lasted so long. Remember? The farthest they'd ever taken the dog was to the valley for the day. The farthest the three of them had driven was two hours east to Kawkawa Lake near Hope. Any farther, and they'd flown.

"We can bring a blanket," Charlie said. "For the back seat. And water in a thing with a lid. And her kerchiefs. We *have* to bring her!" There was an edge to his voice. "Something might happen."

"Happen to Old Daisy?"

"Yeah." Maybe Charlie was as tired as Keith was of crying. His words came in a mucusy growl. "If we go without her, something bad will happen."

Other words came out of Keith's mouth then. "You can pack her food. *You* can be responsible." Who was he kidding? A not-quite-seven-year-old couldn't be responsible for a dog. But he didn't want to say no. Children didn't learn from yes and no. They learned from *shit, that didn't work out!*

"The poo bags, and her leash, and a blanket. Okay."

Charlie hugged his dad with the odd fierceness he'd taken on through these days. Off he went, and Keith could hear him scooping kibble out of its enormous bag. He could hear some skittering over the floor, some mutters of frustration, and scrambling. Keith left him to it.

They packed food. Beer and iced tea in the fridge. Some cheese, Charlie pointed out. More for Old Daisy, the sharp kind she especially liked. Dogs and cheese. As soon as Charlie started to open the packaging, she was at his elbow.

Keith spirited a load of underwear back to Charlie's drawer while he dealt with the dog cheese, and he tucked in pajamas instead. Charlie loved all-day flannel, bottoms only for summer. Rags by fall.

Charlie wanted to take the chess board and pieces. Keith struggled with the urge to leave it at home. Memories: hospice afternoons at bedside, the koi pond beyond the window, where they watched the swimming orange and white, yellow, and black shapes, while Charlie chose his next move. Keith tried to cut the other images from those swallowed-up days. Reluctantly, he left the chess set where Charlie packed it. Maybe Charlie would forget about playing once on the road.

In seventeen years together he and Raz made only two trips to visit Cat. They'd enjoyed the times, bright mornings and evenings by an outdoor firepit. They spent one Christmas with Miriam before she left the country. Cat and Eryk drove or flew out at least once a year to get an urban fix, and in between made a point of using technology to connect with their nephew. Cat often read Charlie a bedtime story, holding the book to the camera on her laptop for him to scrutinize the illustration. Now was time to recognize that effort. Keith had wondered how it felt to want a child for years, to love a nephew, and finally to be pregnant. Eleventh-hour babe.

So odd to be doing this now. It could seem an affront to her memory. Raz wasn't fond of her birthplace, but she would appreciate the freedom, the not knowing which road to take, the lack of deadline. She would have encouraged the trip. "Do that bonding thing," she'd say, then tuck in the popcorn, hide a bottle of Scotch in one of the small cupboards, her blessings on their journey.

More than once Charlie and he had driven somewhere, stayed in a hotel, gone to meet old friends when Raziel was busy with work. It wasn't out of the ordinary for the two of them to be going off. It would be different when they returned home, and Raziel wasn't there, and those cards would be, still standing. He didn't want to think about that time.

He needed to let Trev and Norah know, no Old Daisy for them. He was glad Charlie had pushed. It felt right to take the old girl.

They could pack an air mattress to sleep under the stars. Some image passed through his mind: *that coyote.* What was the chance they'd see her? Of course, he didn't mean that same coyote. But how did this thing connect in Charlie's mind? Maybe through this time of travelling he would come to know. There were parts of his son he was learning about. Rules had shifted.

Charlie was an early riser, and until they set out, Keith knew he'd pack yet more of his things, his books, crayons, boots. Keith wanted to be ready to go before Charlie woke up.

He set the coffee pot to do its thing, Old Daisy following him between the machine and the cupboard. He filled his thermos, had a sip with brown dog-eyes staring up. Charlie had tied the purple kerchief around her neck, a festive time. A few more sips, and a thought came.

Raziel's ashes were in a box that he'd placed on his bedside table. He had vague thoughts of prairie wind as he took the box, deep green, weighty, and wrapped it in a large bag. He locked the apartment, always a moment of unease, even to take out garbage, leaving Charlie, grateful for Old Daisy. And he went to the van to hide the box.

Then up the elevator, hoping Charlie wouldn't be awake yet. His phone had a text message, from Cat.

Sorry for late notice. But wondering about having a few pieces of Raz's clothing. I'd truly love even one. Is that weird? I hope not. Though if it is, I'm sorry. We can't wait to see you and beautiful Charlie! Cannot wait!

He'd tried not to think ahead to the time when he'd have to sort through Raz's things. Maybe when Charlie was in school. He typed: *It's not weird. It's weird I haven't asked.*

He opened the small walk-in closet. For summer he'd had the excuse of using the dresser, for t-shirts and shorts. The waft of familiar perfume stopped him.

First thing he saw was that bright pink dress of Raz's, a favourite. He wondered if the more subdued Cat would wear it. The two sisters had been different as maple syrup and mustard, but she might like to have it. Seeing it in her closet might embolden her. The pink could grow on her, and she in it. Raz would like the thought.

He laid it out on the bed and caught sight of Raz's winter coat with the collar that flared around her face. She'd always bemoaned that in Vancouver there were so few opportunities to enjoy it. It would take space in the van, but he imagined Cat might relish it. On the shelf that ran across the wall, sweaters were folded, neatly stacked, organized by colour. He chose several.

He saw the oversized men's black cardigan that Raz wore, folded away for summer. He set it over the back of his work chair, to leave for later in September. The sweater would warm him in the fall mornings; the anticipation was an unexpectedly pleasant sensation.

Packed up now, he texted to Cat. So much easier to meet requests when people asked and he didn't have to come up with ideas.

Time to wake Charlie. But he was already awake, and, yes, packing more socks. Keith let him be, told him he'd put together bowls of cereal.

Charlie chattered between bites, and they cleaned up. Old Daisy smelled a plan, and she clicked over the floor in old-dog dance. They locked the front door, Charlie testing the knob after his dad, as he did lately. Good. He was a city kid. It wasn't optional to be street smart. Though was there a connection between the new testing and loss?

Thermos of coffee in hand, backpack of last-minute items, and Keith's other hand held Charlie's. Charlie clutched Owl. Old Daisy followed. Charlie helped lift the dog's back legs in through the side door. Once in, she sniffed, wagged, gave a short whine of approval.

"She *wants* to be with us." Charlie's I-told-you-so.

Keith handed Charlie the map they'd drawn lines on, and Old Daisy settled between the front seats. Should they say some words to mark the occasion? The past weeks of days had been drifting and this felt to be the first solid one in too long. But they'd had a lot of ceremony lately. Maybe there was danger in thinking everything required some. Maybe just buggering off before six should be what you do; that was the time on the old wristwatch duct-taped to the dash.

The ancient 350 engine rumbled, happy and words enough. They pulled out, the vehicle moving like a manatee inspired to become a land animal.

Once on the road, Keith put on "Life is a Highway," inching the volume until Charlie laughed, started to sing, and Keith joined. The volume had to be full on over the engine roar. They might have to forego music at some point.

After they'd been rumbling for a couple of hours, it was as if the friendly mask came off Hopper, and he began to let them know how arduous the trek was with assorted squeaks. The sounds didn't seem to bother Charlie. "Hungry birds!" he said. "Do you hear them?" At first Keith didn't understand. He'd been watching the way the road slipped under the stubby hood of the van, right in front of him. But Charlie added, "Sounds like birds in a nest," and Keith heard it then. He always welcomed any words that ascertained his urban kid was learning nature. "Lots of birds," he agreed.

They stopped east of Hope, a perfect spot with a mountain to wonder about on the other side of the creek. Old Daisy walked stiffly to find a patch of dried grass to squat over, then straightened and dashed off with momentary spryness, finding much to sniff, before stiffening again with her old legs as she wandered from one spot to another.

They ate the sandwiches Charlie'd made, with bananas, peanut butter, and potato chips. Charlie was always about the crunch and wasn't happy that it had disappeared. "Maybe next time pack the chips and we can add them before we eat." He listened to Keith's suggestion even as he picked out the soggy chips and fed them to Old Daisy, who had no complaints about missing crunch.

After eating, Charlie spotted a thick log across the creek. "Up, Old Daisy!" said Charlie. But he didn't push it when she hopped away. "I want to walk across the log bridge."

Keith eyed the water. Not too deep, and Charlie was a fish. Raziel would have said a flat no. "Don't fall in," Keith said, half-joking. Charlie stood on the log.

"I'll follow you," he added.

"I have to cross by myself," said Charlie. "I'll fall off if you're behind me." He had a set to his mouth.

"Okay. I'll be here, then." Keith positioned on the bank, and reminded himself of the hours of swimming lessons. *Don't fall in!* Maybe a couple of months ago would have been different, but he couldn't shake feeling raw. At least someone had sliced off the top of the log to create a flattened walkway.

Charlie set a foot in front of him, then another. Large rocks stabilized both ends. He wavered slightly. Old Daisy moved anxiously with Charlie's steps, and she whined.

Faith.

Old Daisy agitated at the end of the log, and Keith stopped her when she moved to climb up onto it. "No, girl."

Charlie was at the other end. He stepped off the log and did a jiggedy jig. Keith let out his breath.

"I did it!"

"You did it!"

Now you need to come back. Keith fought the urge to take off his shoes. But he had to, slipping them off, catching the heel with his toes, stepping out into the grass.

Charlie was almost back to the edge. He looked up, for the first time not completely focused on his feet, to grin at Keith, and his feet slipped. In he went, Keith followed, slipping on creek slime. He grabbed Charlie just as his head went under, took hold of a handful of shirt, and they both emerged, Charlie sputtering.

They scrabbled up the bank and stood shivering. Keith reached to pull Charlie's T-shirt off over his head and, blindfolded with arms in air, Charlie twisted to get free. "I wasn't gonna fall in!" he shouted.

"You were almost there," said Keith.

"I *was* there." Charlie's head popped out, and he scowled at Keith. Did he see the shoes sitting on the bank? Evidence of lack of belief? Would he put that together?

"Take off your wet shorts," Keith instructed, heading to Hopper for towels, relieved to turn his back on the scene. He opened the door, found the cupboard.

He'd completely forgotten towels. He was wet waist down, and Charlie was soaked. Raziel would have said no, but Raziel would have remembered towels.

"You didn't bring *towels?*" Charlie stood outside the van door, incredulous, shivering.

Keith grabbed a blanket and wrapped it around Charlie, sat him on the doorstep. He took off his own pants and wrapped the bed sheet around himself, toga style. "We're good," he said. "Ready to drive the chariot." He wasn't sure that Charlie got the drift of that, but he did start to laugh. Anger to laughter in zero to five.

"You can sit up front." Keith decided. The van had one back seat with a belt, and twice Charlie had asked if he could move up. "It's a better seatbelt, anyway," he said. That was true. And Hopper was too old for airbags.

Charlie was happy. Keith changed to new shorts, and hung up the wet clothes around the van. Charlie stayed wrapped in the blanket. The seat would get wet, but no matter, they could go on.

Wet things dried.

"Are we there yet?" had not yet happened.

They found a campsite for the night near the Shuswap, with an outhouse, a covered picnic area, and a river running by.

Charlie said no to sleeping alone in the bunk above the front seats, so they shared the old quilt on the main bed that pretended to be a double, and suddenly the day felt long. So much excitement about Hopper, the chilling tumble in the creek, and all the weeks before. Keith was ready to close his eyes and hoping that when he did, he wouldn't feel fixedly awake. Charlie whispered out of the cotton and pillow feathers and dark. "Tell me about when I was born."

The roll of memory caught Keith. It was a story he used to like to tell. For so long, Charlie hadn't asked for any stories. It had been windy through the late afternoon, and a gust caught the van now, rocked it, and moments later a sound began. It took a moment to register: summer rain. Keith stood on the bed to wind the lever of the rooftop vent after a few drops made their way in. Once under the quilt again he snuggled with Charlie. Old Daisy moved in closer with her usual confusion over lapdog status.

Keith began. "You were born on a night of rain. Fall rain, though." They listened to the patter. It hadn't yet begun to drip. Leaves were moving, and some fir trees, too. "Your mom and I were preparing for bed." That part always made him think of *The Night Before Christmas*. "When your mom . . ." How that phrase caught in his throat, but he liked to say it as he always had. "When your mom realized you were coming."

"How did she know?"

"She felt you moving differently."

"Did it hurt?"

"Feeling a baby move doesn't hurt. At least, I don't think so, your mom never said. But giving birth does, yes. But so do many things that end up being all right and even good." That's what he'd always said at this point in the story. But was it true? He'd liked to think yes. He paused.

"Keep going."

That was good to hear.

"So I helped her to the car."

"Don't miss the elevator part!"

"Right. Her water broke in the elevator."

"And splashed everywhere."

Always, at this point, Keith would like to see the inside of his son's mind. How did he envision this? "Yes, splashed everywhere. No time to do anything about it. Well, except grab tissues out of your mom's purse and mop up. I wanted to get her to the hospital."

"You did. You speeded."

"I drove quickly, yes."

"Speeded."

"Okay."

"But there weren't any cops."

Keith had forgotten how much he enjoyed this. He'd thought it would hurt. *So do many things that end up being all right.*

Charlie said, sleepy and low, "Tell me the best part."

"After you were born, your mom held you. I had to fight to have you in my hands. She didn't want to let go. She kept looking at you, and into your eyes. She said, *Thank you for coming into our lives, little one.*"

He fought the urge to sit up for more air, and turned on his side. Charlie patted his hand, and Old Daisy whined into a more comfortable position between their legs. They listened to the rain after that, a mothering sound, and Keith wondered at that phrase. *Mothering.*

Once Raz had told him, "You're the best mother." Maybe it was time to change up words.

Charlie fell asleep, and Keith peered through a slit in the ugly avocado-green curtains and listened. He remembered Raz's face in those moments of gazing at infant Charlie, not wanting to let go. Then it had shifted: for a moment there'd been a look on her face so intense it had imprinted on him, gone into his heart-bank of images. What was the look? He'd seen the same on her face in the hospice. *Not wanting to let go.* The two moments fused now, and he shivered and pulled at the curtains as if he might change the image. He felt a moment of cavernous despair, and a need to pull himself back. His thoughts roamed to find and catch a hold.

To the last bit of travel they'd done, going to Iceland back in June, the last month almost untouched by this, so grateful they'd gone. Gratitude lessened the despair.

They'd travelled to a city once a year since Charlie's birth. Paris, the first year, for romance, then Dublin for the pubs, Austin for the music. Last year closer to home, Montreal, for music, pubs, and romance.

This year, Trev and Norah had offered to stay with Charlie and Old Daisy, and they'd shown up with a small box of favourite childhood films borrowed from the library, and a large bottle of popcorn kernels and collection of toppings with lists of vile ingredients. Trev had given Old Daisy a pig's ear, which the dog had toted to a corner. Her open-mouthed chewing was raucous, and her lack of self-consciousness inspiring.

Funny how Keith's mind stalled on the memory of Old Daisy chewing. He willed it to stop there, but it roamed. Now, since Raziel's death, memories leaked in, and sometimes he let that happen, and other times he tried to stop. For moments memories could be salve, and already he was learning, in equally quickly turning moments, the memories could be no salve at all, but could twist and take him crushingly downward.

Beside him, his son slept. For a moment, he let his hand drift over to Old Daisy, and he gave her a scratch. All had to be somewhat right with the world when it could be a boy and his dog in a camper van. If only that were true.

He let his thoughts go back to Iceland. For months they'd planned that trip, adding pieces to look forward to. Keith researched museums, restaurants, the not-to-miss. He would write a travel piece. The country had long been on his list. Raziel was happy with camera in hand. The magazine editor he sometimes worked for was happy, too, when Raz contributed visuals for a piece written by Keith.

He let himself remember when he'd shown her the photos of the Reykjavik punk museum. "Housed in an underground toilet!"

"Well then! We have to see that, take photos for Trev and Norah."

"How about the Phallological Museum?"

She was dithering over red wine or white. Unlike most people, who had a preference, for her it was about the day. Sunshine, white. Rain, red.

"The *what?*"

"You heard me. They have a museum in Reykjavik, with over two hundred preserved penises. From a hamster's to a sperm whale."

She grasped the bottle of red.

"Good choice," he said.

"How big is the sperm whale's?"

"Over six feet."

"Six feet." She poured a glass and went to turn on the gas fireplace. For April, it was cold. "Six feet," she muttered.

"Stop." He started to laugh.

"Yes, we do need to go there." She took a long sip of the red.

He added the museum's address to the list.

•

The streets of Reykjavik offered the sort of walks they loved: colour and view, people and sound.

The day they arrived, their walk had to be cut short. After sitting on a plane, Keith needed to move, but Raziel, for once, said she was tired. The rarity of the admission caused Keith to turn and start back to the hotel.

He would have liked to do otherwise. The day felt unending with the time difference and the late and mystical twilight. Keith didn't voice this to Raziel, but Charlie would have called it spangle-ish. He used the word as a descriptor since that time at the beach. Raziel would have laughed to acknowledge his words, and while Keith had loved the lightness in her laugh, he did wonder how it affected Charlie. Always he felt unease over his son's easy acceptance of other-world, magical or mystical, but that was Charlie. That acceptance felt to have no connection with Keith or with Raziel.

Keith had an urge to awaken Charlie and ask: how did this work for you? The magical? But that was crazy thinking. He couldn't awaken him.

He also had a sudden sense of missing his son. That was more crazy. He was right next to him. But he missed the naive boy who knew nothing about his mother being taken away.

He and Charlie were different people than they'd been in the spring, the last day of school even. There was more to grieve than the obvious. There were layers that Keith was learning now.

In Reykjavik, he'd had that sense of holiday, when they were away from their own part of the world. Travelling was when he was most likely to catch a glimpse of Raziel's playfulness, what had drawn him to her years before.

In this van named Hopper, rain splattering harder on the roof, thoughts and images crowded into his mind, edging each other out, fleeting bits he couldn't piece together. He wished he could have one last dance with her, they'd so seldom danced. At their wedding, yes, and at her fortieth. And one night when she'd had a fever, and he'd gathered her in his arms to take her to the bathroom, and she'd suddenly moved into some waltzing step.

Is every night going to be like this? Memory wallow?

But his thoughts went to the next day walking in Reykjavik, an hour in, and Raziel had to sit. He'd never seen her out of breath. Usually he trailed one step behind. After breakfast, coffee, and going up a colour-filled street, she sat on a bench, muttered words about the view. He could hear her breathing, though, half-turned from him.

"Are you all right?"

"Of course!" She stood and plunged her hands into deep pockets.

"Let's sit. Let's stop and take a real look at this place."

He suspected that she didn't want him to see her as she was, as she fingered the worn strap of her oldest camera. Was she going to take a picture?

She did sit, because he did, and they talked about the houses with their bright roofs and doors, the narrow streets, the people. He was rattled. How Raziel hated when he worried. She didn't like worry, said she didn't believe in it. As if it were that easy to dismiss.

The next day in Reykjavik they'd slept in, Raziel lying on her belly as she did in her deepest sleep. He'd made coffee quietly, pondered red rooftops out the window. She slept on. When she finally woke, got up, showered, there was a leadenness to her, so alien to her fine bones.

He remembered now, his mind reviewing those times as if each memory would be yet another day spent with her, how he'd watched her through the days of that trip. He'd thought he knew better than to ask her about the strange fatigue. But should he have? Even now, he's not certain. They'd always made efforts to let each other be.

His mind conjured that last morning in Reykjavik, even as he thought *let's be done with this.* He could see the sink after

Raz brushed her teeth. There'd been blood. She'd disappeared into the shower, and he felt shock at the red on white porcelain. He could still feel the sudden fold in his gut, air choked off.

"My gums," she said when she pulled aside the shower curtain to find him staring into the sink. "Must be the travel," she added vaguely. "Altitude maybe? Flying?" She stepped out, dripping, and turned on the tap to run the red down the drain. She seemed unconcerned. He'd let that soothe him. *I don't believe in worry.*

Last day they stumbled over that beautiful park, and she chose to sit and work in her journal while he walked. She always had a thick spiralbound notebook, filled with drawings, bits of watercolours and pastels, collaged bits. It would grow heavy with her view of the world, and then a new notebook would take its place. Such images were how she recorded life, maybe even accessed, apart from her work with camera and film.

She'd sat in that park, and pulled pieces of charcoal and graphite from her pack. She hunched over the notebook. He knew the dismissive posture: *You can go.* But as he left, she stopped him. "That picture you took of the bridge we saw yesterday. Can you send it to me?"

He took out his phone and sent it. Did she have any idea what it meant to him when she made such requests, even in that distracted way? She so rarely discussed her work with him that when she did, he paid attention. He walked for more than an hour before returning, and a couple of blocks away bought a coffee and waffle. She was still at the park, camera on the bench beside her, smudges of charcoal on her face, no doubt from resting her jaw on her palm, as she was apt to do when thinking.

She was agitated as she took the food and drink. Normally her mood was lightened by such time. He'd thought the waffle would please.

That same smudged and greyed thinking followed them onto the plane home.

The trip came to an end. Let the remembering end, too. He fell into a foxhole of sleep.

Next day, father and son, Hopper van and Daisy dog, carried on east.

Next morning, Charlie realized he hadn't brought his stick. "I was supposed to," he said sorrowfully. The anger and frustration of recent weeks was sadness on this day. Everything was off. They'd woken at different times, Keith awake for far too long, and Charlie lying so still, so heavily, that Keith had a moment of terror to talk himself through. Then Old Daisy started to lick Charlie's face, and he awoke with flapping hands.

Now he was stuck on the missing stick. Keith wished that Charlie would howl instead of this. The sad was too grown up. Keith, folding the quilt, began to say that he'd forgotten the air mattress. But there was no point in sharing that disappointment.

"You do have Owl," he said instead. "Owl might know about truth."

Charlie stared at him. How could he not understand? Then happened to look up. "We can see the moon still." The wonder of that as a child, the moon and sun sharing the morning sky. Keith grateful for the distraction.

As he prepared breakfast, Charlie set up Owl nearby to watch over them. They ate a breakfast of eggs fried in buttery cast iron on the propane stove. They hoped to reach Banff by nightfall. They were now beyond the farthest they'd ever driven with Raziel, and were going off some old map.

In the midst of the peaks, Charlie cried, "There's snow up there. In summer." And later, "Look! Snow right here." Roadside.

Miles later. "I need to pee."

"So do I," said Keith.

At a turnout, he pulled over, they climbed out, and stretched legs.

"Sword fight," said Charlie, pulling at his shorts. Keith unzipped, and the two streams of urine battled it out. "I win," he said. Let no one say he'd made it easy for his kid.

"I'll win next time," said Charlie as they climbed back into their seats.

"Maybe, maybe not."

They spent the evening in Hopper with all doors open, playing chess and eating popcorn made over the propane stove, drinking hot chocolate and batting and slapping mosquitoes. Keith's initial dismay over bringing the chess game was shrinking. Being in a new space made a difference. Hopper was no hospice.

"Quit thinking!" Charlie chided his dad at one point. "Move a guy, any guy." He motioned to the board impatiently. It was a relief to see this focus on the game, and the streak of future healthy adolescent in him.

"Right!" Keith had been savouring the simplicity of the evening. Now he moved a knight thoughtlessly and lost it in the next minutes. He sat back and looked at his son. Sometimes you have to look at those you love, to remember why you do. It didn't take much to make Charlie happy, even in these rough days. It didn't take much to make Keith happy, even. That was a good thing. It didn't take much to make anyone happy. Little things could change up the big: remembering to pick up a favourite ice cream, noticing where someone left their glasses. Giving someone the last cookie in the jar. Or a back rub.

Next Keith moved his bishop and took one of Charlie's rooks. "Careful what you ask for," he said. But Charlie snapped up the second knight and laughed. He had a plan.

They were both tired that night, ready to sleep.

"Are you looking forward to seeing Auntie Cat and Uncle Eryk in the prairies?"

"Prairies?"

"Where the land is flat, not so many trees, lots of farming."

It would be good for Charlie to see this piece of his mother. Someday they should return in winter, when it was transformed.

"I went to Manitoba with your mother once for Christmas. You'll see where she grew up, and went to school, and the outdoor ice arena."

"An ice arena? We can see it now, in summer?"

This could be the bedtime story. "When we're under the quilt, I'll tell you." They washed the mugs and buttery popcorn bowl, put the dishes away in the small cupboard, and set up the bed. Side by side in the open doorway, they brushed their teeth and spit into the grass.

Snuggled under the quilt with cracked-open windows, they felt the summer breeze, listened to the wind in the trees overhead. How could he feel such peace in spite of the heaviness of all these weeks? But he shouldn't analyze it too much or too long. There was an inherent hunger for such moments of reprieve, a mechanism for survival.

"That arena," Charlie's sleepy voice came. "In the summer."

"Right," said Keith. "It's there in the summer. We'll go and see it. But no ice, it's too hot. You can run around on the concrete. Maybe we can play ball hockey."

"Do we have to drive there?"

"Probably not. It's in the park down the street from where your mom grew up. We can walk there, I think. In the winter you carry your skates and stick, and the best part is . . ." He paused until he saw his son's eyes turn to him. "There's a little hut where you can take off your boots, put on your skates. When it gets dark late winter afternoons, there are lights so you can skate into the evening." Keith felt warmth grow from this sharing. Charlie must have felt it, too; he gave his dad a sudden hug.

After his son fell asleep, Keith lay listening to summer night sounds, a bit of laughter, some singing, the sound of water, a stream. Soon dark with the tall trees, and he could see the slim waning moon from Hopper's windows.

He'd taken bittersweet pleasure in his memories of the previous evening, but this night, with Charlie's soft breathing beside him, he resisted this time. He envied Charlie's easy sleep.

Old Daisy let him know that she needed out. The smell of pines after the heat of the day was rich. Mountains loomed, darker in the dark, and he was grateful for their sense of enclosure.

He walked a distance from Old Daisy and knew that as long as he was walking, moving, the memories wouldn't come in quite the same way as they had the night before. Walking was good for that. He moved in big circles around Hopper, and eventually Old Daisy tagged along, circling into his current. Keith saw a light go on in a camper, another in an RV, and a silhouetted head popped up. He should tuck in, though he'd rather keep walking in the rich night air with breeze enough to discourage mosquitoes.

Charlie had found the perfect log for Old Daisy to use as a step up into the van, and in she went, Keith following. He left the door open a few inches. Charlie didn't move, he was solidly asleep, as Keith pulled covers over and again looked to the moon. He stared, willing his mind to fall asleep quickly. As if. He wondered about finding music on his phone, if music would fill what might empty into memory every night. But he didn't want to waken Charlie. The stars were more than he'd seen in years. But instead all he could see, too clearly, was the morning they'd taken Raziel to hospice.

He could feel the handles of that wheelchair. He could see that small bag she'd packed. What was in it? He'd put it into the box that the hospice employee had handed to him to return home.

Arriving, he'd helped her into that chair, and Charlie had lifted his mother's feet out of the way of the footrests. That chair was such a complicated piece of equipment. Without his son,

Keith would have been audibly cursing the thing. With Charlie there, he kept the words to himself. Charlie had carried that little bag of Raz's, and added a couple of the well-worn board books she'd created for him, with photographs of Charlie and Old Daisy and Owl. The books were titled *Charlie's Apartment*; *Charlie's Dog*; *Charlie's City*.

"I'm going to read to Mom," he'd whispered.

If it hadn't been summer, Keith would have had to make a decision, whether to pull Charlie out of school, or leave him in. He'd wrestled with putting his son through this, day after day. What would he have chosen during school days? He didn't know what his choice would have been. Given the time of year, the decision had been made for him, so there was a strange rightness to it. If Charlie wanted to help, that was right, too. That felt to be the thing to do, to go with the gut. To leave their son out of this time might be the act of creating a hole he would wonder or worry about later; instead he was with them step by step.

Charlie bent over to kiss his mother's knee after he helped her feet find their place on the footrest. Raziel bent over too, and kissed his head, and together they folded over each other, gathered in, and Keith absorbed that moment, mental shutter-click. That image was with him now, staring out a Hopper window, middle of nowhere.

At the hospice, Charlie had helped push the chair up the long ramp. Had he understood that his mother would not be leaving this place? That they had come here for her to die? Had Keith even understood that, so-called adult that he was?

He remembered the top of Raziel's head as they crossed the threshold, and he'd wondered at her face and her thoughts at that moment. Yes, he had to think about Charlie. Charlie was going to need him. But this was Raz's life. He'd touched her shoulder briefly as they crossed, and could feel her shiver. He stopped the chair, and rested both hands on her shoulders. He wanted to feel those beautiful shoulders go down on a breath.

He kissed her head, and could feel her soften. She whispered, and he had to ask her to repeat the words: she wanted that bag she'd packed. No, she wanted something in it.

She lifted her old Nikon, a gift from her father, in time to capture an image of the woman moving to meet them as they passed through the doorway, and then she lowered it to her lap, and there wasn't another moment alone until after they were in her room.

"There are fish!" Charlie had announced from the window, as Raziel was settled into the bed. Outside the window, a Japanese garden, and a pond with the orange, black, yellow, and shiny white of koi. Raziel started to speak but stopped. Charlie stood a long time in front of the window watching the fish go in their circles, and then he went to explore what was behind the door in the room, the bathroom.

"This is *huge!*" They could hear him turning on the taps and flushing the toilet. "Plumbing may be in his future," Raziel had once remarked. "A generation to avoid Artist. Wise kid."

She took the moment, with Charlie out, to speak. "This is a perfect place," she'd said.

The missing words: *to die.* She took two more photos, the light through the window, Charlie emerging from the bathroom.

Charlie sat beside his mother on the bed. "Where will *I* sleep?"

She set down the Nikon as if it was a weight. "Your dad can ask about that." Her voice was soft, tired. Keith should have seen that coming. He felt unable to keep up with the needs.

"I'll ask the nurse," he said quickly.

"You should both go home," she said. "Come back later."

Charlie's face clouded.

Keith reached for his hand. "Let's let your momma rest. We're not far away. It takes only twenty minutes to drive here." He could see Charlie's hesitancy.

"Momma will be here when we come back later." He hoped he was right. It didn't feel like the day that Raziel would leave them.

He hoped his words were true, and that they would build trust in his son. He saw Charlie's trust in the world disappearing day by day. He didn't want to add to that.

"Can we bring Old Daisy?"

"We'll ask if we can," Keith said. "There are other people here, people who might not feel so comfortable with a big dog lolloping about."

"Old Daisy doesn't *lollop*," Charlie said miserably.

"We'll be back soon," Keith said to Raziel. He kissed her forehead. She was already half-asleep, camera on her belly. The nurse must have given her something.

Charlie stood in the doorway, a frown on his face, arms crossed over chest, thumbs tucked into armpits, his stance. "I'm gonna sleep here," he said.

."Yes, son," said Raziel drowsily.

Keith rubbed Charlie's shoulder and turned him towards the door. "We'll come back after we've eaten dinner."

"Okay." Charlie's hold-you-to-it tone.

They drove home, Charlie in his back seat booster, front passenger seat so empty.

They'd returned with blankets and Charlie's pillow, and with Owl, too, of course. The idea of Old Daisy was met with a silent shake of the head from the woman at the desk. There was a fold-out mattress for Charlie, and for Keith the reclining chair.

But he hadn't been able to sleep. For a while he stood by the window, looking for the moon, but it wasn't there. No, there was the thinnest sliver. He listened to the sounds of breathing, his wife's, and his son's with a gentle and occasional snuffle, and he wanted to imprint the moment, wanted for it to stay, even as he felt the force of time and life itself moving them, pushing them. And then his sternum grew that peculiar ache and he had to remind himself to breathe.

Now these weeks later, he could still feel that sensation, throughout all his body, if he let his mind stop there. He tried to right himself mentally, remind himself they were in Banff, the most beautiful place. They were in good old Hopper. They were on an adventure. With each thought, the memory diluted. He checked out the window: moon still there. *Could he go to sleep now? Please?*

He pushed the window farther open, he needed air. This summer had been too hot. He'd welcome more nighttime rain. He'd always appreciated when fall rolled around, and he could put together a pot of minestrone, or hot and sour soup, and put on his hockey skates for a late game of pickup.

But sleep didn't come.

By day three of hospice, the sound of the Nikon's shutter had come to an end. The week had passed with chess games, and a sense of ending.

"No, the rook can't jump others," he said. "Only the knight can do that." The chess moves of that time and earlier this September evening blended.

Charlie hadn't responded, had he? He'd eyed the two pieces, cementing the information in his mind as he did when feeling impatient with himself. Then he'd stopped, and looked over at his mother. She'd been sleeping all day, day six in that place.

It was close, Keith had known. He'd held his breath watching his son watching his mother. Now, mid-memory, he held his breath again.

"Is she going to open her eyes so I can talk to her?" Charlie had whispered.

"I don't know." He looked over at Raziel, too, and they both sat for some minutes. Then he moved over to sit beside his son, instead of across from him.

"If you want to talk to her, you shouldn't wait for her eyes to open. Her ears are open, and she can hear you, and she loves the sound of your voice." Were his words the right ones?

Charlie looked up at him. His son could plainly see his own pain in his eyes. He couldn't hide some things. Charlie needed to see this, needed to see him work through. Some things they wouldn't be able to talk about; show-don't-tell your children how to live, the writing class adage in the real world.

Charlie went to the bed, and with care he climbed onto it and lay beside his mother. No one needed to explain this to him. His head was in the hollow of her collarbone, and he spoke close to her ear. Keith could only hear the odd word. He sat back in his chair and watched through half-closed eyes. Only when Charlie fell asleep there did he think to take out his phone and take a photo for his son. Maybe someday he would want it. He couldn't share the picture in his heart.

Later, when the chair was reclined, and the room was awash in shadows, Charlie snuggled in with his dad, and Keith pulled a blanket over both of them that the nurse had kindly left.

He awoke first. The light was of the earliest morning, a narrow strip struggling between the blinds, summer-drenched yellow. The silence of the room told him she was gone. He was simultaneously aware of Charlie, sound asleep, head on his chest. Keith didn't want to awaken his son. He needed time to absorb.

He could see his wife, her body still, mouth hanging open in a way that might alarm her son. Instinctively, he pulled his arm tighter around Charlie. He could feel his own breathing and a tension. No, the tension was thinning, easing. What a strange sensation — it felt to be releasing, in flaking layers. For one crazy moment, he thought he'd come to pieces. He gulped a breath. After a moment, holding his son still, he felt a small degree of calm. He needed to speak, and whispered, "Goodbye my love, my life." He had to speak. If he didn't he'd choke.

The room was absolutely still.

A nurse appeared in the doorway, silently, as if he'd called her. His eyes met hers. "I'm so sorry," she breathed. She moved to Raziel, to make certain. Then looked at Charlie. "I'll get the doctor. But shall we wait for a moment? Your son is going to awaken." She lowered her voice. "Shall I cover her?"

How calm his voice sounded. "Are you able to close her mouth?" He was grateful for Charlie's weight leaning into him. Without, he wasn't sure where he'd be.

"I'll do my best." She moved towards the bed and shielded her attempts to meet his request. She turned to see if Charlie was awake yet. He was stirring. This was the time, then.

The nurse stepped away. She'd tried, but had not been able to do much. She'd pulled up the blanket and tucked it around Raziel's jawline to soften the effect. His son was fully awake now, and staring at the figure on the bed. The nurse moved the window blinds so less light came into the room.

"Is Mommy . . . ?"

"Yes, Charlie, your momma is gone."

"But she went when we were asleep." His voice, small and quavery.

"She knew we were here."

The nurse left the room, but before she did, she gave Charlie the gentlest of touches on his shoulder.

Charlie stared for a long moment, then turned to bury his face in his father's chest. "I wish she could have waited."

His son spoke the words he wished he could. He would rather not articulate his sense of it feeling unfair, and how could she go ahead and on her own, and leave without them saying good-bye. He couldn't think of the words to this sense of strange hurt. He'd wanted to be there for her. No, for himself. True. The hot reminder of how separate two people are, in truth, burned him. In that moment he felt *forsaken*. Who was the child in the room? He'd hugged his son tightly.

Keith awoke to a *roar*. Where was he? His mind scrambled to piece together. He'd been remembering, and must have slipped into sleep.

The *roar*. A train. So close, too close. Should he be moving the van? Surely it couldn't be quite on them. Wheels, tracks, whistle.

Where were they? Right. Banff. This must be a thing here. Old Daisy whined and paced in her narrow space. Keith patted the bed, and up she came.

Charlie woke in tears, and Keith held him. "It's just a train," he said, over and over. But Charlie wouldn't stop, even after the train had long passed, crying grief. Keith's own dam burst. And when he stopped, Charlie continued, and his dad held him. How could this beautiful place have such a monster running through the middle of the night? He felt a wave of anger. Even after Charlie had fallen back to sleep, there were aftershocks of sorrow that rocked the boy's entire body as Keith held him.

"It's okay," he kept whispering. "It's okay. We're okay." *It's a train. It's life. It hasn't quite run us down. We're here. We're together.*

6

How healthy was it to need Charlie the way he did? How would he be going through this time without his son? He let such half-formed thoughts pass into shadows before they could take shape.

When they awoke with the early morning sun, Keith felt beaten. Was this healing? Sorting through memories and pieces every night? The dreams made him not want to sleep. But this wasn't the first time in his life that dreams had pushed their ways in. Dreams had come after Charlie's birth, too, dreams he didn't quite know what to do with.

"I hate that old train," burst out of Charlie now.

"I've always loved the sound of trains. The wheels and clanking, it's easy to imagine it taking us somewhere," said Keith. "But last night was horrible."

"I hated it," repeated Charlie.

Keith could see it, the dream he'd had after Charlie was born, after Raz had found her studio and given up working in the living room, after he'd become the parent left behind at home — the House-Band, Raz called him, her play on house-husband, not knowing she'd created his blog title in that moment.

The dream of the yellow plastic oxygen mask, as if on an airplane, jiggling in front of his face. Really, it began after Raz started to travel, to take photographs of cycling Cuba, musicians in Saint Petersburg, Munich, documenting clouds off the coast in Wales. The more she travelled, the more Keith dreamed of the oxygen mask, yellow spider dangling in front of him. He'd push at it, push away. He looked at his son now, in front of him, still muttering about hate, his face twisty and his eyes unwaveringly on his father.

"Those mountains, though, eh?" Keith motioned to them. "They're incredible."

Charlie knew when he was being placated. And Keith knew that he was being lazy, and maybe even trying to distract himself, too. "It scared the crap out of me, really," he said now.

Go away, yellow oxygen mask.

"Felicity said Hopper would find things. Remember? She said he'll take us *right to them*. When do you think Hopper'll do that?" Anger bubbled under a thin surface. It could crack, and they'd fall in.

"Any idea what you want to find?"

"I don't know," said Charlie.

"Maybe we'll know it if we see it," said Keith.

"Maybe."

There was a disbelieving note in Charlie's tone that wrenched at Keith, but neither said anything further as they washed up and put away the few dishes.

Not long after setting out on the road, Charlie said, "I don't see anything. Do you really think we'll see it?"

"I think if we have it on our minds to look, then we might. Though things can take you by surprise, too." He was the adult. He was supposed to have hope.

An exit loomed, and they stopped to buy a coffee and licorice for Charlie, then pulled up to fill the tank. Charlie wanted to wash bug guts off the windshield. He stood on Old Daisy's climb-in log, squeegie in hand. It took a while, and a car pulled up behind them, with an impatient driver. He rolled down his window and watched the squeegie work. His face said, *Really?*

"Here," said Keith, reaching for the thing and handing the bag of candy to Charlie. "I'll finish up here, and you go offer that guy a licorice. He needs it."

Charlie took the licorice and surprised the man. At first he shook his head, but Charlie said some words that made him change his mind.

When they started up again, warm air gusted from the vents inside the van. Charlie waved his hand in front of them. "Dad, it's *hot!*"

"It'll cool in a minute."

But minutes later, back on the highway, it wasn't good. While it may have been the air conditioning, Keith suspected worse. They couldn't turn on the divided highway back to the gas station. He only hoped they could make it to the next exit. Charlie was frowning. "I don't like Hopper anymore."

"Hopper is an old van that has hauled our bums through the mountains," said Keith. But he wasn't liking Hopper so much himself, nor the prick of anxiety.

The mountains receded behind them, and he could see another exit. At this rate, they might be coasting in to whatever town was next. Something was dying. He'd turned off the a/c and they opened windows. Felicity hadn't said anything about potential problems. She couldn't have known this was going to happen. The words Keith had said to Charlie, he repeated to himself: Hopper was an old van, things happened to old vans. He took the next turnoff to drive down a street with a collection of bungalows and trees he didn't know the names of. Then turned onto a prairie town Main Street with a gas station and next to it a garage with a sign: *Bill's Auto.*

He pulled in, and tried to put this in perspective: this, a little vehicle problem, shouldn't make a difference. How could this bother them, and stop them, after going through what they'd gone through? They had no timeline. Did it matter when they arrived at Eryk and Cat's? No.

But the look on Charlie's face was hard to see. Keith tried to remind him. "Felicity said Hopper was about Adventure. Remember? It's all part of it."

They rolled to a stop beside a fence, Hopper done.

Turned out that this was the only mechanic shop in town. He came out of the garage, wiping his hands on a rag and looking grouchy about the interruption. The desk phone was ringing, and he picked it up with a curt nod to Keith. He ignored Charlie, scowling darkly over the desk.

"No," said the man into the phone. "I can't. I tell you, Pete's taken the week off, some flu thing, he says, and I'm on my own. Can't do nothing until next week, earliest."

Keith could hear the voice on the other end, though he couldn't make out any words. His stomach was sinking.

"You heard that," said the man after he hung up.

"I did," said Keith. He explained why they were there. "Hopper, I mean, the van, has kind of die — . . . stopped."

The man turned to stare at Charlie while Keith explained. Charlie's face was stuck on Big-People-Don't-Know-How-to-Do-Anything-Right.

The man's mouth stayed closed, but Keith could see he was tonguing breakfast bits out from between his teeth. He wanted to ask, "Too busy to brush?"

"Well, it'd mean delaying a customer who's a neighbour of mine. Maybe I can talk him into that. And there'll be more than one of them. This is a one-mechanic town. All the young people move away to live a broke life in the city." He sighed wearily, and held out his hand for the keys. He set out the front door, walking around to the side. "Don't know what they think they're going to find in the city, but they go."

No doubt this was a regular topic of conversation with this guy. Might even be Pete's case of flu. He wondered about Pete's age.

He and Charlie stood back while the man worked to start the engine, then lifted the hood. The sun was hot, with no shade. Keith tried not to think ahead to what this day might be like.

The man's face was as stuck as Charlie's — hard to tell if he had good news or bad. Well, it wouldn't be good, but less bad. They'd be here for a long long day. At the least.

"I know what it is," the man said.

That was good news.

"I don't have the parts."

Bad.

"They can probably be delivered late in the day."

Okay.

"I'm not going to do the a/c. I don't have time. But I'll fix what you need to get to where you're going. Which is?"

"We need to get to Manitoba. Gimli."

"You can do the a/c there. I'll fit in what I can do, and you can have it ready tomorrow. If you leave it with me."

"Can we sleep in it tonight?"

"Not if you want me to be able to get at it as I have time. I might work at sunrise. Inspiration, and all that, you know." He snorted.

"Is there a place to stay, a hotel?"

"We have a coupla B&Bs, but I happen to know they're booked with wedding guests."

Small town knowledge.

This wasn't good.

The mechanic was looking at him. "I need to get back to work. Should I call in the parts order?"

"Please, yes."

Charlie held out the bag of licorice. His blackened teeth showed. "You want one?"

Bill, assuming he was Bill of *Bill's Auto,* didn't hesitate and reached into the bag, pulled out three of the sticky black pieces. He stalked off, then turned back, and shaded his eyes from the sun. "Look," he said. "You got a tent in there?"

"No, no tent. We sleep in the van."

"Well," he said, "you get what you need for the night, and you can borrow my tent. There's a campsite by the river. With an outhouse." He pointed out a direction. "About a ten-minute walk. Stores are that way." He motioned in another direction. "My house is next door. Give me a minute, and I'll get you the tent.

There's an old wagon around, to haul your stuff." He heaved a sigh. But with the offer of a tent, Keith suspected his growly exterior did not match his interior.

Mostly he felt dumbstruck over all this, over the small town of it. Then he turned and saw Charlie's face. "A tent!" Charlie whispered, scowl gone.

"You're good with that?"

"Oh yeah! Let's get our stuff." Charlie darted off, no doubt to find the wagon the guy had mentioned.

He'd already spotted it, and they took it to the van, found bedding, food stuff, the small extra cooler, some dishes. Keith went into the hiking pack he'd brought along to find their mini stove.

Charlie moved in double time, and he rounded up Old Daisy's supplies, which impressed Keith. "You take good care of our old girl," he said.

They set up the tent, after locating the riverbank site. With no instructions, the tent took a chunk of time to figure out. Keith didn't want to ask the mechanic, Bill, about the how-to. It could be a puzzle to solve, and Charlie was humming as they set out the bits and pieces to make sense of. They decided to set it up by a perfect tree with spreading branches to shade Old Daisy. There were several picnic tables, and a water faucet on a post, with a small wooden platform.

Charlie filled the dog's bowl and set it by the tent door. "I love this," he declared.

They'd never spent a night in a tent. Charlie was ready to bunk down right then, but the afternoon heat made the tent a greenhouse, and Keith suggested a walk into town instead of bedtime at midday. He said nothing about shopping, nothing about the restocking they needed to do.

"Let's see what's in this town."

They set off. *Town* was a string of small stores including the grocery market they'd have to visit, a restaurant, a hardware store, and — what might add a whole other level to the day — a bakery.

The window stopped Charlie, and the open door wafted vanilla, cinnamon, and who-knew-what.

"Cardamon," the man behind the counter said when he saw them sniffing.

The abrupt change in momentum, from travelling to not travelling, had made Keith feel as if there were something he was supposed to be doing, and it wasn't getting done. He wanted to ask the man how he lived in this small place. But his feeling wasn't about the place. It was the stopping of trajectory.

The man behind the counter looked like he might be the baker, too. He had the same look that Trev had at this point in the day, with flour in his hair and too many hours awake. Like Trev, this guy appeared to like his days. He was wearing an apron that made Keith smile. Here, in this town the size of a pancake and with the flatness of same, this man had some colour, some life. The apron was a blown up black and white photo of some showgirl from another era, neck down.

The man was so patient as Charlie dithered. He asked Keith about their travels, and Keith explained about the van.

"The river campsite!" he said. "Beautiful down there, lucky yous! My husband and I go there sometimes, to spend an evening. He'll catch river fish and I'll make us a feast over a fire, oh my!"

"How long have you lived here?" Keith asked.

"I grew up here, some kind of quiet kid who always felt alone. Then I moved to NYC, worked in theatre, loved the sweat, the backstage, the crazy times. But had to come home."

Keith had to wrap his head around that. From New York City to a one-mechanic bump. Little bakery on the prairie. He couldn't help his eyes dropping to the apron, and the man laughed.

"Had to come home?" Keith wanted more of the man's story. So Mechanic Bill was mistaken; some who left did return. With courage.

"All the world's a stage. We're all living on the boards under the lights. There's nothing to say that we can't love all our places."

Charlie had ventured to the end of the counter and slipped around the corner of it, so he wasn't having to look up and over at the man. He appeared to be entranced. The man put his hands on his hips and posed, apron swaying with him, all costume and cleavage. He put his hands in the air and twirled around, then back to the hips. "What do you think, beautiful boy?" He smiled down at Charlie, who stared at him a minute and then put his own hands in the air and twirled too, almost falling over. The two men laughed, and Charlie giggled as the baker clapped. "Bravo!"

"I like the shiny things on your apron," said Charlie. Sequins.

"Aren't they something?"

"This town needs you," said Keith.

"I'm in the mission field, making believers. Really, I came back for the quiet kids who are tired of feeling alone. They need to see me here. They need to know you can leave, you can come back. You can do whatever you want."

Keith put out his hand. "I'm Keith, from Vancouver. This is Charlie."

"Dari's my name." He shook Keith's, then Charlie's. Then he withdrew a tray of tarts from the display case. "I'll bet you'd like a few of these. The Queen of Hearts has nothing on us!" He glanced at Keith for his okay. "Four for the price of three," he said enticingly.

"We always used to get three," said Charlie, studying the offerings. "But my mom died."

Dari didn't miss a beat. "I'm sorry to hear that." He pointed to a heart-shaped beauty. "You could have one of those and leave it in a special place to remember your mom. Or eat it with your dad and share a favourite mom-memory. Call it a mom-ory maybe." He made a sudden motion and placed that one in the box. "That one's on me. You choose four more."

He didn't rush Charlie who, after a moment and a whispered *thank you*, took his time pointing out his four, changing his mind several times about the last choice. "That one looks like a cheesecake."

Dari pushed and pulled a cardboard shape to create a box from tabs and cutouts. Charlie was pleased when the box was altogether, with a cellophane window and handle. Dari wrapped a red bow on the handle and held it out for Charlie to take. "You know, if you go to the far end of the street and find the footpath to your right, you'll have a much prettier return to the river."

"Sounds good," said Keith.

When they were about to go out the door, Dari called out. "Wait a minute, someone left behind a book. Maybe you can take care of it." He held a picture book with worn edges. "Tarts go well with books, and books with tarts."

Charlie's happiness was complete.

It might be a good time to interject the looming food gathering. "We have to explore the grocery store. We can't live on tarts," Keith said.

"You could live on tarts," corrected Dari, "but what would you feed your dog under the table?"

Charlie laughed.

"Right. We're off to find table gifts for Old Daisy," said Keith. This might put a new spin on the ordeal of shopping; how Charlie loathed those errands.

Dari wished them an exquisitely adventurous trip.

Usually, just outside the door of the grocery store, Charlie began his manifestation of junior Jekyll and Hyde. Sometimes it'd even start in the car. But this grocery store was unlike anything they'd ever seen: the door, of warm honey-coloured wood, was held open by a huge pot of cherry tomatoes with a *pick me!* sign. Charlie picked two, put one in his mouth and handed the other to Keith. In they went, Charlie leading. That was a first. He stared at the sandwich and ice cream counter, and ran to goggle the flavours set in the hand-painted freezer. Next he discovered the cat that slept on a cushion on a low window sill, and he sat beside her and showed her the tarts through the window in the box. Keith went to gather food while the peace lasted.

If only every grocery store had a resident cat, shopping might be very different from the nightmare it frequently was. He eyeballed Charlie over a shelf as he found oatmeal and cans of soup and those crackers they both liked. Charlie was petting the cat, talking to her, singing the tune that Old Daisy liked. Oh, she didn't like it! She leapt off the window sill just as Keith was done. But she'd bought him time, and he could have kissed the little stripey tiger of her. He could have told her about other times, of wrangling with grocery carts and bringing down displays of soft drinks, and all sorts of bad memories. But today was a good shopping day. Take it.

They set off to find the footpath, Keith with two bags, Charlie with his beautiful box, and a bit of a hum. The afternoon heat was at its peak, and Keith hoped it would cool as they neared the river, but it didn't feel to matter. The day was just right. *Good things happen.*

"There's lots of grass, isn't there?" said Charlie. The town was behind them now, and the river not in sight.

"There is." Keith wasn't sure if Charlie saw the expanse of early fall and drying grass as he did, utterly dull. But Charlie said, "We can see everything from here." Not the river, but endless sky and more sky.

"*Grass* everything!" Fragrant in the heat, the sound of grasshoppers all they could hear.

"Where are they?" Charlie wanted to know.

"Deep inside, I think."

Charlie stood still. "I see only grass."

"The grasshoppers are hiding."

A plane flew overhead, so high they heard nothing, but Charlie paused to look to the flume. Keith paused to look at his son, to watch the intensity. Grasshoppers, grass, pause. Charlie went back to looking for the hoppers.

The day had come to a standstill. Charlie reached into the grass and picked out bright and feathery orange. The word *paintbrush* came to Keith, he wasn't sure from where. "At least, I think that's what it's called," he added.

Charlie held it up. "It was hidden, too." He turned it in his hands, examining, before walking on. Again he stopped, pulled aside the grass. "Look!" Gold. Farther. Purple. Pink. More orange. Made Keith think of the colour at Raziel's service.

He started to see the blooms then, too, hidden in the heavy grass. The wind parted and revealed, and then blew over again. "Look," he pointed out to Charlie. "Like waves." They watched the grasses move in the hot wind. Except this time they knew what was hidden. The river sounded, growing louder as they neared.

Charlie didn't pick more, but he grasped his paintbrush along with the box handle, and reached for his dad's hand. Back at the campsite others had shown up, a family with a large RV with pop outs. Children, four, Keith counted, were playing by the river. He could see Charlie's curiosity and fascination with them, but understood his reluctance to walk over and join; he'd grown up as an only child, too.

But when Charlie went to Old Daisy, who'd spent the time under the shade of the tree, and released her, she headed off with no hesitation. After a moment, Charlie followed. One child, the smallest, climbed away on a picnic table, but the siblings talked her down in the way they knew, and Old Daisy won her over, and they all danced and tagged.

Charlie neared Keith, now sitting in the foldout chair, unread book in hands, hat over face, eyes closed. But not sleeping. "Can I share the tarts with them?" he whispered.

"Butterknife in the drawer," said Keith, not moving the hat. "Cut each into halves and share. Save the cheesecake for us later."

Charlie made a happy sound as he hurried off. After they shared the tarts, he showed them how to sashay and twirl with their hands in the air.

Keith set about assembling grilled cheese sandwiches with pieces of olive and tomato, laying them out in the pan balanced on the tiny hiking stove they'd brought.

Charlie set the table, plates and a knife to cut up the sandwiches, a bowl of ketchup for dipping, and chattered about the tent, the kids, the games.

He'd set the picnic table with three plates, and stood staring, anguished.

Keith started to remove the nearest of the three, but some small motion of Charlie's, or maybe some sound, made him pull back. He left the third plate in its place.

Charlie crossed his arms, tucking his thumbs into his armpits, a Charlie thing to do since he was two. And he stood glowering at the table. When he began to cry, his arms fell to his sides, and he looked alone, unguarded. Keith wrapped arms around him. He caught a glimpse of a child's face in the RV, heard a murmur of voices, and the face disappeared.

Those grilled cheese sandwiches were cold and stuck to the pan when Keith and Charlie were finally ready to eat. Keith reheated them, and they ate with few words. Then he opened the almost forgotten cheesecake. Wordlessly, he handed a second fork to Charlie, and they ate it together out of the box.

They washed the dishes, readied the bed. Such a grimness to Charlie. He wasn't saying anything about the tent now. Keith let him be with his thoughts. They brushed their teeth by the water tap, settled in under the quilt, then tossed it aside, too warm.

"Let's read that book Dari gave you."

He could feel Charlie's nod as he lay with his face to Keith's shoulder.

The title was simple: *Seasons*. Keith bundled the pillows to readability, with Charlie unmoving. He opened the book. Of course it started with spring: why did all season books start with spring? Why couldn't they end there?

They went through the seasons, the colour-filled illustrations, with children and grandparents, springs and winters. He closed it and set it between Charlie's pillow and the billowing tent. A book had calmed, once again. He turned out the camping lantern.

And waited for Charlie to say, "Can you tell me about the time," but after long moments, he turned and knew Charlie had drifted off to sleep. Sleep was a gift. He lay there listening to his breathing, and matching it.

Along came a spider and sat down beside . . .

A flash of mental-yellow, and the mask was back. There was no pushing away the thing. He remembered how, in his dreams after Charlie was born, he finally grabbed at it and held it to his face, over his nose and mouth, breathed, deeply, and it had disappeared.

And the time after that, and again. Once he took hold of the thing, once he breathed, it disappeared. The sooner he picked it up, the quicker the result. Until finally it stopped showing up. Until now.

He reached out into the darkness, and the yellow disappeared.

He had to remember how that worked. For next time.

Before sunrise the family RV pulled out and later, before Bill came along with the Hopper update of ready to go, Keith caught Charlie in the midst of possibly giving thanks: walking around the empty campground, Old Daisy in tow, touching the tree, the picnic table, a big rock the children had used for a game.

Did he have the same sense that Keith did, in that moment, of knowing they would never be in this same place again?

Keith looked sideways at his son as they drove. Did Charlie find the movement healing, the sound of tires just right? He wondered. He took a closer look: he needed to find scissors at Cat's for the hair hanging over Charlie's eyes. But his son could see enough to count dead bugs on the windshield.

There was the road sign for Gimli. They were minutes away. Keith had a sudden mental image of Cat's eyes, so like her sister's. He had to press harder on the gas pedal to keep going. He hadn't realized he'd pulled back as he had.

"There it is, the Cat-and-Eryk homestead." Cat's word for it.

Hopper went down the long gravel driveway, passing a substantial vegetable garden, much of it finished for the season, corn stalks leaning and dried, tomato plants pulled out from the ground and set aside in a wheelbarrow, some still standing, looking ragged, glimpses of colour in their greyed bones.

"That's where they grow their vegetables," he said to Charlie, realizing that Charlie had no idea what 'growing vegetables' looked like. "We'll get Eryk to show us around, okay?"

"Not Auntie Cat?"

"I'm not sure what your aunt can do. She's supposed to take it easy. Sitting around. We're lucky she's not in the hospital. We'll ask Uncle Eryk what we can help with. Garden clean up, for sure."

They stopped outside the house. Keith had driven in slowly, but still a cloud of dust hung in the air over them. Somewhere behind the house was the lake, and west and south was farmland. But in front of them was the white, wide porch, ageing honeysuckle climbing up the siding and over the roof. Was it obvious to Charlie that Keith was delaying getting out of the van? He fiddled with the key, the emergency brake. Not that a brake was necessary.

"Come on, Dad." Charlie with his frown that kept turning up.

One couldn't shirk the task of healing, not with a child. Pretending wasn't an option. "Right," Keith said. He high-fived Charlie between the seats. He always felt silly doing the high five thing. A bit of pretend right there. He climbed out slowly. Charlie was already halfway to the house.

The door opened. "You're here!" It could have been Raziel speaking. He didn't dare close his eyes.

Charlie was staring at his aunt, too. Before Keith hugged Catalina, he reached for Charlie and dragged him closer, brought him into the hug, connecting over Cat's enormous belly. "Whoa!" said Charlie, feeling movement. "What?" He had a funny look on his face, wonder, knowing exactly what it was but not quite sure he was supposed to know. Or say. Not so long ago, he would have asked. Before Grade 1.

Cat and Keith had to laugh. "The baby must have wanted to be in on the hug," said Cat. "What'd he do? Kick you in the head?"

Charlie laughed and rubbed his temple. "It didn't hurt," he said. "Hey! How do you know it's a boy?"

"I don't," said Cat. "It's going to be a surprise. It's a baby, I know that."

Eryk found them as he came around the side of the house, probably from the barn, with Brando at his heels, mixed mutt with shepherd colour in him and the ruff and overturned tail of a snow dog.

Old Daisy woofed from Hopper.

"I'll let her out." Charlie went to the van.

"He's such a solid little fellow," said Cat. "I don't think I've ever seen a child with resolution like his."

The two dogs greeted each other, Brando wary for his people and property, and Old Daisy puppylike. Eryk picked up Charlie in one arm, and looped his other around Keith. Eryk wasn't much for email or a phone call. He was an in-person man, and a no-time-passed one, too. He could catch up wherever they'd left off.

"Brother!" said Eryk. He rubbed the top of Charlie's head after he set him down. Charlie giggled.

"I'm not your *brother.*"

"No, you're *little brother,*" said his uncle. "You okay with that?" He looked, with genuine care, then burst out, "Oh my, I could eat you up!"

"No!" Charlie cried, thrilled.

Keith couldn't think what exactly he'd been dreading about this visit. Each one of the *first-time-after* moments was going to be tough, and they'd just gotten through another.

They washed up and sat to share late lunch on the porch, thick bacon, fresh tomato, and lettuce sandwiches that Eryk threw together. After, Charlie curled up on the wicker sofa with the weighty calico. Cat told Eryk where there was a basket of children's books that she'd collected, and Charlie was pleased as he opened one to share with the magnificent and poorly, or perfectly, named Rover.

"She's no farm cat," Keith whispered to Cat.

"She only looks pretty. You haven't seen her find a rat," she whispered back. She sipped the iced tea that Eryk handed to her before he headed back to the barn.

Charlie must have heard: he looked at the voluptuous orange and white Rover, and paused. A quick lip purse, the smallest of head shakes, and he went back to turning pages for her. Rover dutifully studied the illustration. In the fields, grasshoppers cricked, and the afternoon settled and felt surprisingly right after all the driving. There were such hummingbird-alighted moments as these when everything felt as if all might be okay. Just for the moment. That was enough.

"I have some things in Hopper the van for you. I'll get them," said Keith.

When he returned, Cat had left her chair and footstool, and stood in the open doorway. She held the screen door for him, and followed. He had the dress and coat over an arm, with the sweaters piled on top. She took the sweaters from him. "Raziel loved colour."

"She did."

"Mother said that almost everyone at the service was in bright colours. Said she'd never seen anything like it!" Cat touched a sweater that was a swirl of all the brightest greens. She fingered the beads woven into it.

"Raz had that made by a friend who does textile art. The beads are handblown glass."

Cat held it up to herself, and caught a look in the mirror. "Am I brave enough?" she asked. "Raz had no problem with people looking at her. I'll think about her when I put this on. Maybe the thought will give me the courage." She folded it with care and set it down. Picked up the next, a deep blue. "Well, this is understated. Relatively."

"I thought that one would go with your hair."

"The white streak in the front, you're thinking?" Cat laughed. The streak was a family thing. She'd had it for a half-dozen years already. Raz had coloured hers.

"It looks good," he said as she held that one up, too. Next, a red one. "This one is for grey days."

He could see her gulp when he handed her the pink dress. "I remember this," she said. She'd need time to get used to it even being in her closet.

"I think you need this," he said, about the coat. "Raziel loved this coat, but Vancouver's never cold enough to wear it."

She started to hang it up but stopped and handed it to Keith to hold for her, some motion and assumption of Miriam in that, surely, and he slipped it on, belled sleeves over arms. She pulled up the wide fur collar around her face and stopped long enough to see her profile in the mirror. "Oh my. You know, I think I might get used to this, once the snow comes. Thank you for bringing it all this way."

"That's my mommy's coat." Charlie appeared in the doorway.

"Are you okay with me having it?" his aunt asked.

He took his time answering. Old Daisy came and stood behind him, and he turned to pet her first. "Yes," he said finally. "It looks nice on you. Like it did on my mom."

"Thank you," said Cat. "I'll think of her every time I wear it."

"You look like a Winter Queen," he said.

Keith helped Cat take it off, and she found a wide hanger in the antique wardrobe by their front door. Keith could hear a sniffle as the wardrobe door clicked closed. "You all right?" he asked.

"I will be," she said. "We have to be. But it's my naptime now. Probably about forty-five minutes, maybe an hour, every day."

Charlie ran to her with a hug. They took their time before untangling. Keith spotted a box of tissues. He handed them around, and took one for himself.

"You do the nap thing. Charlie and I can do some garden or yard work maybe."

"Oh." She appeared stymied for a moment. "Well, there are still raspberries to pick. Might be corn, too, and then the stalks need to be pulled out of the ground. Not sure what all else. Eryk will know." She turned to go, and Keith read exhaustion in her shoulders.

"We've added to your day," he said. "I'm sorry." Being asked for gardening direction wasn't what she needed. *Eryk will know.* He had to remember to ask Eryk for directions.

"Don't be sorry." She disappeared into her room.

Keith found a bowl for raspberries and he and Charlie went to see what they could find. Charlie was happy to pick, and there were so many still. There were some few straggling tomatoes, cherry tomatoes, too. Keith stripped them, and pulled up some of the plants to add to the pile at the side.

Charlie finished filling the bowl with raspberries, and left to get a glass of water. Keith could see him taking off his hat and scratching the back of his head.

Later, Cat was back on the porch, with Charlie beside her. She was pleased with their harvesting, and sent Charlie in to fetch his dad some lemonade. Charlie set the pint glass full on the table when he returned. "Do you see what Auntie Cat's making? A sweater."

Cat held up the mix of colours. "I must have had in my mind your Momma's service when I dreamed up this for the little one."

"I want to make one like it. Auntie Cat said she'll teach me how to knit."

"Then you'll have to make me one, too," said Keith.

Cat spoke. "We'll start with a scarf, okay?"

Charlie nodded.

"When did you learn how to do this, the sweater?" Keith asked. "Or have you always knitted? Did Miriam teach you?"

She laughed. "Imagine: Miriam teaching me."

"Right."

"It was YouTube lessons. Eryk went out to find the wool. I hate this not doing anything, not when there's so much to do on the farm."

"When can we start my scarf?" Charlie wanted to know.

"How about tomorrow? Or if you go find the jug sitting on the stairs, full of knitting needles, bring me the thick green needles. They'll be a good size for your fingers. There's a ball of orange wool there, too."

Charlie left before her last few words.

"I can do that. I get to be the one to teach him how to knit!" Cat sounded pleased.

After dinner, on the porch where Cat and Eryk lived at this time of year, Cat said, "A neighbour brought over a surprise. Then it can be bedtime for you and for me, Charlie."

Eryk carried out an enormous glass bowl and set it on the table.

"What *is* that?" asked Charlie. He eyed it as he would a fish bowl. "Everything is mashed, jello and pudding." He peered closer. "And cake and some kind of berries."

"Saskatoons," said his aunt.

"That's a town."

"It's a kind of berry, too." Cat smiled. "I know. It's confusing. Wait until you have to spell Saskatchewan."

Charlie poked into the bowl, remembered that wasn't a cool thing to do, and pulled back. "It's like a bunch of people were carrying desserts and bumped into each other." His eyes shone. "Maybe they had a food fight and threw it in the bowl."

"So that's how our neighbours make dessert," Eryk said. "I wondered why they gave it to us!"

Charlie's eyes got big. Then he squinted. "No way."

"When you taste it, that won't matter." Eryk handed Charlie a spoon, who filled it tentatively.

They ate on the porch, and watched the shadows lengthen. Brando stretched out on the grass at the foot of the steps, and Old Daisy lay by her boy, her chin on his foot. Keith could see Cat noting that, smiling, looking at her nephew, lip caught in her teeth.

Eryk went to do his evening walk of some of the perimeter of the property. Brando liked to patrol, too. Old Daisy tagged along, and Charlie, too. Cat and Keith watched. "I'll have to join in some evening while we're here. It's a good time for a walk."

"I miss that piece of routine," said Cat. "But I'm glad for your company."

By the time the patrol returned, shadows stretched as far as they could, with the sun close to setting. The line of poplars, the windbreak, swayed gently. Keith got a waft of what could only be called fall air. Summer was at its end, and each had a sweater. Eryk handed Charlie a small blanket, then kneeled to help him pull it over his bare legs. He did like his summer shorts.

"He's so like you," said Cat. "Little Keith. He has your patience, your approach."

"We spend a lot of time together. He slows me down."

He felt a pang, maybe guilt, with not attributing some part of Charlie to Raziel. But he'd nurtured the slow part of parenting, he'd written about it often enough: slowing was significant to contentment. Raz used to say that he was slow enough for both of them, and that freed up her velocity. She would grab him and hug him, with a tussley hug, and laugh that laugh of hers, light, then off to somewhere. Anything but slow. She'd said that taking a photograph was the right amount of time to create. She'd sketch with a handful of lines, and could capture what other artists took hours to create. But even that took too long. She'd never wanted to paint. He used to wonder what would come of it, if she did.

Click. Shutter-speed.

She never acknowledged how it could take time to get a shot she wanted.

Sometimes he had these thoughts, this trying to put pieces together. He wanted to remember his wife; he'd enjoyed her enigma. He'd thought he'd have a lifetime to learn her. But this was it, the pieces he was left with. To study for time to come. He wanted to nurture the memories, and this time with her sister would do that, would add to what he carried. Along with the wind, he felt a gust of what these next days would yield. And felt gratitude.

"Tomorrow," Charlie said. "We can go see the ice."

"Right." The time was important for Charlie, too.

They went to Hopper to prepare for the night. Eryk had connected them with power and water so they wouldn't have to worry about their off-grid supply. He'd offered them a room in the house, but Charlie insisted on Hopper, and it'd be easier on Cat. After brushing teeth and a read, he lay beside his son, and in spite of thinking he'd return to the porch, he fell asleep.

Best sleep in weeks, with the sense of having arrived. No dreams, no memories. Just deep.

"The Rest of My Life" / *Sloan*

"My Best Was Never Good Enough" / *Bruce Springsteen*

"Love'll Set Me Free" / *Michael Franti*

8

After breakfast, Cat rested the end of one needle in her lap and with both hands cast on a number of stitches. "I'll do a few rows to give you a good start. You watch."

Charlie stood and watched intently until he was leaning against her thigh. She laughed. "You're going to knock me down. Here, sit." She pulled a nearby stool into position between her knees. She circled his two arms with hers, and began to teach.

"Your stomach is really big." He leaned forward. Cat laughed, and so did he. "Sorry," she said.

"Can I use the green wool now?" Charlie wanted to know.

"When you've finished this row," she promised. He kept at it, child fingers pushing the yarn on the plastic needles, his aunt guiding. Slow.

"I'll bring in more raspberries." Keith wandered off to fetch a bowl. Cat had promised that there would be even more of the all-season berries today. Charlie's picking the day before had been thorough, but Cat said that as long as they harvested, the berries would continue growing until the frost came. Keith hadn't known that about raspberries.

The day passed with small tasks, the keeping of home. While Eryk worked in the barn and ventured out on some errand, Keith poked around the house looking for things that needed to be done. Firewood needed splitting, and two back steps needed a last coat of stain, tasks Eryk had no time for. Keith could hear the murmur of the knitting lesson, with the occasional shout of laughter from Charlie as his aunt shared a story. Then a wail as a stitch was dropped. Stopping for stories and snack.

This was what they all needed. He was astonished now not by Cat's patience, but by Charlie's.

The result of sitting for hours in a vehicle? A child's grief was so different. There appeared to be times of complete freedom from it, and other times of being lost in it, needing to lash together some flotsam to hold on to.

Keith sat nearby when he'd finished the stairs, and took pleasure in the sight of the two. It wasn't lost on him that these were moments when he and Charlie were not leaning on each other.

Then lunch. Keith's turn to dig through the fridge and pull it together. After, Eryk took Charlie with him for another errand.

"So much preparation for the fall." Cat watched the two of them drive down the driveway. She left Keith on his own again as she disappeared for her nap.

Eryk and Charlie still hadn't returned mid-afternoon. It felt strange not to have his son's presence.

Cat suggested Keith put together some raspberries with cream and brown sugar, and together they sat on the porch with the sound of her rocking chair back and forth, a sound that took him back to childhood, long ago grandparents. They talked about the knitting, the Hopper drive, the grasshoppers in the afternoon heat. After a brief silence, Cat asked, as if it had been on her mind: "How did you tell Charlie that his mother was ill?" She studied the berries positioned on her spoon.

It took him a moment to get to a place to respond. "Raz didn't want to tell him. We argued about it, is the truth, for all the bit of time we had to argue. The days passed, and I felt terrible saying nothing. Then it was time, and I told him. He said he knew."

"He doesn't miss anything, does he."

"I'm glad we talked about it before she died. We were sleeping, he and I, in the chair in the room, and when we woke in the morning, she was gone."

"She died in the night?"

Keith recognized the hunger in her voice, to have been there, to not be asking these questions.

"She did. That's what Charlie said. He couldn't believe she'd gone while we were asleep." He wasn't prepared for the emotions that crept up around him then. "He felt that we'd been left behind in a way. He wished she'd waited."

"Of course," said Cat.

"I felt the same. To be honest."

"Right," she said. "I understand."

"Miriam didn't tell you anything?" Even as he asked, he realized he'd not shared anything of those days with his mother-in-law. Realized that somehow he expected those closest, like Cat, to just know. Osmosis. What a ridiculous way to think. The grieving mind was a Swiss-cheesed thing. Cat couldn't know, not without being told. Only Charlie and he had been there.

"I'm so sorry," he said. "I should have thought. I didn't even share this with your mother." Another wave of emotion. "Though she never asked," he said, not as an excuse, at least not at that moment. But as a thought he was sifting through.

"I asked," said Cat. "If she'd wanted to know, she should have asked."

He wasn't sure though. "I don't know," he said wearily. "Could she? Is she capable of that?"

"I did myself the favour of deciding to stop asking that years ago."

They watched the growing cloud of dust as Eryk's truck slowly came up the long driveway, Charlie waving from the back seat.

As much as Keith wanted something to carry home from this time together, Cat needed pieces, too.

She was tired the following day, slept late, breakfasted, and returned to bed. Maybe they were tiring her.

Mid-morning, he did some vacuuming and headed for the porch with an iced tea to find Charlie, knitting needles in his hands and red-faced. "I can't do it! I can't remember." He pulled on the wool. "Where is Auntie Cat?" he asked.

"She's in bed still, Charlie. She needs to rest when her body tells her to."

Charlie stopped pulling on the knitting. It took Keith a moment to register the disbelief in his eyes. And fear.

"Is she sick?"

"No, Charlie, she isn't sick, she's having a baby. Sometimes having a baby means needing lots of care and taking it easy."

Charlie still appeared unconvinced. He picked up the knitting and started in on it again, pulling.

"I don't think that's going to help. If you pull it off, it'll unravel, and I won't be able to help you."

"How come you don't know how to knit?" Charlie gave a last twist of the knitted bit. The frustration was too much. He pushed himself out of the chair.

"Nobody had the patience of your Auntie Cat to teach me," said Keith. "She's a good teacher. When she's awake, maybe she can help, and I'll take a video with my phone so we can remember her lessons, okay? Maybe I should learn, too."

Charlie pulled the screen door and let himself into the house. Keith caught the door before it slammed. He could have followed Charlie, but he didn't. Give Charlie time. He sat in the chair and took a gulp of tea. The truth was, he'd been a boy, and no one would have taught a boy how to knit. Or no one in his family. But why tell Charlie that?

Keith listened for any sound, but after some bit of clatter inside the house, there was silence. He sipped the drink, tried to quell what Charlie had left him.

Eventually he could hear stirring, Cat's soft voice, and he went in to find Charlie wrapped up in his mother's coat, Winter Queen, on the couch, with his aunt beside him, holding him.

Charlie had not yet seen him, and Cat motioned to let them be. He returned to the porch, eased back into the creaky chair. There was a strange sensation in his chest that at any other time in his life might have pushed him to see a doctor. Heartache.

The clatter he'd heard must have been Charlie pulling the coat from its hanger. He tried to align his heart with his mind, tried to calm himself. He couldn't know the minutiae of his son's healing and journey, and his worrying about it wouldn't serve. Though that might not stop him from worrying.

Charlie and Cat came to the door, and Cat said, "If you can make us lunch, I'm going to give Charlie another knitting lesson."

Keith left them to it. There were leftovers and more trifle, and when he'd brought the food outside, he took his phone and filmed Cat's hands with the wool and needles so they could remember how this was done. Charlie took a look at the video and approved. Peace restored for tenuous moment.

In the evening, Charlie was insistent: they had to see the ice arena. Cat was yawning and off to read in bed. Brando and Old Daisy followed her, crowding the doorway as she waved the men and boy off.

"Not much to see in summertime," said Eryk, "and we'll have to drive. It's just down the street from your grandmother's house. On our way let's drive by the house where your mother grew up."

It wasn't a long drive.

When Keith saw the house, memories of the one time he'd been there came to him. The sky was darkening, but windows were alight. Streetlights came on. Eryk pulled up in front of the sidewalk and started to get out, but he looked to the back seat and stopped.

Charlie'd gone still, eyes on the house. "What is it, son?" Keith asked. He never said 'son' like that. How odd. "Charlie?"

"You mean Mom and Grandma Miriam lived in that house?"

"Your mom grew up there, yes. So did your Auntie Cat."

Charlie's eyes were opened wide.

Like all other houses in this town, the simple rancher hid an in-ground basement with its ubiquitous damp bedrooms of youth, a recreation room with couches once coveted for upstairs, now taken down. The exterior was brickwork and intemperate stucco, yard with snow-stunted trees.

Keith spoke. "If we knocked on the door, the owner might let us look around. People often do that, especially in a place like this. I can show you your mom's room when she was little."

Charlie had a strange expression on his face, hard to read. Though with those wide eyes, Keith would guess fear.

A woman had come to stand in the front doorway, and she opened the screen door, gave a hesitant wave.

Charlie saw her, and said, "No, I don't want to."

"Maybe tomorrow," suggested Keith.

"No," Charlie repeated, and he sounded certain. "That house is sad."

Eryk grunted as if he'd been punched. He turned the key, started the engine, and pulled the truck away from the curb, muttering about going to the park. He looked shocked, as if he expected children to always go along with whatever was on the adult agenda, unnerved by Charlie's unequivocal no.

He still hadn't said a word as they pulled up to the ice arena, and he climbed out without a glance to the back seat.

The truck was high, and Keith had to hold his arms to Charlie and lower him to the ground. As Keith's arms wrapped around Charlie, he felt the boy fold in on himself, and he held him tightly for a long moment, waiting to feel him loosen before setting him on the browned grass. But Charlie skirled off as if his insides were wound tightly, and Keith turned brittle. Eryk still appeared beaten. They followed, as far as the boards of the rink. Both leaned on the boards and watched as Charlie ran in circles.

"How did he see that about the house, do you think?" Eryk asked.

"I don't know," said Keith.

The streetlight by the arena flickered out. And the sudden silence, without its buzz, was unexpected respite. Charlie stopped his frenetic running to stare. Then up at the sky. He lay on his back in the middle of the empty rink.

Keith could hear Eryk suck in his breath.

"Parenting isn't always like this," Keith said. "This has been a tough day."

"It's not that," Eryk said. "It's that he's right. Cat's told me things. It was a sad sad house." His words were cut off by a shout from Charlie.

"Look!" Charlie's arm had straightened into the air above him. "Stars!"

Stars were coming out. The streetlight's death had created a night sky.

Yet even as he looked up, Keith felt shaken. He knew how he felt about Miriam. He knew Raziel and Cat's father had not been a part of their lives, not even before he disappeared. He knew that one sister had chosen to leave this place, and one had chosen to stay. Raziel had said little about childhood sadness. She had burst out beyond whatever her experiences had been, and didn't want to look back. Had he, Keith, been immune to her suffering? He'd asked, and she'd refused to talk. But perhaps he should have done more. What kind of partner had he been?

"Was it really bad, do you think?" he managed to ask. Then he realized that Eryk's eyes were fully on him, concerned.

"Nothing they couldn't handle," he said. "Their father was nonexistent, and Miriam was self-absorbed. But the girls were there for each other."

"That's too much to ask of kids," said Keith. He wanted to wipe his nose on his shirt. He sniffed.

"You're right. But it made them strong."

Strength's a funny thing, Keith wanted to say. Too much strength can cause a weakness somewhere else, he'd always thought. They stood watching Charlie, alone in the middle of the empty rink, pleased with the night sky and the openness around him.

Keith resisted the urge to go lie down on the concrete beside his son. If he did, he feared he'd completely lose it. He turned away and went to sit in the ancient bleachers nearby. He couldn't see Charlie from there, not as long as the boy was still lying down, looking at the stars.

Eryk knew to leave him be. He went into the arena, and walked the perimeter. Eventually Keith joined him. He had to move. Then Charlie, and they stalked about, walking out a few of their own sad things.

Midday, Charlie played with the dogs, and when they tired, he lay with them on the porch in the sun. He forgot knitting, he forgot his mother's coat. He fell asleep. Boy and sun and dogs.

Keith and Cat were out on that porch, too, Cat with her feet in a tub of water.

"Can you please add ice, Keith?"

He picked up the nearby weighty copper pitcher, water dripping from its surface, and carried it to her basin. Ice rattled out into the water. Her feet gave him a start, toes lined up identical to Raziel's. He didn't comment.

"Oh," sighed Cat. "Amazing how good that feels. My feet have been so swollen in this heat. At least the nights are cooler now."

"In a few weeks you'll have blizzarding snow." Keith replaced the pitcher by the door.

"Don't joke. You know it's true."

"How many more weeks before the day? I'm embarrassed I can't remember your due date."

"Don't be. Too much has happened. Five weeks to go." She looked to her feet, and wiggled her toes, shifting what was left of the ice. "You know, I'm so sorry we couldn't come to Raz's service. You've no idea how I feel about that."

"I have some idea."

But he was shocked to see the wretchedness in her eyes.

"I am sorry you couldn't be there," he said. "You know we understand, right?"

She nodded, but looked away. "I needed to be there. Maybe to connect these two in my life, my baby and my sister, who just missed meeting. I don't know what they would have been in each other's lives. We have such an odd little family. Father disappeared. Miriam's never been a mother, ever. I feel as if I'm striking out on my own here."

Keith had to look at her closely. The words came with a gulp, a half-sob. It was no time to point out the obvious about her sister.

"Well, Raz didn't really mother," she said. Followed by, "Oh maybe I shouldn't have said that." She peered at him apologetically, but there was a stain of defiance there, too. "You've done the real parenting. That was the best choice all around." Was she trying to gauge his response? She went on. "Mothering isn't natural in our family. Miriam is all about herself, and Raz was all about her art. It's a mistaken belief, you know, that women are natural mothers." She paused. "You know that."

"Raz was a good parent," Keith said softly. "She provided for the three of us. She gave me the time I needed to be the parent I wanted to be, to slow, to play. And she showed Charlie — we showed Charlie — that things can be different, that you can do what you feel a need to do."

Cat was looking at him.

"I was the one who could make something from nothings in the fridge, the one who could dance with a vacuum cleaner . . ." As he spoke, he could almost hear Raz's voice, that quality of recitation, when she told people why they'd made the choices they had, when people stupidly asked. And they did. "She'd say I was the Superior Mother, mocking but not. She was still pregnant, when someone asked if we were on a waitlist for childcare." He laughed with the memory. "She didn't miss a beat, and told the guy, 'That's Keith's department now. I'm really a surrogate. He would if he could, but here we are.' And she laughed at the guy's surprise. On the way home, I remember her saying how much fun she was having already, turning everything on its head, all the how it's supposed to be."

Cat nodded, paused. "Why do you think she resisted treatment?"

No one had come out and asked like that.

Cat began to flush. "Maybe I don't know everything, maybe she changed her mind, and did take some treatment. But that's what Miriam said."

"Your mom was right. Raziel didn't want treatment. She refused. She said it would prolong, and it was too far gone."

"Was that true?" Cat asked. "What did her specialist say?"

Keith felt weary. "It was her decision to make, Cat. It was far along. The specialist explained the odds. Raziel spent the time she could thinking it through."

"You were all right with that? Her decision?" If it wasn't Cat asking, with that tortured expression, he couldn't have withstood these questions. He had to remind himself how far away she'd been for those weeks. He had to believe that maybe, if you were far away, you might be left with questions even more unbearable than his.

"Did you talk with your sister about this? Did you ask her?" He didn't want to sound cruel, but he probably did.

He would've liked to ask Raziel about her choice, too. But Raz had that edge to her voice that told him not to push, not to ask. It wasn't up for discussion. The edge had always cut. He'd never been able to bring himself to talk about anything that brought out that edge. Didn't like to think about it. Especially now.

"Did it bother you that she didn't try?" Cat whispered.

They stared at each other. Had she meant to say those words? That thought, *did it bother you*, had been hiding in his mind, and he hadn't wanted to pull it up into the light. He didn't intend for his in-breath to be audible. He knew he'd come all this way for some words, some affirmation, some missing thing; he'd know it when he heard it. But he didn't want for it to be this.

"I shouldn't have asked that," she said. "I'm sorry. I keep thinking, and wondering." Her voice faded away. Her eyes stayed on him a moment and then, as if she couldn't stand the conversation anymore, she looked to the water at her feet. It slopped over the sides of the basin. Keith spotted a towel and reached for it.

"Raziel lived how she wanted to," he had to say.

"But what about Charlie?" Cat's voice caught. "That's what keeps coming into my head. Knowing the person I love did whatever they could to stay with me. I'd want to know Eryk fought."

"We're all so different. I have to accept her choice."

"We are all so different." Cat sighed. "I'm sorry about my questions. I wish I'd been there. I wish I could have talked with her. But what would I have said?"

"I am sorry you've lost your sister," he said.

"I'm sorry we've all lost our Raziel." She placed her hands on the armrests of the chair. "Give me a hand, please. It always feels a little slippery and scary, this foot-soaking thing. It's time for me to go to bed."

He laid out the towel now, and put a hand under her arm, steadied her with his other. She stepped out of the water, and they hugged for a moment, and he had to laugh. "Right. Now I know what Charlie felt when he hugged you. That little one wants out."

She rubbed her belly. "Yes. It's good to be in the safe zone, these last weeks. Every day is a bonus now. I think the baby gave Charlie a rather good kick."

"Little cousins have to hold their own."

"Feel that." Cat caught his hand and pressed it to her belly.

That sense of elbow or knee always amazed him. He'd marvelled at how this was a part of being a woman that a man, a father, couldn't know. This was a piece of that natural-mother belief—it made it easier to think that, yes. Even if they could still talk about whether there was truth in the idea.

"Thank you."

"Every day needs a little wonder," said Cat. "I have more than my share these days. I like being able to let others feel it.

Can you dry the tops of my feet before I go in? Save me bending over?"

He patted her feet dry, then took care of the basin, spraying the water off the porch, and hanging the towels to dry over the rail.

"I've been thinking," she said, her voice tired, "Eryk makes a wicked German chocolate cake, and Charlie does like chocolate. I was thinking we could have an early birthday celebration before you leave. I've never spent one of his birthdays with him. We're always so busy with the farm at this time of year."

"I think Charlie would like that. It'll be a hard day without Raz."

"Let's do it then."

"Let me cook," Keith said.

A laugh. "Let me tell you what to do!" she said. She was his wife's sister.

"It's good to be here, and for Charlie, too."

"Next summer, you will come and see the three of us."

"We will."

She turned to go into the house, then turned back. "You're different."

"Different?"

"Without Raziel. You're different."

"What do you mean? How?"

"I don't know. I've felt that from the moment you arrived." She smiled. "It's not a bad thing. It just is."

It just is.

She moved heavily into the house. Even as Charlie awoke.

While Cat had her nap, they worked together in the garden and later, when Cat awoke, and Charlie had had quite enough of the sun, she called out, "Knitting time!" Or maybe they'd sit and tell each other stories. Knitting time could devolve.

Keith decided to go for a walk.

●

He wasn't sure if the urge was conscious or subconscious, but he ended up back in front of that little house. The woman who'd been in the doorway appeared. "You again." She uncrossed her puffy sun-pink arms and beckoned him closer. "You were with Eryk Melnychuk, in his truck, weren't you? I'm thinking you must be part of the Porter family who used to live here."

"I was married to the daughter, Raziel."

She peered over his shoulder as if Raz would appear. "Did she come with you?"

He took a breath. "No, I'm afraid not. She passed away. Last month."

"Oh." She paused. "I'm so sorry." She held the door open. "Come in. Please. Was that your son with you? I saw a child in the truck."

"Yes." He stepped over the threshold. He could smell the butting-head odours of old cigarette smoke and stale lavender.

"My son didn't want to come in. It's all too much right now."

She patted his arm, and he had a sudden flash-memory of a long-ago schoolteacher. "Children see thing differently, things we've forgotten about," she said. "It's hard for them to imagine parents in another place, another time. And in my experience, they really don't like knowing there was life before them."

He'd never thought of that. "You think?"

"I've a son who saw a wedding photo of mine, when he was about four, and asked where he was in the photo, and burst into tears when I tried to explain." She gave a laugh and led him through the living room. "You been here before?"

"Once, many years ago, for the holidays."

The front door opened directly into the living room. The only nod to it being an entranceway was a small sad closet, its door half-opened, and possibly broken. A nearby and shadowy hallway led to the kitchen. It was challenging to imagine the woman jetted in from London in that pearl-grey suit in this place. She'd be revolted knowing he was between these walls now.

There'd never been a satisfactory answer as to how she'd been displaced here.

Even harder though to imagine Raziel between these walls. They passed a small room off the hall. "This was hers," he said, and poked his head into the tiny den, filled with a desk and two-seater couch, with a window too high for a child to see out without standing on a chair. The wall colour was unchanged from the dull nothing in his memory.

How had Charlie sensed this?

"Can I pour you a coffee?" The woman's offer interrupted his thoughts. Her name was Heidi, she said, as she poured from the carafe on the counter. She asked him if he took cream and sugar, and went through the cupboard for white. He didn't tell her he favoured honey.

"You know," and she stopped suddenly, hands in the air, one holding the sugar cubes — he couldn't remember when he'd last seen a cube — "I do believe my husband put a box of the Porter family things out in the shed. I'd forgotten about that until now!" She set down the cubes on the table and filled a creamer with milk. "After we've had coffee, let's go look. And you should have some fruit salad. I was just about to have some when you came to the door. You need to have food that keeps you hydrated in this heat. Where did you say you were from?"

It was pointless to refuse. She'd opened the fridge door, and there were the sound of bowls and spoons being assembled. He could imagine her at some earlier point in life, surrounded by children, and happy.

"Do you have grandchildren?" he asked.

"Only two," she said, "and they live in the States. They rarely visit."

She would have enjoyed Charlie. She handed him a bowl, and they sat at the chrome and Arborite table. He couldn't remember the last time he'd seen one. Maybe at his grandparents' house.

Pineapple, papaya. He looked at the fruits. Not a single berry, nothing that grew naturally in the entire country. Was this conscious on her part, or was he just weird to read yearning in this bowl?

"Do you travel?" he asked. She shook her head, mouth filled with fruit, and didn't add any words to that answer. When her bowl was empty, she only said, "Come, I'll show you the rest."

Which meant basement renovations, quite changed from what he recalled with the silver tinsel tree that year. Then out to a patio, where she lit a cigarette. "I try not to smoke inside with a guest." She took a deep draught, and led the way to the garden shed at the farthest corner, filled with clay garden pots and implements, the smell of cut grass, dried, and canning and jam jars, boxes and boxes of them, stacked and dusty. Shelves in the back had plastic crates, more boxes, and cobwebs. One cardboard box was marked PORTER. It wasn't large, but looked heavy and awkward. He hauled it down. Sticky cellophane photo albums and outdated magazines.

"Can you take it?" Heidi asked. "It's not doing anything for anyone here. I could get my husband to give you a ride back to the Melnychuks'."

"That would be nice," he said. "If he doesn't mind."

He pulled out an album, flipped through the yellowed pages: high school photos of Cat and holidays, lakeside and skating, and Raziel and classmates. So many boys that Keith had to laugh. Drawn to the light, all of them.

He thanked her for the coffee, the fruit, the box, the time.

"You take care," she said. "And your boy. Both of you."

He could tuck the box into the bed space over the front seats. Gift from the sad house.

"Stickshifts and Safetybelts" / Cake
"If You Don't Know Me By Now" / Patti LaBelle
"Locked in the Trunk of a Car" / Tragically Hip

10

The following day, in his clothing compartment, looking for a shirt to wear on a day of dull heat, Keith's hand brushed the box of ashes. Maybe today would be the day. He had a mental image of ashes set free in the wind.

"Have you seen my rocks?" Charlie's head popped into Hopper's doorway. Keith still hadn't cut that shock of hair.

"Right under the front seat, buddy." Keith closed the compartment door with a magnetic snap, leaving the ashes in their place.

Charlie reached far under the passenger seat, and pulled out the bag. "This isn't them," he said, disgust in his voice.

"It is," Keith said.

As he pulled a shirt over his head, he could hear the rustling of the plastic bag.

"Did you pick rocks, too?"

"No." Keith pulled the shirt into place, and saw his son's face.

"These are grey and brown. Not the ones I picked at the lake." Charlie stared into the bag. "Where's my square red one? That's not even here. That was the best." Tears weren't far.

Keith sat beside him on the doorstep. "This is what happens when they're out of the water, when they dry."

"But there were *colours*," Charlie said.

Keith reached into the bag, felt chalky stones pass through his fingers, muddy brown, grey, darker grey. He pulled out a brownish square. "This is it. This is your red square."

Charlie took it. "It was?" Enough tears and the rock would be red again; Keith didn't share the thought.

"It still is," he said. "Even though it looks different now."

101

Today was not the day to let the ashes go.

Keith found a crumpled Kleenex in his pocket and handed it to Charlie. He'd never kept tissues on him or anywhere near him as he had this last while, never bought them unless one of them had a cold. Now they were everywhere.

Old Daisy whined for attention, poked her nose into Charlie's knee, rubbed her jaw on his thigh. The dog knew the moments. Charlie put his hand to her velvet head. "Old Daisy," he said. "Don't be sad. We're okay." He gulped, wiped his sleeve across his eyes.

"Auntie Cat said Uncle Eryk is going to make you a chocolate birthday cake, and I'll cook an early birthday dinner tonight. It'll mean you'll have two birthdays — what do you think?"

A nod was enough.

Eryk worked with no recipe in sight. He measured, melted chocolate, mixed with a timer set. He and Keith worked together on the meal while the cake baked. "It's labour intensive to be a kid, isn't it?"

Keith suspected that he was thinking about the arena and that old house. "How are you with becoming a dad?"

"Honestly? Scared. We wanted this for so long, and then we gave up. We were going crazy. We were going to lose each other if we kept trying. We decided we'd move on." He began chopping the tomatoes he'd been washing, homegrown cherry tomatoes, rich colours. "But we'll all be okay, we will." He was telling himself, and Keith didn't correct him. "We're going to be okay. Somehow."

"That's what I tell myself, all the time," Keith said. "And Charlie tells Old Daisy, too. We're all telling each other that."

His brother-in-law stopped chopping and looked at him.

"We have to think that," said Keith.

Later, when Charlie smiled after the first bite of that cake, Keith and Eryk exchanged a look over his head. "We're okay," said Eryk. He had an easy grin, and Keith hoped he would use it in the next few years. "We are," he concurred.

Bath time. Cat suggested Charlie use a huge plastic bin, and have a bath on the porch. Then reading, and Charlie was asleep with Hopper's side door open, far enough from the porch not to hear, but to be seen. Keith headed to the porch to join Cat for this last evening. Eryk said he'd sit with them when he returned from his evening walk.

They sat in the yellow light, Rover spread over Cat's lap, and Cat scratched her belly.

"She's very doglike."

"She is."

"How big is she?"

"Shhh." Cat laughed. "She's a trim twentyish."

"You've always had her, it seems."

Scratch scratch. "You know, before Raz died, I was so afraid I'd lose Rover. She'd get sick, and I'd panic. Miriam laughed at me about it. More than once."

"I imagine she did."

"I don't know why I felt that, but I did. For years." She looked toward her garden in the front yard, fingers still scribing over Rover. "I used to be afraid everything I had would disappear someday."

"Why do you think you felt that?"

"I don't know." His sister-in-law took a long breath. "I grew up with that. I don't want to pin it on Raz. She did nothing deliberately to make me feel that. But after she died, it occurred to me that I no longer had that feeling. I realized it when I looked at Rover. I've let her go. I've stopped feeling the anxiety that someday I'll lose Rover and more. Now, I know I will, and of course it matters. I'm so terribly fond of this old girl. I could think it has nothing to do with my sister. But it's a jumbled connection."

She looked at Keith apologetically. Did his sudden feeling, of being lost, show on his face? "Maybe there's no connection," she said. "It's not like I can point to anything she ever did that made me feel that." Her voice was not blaming. She had a tone of mild amazement.

Keith wasn't certain how the conversation had turned. "She changed her name for you."

"No," said Cat. "She changed her name for her."

He waited for the explanation.

"Miriam wanted us to be Angelina and Catalina. But when I was born, Raziel was eight, and she decided she didn't want for our names to be so similar, so she changed hers. I don't know where she found a name like Raziel. She told everyone to call her by that name." Again, Keith couldn't think of what to say.

New subject. "I went back to your old house," he said. "By myself."

"You did?"

"The woman who lives there, she gave me a coffee, bad coffee, and tropical fruit salad, and showed me around. Remember that stuffy little room of Raz's? And she took me to the back shed and gave me a box she said they found, left behind. Not sure why they haven't given it to you before now. There was a photo album in it." Before Cat could get a word in, he went down the porch stairs to Hopper, and returned with the album.

"I remember that," said Cat, wonderingly as he sat next to her and opened the album. He'd taken only the quickest look in that shed. Now he slowed.

"Why would we have left these things behind?" She poked at the brittle plastic. "Look at the bunk bed in that *stuffy little room* as you call it. For years we shared that room. Raziel insisted. I was maybe three years old when she asked if I wanted to stay in her room, in her bed, until she talked Miriam into getting the bunk. We shared the bunk until she was maybe fourteen. Then she was too old, she decided, to share with her little sister. I remember being so upset. She left home a few years later, it was just me and Miriam, and I was grateful for the years Raziel did share with me. I accelerated through school, took extra classes, so I could leave home as quickly as possible. Miriam found a way to go to London. The house was more than big enough for the three of us, but spending those years with her, sharing that little room, made all the difference. I remember Raz saying that if she'd been in the basement, she would have felt buried alive."

Keith shivered when she said that. Cat went quiet. Keith found that he was breathing so lightly, as if he might mess up some human thing if he did anything else.

"It made all the difference," he repeated.

She didn't offer up what she meant by that. Instead she closed the album, set it squarely on his knees, and sat back to look out over the yard. "Eryk does this every evening, you know, this patrol of his. His patrolling makes me feel loved," she added, softly. "To see him out there, with Brando, and these days with Old Daisy too, traipsing after, it warms my heart."

Old Daisy had enjoyed these days of tapping in to ancient dog ways that had nothing to do with living in an apartment.

"I loved her. Raziel. You know what that's like," Cat whispered. "But I always felt like I had to be on the lookout."

"Lookout?"

"Wary."

"When you were young?"

"That's when it started. But always, really. Once, after meeting Eryk . . ." She paused. Then gave a shake of her head. "It was nothing. Sometimes she wasn't sure what was mine and what was hers. And I had to know and protect."

Keith had blundered into a dark room. "What *about* Eryk?" he asked.

Cat plunged a spoon into her tall glass of iced tea and stirred in a way that was too familiar to him. "I shouldn't have said anything." She set the spoon aside. "You know, there was never a reason for me to think twice about anything. Eryk once told me he was afraid of Raz!" A laugh at that memory. "We were such kids when we started going out, and she always seemed so much older."

Keith resisted the sudden urge, again, to close his eyes while listening to that voice. He kept his eyes open. Here was Cat, with her own slight and natural awkwardness, disguised as pregnancy. An oddly endearing trait, though she probably wouldn't see it that way. In all ways so different from her sibling. His mind wandered to her words about Eryk's fears, and their being kids, and Raz always seeming older, to him, too, even with only their two-year gap. It wasn't about years.

Here on the porch, sun still up, light warm yellow, it should be easy to get out of that dark room. He'd known before now that other women could feel jealousy around Raziel. He'd sensed that this might be true of her sister. Now to hear Cat talk about it, he was even less sure what to make of it.

"I'm sorry," she said in a softened voice. "This must sound terrible. I must sound terrible. You know I loved my sister."

"Yes, I know."

"Those years we shared that tiny room, she was my mother then. She didn't have a mother, but I had her."

"Didn't have a mother?" It wasn't as if Raz herself hadn't said as much. But a time came to mind: after posting that blog about Charlie having no grandparents, Raz had had what some might call a fit. He'd never put a word to her response until now. For once, the only time he could recall, it seemed to matter to her. Maybe because the words about her mother came from him.

"That's what you meant by 'it made all the difference'?"

"Yes, exactly." She sipped. Then asked, "Do you ever feel her? Her presence?"

No one had asked him that. He paused, remembering the sense of a hand at his back that night on the balcony. "No," he said. Was there something not right about that? Why did he not feel Raziel? Should he? That hand had been the wind and wishful thinking.

"I wondered," Cat said, pensive. "I was thinking that with you both here, I might feel her, but I don't. Or not like I was thinking I might." Her forearms were wrapped over her belly, and there was motion that made her smile, and unwrap. She circled soothing hands over her belly. "My mother told me once, and shocked me, that when she was pregnant, she never felt either of us move. Not once." Cat lifted her arms away and watched as the babe found some better position. Keith watched, aware that Cat was comfortable with his eyes on her, and aware of how blessed he was in this moment to be allowed in.

"Don't you think that's strange?" she said. "Have you heard of anything like that, ever? Being pregnant, healthy pregnancies, and not feeling a twinge of movement?"

"Men don't talk about these things," he said. "But no. Never heard of."

"I remember her laughing, and saying she must have had a concrete uterus."

Keith was saved from having to respond by the return of Eryk and Brando with Old Daisy at their heels. Well, Brando at his heels, Old Daisy bringing up the rear, slower tonight. She did seem anxious, with sideways steps, wind ruffling her fur. Did she sense the imminent leave-taking?

They turned to end-of-day conversational bits, questions about whether they wanted breakfast before they left to make the journey home. *Yes, you must stay*, insisted Cat. Then Keith made his way to Hopper and crawled into bed beside his son, who patted his hand in a most reassuring way, though otherwise asleep. Old Daisy whined and moved restlessly. Maybe she was ready to go home.

Keith closed his eyes to sleep but felt he was still in that dark place, the room Cat had taken him to with her questions and thoughts. But someone had moved a piece of furniture, and he was bumping into it now. Heavy table, ancient chair, all had sharp corners now. The air even had sharp corners.

He opened his eyes. Wind gusted outside, and he listened. It hadn't been just the conversation that had been weighty, that had felt to have some crackle. More wind came, and then a soft knock on Hopper's window nearest his ears, a low voice, Eryk.

"Do you want to come into the house?" he said. "There's going to be a bone-rattling storm out here. It's been growing all afternoon."

Keith could hear a low and long sky rumble, a throat clearing before bad news. Old Daisy must've known.

He pulled aside the curtain, and could see the shape of his brother-in-law. "We'll be all right," he said. "But thanks. I'd like to see it."

"Cat thought you'd say that. But I'll leave the door unlocked, if you change your mind. Stay safe."

The shape glided away. Strange to see Eryk without Brando, but the dog was probably in hiding.

Keith fastened both curtains open. The rumble had died away. Maybe it'd be nothing. Or too far away. But a flash unlike any Keith had seen illuminated the entire sky and the ground, so clearly. The windbreak of poplars glowed, blowing and bowing. And the vegetable garden with its dried stalks moving, shone silvery, dancers with backs bent over and arms waving goodbye. Wind chimes, silent all week, broke with a melee of notes.

Charlie sat up and wanted to know. The flash had died away, but he wanted to see, too. Another rumble. A minute later another flash, and Charlie was pulling on his shoes. There was nothing like this in their part of the world.

"Okay," Keith said. "We can't let Old Daisy out though, and we shouldn't be long. She might need comfort." He eased himself over the mattress and reached into the food cupboard for a pig's ear to give to the old girl, hoping she might stop the whine and settle in long enough. Charlie gave her a hug and told her what they were doing, and she began to chew. A good sign.

Quick lesson for Charlie: "We don't go near the tall trees. And we shouldn't be standing to watch."

He slid open the side door. The air crackled, and Keith hunched over and led Charlie toward the vegetable garden. "There's a dry ditch over here. A good place to watch."

They reached the trench with its sloped sides, and hunkered down, in time for the next fork in the sky. Charlie gasped and wiggled. He turned to Keith. "I can see you!" he shouted. "Like daytime!" Then, "Dad! Your hair's sticking out funny!"

"Yours, too," Keith said.

Charlie reached to feel his hair. The air crackled in his hands. The grass in front of them, the dried ghost plants in the nearby garden, swayed in the wind.

They took in the show.

Cat was making savoury omelettes. Eryk was gone to the barn. The night before had cleared the morning air.

"Eryk will join us for coffee. He said to let him know when you're up." She found a mug for Charlie. "Hot chocolate for you." She kissed the top of his head, and sat so she was eye level. "We will be out to visit you in the spring. You need to meet your cousin. You can have a talk about kicking you in the head!"

Charlie laughed.

"That would be good, to see the three of you in the spring. Eh, Charlie?" Keith said.

Charlie nodded, mouth filled with omelette, eyes shiny.

"We're so grateful you drove out to see us."

"We have Felicity and Ron to thank. Without Hopper we probably wouldn't be here. Not that we wouldn't want to be," he added.

"We're grateful." Cat lifted her mug. "To Felicity and Ron. Lift your mug, Charlie," she urged.

Charlie picked up his hot chocolate. *Clink.* Eryk showed up to join them.

After breakfast, they rounded up belongings and headed to Hopper. Eryk had filled their water tank and topped up the oil. He told Charlie to go find a bowl for whatever raspberries were left.

As Charlie skipped to the garden, Eryk wrapped an arm around Keith, and said not a word.

"I don't want to go home," Charlie said. He wiggled in his seat.

"How about we go to the big city? Toronto?" Keith did a quick calculation. Twenty hours. Close enough, Canadian-way.

"Mommy used to travel there, right?"

"She did."

"All right."

Silence for the next few miles. Then: "Are we on the right road?"

"We are."

"Still looks like prairies."

Was this Charlie's 'are we there yet?' Keith pushed in a CD. Music would help. He woke up these days with some nagging feeling. Maybe connected with leaving Cat and Eryk's, wondering when they'd see them again. Cat's voice had been reassuring these past days. Leaving them behind, he felt the undone. Life always felt to have too much undone.

The conversation he'd had with Cat the night before wasn't going to let him go. He could hear her words in his head. Had she thought through those words, or was it a time of hearing her own thoughts shaping into words? What was she saying about her sister? Maybe if he'd grown up with a sibling he'd understand more of the twists and turns. Had this shadow he was feeling always been with him?

He stole a look at Charlie, turned to the window, map on his lap unopened, and wondered about his lack of siblings, too, how it might shape him. But then an hour passed as they travelled on, and the undone seemed to be shrinking. Maybe that conversation would too. He tried to remember what he'd wanted from this time.

"There." Charlie's voice was so soft that Keith almost didn't hear him. "Look. There."

"What?" Though his gut knew immediately.

Charlie leaned forward. "The coyote."

Keith looked.

"Right by the road!" Such urgency to his son's voice, and his bounce on the seat grew almost spastic.

Keith slowed Hopper. Hitting the animal would be the worst that could happen right now. Still he couldn't see. "You sure?"

"You went right by her! You didn't see her?"

Keith's breathing messed up then. He tapped his chest with a fist. They'd passed right by her, and he hadn't seen. *Her.*

Charlie had given up on him, his head turned away, forehead pushed into glass, looking back as they drove on. Keith tried to focus on the road. *Please don't say that's your mom. Please.*

"I want to go home."

Keith kept his fist to his chest, steering with one hand. "Home?"

Charlie nodded. "I'm ready to go to school." As if that was the reason they'd driven off in the first place.

He could see how it might be that in Charlie's mind. Or how it could have become.

"Okay," he said. "We'll take the next turn off."

"It's around this curve," his son said. The map had fallen to the floor. Keith didn't want to ask how he knew about any curve.

What was it Felicity had said about Hopper? *Good things happen. Hopper'll help you find what you need.* The knowing was catching Charlie, at least. Keith was starting to feel he knew less than when they started out, in these last twenty-four hours, particularly so. There was a curve and a turn off, too, and they circled, facing the choice of back the way they'd come or go north.

Keith felt a need to regroup. "If I'm not mistaken, there's a section of highway called 'Life is a Highway'." He reached for the CD. "Put this one in next?"

Charlie knew how to press repeat, and how to crank the volume. He began to sing along, and by the time Keith pointed out the road sign, Charlie'd moved on from frustration. When Keith joined in with the singing, Old Daisy staggered to the back of Hopper, lay with chin to floor, and wrapped her paws around her jaw to keep from howling.

They passed through Saskatchewan and Alberta, stopping for one night in the midst and the next on the west side of the Rockies. Then onward, as the sun tinted the early morning sky.

To British Columbia: Revelstoke, Kamloops, Cache Creek. They felt a push to return.

"Look at *that* cloud," said Charlie. They'd taken a corner, and that was no cloud. That was smoke, dull orange pulsing in its centre. Although they'd passed drifting spires of smoke on the path home, this was closer than anything they'd seen. A gas station was on the right, and Keith signalled. "We just got gas." Charlie gave his dad a curious look.

"We did," Keith said. "I need coffee." He pulled up outside the little store that was trying to look like a log cabin.

"Charlie, can you find some peanuts?" Keith asked, once inside. Out of earshot, he asked about the fire.

"They're about to block off the road, yes," the young clerk said. "You were smart to turn in. They're rerouting onto the 99, two lanes, curves all over." He looked at the coffee Keith had poured. "Good idea. At least it won't be dark going through yet."

"Where we going?" asked Charlie, clutching a bag of roasted peanuts and overhearing.

"We need to go another way. We don't want to be caught in smoke."

"Smoke?"

"Smoke." Keith said nothing about fire. "Would you like anything else, besides peanuts?"

Charlie shook his head.

"You'll be heading north before you turn back south," said the young man, ringing up the purchase. He looked at Charlie. "It's a good road. Kinda like a roller coaster, you know?"

A frown flickered over Charlie's face. Roller coaster wouldn't win him over.

Once in Hopper, Charlie caught sight of the fire.

"We'll be safe going the other way." Keith knew Charlie wanted to believe him.

They headed in the direction they'd come. A crew was putting up signs, and they took one hairpin turn, then another, then re-routed to a road that passed through a small town, or what had been a town, and was now a collection of house foundations, burned out cars, and blackened trees. They were halfway through when Charlie asked, in a stilled voice, "What is this?"

They passed a school, recognizable by blackened bicycle racks and chain swings and a sign that read ELEME . . . SCHOO . . .

"This was a town." Those days when they were struggling with the diagnosis, this had been happening. Summer fires. News had been on the periphery of their world. Almost mechanically, Keith reported what came to him now. "No lives were lost. Everyone's safe." He'd heard that, registered it somehow.

"They have nowhere to live." Charlie looked at one place with an intact fireplace standing in the middle of the foundation. You could imagine a family gathered around, a scene that would have been behind walls. Keith didn't want to see — it felt invasive. But Charlie was struggling to understand.

"It's impossible to understand some things," Keith said.

"Do you think there were dogs in this town?"

"There must have been."

Was Charlie going to say he could see them? He hadn't mentioned the coyote again. "The people took the dogs with them,"

Keith continued. "They must be staying with friends or with family, in other places." His voice drifted off. Avoiding the truth or making stuff up with Charlie never sat right.

Once, he was maybe ten at the time, and with his father, he saw a vehicle abandoned behind a mechanic's garage, with the entire roof crushed to the seats. Keith could still hear his father's tone: thoughtful, truthful. Had someone died? He'd asked, and the answer was, "Most likely." Keith had been shaken, mostly by his own thoughts and images.

He had a sudden sharp ache for his dad, gone all these years, and a sense of intense connection with his son, sitting feet away.

They passed the end of the street, the last of the foundations, and Keith glanced back as if some bony legged and ghostly creature might slink out of the ruins. He shook his head. He didn't know how to handle this. What was it? *The coyote.* How would Raziel have been, with Charlie seeing her in a coyote?

Ahead were cliffs, greater than any they'd experienced through the Rockies, rising sheer-faced. The destroyed town was left behind.

How he wanted to remember his marriage for being core, for memories to be sustaining in the years ahead. And this child he shared his life was, at the moment, a bit of a mystery. He wondered what it would be like to let that mystery be, let it unwrap itself, layer by layer. He'd just told his son it was impossible to understand some things.

"This coyote," he started, "what do you think about her?"

Charlie looked at him as if to say, *we've had this conversation before.*

Keith pushed on. "Do you actually think that it's . . . she . . . is your mom?"

Charlie turned to the rockface of a cliff beside them.

"Like she's inside the coyote? *Is* the coyote?"

Silence.

"Do you know when that happened? Or how?"

How did his son get to this place? He wasn't in any place about knowing. He could see Cat's eyes when she asked about Raziel's presence. He'd been brought up to believe in the here and now. If his parents' thoughts had changed as they aged, they'd never shared. For him this had translated to an unarticulated sense of disloyalty to life itself to be prepared for death. He was too young. But when was old enough? It had been staring Raziel in the face, and she—they—couldn't talk about it.

Charlie was frowning. "You're talking about it too much," he said.

Was he? More rocks passed before Charlie relented. "I feel her in lots of things. I just do."

In the road a turn, another turn. Keith had vivid memory of being driven up this road as a child. He could see his dad's broad shoulders in the seat in front. He could hear his mother's voice exclaiming. How strange to be handed this memory now: his mother laughing, both of them secure in his father's driving of this scary-shit road.

Charlie peered over the edge of the passing road as much as he could. They could suddenly see a ravine and so many trees. He pulled back and sat quietly.

"It's a long way down, isn't it?" said Keith.

Charlie nodded.

"Do you *not* feel Mom?" he asked, as the road shifted again, dictating the rhythm of the conversation.

Keith didn't want to answer. But he'd asked questions of Charlie. "Not really," he said. Should he find some comforting words? Whatever they were, or needed to be, escaped him at the moment. He thought of how his father had chosen those words about the automobile accident.

"Hmmm," said his son. Maybe he was done with this now. He asked, "Is it going to be bedtime when we get home?"

"Close."

"Is the moon gonna be full?"

Keith was grateful for the turn in conversation. "I think so."

Charlie opened the window and waved. "Goodnight, moon!"

"You remember that book?"

"Yeah." Two syllables.

"Goodnight, mountains." Charlie waved towards the mountains.

"Goodnight, waterfalls." Charlie was fascinated by the roadside trickles here and there.

"Goodnight trees growing at weird angles." That one from Keith made Charlie laugh. "They do!" he protested. "Growing right out of rock."

"How do they grow out of the rock?" Charlie asked.

"I don't know how they grow anywhere on these mountains." He'd wondered as a kid, probably on this same road.

Sleepy Charlie went silent. Keith drove on, dreading getting home, but tired of being on the road. They drove through the ski resort, Whistler. Horseshoe Bay. West Vancouver. He could feel the release of the tension of mountain driving, a physical sensation, every muscle tightened, and one by one letting go. He would begin to feel sleepy with the release, but the minute his head touched a pillow, he'd be wired awake.

Over the Lions Gate Bridge, through the park. Old Daisy sat up and swayed with the motion. She whined. They'd be home in minutes. How did she know?

"Spanish Banks," Keith said aloud, and Charlie looked at him.

"That full moon's going to come up, and we shouldn't miss it. We can walk on the beach, and say hello to the ocean before we head home."

"Really?" Charlie wiggled to sit up.

"Yes, let's pretend we're nowhere near home." The words grabbed at his gut.

"I think Old Daisy knows," said Charlie.

"She can pretend with us."

117

Keith turned onto Burrard Street and over that bridge. Down Fourth Avenue. They passed Jericho Beach. Spanish Banks. Charlie downed his window. Behind him, Old Daisy stuck her nose in the corner of her boy's window and sniffed deeply. Salt. Home.

"I hear music!" said Charlie.

Keith put his window down. "I hear it, too."

"Can we stop?"

Keith pulled in to park beside spreading cedars. "Grab those sandwiches from lunch."

A band of musicians played on the tired brown grass of the dusky beach, and people listened, on blankets and beach chairs. Charlie's eyes shone. "It's *real* music."

Keith had to chuckle. *Live* meant *real*. He'd done something right.

"What's that?" Charlie pointed to the upright bass.

People clapped as a saxophone solo came to an end, and a coronet took over. Keith watched Charlie's face. It had been a while since they were this close to live music. Jazz festival at the park, the year before.

He spread the blanket, but Charlie didn't sit. He stood, head moving with rhythm. Keith handed a sandwich to him, and he ate so absentmindedly that Keith was glad he'd removed the waxed paper.

The moon came up to play from behind one of those trees, and under another cedar was a family of four and their half-grown big pup. They caught his eye, and they'd caught Charlie's too: the father was dancing with the daughter, twirling her in circles around him, moving her from one hand to another, figure eights, while her brother held on to the puppy's leash, and moved around them in a bigger circle. Then the woman stood, and without missing a beat, she was in the man's arms, the girl released.

The couple danced a loose-limbed two-step that spoke to togetherness and timing. The girl never paused in her movement, but continued to spin. Brother and puppy circled, too. A familial galaxy. Keith watched, pleasure washing over him. The woman closed her eyes, and put her head back, and she followed the man's movements, so trusting that a dull ache of some kind of longing made itself known in his gut. Had Raz ever been so trusting of him?

The singer announced last song, and people got up to place bills and coins in the open saxophone case. When Charlie looked at Keith, he handed him a bill and nodded. Charlie followed the dancing girl, watched her put in money, and did the same. He caught the bass player's eye, and the musician nodded. Charlie returned to sit with a wiggly settle-in between his dad and dog.

The music ended and talk started, the musicians began to pack up. There was laughter, and Keith could hear someone humming the last song, caught in the cool September wind. Most of the audience had left. But Charlie watched one of the musicians gather the coins and bills and split and distribute.

"I liked the dancing," he said at last. "The boy danced with his dog."

"He did."

Charlie looked at Keith.

"You want to dance?" Old Daisy watched as they twirled. Charlie started to laugh. "I'm getting dizzy!" But he didn't stop until Keith said, "So am I!" He gave his son a hug. "Thank you for the dance."

He picked up a corner of the blanket, handed another to Charlie, and they shook it into the wind, did a fancy step to fold it together, and made their way to Hopper, cozy inside.

"Can we make hot chocolate?" Charlie asked.

There was enough milk in the fridge. Charlie and Keith both hummed "Fly Me to the Moon."

Let me play among the stars.

Spangle.

III

●

Fall

12

"Car Wheels on a Gravel Road" / *Lucinda Williams*

"Morning Coffee" / *Jesper Munk*

"We're Going to be Friends" / *The White Stripes*

Sunday was about cleaning out Hopper, doing laundry, feeling their way into more space. The apartment had expanded from the days they'd left behind, and the air they breathed was no longer dead lilies. But almost all those cards were still standing and even a little dusty. Whatever Keith was feeling, Charlie must have felt the same, because he went into his room for that shoe-box, returned and eyed the lot, selecting one with umbrellas on it. Then he found one with more ghastly flowers, and he put that in, too, without comment. He didn't look at Keith as he toted the box back to his room, so diligent about this self-appointed task.

Keith did his own task of putting away the ashes into the lowest shelf of his bedside table, imagining how he might answer if Charlie asked about the dark green box with the embossed tree on its side. He really had thought that when he saw a particular place, he'd recognize that it would feel right for Raz's ashes to be there. But they'd been through mountains and rolling flatland, towns and unpeopled places, and nothing had reached out to Keith as *the place*. Even if the lake stones losing their colour hadn't sullied that one day, he still wouldn't have found it.

Or maybe he wasn't yet ready. There was that.

They returned the van. Lucy was housesitting, and said her parents had gone to visit friends on the Island.

"You and Charlie had a good trip?" She ruffled Charlie's hair, which normally he hated, but he accepted from Lucy. "We took Old Daisy," he told her, and showed off the half-knitted scarf which he'd put into his pack. "I'm gonna finish it before it snows."

Lucy fingered the thick wool. "I like snow. We never get enough." She toggled the corks that Cat had pushed over the ends of the needles to keep the knitted work in place. "Good idea. Your auntie showed you that?"

"My Auntie Cat."

Keith handed Lucy the keys. "Tell your folks that we love Hopper!" He handed her the thank-you card he'd written. "Charlie did the drawing." The van with Old Daisy lying in the open side door, stream running nearby, with the log over it.

Lucy fixed the card to the fridge door. "This fridge really needs some art on it."

At home, Keith's eyes kept stopping on the black cardigan he'd left folded over the back of his work chair. He'd been hoping it would make the back-to-work easier, but at the end of the day, he put it on his bed. While he read a goodnight story to Charlie, his mind drifted to it. Later, he left it on the pillow next to him, and fell asleep with a hand on it.

He was grateful for the trip, the safe drive home, the music at the beach. Mostly he was grateful for being so tired he fell asleep.

Monday morning he replaced the sweater over the chair. Would he write today?

"Should we throw stuff in your backpack and head to school?"

"Tomorrow," said Charlie, as if he'd thought the matter through.

They made pancakes and took their time. Charlie put away another card, this one of blue roses. Condolence and blue.

Tuesday morning they had a bacon and egg breakfast and filled Charlie's pack with last year's leftover school supplies, a lunch, a snack, and set off.

"We kept a space for you." Maggie, in the school office, gave a room number that appeared to be across the hall from Charlie's Grade 1 classroom.

As they caught sight of the door, Keith saw a familiar figure and the nameplate: *Ms. Duffy, Grade 1/2 Division 5*. His burst-dam relief caught him.

"Ms. Duffy, the Sequel!" Had the school made this decision for their sakes?

"You!" was all Charlie could say. He hugged her around the waist. So the no-hug policy could be broken. Better Charlie than Keith. Who felt like hugging someone over this.

"It's so good to see you, Charlie!" Ms. Duffy said.

The sensation of walking away from the school without Charlie's hand in his, or without a skipping shadow beside him, was one of dismemberment. Too much like the early days without Raziel. The Hopper trip had delayed that moment of stepping into his empty home. In spite of the proximity of neighbours, in spite of the city outside the door, ambulances and car horns outside the windows and down on the street, there was silence in the apartment.

As Old Daisy clicked her way over the floor to him, he loved her and her clicks. He stood in the doorway, though, unwilling to step over the threshold until he must. Old Daisy looked up at him, brows puckered.

He closed the heavy front door and sagged down the wall to sit on the floor. With Charlie at his side, he could fight. But now he sobbed, and when he did stop, he couldn't do anything to control the shaking. He wiped his eyes and face on his T-shirt and moved woodenly into the kitchen, where he stood in front of the coffee machine.

Trying to remember how to make more coffee.

A filter. He blanked on the amounts. *Fill the measuring scoop. Fill the tank with water. Push the button.* He watched it trickle out. Breathed in the smell. Poured. Took it to his desk. Out of habit. Stood up again. Needed air. Went to the balcony, opened the door. Sat and drank the coffee, images coming to him: Cat on that porch; Trev and Norah out here, night after the service with Charlie; he and Raziel at the end of a long day, each in a chair, feet meeting on the table, his toes to hers. He could make her laugh.

He went back into the apartment. What would it take to write again? To be normal. He poured a second mug. The first was tepid. Coffee was part of work routine, pump priming.

He ran a hand over the cardigan, and sat at his desk. After long moments, he hit the button to turn on his computer. Had it always taken this long to start?

Email notification had a three-digit number on it. He closed mail.

He'd avoided all social media when they were travelling, and the weeks before. He opened it now. Someone had left a photo of Raziel and him at a party years ago. He remembered the party. He remembered Raziel's perfume that night, and that red dress with the hip-hugging skirt.

He didn't want to do this.

He opened Raziel's page and pain sliced cleanly into him, pain that was letting. Like sobbing by the door.

Messages left by so many: Nancy and Joey. Sabine and Twyla. Ron and Felicity.

Missing you

Love you always

Memories

Christmas party photos from Ron and Felicity's, their annual party always on the Eve, pulled pork and potluck. Birthday photos from a rented hall, hired musicians, dancing. A photo of Raziel with baby Charlie in her arms. Keith had no idea where the picture was from, who had taken it. It made him cry again.

His phone rang, welcomed interruption. He didn't recognize the number.

"Hello, Keith. This is Prabh. Prabhjit." Her voice drifted, as if she questioned whether he would know who she was. One of the other photographers who worked with Raz in the studio.

"Of course," he said.

"We've put together some of Raziel's things. If you want to pick them up, and maybe have a coffee with us, we'd like that. Or I'd be happy to drop them off. Whenever." Her voice bubbled quickly. His understanding was on delay, but it came as he took a breath.

He hadn't thought about that piece at all. The studio. He remembered Prabhjit from the service: she'd come up to him, hugged him, introduced herself and another photographer, Sam. He'd not met her before. Only once had he met the assistant the three of them shared. Ann-something. Sam, he recalled from an opening, and painting the studio, a few meetings over the years.

Some people found it strange that he didn't know these people, but they'd each had their own life. Raz had never demanded to meet the parents at the park, or the hockey circle. They'd been respectful of each other's lives, and trusting. She laughed over stories of the mothers at the playground. If she was somebody else, she might have pressed him, and been anxious about the possibilities. More than one of those women had made it clear she'd be open to spending time with Keith without little ones around. Raz had been amused at the stories, shaken her head, kissed him, and poured herself a glass of wine. There was a certainty to their relationship that Keith trusted and took pride in. The trust was necessary for two people who spent so many hours apart. Since before they'd met, Raz travelled regularly, always looking for new places, new sights. He'd focused on freelancing, and long hours of fiction. Long, lone hours. He'd get back to that someday. But these last years had been mostly about writing as a father. When they were together at the end of the day, they shared stories. They had stories because of the way they spent their time, and as artists, they needed those. Their stories nourished them.

Those women disturbed him; one had been an insistent force. She'd reminded him of that girl in Grade 3, when he was eight, the one whose desk was behind his, who loved to touch him, a prod or a stroke. The one who seemed to have no idea how much she scared him. Or did she? He couldn't tell his teacher, or his mom. They would have said she was cute. But they didn't see the fierceness in her eyes when she looked directly at him, a look she'd change up quickly when an adult was around.

He'd never said anything to Raz, about the insistent one. On the playground, apart from the rare times there was another man around, he'd gotten used to pushing the littlest ones on the baby swings, while their mothers and caregivers talked on the benches. Pushing babies was the safest place to be. But after too many invites, shadowed words, he'd decided it was time to take Charlie to the nature park instead of the playground. He didn't want to deal with it.

Maybe it was too much to think that men and women could be friends.

Keith had seen the studio only once after signing a lease. He'd helped to paint her corner. How particular she'd been about the shade of white. Her creating was exact. She'd called him a crafter at times. That was okay. It was the truth. He knew he could write too quickly, passing the line from art to pure craft. Parenting had become a form of art.

Raz always stayed firmly on the side of art. For her that meant control of all she did, and her personality took care of the entrepreneurship. What created their success was, in no small part, their acceptance of roles, their own and each other's.

"Does tomorrow afternoon work?" he asked, suddenly aware he'd let a silence build.

"It works well." Prabh's voice was light, with a note of care.

The studio was blocks away. He would know it when he saw it, he was sure, but saved her number in the event he didn't. The call had reset his mind, lent a solidness to things.

He looked at email, and saw a note from an editor about a project. Maybe he should first return to the blog; readers would want to know how he was, how Charlie was. But after opening the post he'd been working on, rereading a few rough paragraphs, he thought to sit on the balcony. At a quarter to three he'd accomplished nothing by any standard.

He set out to walk back to the school, and arrived in time to see more than half the class walking off the school grounds with parents and caregivers, and he could see Charlie standing by the doorway, leaning against the wall. *Forlorn.* Then he caught his eye, and some springiness uprooted in Charlie.

"Look!" He waved a plastic Ziplock bag, and ran over, handed it to Keith, a library picture book, a favourite from last year.

"We'll read this tonight."

"I can almost read it!" Charlie set off for home, but stopped in front of the school sign and stared. "C . . ." he sounded out. "Rrr . . . aw . . . sss. Cross. It's the name of the school. Crosstown!" he said.

Keith pointed to the second word. "Elementary."

Charlie puzzled through the -ary part before they started to walk.

They came to the corner.

"S-T-O-P," Charlie said. "Stop."

"You sure it's not P-O-T-S?"

Charlie squinted up at him, as if he was losing his mind. "You read *that* way."

He went on to the next sign he saw. "B-E-E-R. W-I-N-E."

"The E makes the I say its name," Keith reminded.

A few blocks from their building, they walked by the narrow gingerbread-coloured house they often wondered about, squished between another building and an old-school corner store, always wildly decorated for holidays and celebration.

Once they saw a woman, sweeping leaves. Another time he'd seen developers on the front steps, in their business armour, knocking without answer, and turning away with mutters. They'd probably been prepared to offer the homeowner an absurd sum for the place. The east side of Vancouver was changing more quickly than any other part.

Charlie stopped. "Look!" He pointed to a hand-drawn sign in the front window. "What does *that* say?" The sign must have been there for months, through the summer at least. Keith couldn't recall seeing it on the walks last spring. The house faced south, and the sun had done its work. They both stepped closer. Charlie moved to the middle stair of the porch.

"G," he said, not the letter but a grunt. "G-r . . ." Now a growl. Pause. "What's that on the end again?" he asked.

"That's a Y, and it sounds like *ee*."

"Granny!" Charlie said with triumph. "Granny f-f-f-or f-r-ee! What does *that* mean?"

Keith climbed a few steps toward the porch, too. Shades were down. Such a strange mix of hiding from the world and then those decorations for Halloween, Christmas. Last spring, he recalled stuffed yellow and pale blue rabbits on the porch railing.

There was a phone number under the letters. "You can call," Charlie said. "Call the free granny."

"I'll call," Keith promised. He was curious about the house, the sign, the offering. He took out his phone and copied the numbers as Charlie recited them.

13

"Shiny Happy People" / *R.E.M.*

"Cannonball" / *The Breeders*

"Rainy Night House" / *Joni Mitchell*

The following day, with Charlie safely in Ms. Duffy's class-room, Keith set out to find Raziel's studio on Alexander Street in Gastown, in a brick building not far from the touristy steam clock that announced neighbourhood time. He had a mission that involved movement. He couldn't take another day attempting to accomplish at his desk.

In the end, he couldn't determine the correct building, and he had to call Prabhjit. Right building, wrong floor. How could he not remember it was the top floor? He climbed the three flights of stairs and recognized the wood-framed windows and their views from photographs. He paused to look out. One was wide open, and even into September, so many tourists, so many languages he could hear. Noon-hour smells: barbecue, garlic and spaghetti, rich-edged coffee, and the familiar waft of Vancouver weed.

He pushed open the door at the top of the stairs. Raziel's hand would have pushed over and over at this same spot, the rectangle of brass in the dark wood. He recalled so little from the service, but friendly and grieving-aware eyes met his now. Prabhjit, kindness in her smile. A tall thin man, Sam, gave him a quick hand-shake. "Good to see you, Keith," he said. "Can I get you a coffee?"

"Please," said Keith. He followed Sam through the work areas in the mostly open space. First the assistant's, Annika, with her neat desk, her measured smile. Then Sam's own workspace, not neat, with some sort of black screen placed a foot in front of the window.

They walked through Prabhjit's large work corner, colourful and untidy. It felt like being welcomed into her mind. Last,

Raziel's space, quite empty for the most part. He felt regret not seeing it as it had been.

Sam seemed to understand. "It hasn't changed much. She was the minimalist. You know." They stood in front of cameras and lenses laid out on a table: her newest, a Canon she'd begun to work with, and another old favourite stood out.

"We have a friend joining us at the end of the month. Though no one will take Razi's place, of course."

Who called her Razi?

The camera that Raziel had with her in hospice, he must have packed it up, or at least carried it home. Unnerving how that moment and others like it — the diagnosis day even — had disappeared. Maybe not disappeared, but greyed. He had no memory whatsoever of walking out of the hospice, let alone what had been in his hand. Other than Charlie's hand. And he could almost feel those fingers in his.

Sam was staring at him. Keith was assailed by a memory of Raziel's last show opening. He'd spoken at length with Sam then, the one time. "We talked," he said, "at that opening. We talked a lot."

"We did," said Sam. "That was quite the evening." He gave a rueful smile. "We watched Razi working the room, and we laughed about it."

Right. Sam had said that she blew the artist-as-introvert stereotype. They'd watched her perform. And Keith, being some kind of introvert himself, took pride in watching her flit. This ability was an undeniable piece of her success, she was quick to admit. Admit wasn't the right word perhaps, but credit where due: "People like me," was how she'd put it. They did. "I pay attention to them. I ask questions." She did. "I'm good at what I do."

"And you don't indulge in false humility," he'd said. She'd laughed.

Sam was looking at him when this memory came to an end, patiently, a small and sad smile on his face.

"You all right?" he asked.

"I am," said Keith.

"We were thinking we'd wait for you to be here to pack up some of her things. Prabh is hoping you might consider letting her buy the Canon." He paused. "I'm so sorry if that seems inappropriate to ask."

"Not at all." Keith looked at the cameras. "If I were to keep one for Charlie, would you suggest one over the others?"

Sam thought. "Her Nikon is missing. That would be the best for him."

"She had it in hospice," Keith said. "So we have it somewhere at home." He thought. "It'll have film, half-used, come to think of it. She took some photographs."

"Bring it in," Sam said. "I'll work on the processing for you. When Charlie is ready to play around with the camera, I'll be happy to work with him."

"That would be so good."

"Any time." Sam nodded. "We'll be here."

"Is there one of these you're partial to?" asked Keith, motioning to the cameras.

Sam picked up one of the lenses laid out. "This is my secret love."

"Then it's yours."

"No." Sam looked embarrassed, and set it back down.

"Yes, I insist. Prabhjit," said Keith, "can have the one she wants. No protesting."

Prabhjit must have heard her name. She showed up in the doorway, and the looks on both their faces said that they were missing a friend. In the moment, Raziel almost seemed to be in the room. That was worth the gifting. Maybe not Cat's 'presence,' but close.

Prabhjit might have had some thought to say no, some polite protest perhaps, but the expression on her face cleared. "Thank you," she said. "So much."

"What about . . ." He had to think about the assistant's name.
"Annika. Is there something she'd like?"

"Razi left behind a scarf, hanging by her desk. I noticed Annika putting it inside Razi's desk. I know she won't ask."

"Yes." Keith nodded. "Of course."

When he handed the chestnut and ruby scarf, Raz colours, to Annika, she hiccupped loudly, looked mortified, and clutched the fabric in her fingers. "I always wondered about you," she blurted. "We would have happy hour here on Fridays before leaving, and I always wondered."

Keith got the feeling that this woman often danced with awkwardness.

Prabhjit looked at Annika, and she went silent. Prabhjit spoke to Keith. "You were always with Charlie. We knew that."

So they'd wondered why he didn't show up for their Fridays, times Raz had mentioned, but it never came across as an invite. Often the hour stretched into the evening. Once she'd offered some thought that he would feel a bit out of it in the shoptalk.

Would he have? Sam's openness and Prabhjit's thoughtfulness made him feel he'd missed out. Annika's awkwardness made him curious.

"Her process journals," said Prabhjit, pointing out a shelf with spiral bound and bulging notebooks. "I suspect they're quite personal." She motioned to a large box on the floor. "We left them for you."

"I can pack them," said Annika, "while you drink your coffee. If you'd like."

"That would be kind."

She handled the journals with an archivist's hands, putting them into the box in the order she removed them. They were all dated, he could see. He opened one, pages thickened with bits of paper and magazine cuttings. One section appeared to be sections of a novel folded into origami, drawn over with chalk pastels. He'd seen these books in his wife's hands over the years. Never the insides.

After he finished the coffee, they helped him carry boxes to his car. Annika had disappeared.

"Come back, and visit. Bring that film. We'll see you again." Sam closed the trunk, but he left open a door.

Not even an hour to go before he had to pick up Charlie. The boxes from Raziel's studio spread out in front of him.

Grief. He'd never known exhaustion like this. Raziel, pregnant, had tried to explain exhaustion, to the bone, bones heavy with it, she'd said, but he hadn't understood. Maybe he did, finally. He would have liked to ask: *was this what you felt?* He was left with so many questions he wished he could ask. He'd mutter them aloud, imagine what might have been the answer, words she might have said. Often, silence.

He unwrapped the art. One with rich colours that Charlie would like in his room. The other, a piece created with fabric and metals, darker, textured, would go in the living room. They could see it from the kitchen. He'd always loved this piece, Raz's every day, now theirs. He found hooks, searched for the stud finder. The piece looked as if it should have always been with them. He stood back to absorb.

Twenty minutes to go before school pickup.

He stacked the boxes in a corner, heaviest on the bottom.

There was a laptop in a soft case, fairly new. They'd made a point of not holding on to anything that couldn't justify its existence in this small space. His workspace, the corner by the window, was filled by a desk and bookcase. This newer laptop could be Charlie's at some point.

Time enough to open one box labelled *desk drawers.* The first thing he saw was the card Charlie had created for Mother's Day. He was afraid to touch it. Instead he took a moment to find music to fill the room, and a small box for the pieces that Charlie would want. He marked the box with Charlie's name and put the card inside. Someday he would hand it to his son.

Under a small cosmetics bag was her daytimer, well-worn ruffled Post-it pages for the first half of the year. He sat back from kneeling on the floor, and held the volume in his hands. Her hands had held this.

Still so unreal.

He opened it. Appointments, lunches, meetings. He had a sudden sense that ahead of him lay a path that would ask him to stretch. Already, he'd had emails from people out in the world, who had purchased photographs of hers for their homes, their walls, and had heard the news. Magazine editors, collectors, gallery owners. With even the first such message, he'd felt comfort in hearing others' stories of Raziel and her role in their lives. But others' grief was tiring.

He had to get up from the floor and walk, move. He stood by the window, for the view of his city. Lyrics came to him, Patterson Hood's. *Gonna be a world of hurt.* He remembered seeing the band, Raziel in his arms. His joints felt looser at the thought, and his heart softened. At some moments he'd realize how bloody sore he was all over, as if his body was in overdrive to keep him standing, or doing whatever he was doing, nothing he'd ever had to give thought to before.

They'd had a good life. Raziel loved her work, gave it brightness from her depths. He'd been able to do what he loved, too: spend the right kind of slowed time with their boy and write and cook. They'd 'done well.' There had to be gratitude with the grieving. There had to be. They'd been so lucky. They'd had this time together. Even though now, somehow, the time felt so brief. How could seventeen years be so quickly passed through? He wanted to go into corners of memory and remember the feel of each. Have those loose joints and song lyrics in his head. Remember the feel of her in his arms. He knew this was what would heal him, would keep him going: gratitude. If he could feel the slow-ing of music and moments together in him.

He had to check the clock. 2:40. He should leave in five min-utes. He didn't want these things scattered about, though, for Charlie to see the minute he walked in. He set the daytimer on his desk. He liked the sight of it there. A slip of paper fell from it, three lines written in handwriting. Raziel's? Maybe, though smaller and tighter than usual.

let's play a new song
paper and gold say you're his
the world has your heart

A new song. He turned over the paper as if there'd be an answer. He didn't want a new song; he could live with "A World of Hurt." *World has your heart.*

He slipped the paper back into the daytimer, and put it back into the box. He closed the lid. *You're his. Paper and gold say.*

He was moving in slowed motion. And going to be late.

What did the scrap of paper mean? *Stop shaking.* What was in his head?

He had to pick up Charlie. *Go, now. Get him.*

It was twenty past three when he got to the school door. He'd run without looking at the time. The schoolyard was empty, the door locked.

His head felt strange. Light, dizzy, sluggish, as if one part was dragging another after it.

"Charlie?" said Maggie, in the school office. "Oh, my." She called the classroom. Ms. Duffy said she'd been speaking with a parent. It wasn't like her to lose track of a child.

Keith tried to keep his voice steady. "I'm going to head home. I'll find him on the way, I'm sure. He's brave like that." The woman's face was anxious. "I'll call you when I find him."

"I'll call you if he shows up," said Maggie.

What had he allowed to happen? He and Charlie always took the same route to school. They crossed at certain intersections, walked down the same side of each street. So why hadn't he seen him on the way? He and Charlie had talked about this: *what to do if Dad is late.*

He jogged down the streets towards home, watching for a flash of red, Charlie's jacket, and not seeing it. Of course, if this was what he'd done, then he'd be home. Was Grade 2 too young to have a phone?

He began to run, dodging others on the sidewalk. Charlie didn't have a key. Surely someone would let a kid into the place. He'd be safer in the entranceway than waiting on the sidewalk. A few blocks to go. Watching for the red flash.

Brakes screeched close by.

The only red he was seeing was the light he was dashing against. The driver shouted. Keith had scared the shit out of him. Mutual shit-scaring, driver and Keith. Keith waved at the guy. "Sorry!" Guy nodded curtly, took the corner. Keith stepped back to the sidewalk, stalked in a circle. He was an idiot. Charlie couldn't lose his second parent. He couldn't take chances.

The light turned, and he took care before setting off the curb.

Half a block away he saw his son, on the sidewalk. The relief he felt was physical. As shaky as he'd been moments before, he was more so again. He slowed to a walk.

Charlie was with an older woman, and they both turned when he called out.

"I found her!" his son announced.

Then Keith had to put his head down, hands on his kneecaps to still. He breathed. He couldn't get enough oxygen.

Charlie was talking at a heightened pitch, and Keith couldn't absorb the words.

The woman had a voice. "Let your dad catch his breath."

Keith gulped. "*Who* are you?"

"Catch your breath," she repeated.

He straightened. "Who are you?" He tried to ignore Charlie,

staring at him. "Why is my son with you?" *Don't you dare tell me to catch my breath.*

"Free Granny!" Charlie said then, his frown deepening.

"Free Granny," Keith repeated, feeling stupid and angry.

"You were going to call her. Remember?" Charlie, accusing. "You weren't there to pick me up."

"We've talked about this. If I'm not there, you stay at school."

Charlie's face had taken on some stubbornness that Keith couldn't recall seeing.

"Sometimes it's enough that things end well," began the woman.

Keith cut her off. "Maybe for you it is." His voice was so sharp that Charlie took a step back. "This is not *end well*."

"He knocked on my door. He asked if you had called me. He explained where you live. We were heading to your apartment." She straightened her aging spine then.

He stared at this woman, absorbing: she was rail thin and ropey, all bones and tendons, and the bright print baggy jumpsuit was too much empty fabric. Her hair was grey and piled in some terrible way on her head, probably not cut in years. Eccentric. Probably crazy.

"You should have taken him back to school."

"You're right, I should have."

There was no mollifying Keith. He only understood that the reason he hadn't seen Charlie earlier was because he'd gone off path to Free Granny's house. Whatever her name was. Stupid woman. His son hadn't paid any attention to the plan they had in place.

"I'm sorry." Again she said, "I should have thought."

"Yes! You should have." He seized Charlie's hand. "Home. Let's go."

"But . . ."

"We need to be home," Keith said. He loathed the tone in his voice.

Why did it feel then as if no such place as home existed? Just a sense of dangling. *Paper and gold and home.*

Neither of them spoke. Keith unlocked the front door, jabbed at the elevator button, up, unlocked their door, stepped in.

He'd cleared the traces of his afternoon. But had he missed a piece? He'd hurried, even as he felt to be moving in slowed motion. Not that Charlie would read or understand. Keith didn't understand. But the boxes were closed. Somehow an end had passed without being marked. They were supposed to be a team, he and Raz, to take care of Charlie each in their own way. Now there was one of them, doing for both. Half thoughts sat undigested in his gut. But it was his fault he'd been late.

He had to start this afternoon over again.

Catch your breath.

"Tell me," he said, "about finding the Free Granny." Finally enough oxygen in his breath.

Charlie peered at him, evaluating his words. Was he for real?

"I'll make hot chocolate," said Keith. He needed to be moving, but his hand shook as he closed his fingers around a mug. It slipped, and he caught with a goalie's reflexes, but when he set it, hard, on the counter, the handle cracked off. He tossed the whole mug into the garbage without a word.

Charlie climbed onto his stool, eyes on him, wary after that tossing. The wariness was not lost on Keith.

"She answered the door when I knocked," Charlie began. "I was scared knocking, but I saw a cat in her window. Really bad people don't have cats," he added.

Keith started to speak, but stopped.

"She asked me if I was okay."

He'd have to concede on that.

"She asked if we should phone you. I told her to come to my house. I couldn't remember your number."

"You forgot that it's in your pack?"

"Oh." Pause. "Right."

He was a kid, a little kid. Half orphaned. Keith was suddenly too tired to chastise.

"What did she say?"

"She said we should hurry, that you'd be worried."

He could be starting to feel bad, but he was too exhausted for that, too. He poured the steaming chocolate, dropped a marshmallow into Charlie's, one into his own too. Chocolate needed sugar. Then sat on his stool.

"She's probably a good grandma," Charlie said, eyes still on his dad.

"You have a grandma," said Keith.

"No," said Charlie, "not a real one."

Why defend Miriam?

"I invited her to my birthday," Charlie added. "Friday."

Keith hoped that Charlie couldn't read his face. He shouldn't have needed a calendar to remind him. Or his son.

Charlie was asleep before Keith finished reading the first book. He closed it, and debated taking the stick from Charlie's hands, clutched to his chest, but that might wake him. Charlie hadn't asked for a Mom-goodnight story, and Keith was relieved.

He treaded soundlessly to his room. He wanted his own space tonight, but passing through the main room, knew he couldn't sleep with those boxes there.

Old Daisy followed and stood in his doorway, waiting. She had the confused-retriever look as he passed her on his return to the living room. She paced again to Charlie's doorway, where she circled and finally lay, watching as he put the boxes into the entrance closet.

Later, when he'd gone through the contents, they could be put into storage in the bowels of the building. The dog's eyes were still on him.

The words etched into his mind. *Paper and gold.*

Paper and gold. *Catch your breath.*

The slip of paper with its words would make sense once he looked further into the boxes. It would fit with whatever Raz had been working on. He'd always joked about what would happen if anyone took a look at his search history, at any writer's search history.

Paper and gold. Marriage. When you put it like that, what did it come down to?

There would be an answer. *Logic.* The word kept coming to him. He would find it. In the morning. Morning was always a new day. There would be new days ahead, many of them, each an exercise, an opportunity. He tried to focus on those new-day words, versus the few on the paper.

Back to the bedroom. Old Daisy followed, and whined. She moved between the rooms, relenting to stand by his bedside. He gave her a scratch. She would return to check on her smallest charge before too long. He felt for the old girl; it's a lot to take care of broken people.

He made himself switch off the reading light, and the room became black. Sharing Charlie's bed had not only been about comforting his son, but avoiding this space.

Raz had surprised him, finding a nightlight for those weeks when she was sick. She'd always preferred to sleep in complete darkness. The light was soft pink and shaped like a shell, unlike anything he would have associated with her. He turned it on, then off again, as memories flooded, that light so connected with those weeks. In tomorrow's daylight he would get rid of it. Old Daisy whined again. How much did she understand? Did it matter? She felt everything. Some dogs could anticipate epileptic seizures and read cancer. Standard clause on dogs' contracts, to recognize grief and sadness.

Grieving was excavating deeper places, hollowing from inside out. No child needed to see this. Even if it meant being wakeful, he felt a need for time of lying in the dark, to try to put pieces together, to process. He was glad when Old Daisy finally settled on the floor beside him. He reached down, felt her fur in his fingers again, her orange kerchief, Charlie's choice of the day. He could see the colour in his mind.

An image came to mind, and he saw her as she'd stood in front of him, that woman wearing a winter-weight wool sweater under the baggiest overalls. Grey wrapped in colour.

Charlie had invited her to his birthday.

In Ms. Duffy's class one parent read a picture book to the children each morning. Today, Keith offered, a delay to going home.

Ms. Duffy saved the window side of the room for the art tables, and the reading corner was on the other side. She'd strung coloured lights that glowed in the shadows of the rainy morning, a surreptitious push for literacy.

He picked up a book from the shelves, *Pizza for Breakfast,* and showed the cover. He pretended not to notice the children nudging each other and the whispers. "Somebody's *dad!*"

Keith pretended to bark.

"He said *dad!*" yelled one kid.

Ms. Duffy did a look across the room.

"Sorry," muttered the kid.

Keith flipped open the book and hid a smile.

"He's smiling."

"Shhh," said a future schoolteacher.

Another kid, furiously, "He's gonna *read! Shhh!*"

They all fell silent, and Keith began. It might prove to be the best ten minutes of his day. Especially when he saw Charlie's eyes.

At home he closed the door. Those low-lying clouds rained against the long windows. He was okay with the grey, grateful for the sense of moving on from the summer. He hadn't anticipated that. He'd been dreading the fall, but after the prairie exposure, he felt blanketed. Today he made coffee without having to think about it.

Thoughts about working, writing, were coming. He was going to give up on that project for the editor, tell him it wasn't in him. He'd send off what he had in the unlikely case someone else could use it. Forget a blog post for now. He should write a picture book. He could read it to Charlie's class to make it right. Or get a job that took him out from between these walls: pour coffee for people, talk with them, sweep a floor.

But he sat at his desk to see what it felt like.

The boxes were close. Like hiding in the dark, hearing someone nearby, breathing, waiting. He stood, pulled out one, set it on the floor. Went to top up his coffee.

He could go on with life as he knew it, or he could open all of these and find who knows what. Suspended in possibility. That note might have been copied by Raziel from elsewhere. The handwriting could be hers on a different sort of day, even scribbling on a bus. Maybe she'd simply found the note. He would never know if he didn't open and look. He could find an explanation for those scribbled words, and he wouldn't feel this weight. He opened the box, found the daytimer, and out fluttered the paper, exactly as it had yesterday, nothing about it that wasn't already in his mind.

On a whim, he counted the syllables.

A haiku.

In the next-day light, a poem. So much anger and lost sleep over a haiku. *Why* had his thoughts gone so quickly elsewhere?

He flipped through the daytimer. There were asterisks for particularly important meetings. *be 15 mins early!* A note scribbled next to a lunch meeting. *don't wear blue!* That broke off some piece of his anxiety. This would all make sense. Raziel had mentioned a client who loathed blue. Double asterisks next to a dinner meeting. No note with it. He stared at the asterisks.

He'd held a few beliefs about what he was doing. One: if you're looking for something you'll find it, or, more likely, you'll find what looks like it. Two: if you think the best of someone, if you have expectations for them such as 'I believe this person would never willfully hurt me,' they will live up to that. Expect the worst of someone, and that'll probably come about, too.

Now here he was, like some woman in a soap opera. How sexist of him. He'd never gone through anyone's phone or email, never felt the need. Wouldn't be right. So what was pushing him now?

Raziel's phone. He couldn't remember it at the hospice. All he could envision in her hands was the Nikon. In her bedside drawer? No. Where were her purses and bags? That little bag she'd packed? He found the phone in a coat pocket, dead. He plugged in the cord, couldn't believe he was doing this. He walked away, back to the box, gaping open.

Leave the box. Let the phone charge. Or toss it, now, in the garbage. Why not?

Yesterday, after the Free Granny disaster, he'd been thinking that Charlie should have a phone.

Could he not look?

Didn't they need groceries? He had other things he could be doing, useful things.

He grabbed his pack and wallet. They needed toilet paper and bananas.

Rain snapped into his face and brought him to. He needed to find a birthday cake, come to think of it, and a gift.

He took his time with the matter of toilet paper, steps slow, reading through the price shelf tags, what was the best deal for twelve rolls.

He couldn't deal with birthday anything yet. Back at home, rolls under his arm, and bananas in pack, he hung his coat and put it away before checking the phone, battery symbol in the corner now green.

Keith knew her password from seeing the movements of her hand so often. He clicked on Messages and there he was, first in the list of people she'd last communicated with. The sudden sight of so many words he'd shared with his wife was hard to see. He set the thing down on the counter and made a cup of tea. He needed tea to write, he told himself, and needed to get back to work.

A banana first. Then, mug steaming in hand, he came back to the phone. Set the mug down. Moved aside a couple of frames of apps. There was one called Telegram. He hesitated. This didn't feel right. Raziel would never have gone through his phone. Trust was foundational.

He poked at the app, and it opened.

There was only a single person who Raziel communicated with here, no real name, just Sailorman. Who would be *Sailorman?*

Good morning, sexy!

His stomach turned, and some door clicked and closed.

Her reply on the righthand side. *Good morning lover.*

Looking forward to later. Meet you at yours. Let me know when clear.

Yours. House or studio? Must have meant studio. The date: the week before they'd left for Iceland. He scrolled through, catching words here and there. Two month's worth of messages. The setting let him know that messages were automatically deleted after six months. The most recent photograph she'd sent to Sailorman was a pic she'd taken of the sign in the hospital. He'd heard the swoosh of the file sent, sitting beside her in the waiting area.

Sailorman. Soap-opera name. Raz, the woman who mocked her mother's decades of *Coronation Street* addiction.

He returned to the opening window to scroll beyond his own words. Friends, workmates, Cat. Miriam, with motherly messages, the words a disconnect with the woman.

Mark. A name he didn't recognize. Incoming message: *Remember me? Let me know if you are in San Antonio again.* So another.

Raziel had been in Texas two years ago for a conference. He remembered picking her up at the airport. She'd been unusually affectionate, and through the days following. She missed him, she'd said.

Of course I remember you. If ever again I come your way, yes, we'll play.

His finger hovered over the keys. What would it be like to receive a message from a dead person? So tempting to write *you piece of shit*, and press send.

He typed the words. But couldn't press send. He was shaking too hard. He put the phone back into the box, pulled the flaps together, and pushed it into the closet. He couldn't look at more. Somewhere between haiku and double asterisks was a turn.

He was swallowing too much saliva, could feel his stomach churning.

There may be paperwork he needed, and he had to be rational. He spread his hands out in front of him and willed them to stillness, wished he could do the same with his gut.

He took his runners out of the closet, saw his hands doing this action, watched them tie laces. His legs moved down the elevator, out to the street. Could feel his knees, ankles, the way the parts of him worked together. He began to run.

Good morning, sexy! Yes, we'll play. He ran faster but the words kept up. Ahead he saw a brick wall and corner, and he reached the corner, took hold of the brick, and held himself up as he vomited around the side of the building.

A woman was staring at him. It was halfway through the morning, still early. At first her eyes were hard and questioning, but when his connected with hers, hers softened. What did she see? She had her phone in hand, and hurried off.

What had everything meant? What had anything meant? He closed his eyes, leaned into the brick. Vomit had splashed onto his jeans, his stomach still churned. He was still swallowing saliva. He turned back, hollow and lightheaded.

He had to walk by the street of Free Granny's house, and he felt a pang: he should have been on time to meet his son. Nothing should have gotten in the way of that. He needed to come up with a time for the birthday party-of-sorts. But he had vomit on his shoes, so he wouldn't stop at Free Granny's now.

At home, he stripped out of his clothes and pushed them into the stacking washer in the kitchen closet. The smell caught in his throat. "You can't do this," he muttered. "You can't come to pieces. Maybe all this meant nothing to her. Maybe it meant something, but that didn't mean you meant nothing to her. You have a son. You need to hold it together. *Hold it together.*"

What he would have given to talk with her, to ask. *What? When?* Mostly *Why?* Would she have told the truth if he asked? When had she told the truth? *Who was she?*

Who was he? There was that, too.

He took the vacuum cleaner out of the closet and pulled out the cord, plugged it in. He vacuumed the entire apartment, under the couch, the chairs, the beds, in the kitchen, and around the coffee table. Put the vacuum away. Filled a bowl of cereal. Had two bites. Splashed it down the toilet. Mopped up the wall, the floor. Cleaned the fridge.

He'd *known* Raziel.

He thought he knew Raziel.

There was a half hour before he had to pick up Charlie, but he couldn't stay in the apartment. Two blocks from the school, he began to circle the block. He didn't want to face others waiting. At last, he checked the time. He couldn't be late again.

He could feel his phone vibrating. Trev had both phoned and texted, as if he knew something was up. Keith didn't return either message.

He and Raziel had been together seventeen years. What would be an evening in all those years? Three hundred and sixty-five days and as many nights in a year. Times seventeen years, five months. How many days?

149

What was one night? Okay, maybe more. But not many. A handful, a couple of human beings. *Sailorman*, *Mark*. Two among billions. Pinpricks in the sky. Nothings.

On the outskirts of the ring of waiting adults, there was Juliana's grandpa, always dressed in trousers from another era, even suspenders. A hat more often than not, a silk scarf, even. In the winter, it'd be a heavy one tossed over a shoulder. The man caught Keith's eye. They'd spoken before, and the man's years left Keith with the sense that no matter what they spoke of, it would be a subject that he would know about. *What would he know about one night? Maybe he'd had his own one night.* If the man noticed Keith's shakiness, he wouldn't say anything about it.

What would anyone say, anyway? He was a widower. Already, people stepped back from him. He could take solace in that. No one wanted to mess with a grieving person, and one form of grief looked much like another.

What was this acceptance in the old man? Talking with him last year, Keith could recall moments of cynicism, humour twisted from a corner, often ending in a laugh.

He greeted Keith with his slow smile. "Good to see you."

Surely he knew about Raziel. But maybe he didn't. This was no small town.

He did. "I'm sorry to hear about your wife."

"Thank you."

"I lost my other half when I was your age."

Other half. A phrase Raziel and Keith had never used, deliberately. *Did you find out that she wasn't who you thought?*

"I still miss her." All those years, and still. The man shrugged. "Maybe you don't want to hear that, that you can miss even after decades. I should know better. I say the wrong thing often."

"I didn't want to think that there's another way to feel."

The man nodded. Didn't comment on Keith's past tense. It had slipped out.

He might not be in this man's shoes when he was old, not if this continued on this path. He might well be wishing he could say *I still miss her.* He could feel the man sensing his struggle. His head was back slightly, as if he needed another perspective.

"I'm sorry that you still miss your wife. I'm sorry, too, that I can't remember your name."

"All sorts of things might disappear from your brain now. Especially names."

"So it's a thing, a grieving thing?"

"You'll forget things you've known for years. My name is Alphonso."

"Keith. Thank you."

Alphonso nodded.

The bell rang. Alphonso put a hand on Keith's arm. "You'll be all right, you will. Someday you will even discover the reason for all this."

Someday you will discover the reason for all this.

The man had warned that he could say the wrong thing.

Keith watched children stream out.

The affair, the connecting, it doesn't matter. Nothing matters now except that Charlie and I are okay. We will heal. We'll miss Raziel. I'll miss my wife. Charlie, his mother. But we'll still be all right. We have been loved and we have loved, and we still love.

He turned to Alphonso to say, "Yes, we'll be all right," but the man had already turned away with his granddaughter, his hand solidly wrapped around hers, head bent to catch the girl's words about her day, all focus on her story.

Charlie was the last. He caught sight of his dad and ran to him. Keith picked him up as if he was half his size, and Charlie waggled his boots in the air. One fell off, and he laughed. A moment of light.

After dinner, after Charlie's bedtime, after some trying to read, Keith felt that sense of missing return, and the shift in it. Sleep felt far removed. Raziel had often taken something to sleep, to stop her brain racing — she'd push in earplugs and be gone.

He poked about the cabinet in the bathroom, the basket in a high cupboard, but found nothing other than some expired pain-killer, some children's cough syrup he didn't remember buying. He stood in his son's doorway. Charlie appeared to be asleep, his face peaceful. Maybe if Keith looked at that beautiful face long enough, he would find some calm. But he retreated, left the door ajar, and went to stand on the balcony. Fish on a riverbank.

Keith stopped at the gingerbread house after dropping off Charlie next morning. The sign in the window was gone. *Silly old woman, blundering into people's lives.*

He had to do this. "Short notice, I know," he said when she opened the door. "This evening at six, if you could join Charlie and me for his birthday dinner, he'd like it." He couldn't bring himself to apologize.

She was wearing the same too-much-fabric overalls with a different sweater underneath. Sparkly earrings pulled at her wrinkled lobes, and she was actually wearing lipstick. Raziel would have asked the woman to do a shoot with her.

She didn't speak. She'd been so obviously warm with Charlie. But with just the two of them, grown man and ageing woman, there was a wariness.

"He did invite you," he reminded her.

"He did." Reluctantly — it seemed — she added, "Please come in."

The last thing he wanted to do was sit and talk small with this woman. "I can't. I have too much to do." Like find a present and a cake, too. *And shit my wife left behind.*

"Charlie would like it," he added.

"What about you?" she asked drily.

He paused. "I'd like it, too." The words came easily enough then. Anger was exhausting. "We got off on the wrong foot."

"So long as we never have to perform in a three-legged race, we'll be all right," she said. A smile flickered over her face.

He started to give her the address, then told her that he and Charlie would walk over to bring her back to the apartment.

"That would be lovely," she said.

At home, he began to wrap up Raziel's Nikon. He would take Sam up on his offer to mentor. Charlie could finish the half-used film before Sam developed the photographs. It felt right to give the camera to Charlie, though he'd prefer to toss anything she'd ever touched. The thought pressed into his mind, and he knew its truth.

Carelessness seeped through his task. No, it was anger. The camera had been a gift from her father; he could share that with Charlie. After years of divorce from Miriam, he'd died before Keith and Raz even met. He wondered what it had meant to her father to give it. He wondered at how meaning could pass through generations and hands.

He had to unwrap the paper and slow to make it look good. It was a gift after all.

He headed to the bookstore for a new picture book, too. Never too old for one of those. On to the bakery. Where he hesitated over a cheesecake. But his mother's favourite was what Charlie would expect. At least the walk, the movement, was right. He was as ready as he could be.

Norah didn't like to miss her little cousin's party, but she had to do an extra shift at work unexpectedly. Trev had an extra early start in the morning. Keith apologized to him for not responding to his messages. "Railway Club. You and me soon," texted Trev. "We'll bring over Charlie's present tomorrow. Don't eat all the cake!"

So for the party it would be the two of them and the neighbour woman. Last year had been full and loud with the entire Grade 1 class. The school year was too new to know who to invite, so they'd invited all. He did send an email to Anne, Ruby's mother, to see if they might come. "Charlie'd love to see his boy-sitter," he wrote in the note. Though as he clicked send, he knew he really had no energy to hear platitudes. Oh, he had to let it go . . . She'd only done it the once at the service. And he'd sent the email so late, he probably wouldn't hear in time. He felt as if he was scrambling these days, since returning from Gimli.

While Keith prepared food, Charlie had a video chat with Cat and Eryk.

"Where's our scarf?" Cat asked, and Charlie held it up to the phone, showed her the rows he'd added, a stitch twisted here and there, a few pinched places, but his aunt was impressed. "It's longer!" she said.

"You're even huger," he told her, his face close to the screen, studying her belly in the frame, Cat's face looming at the top. "You should draw a smiley face on your shirt," suggested Charlie. She was wearing a yellow turtleneck pulled over her roundness.

"You think?" she said. "I can wear your mother's coat, and when I walk by grumpy people, I can whip it open and flash my happy face?"

"That would make them laugh!"

Cat reached off screen into a kitchen drawer, waved a marker in front of them, and pulled off the cap to draw a thick red smile and two eyes on the yellow shirt. Charlie gasped.

"I've been wearing this shirt so much, I'm sick of it! This is just the thing. Happy birthday, Charlie!" She drew a birthday cone hat at the top of her belly, pompom on the pointy tip.

"Did you *see* what Auntie Cat did?" Charlie asked Keith after they'd disconnected.

Keith gave him a cutting board with mushrooms, but Charlie went to the family albums instead. "Do you remember," he said, "that time the man asked me if I was a drawing?" He pulled an album with worn edges and flipped through pages until he found a series of photos of him, skin covered with bright lines. Keith left the mushrooms to have a look at the day Charlie found the set of new felt-pen markers Raz left on the table. Keith and

Raz had been arguing, one of few times, Keith couldn't remember what about. And Charlie had slipped away to his room, and emerged in colour. Raz stopped mid-sentence and went for her camera.

Photo after photo of limbs covered in story, in some sequence that Charlie shared with Raz, and click click click, now all in the album. How did Charlie remember the story? Or was he recreating on the spot?

Keith left Charlie with the memories to assemble the naan pizza. Charlie eventually came to help, and he was humming, a good sound. Keith chopped the rest of the mushrooms, and Charlie smeared pesto with his fingers. He loved to cook with his hands, inspired by Jamie Oliver.

Together they crumbled feta over top, readied two pans full, and found their boots to go and meet Free Granny, as Charlie called her.

Birthday focus had been an excuse not to try to write, and not to look through anything more in those boxes. Still, Keith realized he was almost squishing Charlie's hand as they made their way to the gingerbread house.

"Sorry," he said, and released, but Charlie looked up at him.

"About what?" he said, and grabbed his hand again.

Free Granny opened the door when they stepped onto the porch, with her boots on and a thicker sweater. She took a moment to sling a bright appliqued bag over her shoulder. Charlie got a sheepish grin when he saw the gift-wrapped package that stuck out of it. "You didn't need to get me a present."

"Of course I did," she said. "And we need to celebrate a new friendship."

Back at the apartment, they slid the pizzas into the oven, and Keith lit the gas fireplace. Charlie helped to set out napkins and plates and glasses on the bar. Keith poured wine for himself and Free Granny.

He had to stop thinking of her as Free Granny. She had taken down that sign. Who was she when she'd put up those words? Who gave themselves away? Many people. But not on cardboard in a window.

Exchanging more than a few words now, he could hear her slight accent. He wondered if she'd been trying to get rid of it forever. "England?" he asked. "North?"

"Long ago," she said, not naming the place. A runaway.

She was birdlike, couldn't weigh even a hundred pounds. Though he couldn't name the bird yet. No, he had it: *heron*. That heron neck of hers didn't terrify Charlie. It would have terrified Keith when he was seven.

The baggy puckered upper arms of his own grandmother, how he'd loved her. She was pillow soft in memory, and his body had fit snuggly with hers as she wrapped one arm around him, turned the pages of a book with her other hand, and read with a smoky deep voice.

Old women. Mostly fearsome and good.

Amazing to him how he could go back and forth like this in his thoughts. Had he done that before? He couldn't recall. He was too old to have such an unsettled way of being.

The timer sounded for the pizza. Keith could smell that they were done even as it sounded. Charlie disappeared into his room, and after some moments he returned with his gnarled stick, and set it beside Free Granny's plate.

"You can't take it home. But you can use my stick while you're here." His voice had a serious tone, and her manner immediately mirrored.

She ignored the pizza that Keith slid onto her plate and picked up the piece of wood. "Where did you discover this?"

"What beach, Dad?"

"Spanish Banks."

"Spangle Banks," said Charlie, echoing.

She held the end loosely and ran the length over her palm, and again. "Thank you for sharing with me." She placed it on the table near the top of her plate, before picking up knife and fork to cut the hot pizza.

She set them down again, and raised her wine glass and waited for them to do the same, Charlie with his apple juice. "Happiest birthday to you, beautiful Charlie!" *Clink.*

Charlie was delighted.

Keith clinked both glasses. "Happy birthday!"

He had to ask. "What shall we call you?"

"My name is Moth, Clarice Moth." She looked at Charlie. "I didn't put up that sign for nothing. I would like to be a grandma. How about you call me Grammy Moth?"

"Grammy Moth!" Charlie said.

"To Grammy Moth," echoed Keith, and raised his glass again. Charlie, he was discovering, loved to clink glasses.

After pizza and putting dishes in the washer, they heated hot chocolate and cut cheesecake. Charlie directed Grammy Moth to sit in the chair by the fire, and she moved her hand through Old Daisy's fur, lying on her feet. Did she also feel what emanated from the dog? The loss? The retriever still wandered the apartment, doorway to doorway, searching for Raziel, Keith was certain. But with Grammy Moth stroking her fur and offering her a scratch, she was still.

Grammy Moth asked Charlie to bring her bag to her. She pulled out an object wrapped in red paper. With iridescent paint, she'd painted moths on the paper. It took some persuading for Charlie to take it off.

"A flashlight!" he shouted. "Like the one in Hopper. But my own!" He turned it on and shone it on the ceiling. "Dad, can you turn off the lights?"

Charlie shone it over the walls, and made shapes with a hand in front. Keith was astonished. He'd never have thought of such a gift.

"It's rechargeable," whispered Grammy Moth. "I didn't buy you a fuss with batteries."

Next, Keith handed his package to Charlie. And turned the lights on again.

When Charlie opened it, and held it in his hands, he went still.

"Mommy's workmate, Sam, told me he would be very happy to teach you how to use it," Keith said.

Charlie looked at the back of the camera. "I can't see you," he said, and Keith showed him how to hold it. "You can't see the photo until later." Charlie looked mystified. "Can I take a picture of you and Grammy Moth?"

"Here." Keith demonstrated, and handed it back. Then he stood with the old woman, and put an arm around her. Looking down to the eye of the camera, Keith would swear he felt her smile with her entire body.

Charlie took a picture, holding tightly as his dad instructed, then watching as Keith advanced the film. By the third and final shot, he advanced it himself, though he still looked mystified.

"I should be going home," said Grammy Moth after the picture taking. She stood in a decisive way, and pulled her sweater closely around her bones.

Charlie chewed his lip. "You need a raincoat," he said. "You can borrow my momma's."

Not so long ago, that moment might have fuelled a blog post. But Keith made no move to note it. "I'll get the raincoat," he said. Best to keep doing. He opened the front-hall closet, and found the raincoat. A slight waft of Raziel's perfume, woodsy spice, and sexy when his nose had found her neck, came from a coat hanging next to it. He wrestled with feeling lost.

Keith held the coat for her to put on.

"This was your mother's?" the woman asked Charlie, before she moved.

"You should wear it," said Charlie.

Her eyes met Keith's. "He's such a little man," she murmured, and he tried to ignore the sadness in her tone. It had to be okay to be a little man.

She put an arm into the offered coat, with a gentle smile at Charlie. As friendly as she was toward Keith, her smile for Charlie was different. He suspected she had another scale of measure for children. "Thank you. I'll return it when we reach my home. It's nice to stay dry." She pulled up the hood. "And it's nice to hear rain on a hood."

"Here," said Charlie. "You can carry the truth stick on the way, too."

She took it. "Truth stick! You didn't tell me about the truth part. Do you want it taken out in the rain?"

"I found it on the beach. It was wet when I found it. Maybe it likes rain."

Keith found the anthropomorphizing unsettling: *let's talk about what sticks like.*

Charlie took the woman's hand and led her to the elevator, and out the door. The wind had picked up and was blowing rain right into them.

Grammy Moth waved the stick. "Other way wind, other way." She did have the warbly voice that a heron might if it could speak English. Now he was doing his own anthropomorphizing.

They walked a half block. Charlie spoke. "It worked," he said, awed. "The wind's not in our faces anymore."

"Believe me," Grammy Moth said, "if it *needed* to be in our faces, then it would be."

Soon they were at the steps to her porch. Grammy Moth waved the stick over Charlie. "This can't protect you on its own. You need to help it out to stay safe. You understand that what you did, knocking on my door, meeting me, wasn't safe?"

Charlie was solemn. "How would I have met you if I hadn't knocked on your door?"

She nodded. "I understand that, and I'm glad we've met.

We're going to be good friends. But you took a risk. You realize that?"

"I think so," he said slowly.

She didn't say anything, but she didn't let him go either. Her eyes stayed with his, and he stared at her. "I understand," he said at last. Her heron edges softened.

She waved the stick over his head again, then over Keith and last, over herself. She handed it back to Charlie. "We are blessed. We will meet again. Goodnight."

They both said goodnight, too, and watched as she let herself in and closed the door. They could hear the lock turning over, see a yellow light come to glow, and she was in the window, waving goodbye with a glimpse of her smile before she turned away.

On their way home Charlie said, "I like her. She's a real grandma."

Keith didn't protest.

"Grammy Moth can be my grandma." Charlie held the stick carefully. "I'm not supposed to wave it," he said, when he noticed Keith's questioning look. "Not unless I need to."

Keith wasn't at all sure he wanted to know the ins and outs, so he just nodded.

"You're supposed to be careful with powerful stuff," Charlie concluded.

"Well, that's true," said Keith. "That is absolutely true, yes." He didn't ask about the *powerful stuff*. He took Charlie's hand.

"You okay, Dad?"

"This is a tough time," he said. "Learning to live without your mom."

Charlie stopped, and gave him a hug around the waist before they went on, but not before he waved the stick in front of his dad. Keith didn't ask for an explanation. Sometimes you had to take whatever was offered, even if you didn't understand it yet.

Charlie held up the stick. "It's kinda like her arms, isn't it?"

Keith knew immediately what he was saying and had to laugh. "Yes, the stick bears something of a resemblance to Grammy Moth. Though I'm not at all certain she'd want to know that." He didn't laugh with those last words.

"I think she already knows."

Truth, Keith thought: that gnarled thing resembled a part of his own life. Or yes, maybe a heron, skinny pathetic legs, standing in cold water, but a step away from fish gasping on riverbank.

"When we get home, you'll tell me the story?"

Keith knew what he meant. *You were born on a night of rain, lots of rain.*

"It's your birthday, the best night of all to tell it."

Monday, seventeen minutes after nine when he returned home from taking Charlie to school. He found Irish whiskey for his mug and put on music. The thing had to be done. He brought out the boxes, set them in a row like game show contestants, then went to the window with his view, sipping coffee until he could feel whiskey.

He opened the largest box. Office supplies, pens, paper clips, staples went into his desk, work-related papers into a particular stack, some into tax folders. Personal mementos in a box. Knick-knacks in another pile, though there were few. Raz wasn't sentimental, or at least he'd never known her to be. A pocket watch surprised him. He couldn't recall seeing it before. He started a box of things to be given away, and dropped in the watch.

He shut down his mind to sort.

The weeks of dealing with the illness, the coming apart of Raz's body, of their lives. The Hopper trip. Through it all, Charlie's face, trusting. But those times, too, times of questioning, times that made Keith feel as if so much more could come to pieces, even as he wasn't sure what: here was the edge. And he was buzzed mid-morning. He was tackling this with the same mindset of doing research he didn't want to.

Quick enough to finish the basic sorting. Two boxes, one heading for the garbage in the basement, the other to the thrift shop. He pulled the boxes over to the front door.

Books. One of the boxes had been nothing but. Some could be added to the living room shelves and a small number to Charlie's. Keith tried to think what his son might want in the future. A half box to be sent away. He left the box of journals.

Photos in frames. A shot he'd taken of Raz and Charlie on Mother's Day two years ago, Charlie looking up at his mother with adoring eyes, Raz's eyes on the camera, with a singular focus that Keith had never noticed before. He began to look through the images: his wife had this expression and direction, yes. She had loved to challenge the camera head on, as she asked of those she photographed. "Look at me!" she'd say. Was it coaxing or command?

He'd never interpreted her focus in this way, leaving out Charlie or anyone else in the frame. It wasn't about who was behind the camera. Almost all photos of her were like this, taken by anyone, family, friend, another photographer.

He stared at the image, wondering how he'd missed this. How did a photographer *think*, having her own picture taken. He could remember a discussion about the phrase 'take or make' a photo, a heated discussion between Raz and another photographer. 'Take' had been Raz's word, but she'd had words about what it meant to take, and the flipside, what it meant to be taken, to stand up to that. He could recall the tone of her voice, that came to him now. He'd loved how her chin would go up. The 'make' person, the other side of the argument, he couldn't even recall. Had it been Sam? He wished he could remember the thoughts on 'make.'

Images came to him: the last opening of Raziel's work. He could see those long arms of hers, gesticulating, thrown around others' shoulders, running fingers through people's hair, her red lips laughing, eyes shining. Always as if she'd been plugged into a new generator, more power filled than the last or the one she kept at home. He could hear a certain hum emanating from her then. Every so often their eyes would connect. She had a way of finding him across a room and catching him. And he'd feel noticed, even if that was the only contact they had through the evening, until time to return home. "You come with your wife, and you leave with her, but she's never here in between," someone said years ago.

His answer: "That's how she is." Butterfly. He'd not been unhappy. He was a writer: he liked to observe, usually from a corner. Raz observed behind a lens. The togethering of an introvert and an extrovert was synchronous. Inversions. Yin and yang.

Another image of that evening came: Sam, in a couple of corners. Keith had chatted with him in one, a good chat, though what had they talked about? Sam gave off a low-key vibe of contentment. His partner was shadowy. Grief made it impossible to recall her name—or was it something else? Had he never remembered it? Had Raziel ever shared her name?

What should he be thinking about Sam? His mind balked. He didn't want to think about Raz, and the possibility of her with anyone he knew. Or anyone who could look him in the eye. Keith let Sam sit in his mind for a moment. He had the feeling Sam was a man who weighed consequences. Still how could he know? He was discovering that he wasn't the discerning person he'd thought. He recalled Raz once, with words about Sam being a stick in the mud. It was an odd comment at the time. Some note of derision there. Come to think of it, there'd been other times he heard that tone. Mocking, a bit angry. What was that about? How did memory buckle and twist? He'd not questioned her integrity before.

Though there had been moments, half moments, when he'd wondered at lateness, evasiveness. But nothing, really. Had told himself it would be nothing if he probed further.

He'd thought once that if she'd had the same thoughts about him, he couldn't stand it. Trust was what he wanted, and it had to work both ways. So he'd let those moments slip away, willed them away.

What did contentment look like for her? Her easy laugh had felt to be borne of peace.

He forgot his resolve to work through those piles, and instead pulled a family album from the shelf. He began to turn the pages, slowly at first, and then faster. They'd had these albums made for Charlie, so he could look through them and know his family. They'd had photos of relatives reprinted, and Keith could pull out his mental photo of the rounded back of toddler Charlie sitting with chubby legs in a V, communing with these pages. Now Keith looked closely at Raz in the pictures, seeking even one in which she might be looking not at the camera but at a loved one. In photo after photo Raz connected with the lens, some taken by him, some by Cat and others. He couldn't name what he saw now. He closed the album, unsettled. Why would he suddenly see something that had been in front of him for so long? It was how Raz was in the world. She was a beautiful woman, and she enjoyed it. The camera loved her. And she loved the camera in ways that had nothing to do with being a photographer. "What's the point," she'd said, "of being beautiful and pretending you don't know? I'm not pretty. I scare people, with my long neck and short hair and wide mouth, and brows like tattoos. Seriously, someone *asked* me that the other day! But I enjoy what I am. Life can open its hand to you. Take what it offers. It's as likely to take as to give." Those words had other layers now.

Back to task, though he struggled to absorb, to understand. Maybe his mind would follow what his hands were doing; the framed photos went into their own box. Charlie might put some on the wall and the shelves. At last he was down to the box of visual journals. And an envelope filled with postcards. He'd had no idea Raz was into postcards. So many different handwritings, from places all over the world. Cryptic messages. They, too, could read as haiku, almost.

It was lunch hour, and he'd been generous with the whiskey. He should make himself a sandwich.

If the postcards belonged to anyone else, the messages would have piqued his writer's curiosity. Instead he wandered to the kitchen, made a sandwich to slow the whiskey. But he still felt hungry after, and it had nothing to do with food. As Keith touched those postcards, he knew what they were; every one of them had a line of praise for her. The fact they each existed was testament to some far reach she held. His gut boiled.

You asked. Here it is! Paris. The date: three years after they had been there to celebrate time with each other, and to celebrate life.

Imagine what we could do here. A beach, New Zealand.

From Athens: *You could be my dancer in these columns.*

He laid them out on the floor, like a kid's recall game, trying to figure if any two of them had the same handwriting. The dates were '07, '05, '11. Each appeared unique, though with similar messages, playful, nothing overt. He didn't read closely, a word here and there was enough. The word 'muse,' he saw more than once, and 'angel.'

He turned them over, and a *National Geographic* world was at his feet as he looked down. He began to step on them. This was absurd. He gathered them into the paper recycling. Then had the irrational idea that they'd resurface. Charlie couldn't find these. He'd be drawn in by the images.

Keith was getting paranoid. But what had Raziel done with her life, and what was that going to mean to Charlie? Charlie didn't have to know, though.

Keith went still at the thought of his son. All his dreams about yellow oxygen masks. *You first, child second.*

His T-shirt front was soaked. *Breathe, man.*

He could throw away some of the paperwork that he wouldn't need. That could feel normal. He took the recycling to the basement, put the box of postcards in the trunk of the car. There was something he had to do with them, and he wasn't sure what.

Back to the notebooks, two colours, beige and navy. The beige had years inked onto their covers and appeared to be records of projects. Keith tried to skim through. So many words about the birth pains of projects, pieces he knew. On the last pages of the first notebook, a project name stood out, and under it, a sentence: *Don't expect people to understand you,* scribbled with a flourish.

Underneath, the date was 2009. One of struggle. There'd been a few tough years, when her work hadn't connected readily with the world, a time of push and pull. She'd never liked to push. She wanted things to come to her. She'd never liked grasping artists, and there was so much grasping in the world she knew.

What had come of that time? It had lasted a handful of years. Keith had been busy, too. If it hadn't been for the bit of inheritance from his mother, none of it would have worked; at least, not then. He hated to recall that time of struggle, what it almost did to them. He recalled working to hold on to what had brought them together. From her, he felt the expectation for him to be there. He'd become a part of her, it seemed. He'd wondered at that—for all their talk of no halves.

Her imagination was expansive, and her artistic net had pulled him to her; she hadn't had to struggle for him. For a moment, a waif-thought circled the edge of his mind, peering at him through some mental bars that were keeping one of the two of them out. The mental waif questioned if Raz took photos for the love of it? Or because of the people it pulled to her, as it had pulled him. It had been okay to have pull. But not push. For her.

He reached for the next book. More of the same. In another time he would have appreciated this, seeing her mind in these words. Whatever was real in what she did, it would be in these pages, possibly even more than in what she produced for all to see.

He placed the notebooks with the books he'd set aside for Charlie. Charlie might want these at some point, to know more about his mother. Keith stopped his thoughts from continuing down that path. No idea how this was going to take future shape.

There were half a dozen of the navy notebooks, once all the beige were separated. No dates on the outside of these, but inside some pencilled in. She always did have an odd preference for pencils, soft pencils. Even her letters had shading, some of them gone over, and shaped. One page so much so that he had to hold it at arm's length and observe it as a drawing, not words. These journals were more visual than the project notebooks. There were sketches. Studies of body parts to begin with. Her own breasts, he recognized. She was the only woman he'd known with one areola larger than the other. Not by much, but noticeable to him.

A sketch of a man's back, buttocks, between his legs shadowy, weighty. In all these sketches there was appreciation for flesh. He knew the back wasn't his. Or was that how he appeared? What is it to have a body part or perspective we can't even know? But another can. Still, he was quite certain, it wasn't his. Shakespeare's *beast with two backs* came to mind: the phrase always evoked fiercely intimate sex, face to face.

What was it to make love, to have sex, to *know* another? Amusing diversion? Sacred pleasure? Should it hold meaning? Anything? Or only if you wanted it to mean? Or what you wanted it to mean? What was the body? What did it mean to exist physically in the world? How are we our bodies?

There was a drawing of a young woman in what appeared to be the 1940s era, with styled hair and full-legged slacks, with a shirt buttoned low, sleeves rolled up, and wide collar flaring at her neck. In her late teens, Raz studied fashion illustration. So many stories they'd told each other, of their lives. How much had he forgotten? What stories would he need to share with Charlie? Maybe there'd been pieces he should have paid more attention to, maybe he could have understood. But understood what? Sometimes he'd had some sense that there was more, but to push at that had felt like a door with a sign *no entry*. There would always be things you could not understand about each other, things that anyone could not even understand about their very selves.

This drawing had a leggy, sexy confidence, and around it were words: *The girl and the woman, in their new, individual unfolding, will only in passing be imitators of male behaviour and misbehaviour and repeaters of male professions   women will strip off*

conventions of mere femaleness in the transformations of her out-
ward status, and those men who do not yet feel it approaching will
be astonished by it. Rainier Maria Rilke, 1904.

Keith reread the words. 1904 was a long time ago.

Raz had written underneath. *Tired of imitation of being*
repeater.   *I am*   *Transformed*

Page after page, sketches, lines written. In the middle of the
book, a sketch of a woman surrounded by men. It brought to
mind that high-school-years album from the backyard shed, that
photo with the boys.

She'd drawn with even softer pencil. Perhaps at some point
the men's faces would have been recognizable, but she'd taken
a blending stump, smudged each. It gave a dislocating sense of
movement. Intentional? Or was the effacement intentional, and
the movement coincidental? Each face both unique and alike,
between drawing, then smudging. The drawing transfixed, and
Keith studied. The bodies were different, different heights and
postures. If this was at all reflective of her reality, it wouldn't be
possible to say she had a type. There were words pencilled into
this drawing too: *No* one *is enough.*

He stared at the word *one*. Was he *One*?

More of her words. *How is it I am here?*   *I never belong*
Always in the wrong place

What was she talking about? He scrutinized the handwriting
as if it could tell him more the longer he looked. Closing the journal didn't resolve anything. Perhaps the reference to 'one' was
his answer. If he was capable of accepting. Instead he was filled
with questions he could never answer. He slipped the navy notebooks into his own desk drawer, closed it. Then pulled them out.
It didn't feel right, the books tucked in with his.

Taint. The word made him recoil.

If she were here to give him answers, would he believe her?

He put the books under the stack of magazines and journals
on his bedside table.

What else to get rid of? Go through that phone one last time. He could feel himself shaking and lightheaded. He had to make short work of this.

But within minutes on the phone he found texts written and read while they'd been listening to Maceo Parker in concert. He remembered that evening, Raz next to him, tapping into her phone. He'd placed a hand on her wrist, to ask her to stop, and she'd shaken him off. Later she'd pointed out that her texting was impossible to hear with the music. He'd felt silly wanting to say that the concert was their time, she didn't need to be always connected with the outside world.

The texts:

Amazing

Can he go longer? 2.5 hrs already

Musical viagra!

Don't give me ideas

Gonna feel you up as we crush outta this place

Impossible to recall the details of that evening, the crowd thickly moving towards the doors, taste of saxophone in everyone's mouth. Who had crushed into Raziel? Whoever it had been was inches from Keith. Someone he knew? Did they say hello? Someone he didn't know? He couldn't do a playback.

His thumb hovered over the delete key. What was he going to do if he didn't get rid of this? He had friends, people who loved him. He had Charlie.

He hesitated. Then hit the key.

He scrolled through: another unfamiliar number, along with Cat's. Miriam's. Ron and Felicity's. A cousin.

Here was a name. Bill. He'd gone deep into messages. Why hadn't she gotten rid of all this? She'd had time, after the diagnosis. She could have gotten rid of every last blurry image, postcard, and Rilke quote, and he'd never have known. Why didn't she? She can't have wanted him to find this. Or could she have? Did she think it might ease grief? Make it easier to move on. How could anyone think that? How had she processed emotion? How did she think he did?

Ready for our dirty weekend? Bill.

· *Crazy with the thought.* From her.

Date. One week after Charlie's third birthday.

They'd argued about which weekend she could go away. There'd been some photographers' event the weekend of Charlie's birthday. She stayed home, but only because he said she should. She'd never reminded him that she was the one who paid the mortgage, but he'd seen the aggrieved brow. Heard clanking cutlery. A dropped light bulb, when she was screwing it into place, something she usually left to him, and the cursing that elicited. The following weekend she insisted on travelling alone to the San Juan Islands, some autumn call to her and her cameras. Taking pictures, following her whims. Her muses. He'd trusted.

He felt like an idiot.

He pushed the delete button again. How much more did he need to see? How long, if ever, before the images and words would leave him?

He emptied a desk drawer to find a paper clip, pulled it into a useful shape and dug out the phone card. Where was that hammer? In the closet with the vacuum. He dropped it twice, left a ding on the kitchen floor. Gripped it tightly to the concrete of the balcony and hammered the secrets out of the card. Pushed it into the bottom of the kitchen garbage, and took it to the parking garage bin. Found himself in that concrete underground and howled until he sweated. It didn't ease the shaking, but worsened it. He placed his hands flat on the hood of his car, bowed over, chest heaving. Was there a shadow of someone slipping out? Street people found their way here, and he'd probably terrified the poor bugger.

In the apartment he sat with the laptop, turned it on, waited. The password box popped up, and he tried a few. Name with symbols. Ch@rl13. oldD@!sy. Birthday numbers, anniversary.

A couple of phrases they'd laughed over. He closed it. This wasn't going to work. He had to set it aside.

He opened another box in the row to find a large manila envelope with instructions on it. *Keith. Family photos here. Wedding. Birthdays. Holidays.* He had no idea when Raziel had put this together. *Family.* He stared at the word. Inside were a number of computer sticks along with hardcopies of black and white and colour photographs. Each stick was in a small envelope with a description neatly printed on. This should calm him, but didn't.

But Raziel had saved him from having to examine the computer. That was how he saw this. The laptop, the phone. He needed neither. So back to the basement, and he dropped both into the dumpster.

He pushed aside the second half of his sandwich, and sat staring out the window. He felt strangely intimate with the woman he'd been married to. He'd spent the day coming to know her in ways he never had before, and he felt his loss in a much sharper way now. He'd lost her in other unexpected ways, gone, completely. The intimacy wasn't a closeness; it was being inside her head, a most sullied place. His own mind was filled with images and words, and a messy, dirty pain, the kind that scores flesh where it binds. Like some work of clay. The pain he'd felt losing her had been simple, clean. He was recognizing that now. He wouldn't have before. But now, as much as it had ached before, it had been a life-lived pain, the price for loving. There had to be some price for love.

This was something else. What was real?

The loss he already felt: had he ever had her? What did it mean to *have* someone? Was that even possible? Not unless they shared their selves with you.

Was it even possible to grieve someone you didn't know? Now there was the rub of this distancing intimacy. When someone died it was supposed to be some closure, but this wasn't. It didn't feel like a beginning either. It was a wading into a rushing stream that would take him, smash his bones into a rock, and leave him. There'd never be answers. She'd left too much for him to sort.

He needed a shower so hot the room filled with steam. And music, loud, over the pouring. He scrubbed red, almost felt clean, would like to scrub his insides too. But there was something he couldn't get down to: being unloved and, maybe worse, un-loveable. Could he understand if or how she'd loved him? If you couldn't understand how someone loved you, did that mean you weren't loved? He climbed out and towelled off, hard.

In his bedroom there was a family photo collage on one wall. Keith took it down and moved it into Charlie's room.

Back to his room, to the bedside photo of the woman who had been his wife, costumed and posed with her inherent drama, was how he was seeing it now. Why had he not before? He'd seen it as flair. Creativity. The dress was from the thirties, vin-tage, with long loops of pearls down to her hips, shoulder fabric dropped to her upper arm. In the corner of the frame he'd long ago tucked a snapshot taken by Trev on their wedding day, one of the few photos, maybe the only, in which Raz was looking at him, not at the camera, and filled with laughter. A photo he'd always loved, taken by a not-photographer in a moment no one noticed. What was the real Raziel?

He put it in the bottom drawer of his desk. Closed it, opened it, took it out, and added it to the box of photos he'd set aside for Charlie. He closed the flaps, struggling to tuck them in. They did that stubborn thing box flaps do. His hands weren't working properly. He needed to go, couldn't be late again.

He wanted to be free.

"Softly as a Morning Sunrise" / *Foolish Ska Jazz Orchestra*
"1979" / *Smashing Pumpkins*
"Autumn Sweater" / *Yo La Tengo*

18

"What's with the hat?" When had he last seen Trev with a hat? This one, fedora-like and from their past, he'd jammed onto his head. They were sitting at the Railway Club, and Keith couldn't figure out what wasn't right.

It wasn't surprising that Trev still had the hat. He had yellowed local band posters on his walls, unframed. Norah's idea of a birthday surprise was to add to the collection or frame one. How'd she find the things? Their apartment was filled with memorabilia, every one chosen. Stories.

"How about I get you a beer, and you forget about the hat?" Trev asked, and was gone before Keith could reply. As he walked away, Keith saw what appeared to be a purplish stain bruising his hairline.

Trev returned with two pints.

"When did you decide to dye your hair?" Keith had to ask.

"Let's not," Trev said, and filled his mouth with dark lager.

"Okay." So Keith said nothing about the grey hairs he'd been noticing on his friend's head.

It was easier to talk about the start of the hockey season, more details about the Hopper trip, anything, than what was on his mind. Keith had to be almost done with beer two before he could begin. But Trev knew something was up, and the conversation found in its rhythm a place to come to a full stop.

"It's like this." Keith stared out the window. Always street people at this intersection, Dunsmuir and Richards, with that corner store below on the first floor. "I've found some stuff. Notes, postcards, messages."

Trev could be a guy of few words. Now, nothing. He looked steadily at Keith, waiting.

"I think maybe I didn't really know Raz."

Pause. Trev leaned forward. "What are you talking about?" He pushed at the hat as if he'd like to be freed of it. More purple. Keith wished he cared enough to give him a hard time. On another day it would have been sport to chirp. But here, now, was the line between only Keith knowing, and someone else knowing, a line thicker than everyone knowing.

"An affair?" Trev's eyebrows raised. "She loved the shit out of you. You guys were a team."

"Not so much maybe."

"You didn't do a lot together, we all knew that. You had roles, you knew what you were doing, each of you. You had your own lives, together. I've often pointed to you guys as knowing how to do it. I've said that to Norah, so many times." His voice drifted off.

"Not an affair, not what you're thinking. Maybe that would be sort of normal. No, this was more like . . ." Keith took a long swallow, and thought of those postcards. "More like a game."

Trev stared.

"Like Charlie and I were one world, and everything else was another. I don't know if her worlds overlapped, or if one was inside the other. I don't know what anything meant to her." He was taken by the shakiness that came over him then, and he had to move, had to stand.

"Let's move up to the front and see some music."

Trev caught his sleeve. Keith pulled away. He went to get round three. He stood at the bar and pointed for Trev to grab one of the two tables left up front.

When Keith set down the pints and took a seat, Trev spoke. "Are you sure about this? I mean, is there any way it's something else?"

"I'm sure," said Keith shortly. "I tried that myself, the idea that it wasn't what it seemed. But I found more and more. So much.

Texts, her journals." He broke off. Trev appeared to be unable to think of anything to say. "Are you going to tell me now how you would deal with this?"

Trev took a breath. "I don't know. I don't have any idea how I would. I mean, Norah would never . . ." His face reddened.

"I didn't think Raz would. Actually, I didn't think about it. Not really." He gave a rough laugh. "I guess you don't know how you would deal with it. Until it happens."

"How long have you known?"

"I started to find stuff after we got home from the trip, after I went to her studio to pick up things."

Trev was still, as if he needed time to take it in. He turned away for a moment, muscles working in his neck, around his ear. Keith could see: weird-ass little muscles that kept it all inside.

"She's not even here," Trev spat out. He turned to face Keith. "She's not here to ask. That's the thing, isn't it? Living with that?" Another moment of processing. "Damn, I know what Norah'll say."

"Yeah?"

"Bitch!"

Keith was stunned. "Really?"

"Really."

"I thought Norah liked Raz."

"She did. But she also said she never trusted her. Though she could never say why."

Keith felt as though he'd been struck. Norah. His cousin-like-a-sister. Mild. Easygoing. Had had this thought all along.

"Maybe I shouldn't have said that." Trev moved uncomfortably in his chair, turned his drink in his hand, grimaced.

Keith shook his head. "You know, I felt like we, Raz and I, were family. Maybe that was a mistake. I never should have let that happen."

"Norah's my family," said Trev, flummoxed. "I can't imagine her not being around. Half the time we don't have to talk. I don't think that's a mistake. I don't think it's anything you can control.

After time has passed, it just is." He seemed to be mulling over a thought. "Maybe that's what she didn't want. Raz, I mean. Maybe she needed something different. I'm not saying you're not exciting, but . . ."

"I'm not exciting. I'm good old Keith. Nice guy. But everything I thought was my life, it isn't."

Trev nodded, said nothing.

"I keep hoping it'll make sense, but I don't think that's going to happen. It's going to take time. And I don't know what else."

"If it never makes sense, do you think you can handle that?"

"I have a choice? I haven't put this into words yet. I just think in circles. I think I'll have to get beyond logic."

"Beyond logic?"

"Yeah."

"What does that *mean?*"

Keith shrugged. "It's the thought that's in my head right now. That I need to get to some place I've never been. That's the phrase that comes into my head."

"Okay."

"I need to pay attention. To what's in me about this." Feeling the alcohol. "You know, that's all shit. I don't know what I'm saying. If there was an answer I'd grab it, but I don't know how that's going to happen. Ashes don't talk." Was that why he couldn't put them into the wind on the prairie? Was he hoping for an answer of sorts? Had he thought he'd need one?

Trev had no response to that. He was almost finished that third beer. He eyed Keith's. "You know," he said, "if you want to keep going with that, Norah can probably stay with Charlie for the night, and you can crash on our couch."

"I'm good. I won't need that."

"It's a thought," said Trev. "You and Raz used to trade off, I remember. Designated driving and all."

"Yeah," said Keith. "We did." As he spoke, he heard the slip in his voice, and he felt memories pushing at him. "I'll have another."

Trev nodded. "I need one." He went to the bar.

Keith didn't feel like talking after that. He was glad they'd moved up front to the stage. He could watch the band with the ratty velvet curtain behind them, nod his head with the drummer. Music was like a disposable diaper when it came to absorption; the comparison came to him, and he had to shake his head. Next thought: he might actually have a hangover for the first time in seven, maybe eight years? Even when Raz had the driver's designation, he never went too far.

Maybe he should have. Maybe he should have lightened up now and then.

The more he drank the more he talked. In between thoughts and words, he listened. The bass player was pulling him in.

Trev spoke in a pause. "You're gonna be okay."

"That's what I tell myself."

Thoughts of the future blended and connected with present and past. He made himself aware of the blending, injected himself into it. He tried to take on some feeling that might be Hope, and the blurry sense of future was somehow transmitted to past. Retroactive. Such a fleeting sensation, this blurring. He wasn't sure how it worked. Maybe as a piece of 'beyond logic?' Even a moment of reprieve from the sadness was worthwhile. Such moments were islands floating. Maybe, eventually, the islands would conjoin, create some place he could go.

Maybe this was why some people drank. He drained another glass. Everything could make sense for a time.

He missed sex. He missed holding someone. True, it would probably be easy enough to have sex. But it would be a long time before he had sex with someone who knew him, and someone he knew. That reaching for someone in the dark, a familiar body, and one who was familiar with him.

He didn't realize how inebriated he was until he stood to go to the toilet. It took a while to get there, and another to get back. When he did, Trev was on the phone, but he wrapped up the conversation shortly after Keith sat. "Norah," he began. "I had this thought. That maybe it'd be an idea for you to go away."

"Apropos of?" This wasn't the time to go away. "We were just away," Keith said drunkenly.

"Yeah, and good for Ron sharing his old van. This would be different. It'd be about you going away. Norah and I were supposed to go up to the Sunshine Coast next weekend. Was a deal from her work. The travel agency has this B&B network up there. But I think you should go instead, get into the woods, you know. This is some crazy shit to get through. We can hang out with Charlie and Old girl Daisy, too. You can't say no. We can rebook our time up there."

"I can't leave Charlie."

"Yeah, that's what Norah said, but I don't agree. I think you should. We'll care for Charlie. It's done. We already booked the place."

"I can't leave."

"You're going. I've convinced Norah. If I can convince her, I can convince you. If I can't convince you tonight, I'll convince you tomorrow." He stood to go. This was so Trev, on the fly, snap decisions. They'd done more than one fishing trip with less discussion than this.

"But . . ."

"Go Thursday, back Sunday. A few days. Not enough, and not enough to worry about Charlie. We have it all under control." He fiddled with his phone, and seconds later, Keith's phone sounded a notification. "Go ahead," said Trev. "Take a look."

Keith took a look. Directions, a map, a photo of a comfortable house, settled into protective trees. A photo of waffles. One of a woman, plaid flannel shirt, gardening gloves, crossed arms, not old, not young. Mid or late forties. Smiling.

"She's the owner. Stella. She's a little different, gotta say. You won't see much of her. The place has a few rooms and a little cabin out back. You'll have the cabin, private. Can do breakfast in the big house, or on your own. Norah's coworkers at the travel agency go there often. We've stayed once, a good place to chill, to figure out shit."

Breakfast in the big house. Or on his own. What would he do between breakfast and dinner? Sleep came to mind. There were times he wanted to lie down and not wake up, at least not for half a week. So maybe a weekend wasn't a bad idea. "Okay." That wasn't enough. "Thank you," he added.

He felt in pieces. But this was a yellow-oxygen-mask time if ever there was.

"I think we gotta take a cab home," he said. "Now."

Norah opened the door, hair bunched on the left side of her head, maybe from lying down trying to sleep. Or from worrying about the crazy phone call with Trev? Keith gave her a hug that he hoped was reassuring. But after she stepped back, her hands still on his elbows, to peer into his face. "You okay to look after Charlie when we go down the hall?"

He tried to make light of it. "You're just down the hall." Her question had a sobering quality.

She peered at him. "I can stay on the couch. You're pretty drunk."

"I'm okay."

Trev reached for her. "Let's go home. We're close, if Keith needs us."

"I'm okay," Keith repeated. He could hear their voices, low for the late hour as they walked away, and he should have closed the door, but he took his time, listened to the unintelligible sound that was two people communicating, and ached with the listening.

He filled a glass of water, gulped it, moved to stand by Charlie's door. He could hear his son's breaths. Around him, his own home, felt strange, close walls, far away sounds, warped everything. He moved away from Charlie's door, and his fingers closed around one of those damn condolence cards that were still on the surfaces, and he crushed it in his hand and pushed it into the kitchen garbage. Then slid down the wall to sit by the front doorway as if on guard. No, as if he didn't want to go farther into his home.

Maybe he fell asleep. Or closed his eyes and let go. There was a soft knock at the door that brought him to. How long had he been sitting with his back to the wall? He was still holding the empty glass, which he set down to get up, to answer the door.

Norah. With wet red eyes, who wrapped her arms around him, made him remember being a kid on a bike, skittering through rocks, and going down. How old had he been? Six? His big cousin took him to find a mom, his or hers, and somewhere to wash his bloody, gravel-pocked hands. Now her arms were around him, and she was saying, "I'm so sorry," as if she could do something.

He pushed himself out of her arms to go to Charlie's door and quietly close it. "See?" he said. "I'm not that drunk at all. I can still think. Sort of." He suspected what her words might be, and didn't want Charlie to hear.

She gave him a wan smile. "Trev told me. About Raz. It breaks my heart. I'm so sorry."

"Trev said you had a feeling." He wasn't accusing, but there was some bit of push, even to how the words came out of him.

"I never spent too long thinking about it. Maybe I should have. But there was a feeling I had. Something off. Somehow." She wasn't happy saying this, didn't like to say I-told-you-so. But she couldn't hide being twisted up inside.

"I'm not saying there's anything you could have done. Or known," Keith said.

She went to refill his glass with water and handed it to him. "I see why Trev thinks you should go away. I still think it'll not be easy for Charlie, but you should do what you need to."

"I'll go. It's not for long. You know Trev. He's not going to let me do anything else. Can't argue with the guy."

She nodded. "Mom went through this, you know."

Auntie Nele?

"You knew that," she said.

"I did?"

"You were a kid at the time. Maybe twelve. It wasn't like this. It was one woman, with Dad. But that was enough, for Mom."

He couldn't recall. "I only remember you crying, breaking up with that guy you went with through high school. What's-his-name."

She grimaced. "So that's what you remember. It connected in my mind. I ended up thinking here was a guy who was going to be like Dad, if I wanted to end up like Mom. I couldn't stand to see all the pain in her."

It was his turn to hold her and say he was sorry. He stood in the doorway and watched her make her way back down the hall, shoulders with a bit more slope, arms around herself, hands holding her ribs. Then she turned to wave goodnight, and he was caught by how grateful he was that she was in his world. It was too lonely to hold on to your secrets alone.

He talked with Charlie the next day. "How would you feel about staying with Norah and Trev for the weekend? With Old Daisy?"

"Why?" asked Charlie.

"I need a time out," Keith said.

"Time out?" Charlie's two words, and the question on his face was hard to take. It might be easier to go on as he'd been before Trev's coaxing. How could Keith explain so it didn't sound as if he needed time away from Charlie?

"You know how after you've been really busy at school, or we've had too many people over, you go into your room and draw or put Legos together, and you stay there for a while, until dinner or bedtime? And you feel better? You feel restored?"

Charlie understood the drift of 'restored,' and he nodded.

"I need that kind of time."

"Okay," was the answer, so quick. Did he understand?

"Old Daisy will be with me, too?" He needed to hear that again.

"Old Daisy will be with you. We know she's the one who really takes care of all — both — of us, right?" A family joke. And the update.

Old Daisy heard her name, clicked over, and nosed first one, then the other, and settled in for a scratch.

He filled his pack with two more shirts, a bulky wool sweater, three boxers, socks, slipped in a novel he'd wanted to read at some point, so overdue from the library. Maybe he'd spend the entire weekend reading. Last minute he slid in an empty notebook. Maybe he'd write. Notebooks used to move him.

"If you want to go on the ferry as a foot passenger, you can call Stella when you arrive, and she'll pick you up. It's part of the B&B deal," Trev reminded him.

Being free of the car had appeal, so Keith picked up the bus, jacket on, wearing boots that would do for a hike, and his pack. There were other foot passengers waiting at the Horseshoe Bay Terminal, but he was restless and early. He walked through the nearby streets with mountains rising, ocean with whitecaps, far away from the city, from home.

Back to the terminal, coffee in hand, and announcements over a PA system that sounded like grade school. People dragged wheeled suitcases or had packs. Two pushed strollers, with one child sleeping, and the other, a toddler who appeared to want to be on foot as much as the next person. She stared at Keith and scowled, so unapologetically that Keith had to give her a thumb's up. *You go!* He was awarded a deeper scowl.

A few were exchanging goodbye hugs, but most were on their own, Keith noticed. Did he used to notice that?

On the boat, he found a seat by the window and didn't open his pack, but took stock of the place he was about to sail away from: leaves starting to turn colour, snags of mist, maybe woodstove smoke rising from hillsides. The ocean was a deep green-black. He was missing his son at his side, as he did these days when they were separated, as he did in a way he'd never before. This was good, though, good to be on his own. He needed this, he needed to trust others with his boy.

The coffee was still hot in his dented and scratched travel mug, the same he used for writing, to keep coffee hot through morning hours. How long would the insurance money last? He felt insubstantial, splintered. But someday he would write again. Right now his task was to heal, to get on with the work of that. To let go of what he needed to, to hold on. Oh, he sounded like an Oprah guest. Or as he imagined one.

All he could see were people with earbuds, phones, laptops. A few with books, thank God. There was hope. Maybe.

He was used to holidays with Raz, roaming with her camera, life through the lens. She had a certain tone when she called *Keith?* and he knew that if he turned to her, he'd be looking at a lens, and there'd be a snap. The camera was invitation for others to speak with her. She'd share stories. He remembered now, on the ferry to Vancouver Island, a much longer ride, she'd disappeared. After an hour, Charlie and he'd gone looking for her. Charlie had wanted to, and Keith tried to calm him. They'd find her, she would be fine, he'd reassured, even as the ferry was docking and people were heading down the stairs to the car-park levels.

He remembered her lament that she'd lost an earring, and the flush in her cheeks. He'd assumed she was out on deck in the wind.

He'd loved her. Everyone had loved her.

But should he have known? On some level?

You had to believe that things were possible to even look for them.

He got up from the window seat and made himself move to crawl out of his own head. How long would such thoughts haunt him? Could he take thoughts, push them into a sack with a heavy rock, and toss them in a river? He imagined it, and then a voice in his ear muttered about visualization, and he mentally tossed the voice instead. One being the same as the other. Learning to toss was key.

It wasn't a long ride before the Sunshine Coast terminal came into view, and as the ferry thudded into its berth, he found the number Trev had given him.

"I'll be driving a vw van," said Stella, B&B woman. "I'm minutes away, getting groceries."

To what degree did her voice reflect who she was? Not a cold voice, nor warm. Detached, modulated. Not uncaring, but not otherwise. He wondered if she could sing — it had that weighted core.

He stood where she'd told him to, until a rusty vw stopped, and she climbed out to open the passenger door and close it after him, all so smoothly done that it left him with a shot of surprise. Had anyone held a car door open for him and then closed it like that, as if taking care of him? It put his head in an odd place.

"You always do that?"

"What?" Eyebrows up.

"The door business." Was it strange to note this? "It was nice," he added. "Thank you."

She gave him a quick appraising look.

He rather hoped he'd be left on his own in this backyard cabin. He was suddenly hungry for such time, hungrier than he'd known.

She said little on the drive of maybe forty-five minutes, but slid a CD — Tanita Tikaram — into the ancient player in the van. He didn't want to appear to be looking at her, but he was aware of the sharp profile next to him, the erect carriage. She wasn't tall, but she gave that impression. *Different* was the word Trev had used. Words were coming to mind, but at this point he wasn't at all sure about putting words to anything. Let it reveal itself. Maybe that's why he couldn't write. Everything felt ripped apart, and what should have been obvious, wasn't. He could think of a word and wonder if it meant what he'd always thought it did. He'd unearthed his Oxford to plow through pages and sit staring at a definition. He allowed himself to think this was some form of writing.

The drive was so bereft of words that he could let the lyrics cut across his thoughts and splice. Still searching for a word for Stella, though. So un-starlike. He let that slip through, and was grateful when they arrived, and he could shut down thought.

The house was almost completely hidden in trees, both coniferous and brightly coloured. A blazing Japanese maple stood out. It was a dark west-coast day, especially with the overgrown quality of the place. The porch was the entire width of the house, and deep, with a roof overheard. Twinkly lights were strung in the underside of this roof. They swayed in the wind over a set of two short bamboo couches with a propane firepit in their L-shape. In summer, even in shoulder seasons, it would be a good place to sit.

"Feel free to spend time here," she said. He'd put his foot up on the first stair, but now he smiled and stepped away. The need for time alone had him in hold. "I leave books to borrow and read." She motioned to a small shelf, near one of the couches. "I'll show you your home for the next few days." She led the way.

He could see why she didn't encourage guests to drive. There was no room for parking, and cars would have taken away from the green. Already he was coming undone, pieces threatening to float away. Maybe it was the word *home*.

She opened the door, motioned him inside, and stayed in the doorway.

It struck him as a small space intended for one person. In a back corner was a double bed with an old-fashioned quilt, smaller than the queen size at home and miniature compared to the king size of the hotel rooms they'd reserve for their travels. Raz loved to spread out. But this bed was just for him.

In the other back corner was the kitchen, a corner with everything he needed, and a round antique oak table. Two overfilled reading chairs and an ottoman filled the middle of the open room, with a small woodstove between them. He didn't need the second chair filled. The woodstove would be companion enough.

Stella said, "It's ready to light, and there's more wood outside the door. I leave a kettle on top, if you want tea." She appeared defensive for the moment. "Yes, I like tea."

That was the bit of human he'd been missing. He stopped himself from laughing.

She gave him a look he couldn't name, and showed him how to regulate the oxygen in the stove. "Your friend asked me to pick up some food. You'll find it in the cupboard and the fridge."

"He did?"

"He's a good friend. I remember him and his wife, staying here. Kind people."

"They are," he agreed.

"We all need a good friend. There're so few." She gave a thin smile. "I'll leave you to it. Knock on my door with any questions, or call my cell. Number's on the counter. I should mention coyote sightings in the paths nearby. I'll show you the paths tomorrow if you want to walk. You'll need to be cautious if you go there."

She eyed him. He must look like a real city guy. He didn't explain the expression that must have been on his face. *Coyote.*

"Thank you," he said. *Please go.*

"You might hear them howling. Never lasts too long."

She turned away, then back. "You good?" The question caught him. Had Trev said anything to this woman? That wasn't like Trev.

"I'm good, yeah," he said. "Thanks."

She gave a quick nod that made him think he'd read too much into her question. He closed the door, and out of habit locked it. Then wondered if that was necessary.

It was dusk, and with the cabin set in the tall pines, even

darker. Would he hear howling? He opened the fridge and wondered at Trev asking this woman to shop. Gouda, his favourite, and the right sort of bread. Some Dijon with horseradish. A few rich red tomatoes. He would make himself a sandwich, then call Charlie and say goodnight. There were several mandarin oranges on the table, he saw, as he set out the sandwich fixings.

His phone was in the outer pocket of the pack. And almost out of charge. He ripped the pack apart looking for the cord. Had he really left it behind?

He would have to find a store and get one. For now, he called Trev and asked him to put Charlie on the phone. He needed to say goodnight. He could hear Trev calling. Could hear Charlie's voice. Closer. He could imagine him taking the phone.

"Dad?"

"Charlie. Buddy, my phone's about to go. But I want to say goodnight."

"I don't like goodnight on the phone."

"We could do a video call tomorrow night."

Silence.

"Charlie?"

"When will you be home?"

"Sunday. After three sleeps."

More silence.

"Trev and Norah and Old Daisy will take good care of you." Pause. "We never do talk on the phone, do we?"

"No. I don't like it." Charlie's voice sounded small.

"I don't either. But when I'm not there with you, the phone is the next best thing." That conversation they'd had, about going away, about Old Daisy taking care of Charlie, he hadn't been listening.

"There's no next best thing." Charlie's voice was lost sounding.

Keith was about to say more when the phone died. He opened the laptop and sent a message to Trev to explain. "Give him a hug for me, please."

He knew Trev would, and still he felt bad. He hadn't asked Charlie how he'd like to communicate. That should have been part of the conversation. Still, this was the yellow-oxygen-mask time. Apply first to self, then to child.

Maybe he shouldn't be here. He'd written a blog post about that yellow mask, hadn't he? Thinking he knew all about it, thinking it'd be useful to others. He could write an update. He should write a lot of updates now, but they'd be stuff no one would want to read. People liked chirpy and positive. Or they loved to hear about all the dirt and pain. They didn't so much want to hear about navigating and getting through, keeping up your sails through the doldrums. Actually, his sails were not up at all. He really did want to fall asleep in the hold, and come to the surface so much later.

Make the sandwich, he told himself. But he ate only half, and one of the oranges on the table spoke to him. He picked it up and pierced it, breathing in the citrusy spike as he began to peel the bright skin. He remembered telling Charlie a story, and the memory was like digging strong fingers into a sore muscle, so good.

Once upon a Christmas long ago, I left an orange in moon-shaped pieces on my parents' coffee table. Me and Cousin Norah, we were hanging out. We left the orange a long time sitting and when I came back, it looked not so good, all dried up. But I was hungry and popped one piece in my mouth. It was the best thing I ever tasted.

And they'd done it, he and Charlie, opened and divided a mandarin orange into moony crescents. "We'll leave it overnight and the skin will dry up and get tight and in the morning, when you bite into it, it'll burst juice, and spray in your mouth!"

Charlie had been about to put a piece in his mouth, but he set it down.

"Trust me," Keith had said. "It's worth the wait." Charlie did not look wholly convinced.

But the next morning he waited for his dad so they could do it together, and he handed him a piece, with its taut dried opaque skin. Together, they popped them into their mouths.

Charlie's eyes had grown wide with delight, and he understood. He went to find his momma to give her a piece.

Oh, the *trust me* piece. And the stupidity of not remembering his phone cord, of not dotting his parental i's and crossing t's. He left the uneaten orange on the table now, appetite gone, and set the rest of the sandwich on a shelf in the fridge. *Trust me.* The piece could be untrue, or taken for granted in one of many ways.

He opened his pack, set up piles of clothing on top of the dresser. No point in putting away into a drawer. He poured whiskey into a mug, lit the stove, was relieved when the flames flared readily. Stella knew how to prepare a fire. He pulled both chairs closer, sat on one and put his feet up on the other, glad he'd thrown thick socks into the pack. He sipped the whiskey and listened to the wind in the pines overhead. He could hear right through the walls of the place. Not that the walls were thin. Quite the opposite. They were thick logs and had stood there since before Stella showed up on earth, he would guess. But the wind was suddenly like November. He rested his head onto the soft and thick back of the chair and realized there was a skylight overhead in the open ceiling, and the pines waved mightily. He'd like to take this chair home with him. He stretched to the lamp nearby and turned out the light to see the pines' blackened motion against the deep indigo of the sky.

He was the only one in the room; it felt like he was the only one in the world, too. He kept his head back, watching the flickers on the ceiling, listening to the fire. That skylight was perfect. Pieces of life — worrying about when he might write again, forgetting that phone cord, always, always being aware of Charlie right there, with him — these bits were slipping to another place, and now there was this feeling that he'd been struggling with for weeks, welling up from his gut. If his phone worked, he could put on music.

Instead, he focused on breathing. He'd written a post about that, too. He'd written too many words on things he knew nothing about.

The humbling he could accept, but the humiliation rumpled. More scotch, more staring at the wind moving the pines, at the fire in the stove.

He fell asleep, and awoke with a soft dream of his mother pulling a blanket around his shoulders, being a boy with the flu. Might have been his grandmother. He closed his eyes and recalled the feeling, one he'd not thought of or felt for decades. Had his father ever done that? He couldn't remember and wished he could.

A memory came to him, dragged in to dance, dragged in by the scotch, no doubt. A memory of his father flying a kite, the two of them together. How had he forgotten? The memory came with a slicing pain; or was the forgetting the source of the pain? Some times should not be forgotten.

He got up, took off his clothes, left them in a humanless pile by the stove, and climbed under the quilt. From the bed he could see the embers of the fire. He had to remember, when he returned home, to go buy a kite with Charlie. With that thought he fought again the sensation in his chest, in his breastbone, of being unable to breathe. Not heartburn. Maybe heartbreak. Or maybe there was nothing left in there. But nothing could blow up hard, and push and take over like nobody's business.

20 *"Twist in My Sobriety"* / *Tanita Tikaram*
"If It Makes You Happy" / *Sheryl Crow*
"Here She Comes Now" / *Nirvana*

He awoke to early light, slithering greyly over the horizon. He wouldn't go back to sleep. If he did breakfast at the big house, as Trev called it, there were hours to go.

The rain had stopped, so his bulky sweater would do. He preferred the wool. He stepped out and closed the door behind him. Maybe the ocean would be accessible if he wandered down the road out in front of the house. There wasn't one other person on the narrow road. He could have felt lonely, but he didn't. He followed a trail in the grass, came to a set of stairs set into the hillside that was almost a cliff, could hear the crash of waves below, but trees, cedars and fir, kept him from seeing the water. Wind made him feel that some convergence was imminent.

He lifted his face into it, and his nose grew cold. He headed down the steep stairs, didn't stop again until he reached the bottom. No coyote in sight here. The beach wasn't a summer beach, but covered in stones. There were trees with great branches that stretched out over those stones. He plunged on through them grinding and shifting under his feet, waves sounding in his ears. He loved them for their roaring, almost over his thoughts. If he let them, they might roll over his thoughts and carry them away. He trudged with the fugginess of mind without coffee, vague headache on the periphery. Maybe the wind could clear that.

Then saw a figure far ahead of him, bending to the ground, and picking up. Even from the distance he recognized Stella, with a braid thick and tight down her back. He turned and began to head back. That headache was finding some articulation without coffee. Had she spotted him? It wasn't that he didn't want to see her or talk with her. But he didn't, really. He fought to get back to the wordless trudge he'd been in, but couldn't. The moment had changed. Before him, the foot of the cliff steps, and behind, the woman's presence. Why did one direction, back to the stairs, feel like running away, and the other like a gnawing pressure, something he had to answer to?

He wanted to climb the stairs, return to the cabin unseen, go inside, lock the door, and not come out again until Sunday and time to leave for the ferry. There was enough food in the fridge, he could probably pull it off. He was halfway to Sunday. But he heard his name. So she'd recognized him, too. The wind had to be blowing right for him to have been able to hear. He turned, and the wind gusted in his face, so no point in answering her.

She was the same distance from him that she'd been earlier. As if she'd followed him at his exact pace. She stopped as soon as he did, as soon as he turned. Like some childhood game: *Mother May I?* Or what had it been? Instant memory of an otherwise forgotten summer day with Norah and cousins from far away. A game he might play with Charlie. But Charlie wasn't here, and Keith didn't have to be Dad. He didn't have to think up games. He didn't want to do anything with anyone else.

She waved her hand at him. Or maybe whatever she'd picked up.

He didn't run away, But he didn't move toward her either. He stood, trapped.

She came his way, and held out her hand.

Like a child, without reaching for it, he asked, "What is it?"

"Something to hold on to."

Finally he put out his hand, and she dropped it. He closed his fingers around. A rock. It could all be a game. But as his fingers rounded the wet blackness of the rock, he absorbed what she was saying: every finger and his thumb found a place to rest in its shape. He couldn't help an "oh" escaping him. He had to open his hand again, and feel the curves and softened shape of it. He turned it again and again. A placeholder for everything.

He should say thank you.

"You were heading back? Already?" She fell into step beside him.

I wanted to run away.

"It's colder than I thought," he said finally. It took such effort to speak. At home, he hadn't felt this. Or maybe just couldn't.

"It's a windy place here by the ocean," she agreed. "If you want to walk in this direction," she motioned south, "it's protected." A cliff rose up on that side, a solid wall of rocks and trees.

"Walk?"

She set off without waiting for his answer. And didn't seem to care that he was a constant half step behind, then a full step. She had a focus to her, if only her mind on the rocks. They could turn an ankle. The wind grew louder and louder, and she made no attempt to speak over it. He would like to be completely comfortable with the not talking, but the lack of so much as a word, even with the wind, felt too much like the kind of silence he'd had with Raziel, the kind you have with a friend of many years, not a new acquaintance.

They reached the point where the cliff took a distinct corner, the beach opened out, and the rain and wind were suddenly freshly crossing their cheeks and foreheads. Simultaneously they turned back without a word. It was unnerving. Maybe he should never have had that type of silence with Raziel, he was beginning to think, when finally the woman began to speak. "This is a respite for you," she began.

"My friend Trev sent me here. Insisted, really."

"A good friend," she said. Trudge, trudge.

"He is. His wife, too. She's my cousin," he had to add. "Though she thought I shouldn't leave my son behind." He thought of the phone, not charging. "I need to buy a phone cord," he said then. He was talking in bits and pieces, wasn't he?

"I probably have one. A charger. I collect them for guests. We're a long way from a store. You should be able to call your son, yes." She'd made the connection between those two pieces of his words.

"He's with his mother?" she said, and that was a question.

"His mother passed away. Died," he added. "In August."

"Oh." Her face shifted through some process, a five-speed gearshift. He'd stopped walking to observe this, and she'd stopped, too. He started to laugh. At that, she looked shocked.

"I'm sorry," he said, "But I could actually see you absorbing and reacting. Some people work hard to hide that from me."

"They say my face shows everything," she said. "It hasn't been long for you, I was thinking."

"No, it hasn't," he agreed, sobered now. "I know it doesn't seem right, not near long enough, to leave my son behind. Norah is right. But there's more to it than that." He shouldn't have said that much. He was too tired to add words.

She gave him a sharp look and turned into the wind again. "There's always more to everything, I've come to think. You don't have to tell me anything. But I could feel such sad heavy stuff in you when I picked you up yesterday."

That unnerved him. She spoke without a tone of judgment or even curiosity, in that peculiarly flat voice of hers, which he guessed was her usual.

"Maybe I shouldn't have said that," she said.

"It's not an unfair thing to say."

"Life is unfair."

"How do you say that without sounding bitter?"

"That karma thing people talk about, it's childish. I mean, I know that thinking like that helps get us through shit. It enables us to think that people who do miserable stuff are going to get it, in the end, and that way we can feel better. But we don't really, and truth is, so often people who hurt or do some shit end up with power, and in places that shock those of us who muddle through. It all feels terribly unfair." Her voice drifted off. She was staring at him, and had stopped again. "I'm not even sure it's the real definition of 'karma,'" she added.

He didn't want to stop. He set off again.

"Sometimes," he said, "they die before anything happens."

"What happens then?"

"You feel as if they got away with it." His answer, so quick, surprised him.

"Yeah, I can imagine that. But there's the possibility that you've escaped, too."

He'd have to think about that. But for now: "I'm here to try to clean up the mess. Mess I don't want my son to see."

What writer said, *You don't know what you think until you hear what you say?* That came to his mind, on this windy, roaring beach.

"Oh!" Now she stood for long seconds scrutinizing him. "Now I understand why you stopped and walked away from me earlier. I'm sorry. You do need to be alone."

He did. He knew it as he heard her words. But he wished suddenly that they could walk in silence as they had earlier, too. He shouldn't have been wondering when that would come to an end. He should have appreciated it.

"Let me walk ahead," she said. "You follow in a while, once I'm out of sight." She motioned to the water, the waves. "It's a good day to yell!" The flatness of her voice cracked at that. "I'm going now," she said.

Of course, because they'd talked about it, because she'd mentioned the word *yell,* the need dissipated, and instead he stood looking out to the waves for longer than he'd have thought imaginable. Rain came then, heavy. He stood until he could feel it dripping from his eyebrows.

Late in the afternoon, he knocked on Stella's door for a phone cord. She went through her collection. "One of these should work.

And this," she said, handing him a contraption of metal and surgical tubing, "is a slingshot. In the event you go out on the paths. They start out at the northeast corner of the property. Some visitors have spotted the coyotes. There seem to be more this year. But if you don't run, they won't harm you. If you do run, they'll chase you down. If you're an idiot. You're not an idiot, are you?"

He had to laugh. "I hope not."

"City folks," she said, and sniffed. "Lately, I've shared the slingshot with guests, and told them to carry a pocketful of rocks. Hit a tree if you need to, to scare them."

He took it, stretched it. "Hopefully I won't need this."

Back to the cabin, to plug in the charging cord. He could call Charlie now. He left the slingshot by the door, went through the stocked fridge again, and created a sandwich. He ate it slowly. Got a fire going in the stove, and sat to read. After a while, he realized he'd been turning pages, and couldn't think what the story was. He put his head back, closed his eyes, and listened to the rain drum the skylight.

Saturday morning he slept late. The more time he spent in bed, the less time he had to wonder about how to fill the hours. When he did get up, he had the longest shower, and decided to forego breakfast and have lunch instead. He heated soup and set out a bowl on the table, and reached for a second. He set it in place and sat staring at it, thinking of Charlie putting out that third plate. He had to reheat the soup before ladling it into his solo bowl. A year ago he would have been scribbling notes about this time: a time to be apart from one's child, and what it was to regroup. A post, an article, would be taking shape in his mind. He would have his notebook, his favourite pen. He would be seeking out words that sounded wise, but everything sounded hollow now. He didn't dare put anything on paper; the hollow would be in his face then.

Mid-afternoon. The day was passing, so quickly, so slowly, he almost prepared a fire, but thought he'd go look for those trails first. He dressed in layers, and put the slingshot in the pocket. The black rock was still there. Before setting out he rounded up smaller rocks for the other pocket.

Northeast. He situated himself and set out, easily finding the entrance to the trails. Someone had posted plastic-covered signs to watch for the coyotes. There was a faded sign about bears. Human fears.

Hard to believe the two walks, beach and forest, were within metres of each other, really. Surreal. He checked himself: he'd grown up here, or in this west coast part of the country, where it was so easy to take mountains and trees and water for granted. Within minutes he was deeply into the dark and shadows of firs and pine and cedar. Lower and thick bushes shed the morning's raindrops on him, and as he lifted his arms to push back wet hair, he could feel droplets go up his sleeve. He zipped the collar of his rain jacket.

The path was clearly marked. He could shut down his thoughts, in spite of the coyote warnings, and breathe in the forested air and smells. Surprising for a Saturday, not to encounter another soul in the place. The root sculptures, the moss, the turns in the path, the musk of decay and new life, was all good. At one point he detected movement and went still, waited, hardly breathing.

No coyote. Only a squirrel. Right. He went on. It was getting later and would be dark soon. He should have come earlier. He'd been fully expecting to meet one of those coyotes. In his mind, it showed up on the path, gliding in from the trees on one side, sliding away into the trees on the other, before he could ask his question.

Another squirrel showed up instead, and took off laughing, even as he reached into his pocket. He pulled out the slingshot, wrapped the rock into the leather, and shot. He had no thought to hit the squirrel. He wanted to feel the thing in his hands, hear the sound, the thwack as it ricocheted off trees in the most satisfying way. The sound echoed. He took another rock, and shot it, too, then another and another. Birds flapped, a couple of crows cawed. The place came to life for those moments, with branches moving.

He couldn't hear a squirrel laughing now. He emptied his pocket, one rock after another. He found more on the ground, and the bending, picking up, standing, shooting, *thwang, pop,* quickened his breath, made him dizzy. Frenzied, conductor-like, with his orchestra. Sounds grew. He was percussion. He picked a larger rock, sharp edges that cut into his fingers as he grasped.

Squirrels could be strings with bows sliding over them. Crows were brass instruments, and taking over. He pulled back, let the shot go, and was already bent over for the next stone when he heard the soft thud to his left.

A moment of absolute silence.

Crows went mad with their sounds, their response to the thud.

He stopped. In the gathering dim of late afternoon, he moved toward the dark shape on the ground. His heart pounded. He crouched, lightheaded. The crow was lifeless. He put a hand to it, warm, and his stomach convulsed. He had to swallow. The sounds of the angry and grieving crows swelled. He was on his knees, damp instantly through jeans, and he picked up the dead bird, held it in his arms. *Will the crows attack me?* It would be understandable. He was shaking, rib cage and shoulder blades heaving, but no tears, as if tears were done. He was dry. But some sound was coming from him, from the gut, not his throat, not his vocal cords. A sound that strangled before it hit the air, and heaved through him. He could feel it moving up, and then coming from his throat, a roughened blat.

The crows had neared to close branches. But they withdrew as his sound came. They still noised loudly, but so did he with rasps, more animal and crow than human. He stood with the dead crow, then had to move, and he circled over the path, and poured out the sounds until they were gone from him. He walked out of the forest, crows following, tree to tree. At the entrance to the path, they stayed, and he went on, to Stella's door. "I need a shovel," was all he said, and she went to find one, handed it to him, said nothing after a look at the shape in his arms.

Back to the path, where there was still enough light to dig a hole. He set the crow down on the earth, and dug. He laid the crow in the grave. He wanted to say he was sorry. He kneeled over, and with bare hands, he pushed the dirt into place.

The rock in the pocket he'd had the slingshot in, the black rock that Stella had handed him on the beach, he took it out, and thought to mark the grave with it. But thought, too, how he needed it to remember. He couldn't forget this. He slipped it back into his pocket to take home, and gathered more small rocks, rounded rocks, nothing with edges, and created a circle to mark. The crows were strangely quiet. He finally looked up. "I'm sorry," he said. "I'm so sorry." A whole new depth to tired.

In the cabin, shovel left at the door, he pulled off his sweater, knelt at the woodstove. He crushed pages of newspapers, put on kindling, a thin log, turned the knob on top to open and let in air. Clockwise or counter? He felt shaky and needed to warm. He lit a match.

The flame didn't catch. Another match. *Ppphhtt*. His mind couldn't stay with the task. He could hear wind in the stovepipe. Maybe the wind was a problem. That, and he was after all such a city guy with his little gas fireplace.

He'd take the slingshot and the shovel back to Stella. It had been weeks of feeling a deep-set shakiness. He pulled on his rain jacket, sweater still damp, and headed out around the big house. He could leave the things on the doorstep. Though maybe he should knock and ask for fire-building tips. Maybe he wasn't turning the knob the right way.

He reached the porch as rain started again, this time in sheets dropping from the sky, feeling like a curse the crows had sent. He set the shovel by her door, and put the slingshot in the mailbox, and sat on the top step to wait it out.

The door opened, and before he turned, he could hear her retrieving the slingshot. "This rain is like January stuff. You're waiting it out?"

"Yes. Should be minutes." He wanted to be here, and he wanted to be in that backyard cabin, not here. Talk and not talk.

"Or stay," she said, "and I'll light the propane fire, and you can tell me about your walk. Or some other stories. I can tell you some. We might laugh. Or have a good cry. Or you can go back to your cabin."

"*A good cry*," he said. "It's a set of words, isn't it?"

"It can be a thing, yes."

She went into the house and returned with a lighter, a bottle, and two small handleless mugs. She tried to plump the cushions on the two small couches, and sat in one, motioned him to the other. She lit the propane firepit with a frighteningly sudden flame, which settled in with a satisfied hiss.

He liked the distance between them, each with their own couch. He passed her one of the two blankets folded on the back of his, and she pulled it over her knees and unscrewed the top of the bottle, filled both mugs and handed him one. "Sorry, my glasses have all broken."

She touched her mug to his, reminding him of Charlie with Grammy Moth and the birthday.

"Mugs are so much better."

"What should we drink to?" she asked.

"To," he paused, "the inside of a mug." *Maybe a crow.*

"The inside of a mug!" she said, and touched his with hers. "'Clay is molded to form a cup / yet only the space within / allows the cup to hold water.'"

"You're quoting."

"The *Tao Te Ching*," she answered. "'Where the pot's not / is where it's useful.' Emptiness is critical. As you said: 'to the inside of a mug.'"

He had said that, hadn't he? He had a sip. He couldn't remember wine this good. Maybe it liked his acknowledgement. Now he was thinking as Charlie, imbuing life to the inanimate. Another sip and another, more a gulp. Maybe there was no inanimate. He guzzled. Caught her smiling sadly at him.

"Your walk. You want to tell me about it?"

She reached with the bottle to fill again.

"I thought I heard one of your coyotes. Or saw, really, some movement. Nothing but a squirrel. You know, I thought I might see a coyote. I was hoping to." Another gulp of wine. "I have a few things I wanted to say to a coyote."

"Really? I didn't realize that you *wanted* to talk to one of them." She sipped. "What would you say?"

"I'd ask her why." Was it possible to have had too much wine so soon?

"What would you be why-ing about?"

He held out his mug and she poured in more. The mug really was small.

"You won't believe this. Well, maybe you will. But my boy says he sees his mom in a coyote."

She startled. Which was satisfying. She seemed so unflappable.

"That's kinda weird, don't you think?"

She pursed her lips, then shrugged. "Not necessarily." She frowned. "You want to ask this momma coyote *why*?" She stared at him. "You mean, *why'd you die?*" Then apologized. "I shouldn't have said that."

She squinted. "You're furious inside," she said. "Do you mean *why* as in the Marianne Faithfull 'Why D'ya Do It?'" She started to sing a few lines.

"Yes," he said, to stop her. He wondered then, what had brought her to living alone. To having strangers invade her space for a day or a week, and then go.

They both communed with their mugs, with the hiss of fire, and strings of patio lights swaying in the wind. The rain pounded at what was left of the leaves still hanging on their branches. Most would be gone by morning.

"So if you'd seen a coyote, what were you going to say? Beside *why?*"

He was drinking like a teenager.

"What's the line about sharing *my hash?*"

They both laughed at the lyric.

Feeling overwhelmed was imminent. He suddenly wanted to be in that cabin in the backyard.

"I didn't mean to kill the crow," he said.

"Of course not," she said.

"I started to send rocks around."

"We do that sometimes."

"It felt good, hearing them thwack trees."

She nodded.

"Did you bury it well?" she asked.

He thought he knew what she meant. "I hope so," he said.

"Well," she said. Pause. Sip. "You know that old movie *Moonstruck?* The one with Cher and what's-his-name."

"Nicolas Cage?"

"Right. Him. Do you remember what she says to him? When he's falling in love with her, or thinks he is?"

"No. What does she say?"

Stella leaned in toward him, as if she was Cher, as if he was Nicolas Cage. "Snap out of it!"

He jumped. He couldn't help it. Had another gulp of wine.

"Sometimes, that's what we need to hear more than anything. I tell myself all the time: *Snap out of it!*"

"Snap out of it," he echoed. "Snap out of it!"

"Words for a coyote. Maybe words from a coyote."

He didn't want to think about words from a coyote.

"Am I being too glib?" she said. "People have told me I am. At times."

"There's a time for glibness," he said. "If this isn't it, it's a reminder to be when I need to be." The conversation had taken turns, turns he could mull over later, with less wine in him. Though he knew that wouldn't happen. Everything felt too fast, as if he'd stepped out of a cloud of fog into the middle of a roadway.

"You have any kids?" he asked. Talk about what he knew.

She shook her head. "I've never wanted the responsibility."

"They're a lot of work."

Shook her head again. "Not that so much. Work doesn't scare me. I like work. Makes it easier not to think. But no, I never wanted the responsibility."

He'd not broken it down like that.

"Responsibility involves a lot of thought. I work to avoid certain types of thought."

With some people that would have been an invitation to ask about her story, but he didn't hear such an invite. Not that he wanted to know. It was enough to be unexpectedly handed some nugget gleaned from another's life.

"Tell me about your boy," she said.

He told her about Charlie and Old Daisy, about Hopper and their prairie path, and he even told her about Charlie's truth stick. But she had handed him a rock. She should get it. He told her about Raziel, and she listened. For a woman who lived by *snap out of it* she could listen to a lot of words. She nodded, and asked short questions.

He drank more of the wine, from a second bottle now. His stomach had rumbled for dinner, but it stopped. With the conversation, he might have felt sobered, but he went in deeper to a place he couldn't snap out of in any way. More shadowy forest path with bits of light here and there as he wandered through, and back out again. He'd never met anyone who could roam from one place to another with words quite like Stella could, and he was hungry for that.

Later he remembered the fire, the wine, the voices, hers and his own. When he came to in the dawn light, it took a long moment to know he was inside her house, in her bed, and when he opened his eyes, she was there in front of him, an arm thrown over his hip, her face buried into his mid-section, a sheet over both of them. It was chilly. But when he went to move, he realized he was caught in her T-shirt, the only clothing she had on, in dried semen.

He pulled away, naked and soft, and hoped he wouldn't waken her as he freed himself. Really, he didn't want her to see this pathetic moment.

Then he stayed pulled away to see her sleeping face. Eyes closed, breathing softly, and he wished she could answer the questions he had. His head ached. He rolled onto his back and as he did, snags of memory drifted in: soft breasts, her weight on him. The weight had felt good, had held him in place, grounded him. Would it be okay to remember more? He couldn't remember when he'd last blacked out in this way. Back in college. Trying to remember made his head hurt, and he turned over, and drifted off again.

When he awoke next, he was alone, and a knock at the door sounded, and she stood bundled in a thick terry cloth robe, ugly hospital-wall green, with a tray of coffee, orange juice, eggs, toast.

She said, "It's morning," as if that might explain. He struggled to sit up. She placed the tray next to him. Was she avoiding his eyes? She didn't seem like the woman in the VW van, the woman on the beach, the woman by the fire. "Hey," he said softly. Still she didn't look.

"I need to make breakfast for the other guests. If you like, there's a door off this back porch." She motioned to a wall behind him. Through the window, he could see the backyard and a glimpse of his cabin. She started to leave.

"Wait," he said. Her hand was on the doorknob. "What happened?"

"You don't remember?"

"Not really."

She was silent, brow furrowed.

"Bits," he said finally. "What I do remember was nice." He felt like she needed some reassuring. He did, too.

Her eyes pinked when she did look at him. "I'm sorry," she said. "I never do that. You're a guest. It shouldn't have happened. I really need to go take care of the others now." The door closed over her movement, a lot like ducking out.

Keith felt stunned. The memory of grounding weight, of warm skin and cool air. And of their voices and words out on the porch was vanishing. In its place: *I never do that.*

Stella's words sounded on repeat.

This could have been simple, but no. It had to rise from a brownout, with mutterings no one would put words to. If it was supposed to be beautiful or human or meaningful, it probably couldn't. Was Stella hoping he'd disappear through the back door?

The coffee on the tray was cold, as if it had been poured long before. Had she made the tray and stood staring at it, wondering what she should say while the eggs shrivelled and the coffee grew a skin?

He set it at the foot of the bed, so he could sit and get his feet on the floor, and he saw the black rock on the bedside table, keeping guard. How had it gotten there?

He reached out, took it in hand, felt all its resting spots and held it, a chunk of missing life. Could you breathe in a rock? Take its steadiness into yourself?

Finally he dressed, he made up the bed. Realized he was no good with starchy sheets, extra blankets, fancy useless pillows. At home, he and Charlie each had a comforter. He set aside the cold breakfast, slipped the rock into his pocket, and left through that back door. He would head to the beach for a last walk.

He set out to circle the big house with a wide berth. He didn't want to run into Stella. They'd destroyed something that wouldn't withstand being named even. Like finding and dropping a robin's egg on a spring day. He'd done that as a kid, looking to show it to his mother. He could still see the pieces of shell, the half-formed embryo; he'd wished then that he'd not taken the egg, not touched it. He knew, too, that the moment he did touch it, it was dead. The dropping was the second death.

He returned from the walk, packed and tidied the cabin, vacuumed, emptied the ashes from the stove. He was wondering how he would ask Stella for the ride to the ferry, when she texted to say another guest was heading in that direction and had offered. He imagined she was relieved, and knew he was. He didn't have the energy to sort this out. He couldn't snap out of it. Stupid words, those.

She sent a second text moments later: *I'm so sorry. We're too messed up to just have fun. I should have known. Maybe some time, we can start over.*

21   *"Half Moon Bay"* / *Béla Fleck and the Flecktones*

"Somebody That I Used to Know" / *Tommy Emmanuel*

"Moonlight Sonata" / *Beethoven*

Trev sent him a text asking what ferry he was catching home, and Keith let him know, not expecting to see him at the terminal, but there he was in an EVO car.

"Where's Charlie?"

"Thought I'd pick you up, see how the days were, get you ready for city life again."

"Right, after three days." Yet it did feel as if he'd been away a long time. He'd talked briefly with Charlie both Friday and Saturday, but hadn't on this day.

"How is he?"

"He'll be glad you're home. But he's been fine. He's enjoyed Norah." Trev stopped. "Sorry, I shouldn't have said that."

"No," said Keith. "I'm glad you said it. It makes sense. He misses his mom. It takes pressure off me. I can't be a mom, too. It's good to think there's a positive to me being away."

Charlie hugged him so tightly he held his breath.

Norah had put together chili in the slow cooker and left garlic bread on the stove, which Keith put in the oven.

To close the day, Charlie crawled into bed with books in hand.

"Do you want to see pictures of where I was?"

Charlie nodded slowly in the way of a child who thinks he has little choice, which Keith chose to ignore. He thumbed over one photo to the next, mostly beach shots, with a few of the cabin. Charlie studied the ones of the skylight and the little porch. He didn't ask any questions or make any observations. He pushed the phone back to Keith and reached for a book. They read the

Seasons book, and before Keith was halfway through, Charlie was asleep.

Keith set aside the book. He was home, his boy beside him. He watched Charlie's flannel-clad ribs expanding and shrinking with breath, and it occurred to him that he'd not heard a word from him since his return. But in the morning they'd talk.

Maybe, if Keith had any choice, he'd be silent, too. Talking was a certain way to mess up. Maybe talking was as much at fault as wine with the night spent with Stella.

He felt sleepy himself, turned over on his side, and wrapped an arm around Charlie, who all at once straightened. He didn't seem to have awakened. His eyes were closed, his breathing still that of sleep. But he stretched his entire body, pushing at Keith's knees, pushing away. Moments later he turned toward his father and pushed at his chest hard, with both palms. Then went still. Keith was close to the edge of the bed. He started to move, and Charlie did, too, a sort of thrashing movement that ended with more straightening and pushing and a few grunts. Keith stood and pulled up covers over Charlie, and left the room. The message was clear.

The alarm went off the next morning, and Keith sang Charlie awake with "Three Little Birds." Charlie rubbed his eyes, and got out of bed, stumbling.

"You okay, buddy?" asked Keith.

Charlie stared at him and finally nodded, and then he knelt on the floor, reaching under the bed for those old-man corduroy slippers, not awake at all.

"Breakfast?"

Charlie nodded.

Keith made sunny-side-up eggs, two, and toast buttered, with slices of tomato, Charlie's favourite. "Paprika?" He held it over the plate as a waiter would, as Charlie liked. Again, a nod. "Pepper?" Same nod. Cold grew in Keith's gut.

His hands and wrists worked pepper over the breakfast, and he finished with his usual flourish, which usually brought a smile, but no. He hoped his son didn't sense his dismay, though Charlie usually picked up on everything.

They breakfasted with no words. Keith wasn't sure if the growing grimness was his alone or Charlie's or both. "Well," he said, "let's get your snack packed up." He moved to reach for his son's backpack.

Charlie shook his head.

"Okay, buddy. Why don't you stay home with me today? You can read. We have a puzzle from last Christmas we've never opened."

He could see Charlie's shoulders relax. What was this? How long was it going to last? Raziel would have been unhappy about his being okay with Charlie not going to school. But she hadn't gone through what they were going through. Maybe she'd have changed her mind. This was school they were talking about, and school wasn't life. They'd missed the first few weeks of the year while casting about in Hopper, and Charlie's education hadn't fallen apart. A kid could probably miss half of Grade 2 and be fine for the rest of his life. Still, Raz would be unhappy. He had to admit to a certain satisfaction, a subversive pleasure, with these thoughts. "It's only school," he said softly, and laughed, hoping for a smile from Charlie. What was that Twain quote about never letting school get in the way of your education?

He tried to think where the puzzle would be. The games drawer? Top of the entranceway closet? Tucked behind the bookshelf. He pulled it out. A train in mountains. He'd forgotten the image. He began to set it up, thinking of Banff, and wondered if Charlie would say anything about that, but no. Those small fingers set about sorting to find edge pieces, and one side of his mouth pinched up into a half smile when he found a corner piece and set it aside.

Then he trotted off to the bathroom.

Keith sent a text to Trev and Norah: *Charlie hasn't said a word since I got home. Was he talking with you?* He felt silly pushing send. Norah's response came quickly. *He was pretty quiet yesterday, but he did speak.*

Trev called seconds later. "Day before yesterday he was asking a lot of questions about where you'd gone and why, and when you'd be back. If you were going to go away again. I told him that I didn't think so, not for a while anyway. He seemed to be okay with everything while you were gone. But maybe I missed something." He paused. "I'm sure he'll talk soon."

"No doubt," said Keith as Charlie emerged from the bathroom. He ended the call.

"Look!" A second corner piece. He couldn't tell whether Charlie was okay with him finding it. He just took it, set it next to the other, and within seconds was frowning over the pieces, focused in his way.

Keith lit the fireplace. "I'll check email, and we'll do the puzzle together." He added, "I'm not going anywhere." Talking would happen when it happened, he told himself.

Charlie continued to find edge pieces, and Keith settled in on the couch with his laptop. When would an email warm-up translate to writing? After clicking through his mailbox he gave up, and stopped to watch his son. Eyes down, and steady on the task, absorbing the colours and shapes of the pieces, his lips puckered and tucked in. He tried to connect a couple of pieces, two more, and again, finally finding a join. Keith wasn't going to get beyond dealing with email, so he set aside the laptop, sat with his son, and found a few pieces' places. Then made tomato soup and grilled cheese for lunch.

A walk, when Keith suggested it. Without discussion, they both set out in the opposite direction from the school, and Charlie's hand found Keith's. The air and wetness was colder than last week, even. Keith found a pair of dollar-store stretchy gloves deep in his pocket and shared them for their hands they weren't holding. "Right for you, and left for me." That got a smile out of Charlie.

Back at home, Charlie shook his head over a suggestion of knitting, but snugged with Old Daisy for a watch of *The Triplets of Belleville*. Keith watched, too. Forget email.

The next morning, Charlie didn't shake his head when Keith asked if he'd like to go. Keith prepared a note for Ms. Duffy, and he passed it to her as Charlie entered the classroom. He'd added a line at the bottom of the note: *Please let me know if I need to pick him up at any point in the day. Thank you.* He walked away, wondering if his son would speak up or go through another day in silence. His heart ached, and he tried to pick out why: not the silence itself, but the need for it.

Later, when he picked up Charlie, Ms. Duffy gave the slightest shake of her head to indicate he hadn't spoken. "But he doesn't seem to be unhappy," she whispered. "Let's give him time." Keith resisted the urge to give her a full-on hug. *Bless you*, he wanted to say, but the phrase felt strange to him.

They passed Grammy Moth's house on the way home, and Keith slowed, wondering if Charlie might speak. He did slow and squint, his mouth crinkled for a moment, but he continued on.

Tomorrow was another day.

"Hymn to the Mother" / *Charles Lloyd*
"Don't Give Up On Me" / *Joe Cocker*
"Many Rivers to Cross" / *Jimmy Cliff*

22

Silent days followed. Charlie — on his own — had been picking up whatever cards he felt should go, and the cards on surfaces were now down to those that he seemed particularly fond of, including the one from Ms. Duffy. Keith made no comment on any of his choices.

Two weeks later, an early dark morning, and the phone rang with Eryk on video call. "We're on our way to the hospital!"

In the middle of the night Charlie had climbed into bed with Keith, and now he was instantly awake to the pitch of his uncle's voice. Old Daisy came bedside to see what was up. These nights of two-in-a-bed were a break for her anxiety level. Keith could hear her doggy whines when she did sleep, maybe dreaming of the other nights tripping between their doorways.

Eryk's phone must have been in a stand on his dashboard. They caught a glimpse of him, and another of Cat's hand waving from her side of the car. Then just a moment of Cat's face, with such a blend of emotion that Keith had an instantaneous ache for her. She was pink faced with it all, terror just under the surface. "The contractions are so quick. Quicker than I would have . . ." She broke off with a gasp, and the camera swung back to Eryk.

"We're going to be fine here. Almost to the big H, folks!"

Keith could tell he was trying to lighten the moment for Charlie.

"Big H means hospital, Charlie, where they'll take care of all of us!"

Charlie pulled on Keith's wrist to look into his phone, and Eryk smiled at him. "Hey, you're looking mighty, little brother. What's up?"

There was a moment when Charlie should have responded, should have spoken, and Eryk's face faltered. He kept his eyes on the road, but glanced back into his camera. Back and forth. No word from Charlie, though he did offer a smile.

"How's that scarf you've been working? You ready for winter?" Eyes back again in quick glance, now with a furrow between brows.

No answer.

Eryk's eyes back to the road, Cat's breathing calmer now.

Eryk's eyes again flickered to Charlie, and Cat's voice. "Charlie?"

"We're all going to be okay, we really are," assured Eryk, no doubt thinking that Charlie's fears were at issue. Which they were, Keith knew, but not in any way he could explain now or had thought to let Cat and Eryk know.

"We're good here," he said, and drew the camera to his own face. Could they hear the shaky in his voice? "We are. We can't wait to hear the news, though, later today. Keep us posted."

"We will, we will." In the background, after a moment, Keith could hear Cat's voice. "What's with Charlie? Is he not speaking?"

Did she think that Eryk had ended the call?

"We'll talk soon," Keith said, loudly. "Love you guys. Love this new little one. We can't wait!" He moved his thumb to end the call.

The only way he could convince Charlie—who wouldn't stop shaking his head no—to go to school was to promise they'd talk with Uncle Eryk as soon as Charlie was home. "Giving birth can take all day," Keith told him as they walked.

Once home, Keith texted Eryk. *I'm confident he'll start talking at some point.* For two weeks he'd been thinking that this would all go away. He should have let them know. He'd booked a doctor's appointment for the next week, hoping they wouldn't need it. He'd thought of Raz, as he thumbed the number into the phone. She would have said 'What are you waiting for?' with one of those looks. Those looks did not come often but when they did, he knew she was thinking she could do a superior job as parent. But it wasn't her responsibility. The look said this was his, but he had to honour her in it, too. With the guilt that would come over him at such times, would come the piece that he added all on his own, about how Raziel was supporting the family, how she made it happen. He needed to pull it together, forget all his laissez-faire stuff. She had said that once: "Your approach, it's not working." The words stung. He'd called it 'easygoing.'

On the way home after school they talked. Or Keith talked and Charlie nodded. About baby names. 'Head-kicker' was not the best choice, they agreed.

At bedtime Eryk called to let them know that little Billie was in the world, big enough, and healthy, and sound asleep with her momma. Charlie looked through the photos that Eryk sent, of Cat with Billie asleep at her breast and another of Eryk holding her swaddled. Keith knew that Charlie wanted to hear his own birth story.

"You were born on a night of rain, lots of rain," Keith began, and he could feel every muscle soften in the knotted up little person next to him. This was so much harder than he could have imagined.

In a couple of days it would be Halloween, and maybe that would be a tipping point, and Charlie would begin to speak. Maybe.

In less than a year their lives had turned completely upside down. Silence was a fitting response, really. Keith couldn't imagine it as his own. He couldn't get away with it. But if he was seven years old, he might take it on. It'd create some space to be, and to process. He had his own deep need for silence, those healing school hours alone in the apartment.

Maybe this was how it was for Charlie. He still hummed, which reassured Keith, not as often as he used to, but he did. Keith would catch him at it every so often when he looked at a book, especially a familiar book and, most often, while building with his Lego. When he did hum, Keith felt that all in their world was as good as it could be, and he savoured such moments, he let them bring him to a full stop.

His timing was off today, and he ended up at the school with some minutes to go before three. He was relieved to see Alphonso by the door.

"Is Juliana ready for the big night?" Keith asked after they greeted each other.

"She is."

"Who goes trick-or-treating with her?"

"I do. I'm my granddaughter's legal guardian." He didn't offer further explanation.

"Would you two want to join Charlie and me? We go up Union Street. It's a neighbourhood that gets into costume, and they know how to decorate. We usually end up with friends who believe the more the merrier."

Alphonso's eyes lit. "Juliana would like that."

"No problem if she feels otherwise," said Keith. "We'd understand."

The old man looked surprised. "She's always up for adventure. She likes spending time with Charlie, talks his ears off, but he doesn't seem to mind!"

Had he noticed that Charlie wasn't speaking?

Charlie drew a picture of the costume he wanted: a pirate with Owl on his shoulder. He held the stuffed animal in place to show exactly where, and Keith went to find the duct tape.

They experimented with the tape and at one point, when Keith came out of the bathroom, he found Charlie trying to tape Owl to his own ear. He had to find scissors to cut the stuffed animal from his son's hair. The result would make for a fine pirate for The Night, but after it would be time to see the barber.

Maybe Grammy Moth had an answer or a needle. This was outside his skill set. "We might have to sew Owl to your jacket," he warned. Charlie gave a nod as if he understood. He gave Owl a reassuring pat.

Next day after school they stopped off. Grammy's curtains were closed, but a string of orange lights hung in the front window, and several smiling pumpkins were on the porch steps, one with a mouth-O of surprise and hair of stringy pumpkin guts.

Grammy Moth opened the door wide. "Come in!" she said. "I made cookies. How did you know?" Her hair was piled lop-sidedly today. Neither of the grownups could miss Charlie's eyes connecting pumpkin guts to Grammy's head.

"We do look the same, don't we?" She laughed.

The house was exactly what Keith had expected, with dark and aging woodwork, a steep and narrow staircase off to the left, a narrow hall running front to back, a glimpse of bathroom with ancient mulberry tiles, and a glow from the open doorway of what must be kitchen. To the right, double doors opened onto what might be called a parlour, home to the bay window facing the porch.

Grammy Moth motioned them in that direction as she headed to the kitchen, her knitted slippers catching in the burlap-like floor covering. Keith could feel it through his socks after he removed his shoes. Charlie made a funny face. His socks were thin, and he didn't like anything scratchy. "I'll bet she has extra slippers," whispered Keith. Yes, a basket sat behind the door, hand-knitted in all colours. Charlie examined them, turning over green and blue in his hands, before pulling on. Keith shook off a layer of dust before pulling on another pair. Slippers like this should not have had dust on them. Lonely old woman.

The front room had the woodstove she'd spoken of, and ancient furniture with shiny wooden armrests, polished by the many hands of those who'd taken refuge in their brocade depths. Must have been in years long gone. Shelves lined the walls, book spines protruding in such a way that Keith guessed they were double layered. Piles of books and magazines covered every surface. When Grammy Moth came in with a tray of mugs and shortbread, Keith moved aside a stack. As they drank and nibbled, he showed her Charlie's drawing.

She fussed with Owl, and with the jacket Charlie had chosen for his costume. Her veiny hands sewed Owl gently into place, knuckles protesting. "I think Owl's going to like riding around with you like this," she said. "We'll undo the stitches at the end of Halloween. Here — you try." She watched Charlie move the needle and make stitches.

"You, too," she told Keith. His stitches were no better than his son's, and he had to laugh. They were in the same place with this. And in their grieving, he and his son were equals, too. This would forever alter the accepted hierarchy of parent and child. That was okay, he decided right then as he finished a final stitch.

Charlie couldn't wait. He pulled on the jacket. Owl fell over.

Without comment, Grammy Moth added stitches and connected the collar with the stuffed friend.

They stayed for dinner. Off the back wall was a cozy glassed-in area, enough for a wide and thick wooden table and benches that lined the three walls, with cushions for bums. Charlie took one look, sat on a red one, and slid up and down the smooth bench. Grammy Moth didn't stop him.

The windows had handcrafted welded shapes in lieu of the bars that so many of the neighbourhood homes had, bicycle gears and other pieces shaped like birds and flowers. Keith spotted and pointed out an owl to Charlie, and Charlie pointed to a sunflower made from an enormous gear.

At the end of one of the benches, on the floor, was a deep pot filled with water and what appeared to be cedar boughs. Charlie hopped off his slider to bend low for a sniff.

Grammy Moth missed nothing. "It's cedar," she said. "I boil it every evening, and sit reading or thinking and soaking my feet." She had to laugh at Charlie's raised brows, the disbelief on his face. "I've done it for years. It keeps me healthy." She must have noticed he wasn't speaking, but said nothing.

Charlie poked a finger into the water, and pushed the dark green, pungent and cheering.

"After a few weeks with the same pieces, I drain the water and take them back and leave them at their roots. It's important to return the gift home."

She set a cauldron of green leek-fragrant soup in the centre of the table, then a basket of steaming hot biscuits, butter, and an open jar of molasses.

The molasses, together with the sharp cheese in the biscuits, was just right, and Keith and Charlie had two bowls of soup each. The soup was good, but only part of the nourishment that Keith felt. Charlie, too, he suspected. Grammy Moth eyed Charlie as they ate, and said, "Would you like to come and visit me here once a week? Maybe your father would like to have an evening to himself now and then. He can get caught up on work or see a friend. Would you like that? I would."

Charlie's eyes were fixed on her. He gave no indication of yes or no. Grammy stared at him. She assured him, "You won't be staying the night. Your dad will only be gone a few hours, long enough to . . ." She looked to Keith.

"Play hockey?"

"Play hockey," she echoed. "That sounds good."

Charlie looked from one to the other. He nodded, but slowly as if he was still mulling it over.

"I tell you what," said Grammy Moth. "We'll do it once, and see how it works before we do it again. Okay?"

He nodded.

"Brilliant!" said Grammy Moth. "What day?"

"Wednesday?" said Keith.

"Wednesday," she confirmed.

A tentative nod from Charlie.

Would a weekly evening worsen the effects of his time away? Would Charlie be okay with it? It wouldn't be just Charlie who would have to see how it worked for the first week.

On their way out, she asked them to choose a Halloween treat from a large bowl. "I'm ready for tomorrow night. Here, you be my first."

"Why don't we make this our first stop?" suggested Keith. "Better yet, why don't you come with us? A school friend is joining us, Juliana, and her grandpa, Alphonso. The scene on Union Street is people and families everywhere. It'll be fun."

A shadow passed over her face, an expression he couldn't read, or maybe didn't trust himself to. He could feel it wrenching his gut, though, and regretted asking.

Her face cleared. "I need to be here. I like to dress up and hand out candy." She returned his hug, and wrapped an arm around Charlie. "I'm looking forward to the evening, too."

At the door they stood in the night air, a cool breeze whipping away clouds, stars showing up if you looked for them, and Keith had a sense of foreboding.

What more could happen? It was a night that should have felt good, after that time in such a home and sharing food, and now with the clearing breeze. Was it the shadow he'd seen on the woman's face? Maybe a premonition of better to come. His thoughts should not go so quickly to the negative. He reached for his son, and pulled him close as they said goodbye, then went down those porch stairs, orange pumpkin teeth saying goodbye.

They walked home, wind blowing behind them.

IV

•

Fall to Winter

23 *"Someday My Prince Will Come"* / *Miles Davis*

"Ordinary Day" / *Great Big Sea*

"Your Time Will Come" / *Johnny Clegg*

Keith pulled together a last-minute pirate costume. First thought was Long John Silver. But Raz had made a skirt years before, bright and jangly with shiny hoops. "Spangly!" he pointed out to Charlie.

He could be Anne Bonny. They'd read a picture book of the formidable woman pirate, and both fallen for her. He added an oversize white blousy shirt with rolled up sleeves, found costume necklaces in Raz's top drawer and wrapped them around his wrists, borrowed an extra pirate hat from Charlie. His beard was just the right touch.

Charlie still didn't say a word, but he reached out to gather handfuls of that skirt, and laughed when Keith donned the hat, and the sudden throw-his-arms-out hug answered Keith's question of what would be his son's reaction. Charlie wanted to include his mother in their daily lives, and Halloween should be daily life. Well pirated and ready, Keith sent Alphonso a message, when and where to meet.

"Want to go by Ron and Felicity's house?" he asked, and Charlie nodded.

"Haunted alley?" Keith prompted.

The haunted alley, which households always managed to put together, was a treasure. Last year someone had set up their family trailer, haunted with life-sized skeletons, bones dressed in plaid shirts and cutoffs for camping. Always a vat of hot chocolate, white fluffs of semi-melted marshmallows afloat, and Keith would throw some dollars into the collection jar set up for some East Side cause. There were so many.

This neighbourhood was the edge of gentrification, but also served as a stabilizer for the downtown east side. Diversity is health. Families, dressed as tubes of toothpaste, bottles of hot sauce, and traditional sheet-ghosts, they were all there with their shadows, those who haunted alleys and sidewalks, testing door-knobs for unsecured doors to enter. The homeless and benign shadowed, too. Much as Keith would have liked to own a home in the neighbourhood, he felt safer in the high-rise. But high-rise life felt surreal. There was a concrete-and-blood sense to the streets here, and for Halloween, it was the best place to be. Almost every home in nearby blocks was decorated with ghosty stuff.

Alphonso stood solemnly while Juliana danced at the corner. He hadn't dressed up, but was dapper as ever, green scarf knot-ted perfectly, and with a fedora.

"What a bonny-fine and winsome ladybug you make!" Keith said to Juliana, and she dimpled.

"You two," said Alphonso, "make a couple of fine buccaneers!"

They walked the blocks to Union Street, Juliana bubbling with chatter, Charlie happy to listen. He started to skip at one point, Owl barely hanging on, and Keith felt Alphonso's eyes on him. "He won't get away with that for much longer, will he?"

Somebody might have to tell the man that he was behind the times, but Keith didn't want to be the one. "I taught him every-thing I know," he said.

Alphonso surprised him with an appreciative and un,charac-teristic snort.

How little Keith knew him, really.

"We all would skip if we could," Keith added, and Alphonso gave an affirmative nod.

"Quite." So he had his inner dancer after all.

They were nearing the corner by Grammy Moth's house, and Charlie pointed. "That's our first stop," said Keith. "We have a friend who lives this way. She helped with Charlie's costume. We promised we'd come by."

"Of course," said Alphonso. "She didn't by any chance perform that owl's implantation, did she?"

"She did," said Keith.

"Well done."

Jack-o'-lanterns sat by the doorway, flickering shadows over Grammy's porch.

When she opened the door, she was unrecognizable, her hair down, filled with fall-coloured ribbons like so many leaves. The tunic that swirled around her had to have been created over the passing of years, with applique fabric and stitching, ageing layer on layer.

Juliana was smitten. "She's *your* Grammy?" She appeared not to be the only one. Alphonso stood even straighter, and had some new light in his eyes.

Charlie nodded, pleased.

"Pleased to meet you, Juliana," said Grammy Moth. But when Keith introduced the girl's grandfather — "Alphonso Girardi" — there was that reserve to her, as if some colour'd been doused away. Even her voice changed, from warmth with the little girl to wall building. "Pleased to meet you, Mr. Girardi," she said, rather stiffly. Guardedly, thought Keith. Why the lack of trust?

Alphonso seemed to take no notice of this, though, as he shook her hand warmly, even gave the slightest bow. Maybe he appreciated the formality of surnames.

The children's hands hovered over the wide bowl of candy. Juliana chose in no time with quick movement. Charlie wrestled between two favourites. Grammy Moth held out the bowl and she didn't tell him to take both, as some might have. She let him take his time. "Good choice," she said, when he closed his fingers around a box of Smarties. "My favourite, too."

On to Union Street. For the houses with too many stairs up to the porch, people had set up tables on the sidewalk with baskets of candy, maybe a chair or two, and neighbours communed with mugs and thermoses in hand, steaming with evening coffee wafting sweet and intoxicating. They chatted. The corner store had locked its door, but under its front awning, usually a space for coffee klatsch, someone had set up a keyboard for seasonal tunes accompanied by a woman singing.

Charlie's face shone. There were enough kids at every door that no one seemed to notice that he wasn't saying thank you.

They reached Ron and Felicity's. Ron was Harry Potter, and Felicity, with her red hair, was Ginny Weasley. Charlie poked his head around the door as if looking for Lucy, then ducked out again, caught his dad's eye. "Lucy? Maybe she'll be around later."

Keith introduced Alphonso and Juliana. Ron eyed Alphonso's scarf, and tugged on his own acrylic Hogwarts wannabe. He turned to the kids. "A ladybug! Pirates!" His voice could be so loud when meeting new people.

He tossed a few chocolate bars into Charlie and Juliana's pillowcases. "Oh, it's late, take more, take it all!" he cried, and threw in handfuls. He rocked onto his heels, crossing his arms and catching his thumbs into his armpits as he looked down at them, like a big kid, an oversized Charlie. "Such a pretty ladybug, never seen one prettier." Juliana didn't seem to mind his bellow. She was an easygoing child. Did Alphonso give her room to be otherwise?

"Finish up the block here," Ron said, "and come back for some hot chocolate and a nightcap. Tradition!" he added, with a quick glance at Keith. "As we always do."

Keith looked to Alphonso.

"Absolutely."

They trick or treated the last of the houses and returned, trooping up the front steps. Keith tripped on the skirt and managed to catch himself, even as he heard the fabric tear.

"How do you do this?" he asked Felicity, moments later in the kitchen, he inspecting a rip in the skirt and she stirring the chocolate, heating on the stove. She laughed, and gave no answer beyond splashing peppermint schnapps into her own mug.

She gave him flashbacks, standing there, to years gone: walking into this kitchen when Charlie was a newborn in the carrier on his chest, then wandering all through these blocks, enjoying the sight of families, wondering what the next few years were going to be. Raziel pointing out a toddler in a wagon. "There we go, that's us, next year." Felicity telling a story of Lucy costumed as a doghouse with her stuffed Snoopy in her arms. Pieces of the past.

They sat together with front room curtains open as fireworks blew late and a dog howled. The doorbell chimed periodically, at that hour mostly teenagers. Felicity gave them the rest of the candy and said nothing about being too old. She looked out the window after the chattering group. "I think I was pregnant when I was the age of that one."

Keith was suddenly aware of Felicity in some way he'd never been. As long as he'd known her, she'd appeared not to age at all, but now she had. When? He felt bad, maybe not the most logical thing. He'd felt isolated through months of hell. But now maybe those months pushed him to be more cognizant of others.

Raziel had said, at some point, "Felicity isn't taking care of herself." When? Last Christmas? And she was affronted when his response was that he hadn't really noticed. "Men." She'd sniffed.

"I'd rather *not* notice!" he said. "But I hope everything is all right with her." And he added, "You're not usually so judgmental," feeling a need to defuse.

"I'm not being judgmental," she countered. "It's an observation."

"Observation you do with your camera."

She had been surprised. "Right."

Ron was showing Alphonso and the children something at the far end of the room. To make himself useful, Keith reached into the cupboard where he was certain they kept mugs, and began to set them on the counter by the stove. "How are you these days?"

Felicity dipped a wide ladle into the chocolate. "Oh, fine." How she responded, always.

"No, I mean, really." He had to count in his head how many they were: six, an even number.

"I'm always fine," she said.

He set down the mugs. "I'm sorry. I didn't mean to pry." She wouldn't appreciate being told that she looked tired. He looked directly at her, and wished he hadn't said anything, there was too much sadness in her eyes.

Maybe reflected sadness. "I'm sorry you've gone through all you have, I really am," she said.

"Thank you." Could people hear how mechanical this response had become? "I appreciate that."

Her red hair was shot with white.

"She had a good life, you know," she said, surprisingly.

"Raz," she clarified, when he said nothing in the seconds that followed, as if he might not know who she was talking about.

"Raz," he echoed. She was staring at him. Her blue eyes had faded, he thought. Was that even possible? Had they always been so pale? He struggled to think. But it was as if a doorway had opened, and he caught a glimpse of his wife's life in that moment, in that crack: the lightness, the high spirits, the effervescence. Then nothing. As if it had all just plunged into some starless howling night. He was shaken.

"She had a good life," he said. But he felt so far away. He wrapped his hands around two of the mugs. Solid. "I'll take these to the kids." He carried the mugs into the front room, and breathed in air before going back for more.

When he returned again with Felicity behind him, Ron was messing with Owl. Keith began to say, "You have no idea how hard . . ." just as Owl fell over.

"Damn!" said Ron. He attempted to right the bird. "Here I thought he was sitting there like any other self-respecting pirate familiar!" He patted Charlie on the back. Keith could see his son's ribs shift with each pat, and wondered if Ron had any idea of his own strength.

"Sorry, dude," Ron said. To distract Charlie, he stuck a hand into the pillowcase. "Whatcha got in here? Feels like a whole storehouse. Enough to last months!"

Charlie didn't respond.

Ron's look was sharp. "Hey! Are you talking these days, or what?"

Charlie's face fell. No one had actually spoken directly to this. He stared at Ron, stricken, then at his dad.

"No," said Keith. "He's not speaking. Not at the moment."

Ron took a step back.

Keith wanted for Halloween night to be over right then, to pull off this stupid skirt and be at home with their annual sorting of candy bars. He turned away to focus on trying to right Owl, and gave up. He gave Charlie a look he hoped was reassuring.

Juliana, staring at Ron, spoke up. "It's okay that Charlie's not talking. I talk for him at school. And he's the best listener."

Ron stared with a vague frown, as if he didn't quite recognize her, or spoke a different language. Then he gave Keith another sharp look and let the subject go. Seconds later, Keith noticed that Charlie took a step away from him, but Ron didn't seem to notice.

Felicity stayed out of all this, put on music, and settled with her own steaming chocolate. She added another generous slop of peppermint schnapps and held out the bottle to Alphonso, who poured a spot and passed it to Keith.

They talked of Halloweens past, and Alphonso told a boyhood story of a prank, about a discarded handbag stuffed with newspaper, left at the side of the roadway, and a friend tying a string to the thing and pulling it out of reach when some do-gooder stopped to pick it up. The prank, the shouts, the laughter, was from another era.

Keith was pleased to have a storyteller new in the mix. A Ron buffer, too. The children were caught in a spell. Keith could see questions in Charlie. Maybe one would burst out of him if they spent more time with Alphonso. But Charlie clung to his silence, even though after that story, his eyes followed the old man for the remainder of the evening.

Outside, the odd fireworks still boomed and showered, but the street sounds were dying. "We should head home," said Keith. Alphonso nodded.

"Let me drive you." Ron leapt up. Alphonso accepted, but Charlie turned his head towards his father's arm and rubbed his nose on Keith's forearm. He wanted to walk. Alphonso and Juliana had farther to go. Felicity stood, unsteadily, to say goodbye.

They'd started down the block when they heard Ron after them: "Hey! Hope we see you both before Christmas!"

"Yes," called Keith. "That'd be good." He didn't feel the words, though. Memories were washing over, so many Christmas Eve parties at Ron and Felicity's, times when Raziel would shine, times he'd feel like going home, times he felt so deeply his introversion and her extroversion. One time he'd played the dad-card to go home. There wasn't a better time of day than that routine of reading with his son at night, and tucking him in, when the world slowed.

He could recall her momentary annoyance, and then saying she would stay, that there was no reason for her to go home with him. How was it that her long work hours energized her, whereas his time spent parenting and writing made him want to climb into bed at the end of the day? He would have been happy making love and wrapping their selves together to sleep. But there were times, just him in bed and she working. Inspired, she said, being a night owl and all. *And all.* What had that meant? His mind went to the times though when he had stayed and enjoyed how Raziel glowed out in the world, and how others mothed around her.

He was glad when Charlie reached for his hand. The touch was good, made him realize his hand was in a fist. He uncurled his fingers and took his son's.

•

Charlie was asleep before Keith finished reading his own child-hood tattered copy of *It's the Great Pumpkin, Charlie Brown*. He pulled up the quilt, and went to the living room, turned out lights for his time of watching city lights, like some watched the stars. Still bursts of fireworks here and there.

Raziel would come home to find him like this. He'd sit on the floor at the window, glass to the ceiling. Lights lined the bridges, the Science Centre's geodesic dome, BC Place Stadium with its changing colours, and the star lights strung over it. Beautiful. Too, the lights of the office buildings, and so many other homes. All the lives, all lived so close, so unknown.

He'd shared a home and a bed with a woman. *Did he even know who she was?*

He looked over his city, and fought down the untethered.

Focus on tonight, some few stars over it, trying to create peace.

Maybe, if someone gave the constellations a chance.

In the depths of the night he came to, struggled to stand, to stag-ger to the toilet. He'd been in the deepest sleep. Had his bladder woken him, or his need to escape dreams fraught with images and broken pieces of the evening? Costumed people, somebody crying in the background, Felicity dressed as Raziel, red hair cut close to her scalp. Gibbous eyes and general spook. Charlie, wan-dering around Ron and Felicity's home, touching things. Some image of Ron's hands and Owl. Throwing the stuffed animal across the room. Laughing. That gesture of hooking his thumbs into his armpits. Dreams or nightmare?

Keith needed to sit in a dark corner, alone, with a puzzle to turn in his hands. To make the pieces fit, pieces he might even be familiar with. Was he? He kept feeling that there were things he knew, should have known, if he could figure them out. Words came to him, words from Raziel: *Felicity doesn't understand Ron. I'm not sure Ron understands Ron. I think he has an artist's heart.*

"Really?" Keith had said to Raz. "You think that? That Ron has an artist's heart?" He wasn't proud of what he'd felt in that moment. It wasn't something he wanted to articulate, not then or now.

She could randomly defend some. Keith would puzzle over such moments, though not for long. She liked to think she understood people. He'd thought that was about her camera, and the sort of capture she did with it. But what was *this*?

He had to let the dream bits go.

He was at the sink washing his hands. The water made him think that he must be awake. But he didn't want to go to the bedroom. He went back to the living room. He lay down, right at the edge of floor by the window, reached for the afghan on the nearby couch. He needed the lights that reached into his windows. He focused on the silence, tried to see into it, past the sadness even, because the sadness was getting big, bigger than it needed to be. Bigger than he could handle. Sometimes he was aware of how some part of himself was protecting him through this time. From what? Coming apart?

There were words he didn't want to put together, words about his life, his son.

If he did fall asleep at last, again, it didn't seem so in the morning. Charlie came into the room, and Keith pulled himself up from the floor, stiff. He'd never felt age like this. He must have slept again, with Raziel in his mind in this early morning dream, with left behind images, a hip, a clavicle, painted toes. She'd had the most beautiful ears. He'd missed them.

He was thinking in the past perfect tense. *He missed them. He had missed them.* He was forgetting those ears. He'd forgotten them. Though he suspected there would be no forgetting. Who'd come up with the phrase *past perfect*? What was perfect? He would forget. The future. Maybe.

Where he'd been missing her, in his being, there felt to be a chasm, an emptying space. Where was the missing going?

Charlie looked at his father quizzically and rubbed morning sleep from his eyes, wondering if Keith knew it was still a school day, even after Halloween. He left the living room to go to the toilet where he flushed noisily and splashed water.

Keith stood. He put his hands to the glass, looking down into the street far below. The day was overcast, grey, Vancouver. He'd swear he saw a coyote slipping off the sidewalk and into an alley down there. What was it doing in the city street? *Looking for something dead*, passed through his mind.

Looking for something dead.

"Beautiful Boy" / *John Lennon*
"Who's Gonna Save My Soul" / *Gnarls Barkley*
"Skating in Central Park" / *Bill Evans*

24

Whatever was of import behind the dreams finally leaked through: the image of Ron, arms crossed, thumbs tucked into armpits. Another image of Charlie following Ron to go to Hopper, gaits identical. Same eye colour didn't mean a thing, right?

Charlie's eyes were remarkable, grey blue, almost unchanged from infancy. Raziel's eyes were blue, Keith's dark brown.

An image came to him: Ron's eyes, smiling, crinkling in that empty-headed movie star way. Though Keith had never really minded Ron's streamlined approach to life before.

All circumstantial.

He got up to make coffee. Coffee was how a day started. Coffee was . . . He lost the thought.

He stood in front of the machine with twenty layers of floors beneath, other people with coffeemakers, unbleached filters in hand, staring at nothing. He needed to see his doctor, to book being tested for STIs.

Charlie stood in the doorway. Normally he would have said *Dad.*

"Son," Keith said, woodenly.

A paternity test, too.

His gut turned.

These thoughts were coming before any real knowledge. He had to learn how to will thoughts away.

Charlie came to stand beside him, and they did their now wordless breakfast routine, Charlie pointing out the particular cereal, Keith pouring it into bowls, Charlie getting milk. Berries, favourite nuts. Cashews today. Maybe Keith should be deliberately pulling out the wrong cereal, forcing some sound from Charlie, but he couldn't bring himself to do that. Everything was too hard. Words and speech would come, in time. The specialist had said that. He'd named this thing: traumatic mutism. Then said to forget the name, when he saw Keith's face, and to drop the worries over the holidays. He'd catch up with them in the New Year. They'd been through a lot. Keep talking, keep reading, keep loving. He'd actually said that, *keep loving*, which won Keith over. Try singing, he said too. He hums? Good.

He needed to trust those words. *You're still you. I'm still me.* And Old Daisy's eyes, brown, full, trusting him. Thank God for dogs.

Charlie sat on his stool at the bar, and Keith poured coffee and sat across from him. Behind his son was the window, and he could look out past Charlie's shoulder.

Normally he liked even the grey days in this windowed place, but he wished suddenly for the camper van, and remembered that one summer night with rain, the sound of it on the roof, the sound comforting.

"In the spring," he said abruptly, "we should . . ." He hesitated. "Maybe we should see if we can buy our own camper van."

Charlie didn't immediately respond.

"What is it?" He forgot, for a moment, the likelihood of an answer.

Charlie gazed at him, forehead puckered. Keith finally sat on the stool and consciously slowed his breathing. What were the right words to say? What was going on behind those eyes? How he wished he could squeeze-hug words out of the beautiful little guy.

He smiled a weary, even absurd smile. "I'm so tired, buddy," he whispered. "I'm so tired. But we're gonna be okay, I know it." He was talking more to himself. Really, he didn't have a clue about anything. He remembered times when Raziel would look at him, as if she questioned everything about him, right down to what was he doing in her house. *Why would he articulate that now?* What was with the retrospective thing? How had he read such gazes from her before now? How had he not seen?

How had he not known?

How had he been so stupid? There was that. What would he have done if he'd known?

Who else knew? It hadn't occurred to him, with what he'd found in her things, that she might have connected with men they both knew. Looking at the postcards, the notes, it felt like another world, removed. But if this was true, and there were so many others, maybe shared friends . . .

He'd actually uttered a groan aloud. Charlie was staring at him, his eyes gone from bewildered to alarmed.

Keith looked into those eyes until he no longer saw the colour, until he saw Charlie. He was eye to eye with him. "Are you worried I'm going to go away again? Is that what you're thinking?"

Charlie's expression didn't change. He shifted in his seat, though.

"Because if that's what's in your head, buddy, I'm not."

Another shift, this one on his face, frown not so deep perhaps.

"I'm not going anywhere," Keith repeated. He dragged his stool to the other side of the bar to sit beside his son. Together they ate their wheat squares.

"I'm not going anywhere," he repeated, voice emerging in a whisper. "Not going anywhere." He could feel his son next to him, tightening.

He was going to have to live a long time, long enough for Charlie to be okay.

With Charlie at school, Keith booked an appointment with the doctor's office for those STI tests. The receptionist asked him about what he needed done, and he mumbled about lab work. Why did she have to ask?

He turned to the computer to research what it took to determine paternity, and the site he found had at-home instructions and an address to send the samples. They made it all sound so easy, with results returned in seven to ten days, and no instructions for what to do after. Nor were there any thoughts on what to say to a curious seven-year-old about why you wanted to take a cotton swab to the insides of his cheeks, both sides, ten seconds of scraping for cells. He felt sick.

His saying, "I'm not going anywhere" felt like a lie with this. But he wasn't. Going anywhere, that is. Except to stand out on the deck, winter now, elbows on railing, for real air, until he was shivering. Was he going to do this? What would he do with the knowledge?

"The dentist showed me this new thing we need to do," said Keith, standing in front of the bathroom mirror in the evening. Beside him, Charlie was about to brush his teeth, toothpaste smeared onto bristles and raised almost to his mouth.

"It's a way to make sure we're doing a good job of cleaning and brushing, taking care of all the germs and stuff." He couldn't believe he was doing this. His son's eyes were on him.

He took a swab and demonstrated putting it into his mouth and solidly running it back and forth over the inside of his cheeks. He placed it in a bag, and passed fingers over to seal. "The people in the lab can actually test how well we're doing with the germs. After we do this, we can brush."

Charlie looked both mystified and curious. He set down his brush and paste with deliberation, and opened wide.

The whole thing was easier than Keith could have imagined after he'd spent a chunk of the afternoon with scenarios in his head to see what might convince Charlie. He popped the second cotton swab into another bag. "Brush away!" he said, and left the bathroom to label the baggie. He'd pulled it off, with relief and shame. With lying. Straight faced. Looking right at Charlie.

He could feel himself believing it had something to do with germs and health. *Shit.*

His hands shook as he wrote the names and date. For a split second his mind gapped on their address, and went into a grey space. Then the numbers came, and he sealed the envelope with the paperwork he'd prepared.

Old Daisy had taken to sleeping across the doorway to his bedroom. She used to sleep by Charlie's bed, but this had to be some nod to what she saw as Keith's need. Yet she wouldn't sleep by his bed — that would set her too far from Charlie.

Keith tripped over her in the dark of Monday morning, another early morning, too wide awake. He felt a need to move and would have liked to be able to go for a walk.

Instead, he made his way to the bathroom, and there was the dog. Catching his balance, his shoulder met the doorway, hard. He forgot she'd be there, even though this change had been weeks now, since they returned from camping. He felt bad after cursing her and on his return, he dug his fingers in around her ears and gave her a solid scratch. The silkiness of the top of her head was momentary respite. A dog's forgiveness was too easy.

Back to bed, and when he got up later in the still dark, his shoulder ached, reminded him that someday he'd be an old man. He wasn't without company in misery; Charlie scowled at him, already wide awake as Keith entered his room.

Keith had enjoyed their morning routine, his singing "Three Little Birds." Charlie used to join in. But here he was out of bed and already throwing bedroom oddments while looking for his slippers. This would be a moment for Charlie to speak, with his frustration bubbling over, scalding in seething silence. Owl flew across the room. Charlie tore at his pajama bottoms and off they came. Found some pants and pulled them on without underwear first, and then exploded in tears at the thought of having to start over. Keith turned to look for the slippers, and found them, just as Charlie stepped, and sounded a sharp crack.

The truth stick.

The main stem had split, and Charlie stared at the almost-mirrored two pieces, his ribs heaving. Shock ceased his tears, for a moment.

Pain took hold, big for his seven-year-old self, bigger than he knew what to do with. Keith could feel all the layers of his own, too, the layers he knew and understood, and those he didn't. And that made him feel Charlie's more so. One needed the sheer body size to fit in the stuff of all that.

He wasn't sure when to wrap his arms around his son. After the initial shock perhaps? He couldn't even fathom his own sense of fresh grief and uselessness over what was essentially a stick they'd found. In a world of many sticks, how had this one come to mean so much? How could it have this power over them, child and adult?

He put his arms around Charlie then, and Charlie let himself be hugged. It was good to hear the tears finally released. Keith's shoulder grew wet.

At last, he handed Charlie the slippers, which he pulled on with a concentrated focus, the familiarity of the motion seeming to ease the pain back to its usual demands.

Still. The morning sat on some edge, and Keith suspected its crash was imminent, down either side. That could mean just about anything. With a sideways look to check out how this was going to go down, Keith picked up the two pieces, one in each hand, and placed them side by side on the bedside table. The motions were ritualistic.

"Let's eat." He stood to go to the kitchen.

Where he discovered that Old Daisy had emptied her water bowl over the floor. Did that have something to do with being stepped over? He started to do the cleanup. Had to take a breath, slow himself, and mop up with Old Daisy's nose stuck into his side. When she got bored of that, she pushed her bowl around, slopped the water again.

What was going on today? He felt a need to shove, to push, to move. Instead he cleaned up, and it took long minutes. Charlie had not followed him, not come out of his room, so Keith went to check. He found him standing by the bedside table, wordlessly holding half the broken stick in one hand and the second half in the other.

Keith took the pieces, gently. "I'll fix this, buddy, I will."

There'd been a time when Charlie believed unquestioningly that Keith could fix anything. Those days were gone. He led the way to the kitchen and placed the sticks on the bar. Reached into the fridge for eggs. Nothing. No pancakes or sunny-side-ups to get the week started. Charlie stared, questioning and angry.

They sat on their stools, one on each side of a corner, and Keith stared at Charlie as the boy fiercely put away cold cereal. "We're a couple of grouches this morning, eh?" Sometimes such words helped break a hold.

Charlie's eyebrows almost spoke.

"Right. I'll speak for myself."

If he kept doing this, speaking for both, Charlie would never. Even as Keith pushed down panic, Charlie offered a tentative smile, enough to ease the moment. Until there was a flurry before leaving for school.

Charlie couldn't find his schoolbook, the slim little softcover that came in the large plastic bag with his 'reading record.' It had to be returned on Monday mornings.

Keith saw the corner of the bag poking out from under the small pile of weekend clothing, and he pulled it out and handed it to Charlie. Who howled. Were the tears a result of not finding it on his own? Charlie liked to be self-sufficient. Or at least, he had liked to be. But maybe that wasn't it at all.

"Let's get that backpack ready," was all Keith said, heading to the kitchen to throw together a lunch and snack. He packed without another word, just glad there were a few slices of bread. He hummed. He hoped the hum would soothe whatever was between him and Charlie and even in between the walls of this home. The humming soothed him.

Off they set, Charlie clutching Owl. At school, he thrust the stuffed animal into his dad's hands and vanished into the doorway, last child in.

Back at home, Keith poured himself a whiskey, a satisfying splash into glass, and sat on the floor, back to wall. He opened a spiral-bound notebook, the one that would have entries around the time of Charlie's birth.

In her handwriting: *Beautiful beautiful beautiful boy.* September 21, 2012. He could hear Lennon. Raziel had played the song over and over.

Inked lines had all appearances of being a family tree. No names. So many branches, such a strange drawing.

unto us a child is given

Christmas?

Any child born in the September equinox would likely be the product of some Christmas celebration.

In the familiar pencilled letters, so faint it seemed they didn't want to exist, the words: *does it matter? what matters?* showed up a few pages following, in the midst of a drawing. You couldn't say doodling. There was nothing casual about anything in these journals.

What did it mean?

He was sick of words. *What did it mean? What matters?*

The next page: *we will both have our own lives now*

As he read the words he recalled thinking that after Charlie's birth something had calmed in Raziel. He'd never been able to explain what or how. He'd thought it was about finding the studio space, and the way her art began to flow out into the world, and settle into corners.

Through the next pages, words were gone, and the images kept their secrets, whatever they were. He closed the bulky pages and sat with it in his hands.

So often, through these months, when he'd looked at Charlie, he felt that no matter what it would be okay, that the world would hold them in some way. But he hadn't felt that since the night of Halloween.

He went to the shelf to pull out a family photo album. 2012. A year of turn-around. Halfway through the pages of Charlie as infant, Charlie sitting, crawling, beautiful beautiful Charlie, he realized Owl was still at his side. He scrunched a last bit of stuffing into a better place and kissed the top of the thing's head, a Charlie stand-in. He laughed aloud and felt such a warming love-surge just then.

Like that.

How did this work? Did this mean it could happen again, over and over? Or in reverse, moving from love to what? Non-love?

This human thing of family and connection was terrifying. It was terrifying, too, how meaningless everything could become, if you let it. But what was the degree of control he had over that? Maybe next to none. He felt a great push to fight. He couldn't sit here, sipping and mourning, going through pages all day.

He went to Charlie's room, and began to tidy. He made the bed. Usually Charlie pulled up the quilt, but not today. He picked up the thrown-around clothing, and he folded and put away. This thing of throwing around was so unlike Charlie. The mindlessness of tidying was soothing, and so was the calm that came over the room as he did. But then there were those pieces of truth stick. Charlie had set them back on the bedside table after breakfast.

Keith picked up the two pieces and sat on the bed. This was another day of work unapproachable, and the need to move overwhelming. How was it that movement absorbed sorrow?

The best course with the mounds of grief was to move and move and move, and to be outdoors where it was easier to breathe. For the earlier walk to school there'd been drizzle, but this rain warranted jacket and boots. Inside the jacket was a long rectangle of pocket, the pieces of stick slipped in perfectly, and he was careful not to do more damage.

He wasn't sure why he did this. He knew he needed to walk, it didn't matter where. But why take Charlie's stick? Kid magic stuff, this. Maybe it took him back to that time at the beach, and maybe that's what it did for Charlie. That day in the sun, too long ago.

He set off heading west, found his way to Pender Street, with bookstores to walk by. He had no wallet on him and no pack, was emptyhanded. He was out for the walk. It was enough to see books in windows, smell coffee wafting from shops, see the youth hostels. As he passed each north-south street, he caught glimpses of mountains, clouds snagged by peaks, the red flamingo heads of the working cranes of the port. This was his city. A block south, down Dunsmuir, and there was a church that he passed often. Times before now, he'd admired the stained glass and the Mary statue, too, in an alcove high above the street. In evenings she was illuminated with a string of white lights, hung unevenly, as if a child had set them up there. Bells rang. He'd never quite figured out at what time. It did seem random. Rather like the pull he now felt, to go in.

He walked up the stairs, noted how they were worn. Some people must feel a need to pass through these doors. One was often half-opened, which he'd noticed before, too, and he pushed it open fully and stood still for a moment before entering. He'd never been in a church like this. He'd toured cathedrals elsewhere, but never thought to enter a church at home.

He was suddenly conscious of those sticks inside his jacket. Pieces of driftwood. What made this special for Charlie? Did Charlie bring some magic to it? Or some other being, in his son's mind? Was the stick inherently otherworldly? Mystical?

He'd been thinking that Charlie himself made the thing magic, 'magic' with quotation marks. For years Keith had had his own version of the thinking that we create our own realities, even the unreal of our realities. Lately though, he'd felt a thin edge of questioning *what else?* Maybe he wanted to be able to grab hold of something and shake it senseless.

There were four people in the place — that's what kind of difference this made in others' lives. Right. Four, in this vast shell. One up front by the candles, and three dotted about the seats. Two were women, older, and the third, the one closest to him . . . was Alphonso. His back was to Keith, head bowed, but Keith recognized the scarf, deep green knitted, handmade. In a city full of people, he knew one of the four gathered here.

Well, this was strange, this place both public and private. *Liminal.* Maybe that's what drew him: death pulled one into liminal space. He hesitated to let the old man know he was there. Alphonso's head was bowed, and Keith observed the balding at his crown, under the curly hair that tried to cover.

Best to let him be. Keith took a seat across the aisle, some rows back. When Alphonso stood to leave, he couldn't miss him. Yet what to say? How intrusive was this?

Keith gave up waiting, took a deep breath and closed his eyes. His hand found those pieces of stick in his pocket, and he held on to them, told himself they were just sticks. But they brought Charlie to mind, and he wrapped his thoughts around his boy.

When he did raise his head, he saw that where Alphonso had been was empty. Had he stood and left without seeing Keith? Or had he seen, and thought he shouldn't disturb him?

He'd see him at the end of the school day, and they could speak then.

There was only one other person in the whole place now, the woman who'd been at the candles, and she was sitting.

What to do with those pieces of stick. His hand returned to his pocket. He should go. But there was no one between where he stood and the candles, and he made his way to the tiny flames. He thought he could hear the sound of the flickering, like a long-ago night as a boy, his dad on one side, his mother on the other. "Can you hear them?" he'd asked his dad. "The stars?"

Was his dad amazed or amused? "No, can you?"

His mom had wrapped an arm around him, maybe to re-assure. That he was okay? He wasn't losing his mind? Or, that in spite of losing his mind, he was okay? That life could be normal, even for boys who hear stars? They could grow up and get a job and find someone to love and live in a house with four walls and a roof. But he'd heard those stars, the faint sound. He'd been certain that he'd heard a hum, a vibration. Then voices, many voices, from behind mountains, came to mind, voices with no words. He'd almost forgotten.

His dad had said, "The *stars?*" And looked uneasy.

Keith pulled the two sticks from his pocket, and held them. He brought the two pieces together, like a child who thought they could be made one again. Silly. He scrutinized the two pieces, turning first one, then the other, and ran his fingers over the raw tears of break. In the shadows, the flickering light caused the wounds to appear darkened, even healed. He pushed the pieces into his pocket, took in the candlelight for another long moment, then left. The woman didn't look up as he passed, his footfalls soft.

At home, he replaced both pieces on Charlie's bedside table with a sense of calm that he hadn't had when he'd picked up the pieces earlier. But they were still two, still in pieces. *Let's pretend life has some duct tape.*

Things need to sit before you try to fix them, until you figure out what to do, and what can be done. That's what he would have told someone else.

Alphonso caught his eye at the end of the school day.

"You'll find me there at some point in the day," he said. "The days I don't go aren't what they should be. But if I stop in even for a few minutes, the mysteries begin to feel strangely ordinary — the way it's supposed to feel, I think. As if it doesn't matter that I don't understand." He laughed, with a puzzled note, and wondering.

Before Keith said anything, he added, "Not sure what drew me in in the first place. It had been so long since I was in a church — so many years. And it never felt like this when I was young." He paused. "Did you just wander in through the open door?"

"I did," Keith said. No one would understand about the broken twigs.

"I wandered in, too, a few years ago now, wondering about the bells. They're real, not recorded. It's a sound I've loved since I was a boy. I went in when they were pealing. I sat as long as they echoed and went back the next day again, and the next, too." He peered at Keith. "Crazy thing happened, really. Do you have tinnitus?"

"No." Where was this going?

"That was about a decade ago, I blundered into the building, and at the time I'd had one of my ears full of strange high-pitched sound for too long, maybe twenty years. After that third time sitting in the church listening to bells, a miracle happened."

"No more tinnitus?" Right.

"Better," said the old man. "It's not gone, no. The rushing sound, the thickness, that's still there. But now, if I listen, I have the bells in me, always."

So maybe the old man would understand about the twigs. Even if Keith wasn't certain he himself did.

He didn't tell Charlie about his day, but later, after they'd eaten dinner, Charlie disappeared into his room. Keith could hear his hum, then there were sounds. Maybe Charlie was completing the cleanup. He could be so precise about how his books lined up in their shelves, and the groupings of stuffed friends had to have a story to it.

Charlie appeared in the doorway with those two pieces of stick, one in each hand. He hesitated, then set out across the room on a mission. Was he going to speak? The steps toward his father were decisive.

He stopped, held out one of the pieces, and Keith knew to take it.

"Thank you, Charlie," he said.

His son held the second piece close to his chest. He'd changed into his favourite pajamas, faded, threads hanging from worn knees.

"Thank you," Keith repeated. There were words he was missing.

Charlie didn't nod, but his eyes shifted, and that was enough. He returned to his room and Keith could hear more shuffling, a drawer opening, closing, maybe Charlie finding a place for his half. Then he trudged through to the bathroom to brush his teeth.

Keith didn't move from where he stood. He had no idea what to do next, and felt that if he moved, he'd cause some disaster. He'd felt that often over these months. *What is going to become of us?* He was a man in a gusting wind, holding on to a stick. He should have had his arms solidly around some tree.

Charlie passed through again on his return, such a little person, doing what it took to take care of himself. Keith could hear the rustle of the feather quilt, pages of a book turning. He moved, went to the side pocket of the pack he'd taken to the B&B, to find the smooth black beach stone from Stella. He hadn't touched it since returning home. In his hand it felt like an answer. He knocked on Charlie's cracked-open door, waited a moment, then entered. He placed it on Charlie's bedside table, next to the half-knitted scarf. In Charlie's hands, the stone could do what it needed to.

"This was a gift," he said as Charlie reached for it. He kissed his son goodnight, and snugged up the quilt.

Keith put his part of the stick back into his jacket pocket in the entranceway closet. The stick would be there when he next needed to leave the house, to move and feel air. He could take hold of the stick when he was out in the world. A part of a tree, at least.

Each wire-coil spine of a notebook stretched with bulked pages. Keith turned through paper and Raziel's favoured chalk pastels, thickened paint, too, and collaged bits, scraps of fabric. A photo fell out. It wasn't a photo he would have paid much attention to, but now it stopped him: a shot of a woman, possibly Raz, from hips down, knees together, high heels, and a hand pulling up the classical tweed skirt just above the knee, fabric twisted.

He'd have seen it as an artsy shot. Now he saw it as titillating, albeit Victorian. It might have been the first of a series, and he could imagine where the images would go, intended for someone with an imagination.

He tucked it into the pages, and noted that each entry was dated, sometimes months between one and the next. The first entry was February 1995. She would have been in art school.

I hate this, written in pencil on a school brochure folded into origami, crushed, glued to the page. She rarely spoke of that time. She preferred her work to speak for itself.

He turned through pages to reach the summer of 2000, when they'd met.

An utterly blank lefthand page, and on the righthand side, an August date, and a line pencilled at the bottom: *met a man I could make a baby with   he's that sweet.* Keith checked the date again. Were these words about him?

Sweet.

The next page had a photo of him torn at the edges. She'd taken so many. If each took a piece of his soul, she'd taken it all, he told her. He'd laughed when he said that, hadn't he?

Again in that ghostly pencilled script, meandering over the page, Lou Reed lyrics, about a perfect day, about being glad to have spent it with another, how it was to forget who you were, and think of yourself as *someone good.*

How did she know that, about him being the man to make a baby with? A few years had passed before the possibility. It was more than a decade before Charlie. Had she put him on a shelf to take as needed? *Now I need a baby. Now I need someone to take care of my baby.* She was a boundary-breaking female artist, and he a boundary-breaking father. The new practising father. He'd been proud of them, their family, how they navigated. First about artists being able to make it: *check.* Then about men home-making: *check.* Even if they'd lived what some saw as rather separate lives, together they'd done damage to stereotypes, and sold pieces of the broken-down wall.

She'd started calling him the house-band after someone used the word 'wife' referring to her. She didn't like the word. But 'house-band' stuck; he was a house-band, musicians who'd never play in a stadium, but they would show up night after night to entertain in the stage-less corner of the local pub. Dependable. Good old Keith, playing in his corner, entertaining.

Another page, a photograph of himself from the back.

"You cannot observe something without changing it." Heisenberg.

On the facing page, a photo of him moving towards her.

Can you observe without taking? If she'd thought photographs were made, not taken, would it have made a difference? But she'd believed they were taken. His mind struggled with the difference. As he saw it, the difference would be one of having to be active in the creating, the making, and the act of knowing when to reach out and grab hold — at odds with Raziel's distress over the grasping of some artists, as she saw it.

But perhaps she had other definitions. That was the thing, wasn't it? He would never know. Could never know. He kept hoping to stumble over an answer.

In spite of their reluctance to become two halves, Keith was aware he'd always had some residual thought: that even in the nature of being two wholes together, there was a giving up. He'd be loath to put the word sacrifice to it. Raziel would argue that one could fill the deficit of taking if they were aware, if they were human. By dint of being, she'd said once. What had she meant? Did she really think that one's sheer existence, and the role they had in another's life, could be enough for the other? What kind of ego was that? He recalled how her words often left him pondering, and if she gave an answer to a question, the answer would only lead to further thought, and he'd still feel a half step behind her.

So much faded pencil. Or was that how she'd written, as if the words were to disappear before they were even completed?

a thousand words can't do what the perfect image, perfectly timed, can say. there is too much of me   everything is bright I have no choice but to live life   it is mine. I eat the cake   at the end there is more. flour eggs sugar milk. no secret stuff   cake is too good   Keith is good enough for both of us a good man   he overuses the word   good this / good that so beautifully simple   so steady he keeps me from exploding I envy him   I wish I could be happy in the way he is I tagged along on his ride for a while   no one ever really knows anyone impossible.

He had to stop reading.

It *was* true: one cannot know an other. But he resisted the idea that it was impossible, and the unspoken, unwritten, that would follow, the *why bother?* of it.

Did it matter if you couldn't truly know another? Did that get you off the hook for opening yourself up to them? For trying to know? For wanting to let someone in? For making certain the person you chose to spend time with felt accepted? Making certain they knew, without a doubt, that you were there, you could hear, you could see them?

Had she deliberately not let him in? What was there to be let in *to?*

He'd loved her, even as the love created a need to open his self. He felt mortified at how he'd wanted her, how he'd felt raw so often loving her. How he'd at times fought that.

She'd thought he was perfect for her. His mind sputtered at that, at imagining what that meant. *Sweet. Steady.* For her, sublimating?

How did it work?

Who was simple?

He smarted from that descriptor. How had she thought that through?

Keith is beautifully simple

He turned the page.

secrets: a way to live more than one life   a currency
Im everything Im supposed to be that sense of power when a man
looks at me wants me. I turn one down   put one off
& the look on his face leaves me floating

In even fainter script, really he could hardly read it, at the back of this, the third notebook:

greed: a person wanting someone all to their self   marriage
is ownership   I can't explain that to many people
Keith wouldn't understand   life should be lived with openness
Curiosity! I want to experience as much as I can   what I tell
myself on good days   I don't want to look at someone and
wonder what he's like   I want to know
wonder: is for children.

other types of good days, I know I like the secrets
the not-getting-caught.
every good story needs tension   at dinner last week Keith went
on about Tension   holds it together   he demonstrated with
me pretending to hold a piece of elastic between us held in our
4 hands. See? he kept saying   like this. If one of us lets go then
you know what happens! SNAP but if we hold it just right we can
even lean back and not fall   every story needs this
every life I wanted to say
we need to be true to our selves
why don't others understand this?

This last line was pencilled so finely at the bottom of the page, and trailed up the righthand side to be complete. The journal was turned in his hands as he folded the covers together. He had to close off her words.

Why did he need to read? Each pencilled word, faded as they were, managed to ink into his being.

He remembered that conversation about tension, could relive it in his mind, could recall his own earnestness, could recall too her motion of sitting slightly back, head tilted down, but eyes up to him, as she used to do, watching as he strode around their kitchen. Vague amusement, her look. Maybe puzzled by his being caught up as he was. A smile had come over her face. Was she thinking these thoughts? He should have asked why she was smiling.

The notebooks just created more questions. The greed thing: wasn't it greed to want beyond happiness? Or had she been unhappy? What part of her happiness was his responsibility? What part was hers? What about contentment, a sense of enough? He used to have moments when gratitude washed over him so hard he had to sit. It can't have been the same for her.

Had she told him about marriage being ownership? It would have been a conversation that struck him as significant. Had he felt ownership? His owning of her? Hers of him? At this moment, she had a stranglehold over him. Some sense of her was always with him now, even more than when he'd been living with what he was coming to think of as clean grief. It had been enough to deal with death. He would have preferred to live twice through that type of pain, over enduring this, this feeling that his life was so bereft of meaning that it no longer existed.

But maybe ownership, the idea of it, caused this pain. He had a feeling that's what Raz would have said. If she'd let him in.

Ownership and meaning. Apples and oranges. Two people should have known more about each other. Why hadn't she told him? Why had she been with him?

The words should make the ideas clearer, should shed light. But maybe he was looking for harsh white light, from a shadowless point, and Raz was using other light, blue hour light, to colour her words into something maybe pretty. To her. She wanted to create. He just wanted to know. Black and white. Sun at midday. No more shadows.

He opened the pages again. Maybe if he read all, he could end this pull, put the words aside somewhere.

it's all about the signalling   looking for long seconds
a touch.   a few shared words some fragment of dissatisfaction
Im clear about what Keith means to me   I will never leave him
they have to understand he is number one   they have to let
me go when I walk away   they are always free to walk
away too   that is freedom   you can walk away

He closed the journal.

That night he dreamed, vivid and surreal: he opened the door to their bedroom. Raziel was out, he knew. Or thought he knew. But no, she was home, on their bed. He couldn't remember her return. She must have been so quiet, was the dream-thought.

Charlie wasn't there, anywhere in the apartment. How he was certain of that, he didn't know.

She was on her side, turned away, but he could hear her breathing and a soft moan, and knew she was satisfying herself. She knew he was in the room, and she didn't stop; he knew that, too. Some part of him must know this was a dream.

She didn't stop, and she wanted him to be there, so he lay on the bed beside her. After she'd finished, when he touched her, when he took his time touching her, when he closed the space between them, her anger flared. How she hated when he tried to take her from behind.

While he knew so much, how had he forgotten this? *Stupid dream man.*

She'd convinced him she loved to see his face, but he wondered. She had her favourites, and he was schooled. She knew his, too. *I like it like this with you*, she'd say. In the dream, he gave up. He reached for her to roll over, but when they were face to face, she only smiled. She didn't laugh, but he could hear it ringing in his ears. That feeling of being boxed by her, about how it was to be between them. Had it always been that way?

He awoke with that in his mind. *It was a dream.*

He stumbled to the bathroom, turned on the lights over the mirror and instantly dimmed the bulbs. He didn't want to wake up, he didn't want to be asleep. He got the water running to hot. He stepped in, let the water sluice over, easing what he was feeling. He stood for long minutes.

Steam billowed when he finally turned off the taps and pushed aside the curtain. Had he forgotten to turn on the fan? No, it couldn't keep up with the long minutes he'd spent with heat beating his shoulders, steam so thick that all he could see was the dull yellow bulb, ancient beacon in the storm, surreal lighthouse. He a shipwreck.

Siren curves took shape in the steam. Hips, a beautiful back with vertebrae ridge and shoulder blades and soft spots.

The steam pulled apart, image disappeared. He'd swear he heard laughter. But it wasn't, couldn't be. He wanted to be awake enough not to hear things he shouldn't.

He stepped out of the bath, shaky, and wrapped himself in a heavy towel to sit on the enamel edge, grateful for the weight of towel on his shoulders.

There'd be such moments, when a towel could soothe. Or unexpected birdsong. Or an easier fit of a worn key in a lock. Every day there were such moments that passed almost unnoticed, but he couldn't let them. That meant being so still that he could catch a ride with the moment. That's the only way it would be. If he hurried, if he was angry, the moment would be lost, sand between fingers. Forget the laughter, feel the towel.

He'd stood by the shower long enough to feel the chill of cooler air on warmed flesh, and he slipped quickly into bed: the insomniac could not let such a moment go, with the body lulled to a point of cooled near sleep. It might bring the mindlessness, the silence he needed.

"So Long Baby, Goodbye" / *Blasters*

"Blow, Blow Thou Winter Winds" / *Bob Crosby and the Bob Cats*

"Thank U" / *Alanis Morissette*

This Wednesday, pickup game night, Trev wasn't in. "Count me out," he said. "I have some flu thing."

Keith hoped there'd be a few who'd shown up at the south Vancouver games last season. But no matter. After a few times of play, he'd get to know them.

He went down to the locker to dig out his gear bag, and stopped by the mailboxes. Another card from Auntie Nele. She sent them every couple of weeks now, and they made him sad.

And then the envelope from the lab, the test results. It took him long seconds to pick it up. Upstairs with the hockey bag over his shoulder, and he put the mail on the kitchen bar, and instead opened the bag. No one would be sharpening blades at that hour of the night. He located the skates, ran a thumbnail over an edge, and shaved off a curl. Sharp enough.

He began to spread the gear on the balcony to get air at it, thick goalie pads saturated with years of games. He sprayed all with deodorizer. Raziel had never wanted the gear anywhere in the apartment. The smell was bad, true, sweat, the sharp odour of artificial ice, and boyhood, winter nights, and beer. Talk, rumblings, laughter. This time, opening the huge bag, seeing it gape, created a connection to times gone, before.

Why was it so strange to dip into such pieces of past? Why did it seem as if it might be easier to forge new ways to be? Reconnecting with past, bringing it up to date, felt harder than moving into the new. The past, Raz, that life, was so distant. He felt a new thrust of despair. No, it wasn't new, it had been a half breath away, lurking for these ugly days while waiting for the words in that envelope, the test results. His Charlie was at times feeling like part of this past and like someone distant in all that silence, and . . . He fought completing that thought. He held a skate in his hand and wanted nothing more than to be on the ice, the excitement he'd felt as a kid rep player, stupid enough to think he'd be in the NHL someday. To ask for skates for Christmas and to open the box and smell the leather.

He put the skates back in the bag, and the unopened envelope with yet another card from Auntie Nele he put with her last missive in the drawer.

Then he opened the second envelope.

Tonight he drove to Grammy Moth's, Charlie with his favourite pillow and the *Seasons* book, Owl under his arm. Grammy Moth would tuck him in to sleep on the couch after reading. When Keith had picked him up last week, he was sound asleep, and he'd carried him to the car to return home to his own bed, wrapped in a quilt. Last week, Keith had met up with Norah and Trev to hear blues at The Pat pub. But this week was first pickup game of the season.

"You enjoy yourself," said Grammy Moth. "Charlie and I are going to have fun."

Charlie had jammies under his coat, pant bottoms gathered into big socks, gumboots to his knees. Keith hugged him at the door, hugged him hard, harder than he'd intended, and Charlie pulled away with the slightest of motions.

At times now, when he hugged Charlie, his son felt to be such a separate person. Though that was as it should be. Keith should write about this someday. But tonight with this fierce hug, Charlie was a mix of questions and fear, anger even, as unsettled by his dad's hug as was his dad. Keith caught himself staring at him, trying to read him. But he couldn't read this. He wasn't sure of the language. Charlie looked at him, steadily, unnervingly.

Keith backed out of Grammy Moth's door to sit in the car, to pull himself together. He felt Charlie's stick in his pocket. Afraid it would break again in his pocket, he pulled it out and set it on the dash.

Grammy and Charlie were watching from the front window. What did they think he was doing, sitting, waiting? For what? He started the engine, did a half honk, waved, pulled away. He lost sight of the two, framed in the window.

"New guy!" someone called out.

"Keith," he let them know, and handed over the evening's fee. Players were always happy to see a goalie show up.

"Beer after," the fellow, Philipe, said. "At the Boondocks. Down the street."

It was a good group, some younger, a few older, lots of amiable chirping, some creative cursing, some less so. The first period went by quickly. A couple of other players showed up, late. Keith recognized Ron, drunk, and louder than usual, obviously not new to the group. It took him some minutes to realize Keith was on the ice, on the other team. He flashed a sloppy grin.

In spite of beer-league status and no contact, there was a lot of good-natured relocating of other-team players from one point on the ice to another, and the occasional resounding crash in the corner boards, followed by shouts and jeers.

He wouldn't be suffering that type of soreness, but after a few sprawling saves, knew he'd be feeling it the next day. Last period, he could see Ron strongarm one of his Ds, and bear down the ice directly on him. He prepared for the save.

And got a nasty shower of snow.

"Next time, just score!" he called out. "If you can." He had to remove his mask to wipe.

Ron had skated off, but he looped back. "I can score. Can you save?" Off he went.

Somebody waved at him to go to the bench, and Keith heard a mutter of *idiot* as he went.

"You okay, man?" someone asked.

"I'm good," he said, replacing his mask and trying to scrub Ron's words out of his ears.

End of the game, ice emptying, Zamboni rumbling, Keith pushed the goal net across the ice to put it to bed. He liked the moments of clatter to the dressing rooms, the sudden silence of buzzing fluorescent lights turned off over the ice, the acrid smell of ammonia.

After, he sat in the dressing room, enjoying the sounds, the words around him, the ripping of tape from socks. Someone caught the edge of his shoulder with a tape ball, like a big kid. These were big-kid times. Keith tossed it on. Around him, words took apart the game, with laughter and tones of disbelief. Ron was in the other dressing room.

He was more sore than he could have imagined, but the feeling had the wonder of pulling him out of his head where he'd been for too long. He could handle a painful body.

The room was almost empty, sounds of splashing showers done, loud and deep voices exiting down echoing hallways, and now just Keith and two others. "You coming, man? The Zamboni guy will lock up soon. Don't want to shower in the dark and find yourself locked in."

"Right."

"See you at the Boondocks?"

"I'll be there." Tempting to ask if the guy thought Ron would be, too. But why should that stop him? Maybe Ron had had enough, and would head home.

The heavy door swung shut, and Keith started to unbuckle his pads. Long minutes later he stood under steaming water. Sure enough, Zamboni guy showed up with a shout. "You got five!"

"I'll be gone," Keith called out, and hustled his aching muscles.

Outside, he shoved the gear bag in his trunk. He'd forgotten Charlie's bicycle was still in there from months before. He put the hockey stick across the back seat, and drove the few blocks to the pub. He walked through the doors. The players were loud and circled around the big screens reviewing the evening's sports highlights. Or in the case of the Canucks, the lowlights. Middle of the week, and they were the only patrons. No Ron. But then he emerged from the men's room, stopped by the bar to whisper into the ear of a waitress and brush his hand over her backside. He went to a seat at the far end of the table. A good place for him.

Too soon, he lurched out of that chair and made his way to the empty one beside Keith.

"Sorry about earlier," he slurred. "The snow."

"That's always an asshole move." Keith pushed his own chair back and away from the other man.

Ron didn't seem to register the action. "Nothing personal. You know. S'all fun."

The soreness in Keith's body threatened to enter his soul. He held on. "You know," he said slowly, "you've always been some kind of asshole."

Ron was bleary eyed. "You're right. Raziel used to say that, too." "Did she?"

He nodded as a child would. Emphatically.

There was a sudden tightness in Keith's hands.

Ron went on. "So what's with our boy not speaking?"

Keith wrapped a hand around his glass, and took a long draught. "Our boy?"

"This not talking thing. That's bad. You should know about that, all that blog-stuff you do. Parenting. You know all about it." He slurped his beer, then studied the glass, dipped his fingers in and extracted a fruit fly. "What the hell, in the winter. Where do these little shits come from?" He flicked it away. "Felicity says you should take the boy to see somebody who can help. Felicity knows these things. She always knew with Lucy. Always. She was a good mom, Felicity was."

"You're drunk," said Keith. "I don't know all about parenting." He needed more alcohol in him. "And he's not *our boy*."

"He's not *our* boy," Keith repeated, as if the two of them were in a room of their own, away from the men watching on the screen, talking about whatever they were talking about. "I've been finding out things about *our* Raziel. Finding that maybe *our* boy might be yours."

Ron squinted. "What're you talking about?"

Keith refused to repeat his words. "I hope I'm wrong," he said.

Did he want to tell anyone, though, that Charlie wasn't his?

"You don't know what you're talking about," Ron said, suddenly sobered. "You're talking out of your ass. You were always Raziel's number one. None of us had a chance." He pushed back his chair, stumbled while getting to his feet, muttering. He staggered to the waitress, muttered to her, too, kissed her cheek, pulled a bill from his pocket, pushed it into her hand, and headed for the door.

Keith's own words had left him shaking. And watching Ron with the waitress.

He reached into his pocket for his wallet. He'd given his cash for the hockey fee. As much as he'd have liked to walk out, he had to find a card to pay.

"You all right, man?" the nearest guy said. Right, Philipe, team captain. Keith appreciated the concern but at the moment just wanted out. "I'm good," he said shortly.

At least the delay would mean that Ron would be gone when he got outside.

The waitress was right there with the machine, as if she'd noticed. He paid, nodded goodbyes, left.

Outside damp night air hit him. It was late. Starting to rain, too. With his head down, he didn't see Ron until he'd almost stumbled into him.

"Hey, can I get a ride home with you?" A drunk and whiney tone. How had Keith ever seen this man as a friend?

"I tell you that I think you might be the father of my son, and you stagger away, and now you want a ride?"

"It's not true, it's not." Ron stood like an aged donkey, shaking his head.

Keith's fist was all on its own now, no glass of beer to hold to, no hockey stick. No Charlie's hand. It shot out and caught Ron's nose or jaw. Something that crunched and bloodied, and he didn't care what. After that first, a second and a third hit. More blood, more satisfyingly ugly sound. Then arms were reaching around him, hands pulled at his sleeves, Philipe's voice in his ear. "Come on, man. We need to get you home."

Keith's arms windmilled, and he reached blindly for the handle of his car door. It eluded him. He could hear shouting and was vaguely aware that somebody was pulling Ron to his feet. He heard words from somebody near Ron, words about *you had that coming*. Then they were pushing him into a car, taking him away.

Philipe stayed by Keith until the car was out of sight, then he pulled open the car door, and Keith sat, hoping he'd stop shaking. He'd never hit someone like that. His knuckles ached, and he wrapped his other hand around them, tight. "Should I drive you home?" Philipe asked.

"No," said Keith. "I've only had one beer. Not even finished it."

Philipe studied him. "This shit between you two, whatever it is, isn't good. Maybe don't leave yet. You're ready to kill someone."

"I need to pick up my son," said Keith. "But thanks."

Philipe moved the door slowly, popping it closed only after a check to make certain Keith was clear. Keith watched him return to the pub.

He did sit. The rain hardened, drops running together, and loud. He couldn't see through the windshield and was closed off from the world on the other side of that glass. He could see a rectangle of light that was the pub doorway, every now and then as it opened and spat out another man. Voices. He couldn't make out words. How strange: for a moment he had a flash of what it was to be a kid, alone in a dark bedroom of the past, rumble of adult voices down the stairs, evening company.

Flash gone.

Charlie's stick sat on the dash. He reached for it. Then didn't touch it. He wasn't in the right mind to touch it.

He understood Charlie's grief over the breaking of it. He felt it himself. Felt like, if he did touch it, it might break even more. So he kept his hands in his pockets, and grew colder. Time to go. He should go. He looked at his phone, to make all this fall into some place. It was late. Grammy needed to sleep, night owl or not.

But still he sat, and a thought came, a wisp, some preview of a real thought.

What would happen if I turned the key and drove off? Off course. To some other place. North? East?

He tried to push it away. But the thought came into focus, sharp.

The thought settled, along with some concrete, into his feet. Inertia. He was finally losing it. It had occurred to him, through the weeks before, to wonder how he hadn't. Charlie, no doubt, made him hold on. But that sense he'd had, since the birth of this boy, that some piece was explicitly right with the world now . . .

He'd lost that. *Gone.* His world wasn't what he'd believed.

This was what he fought. And losing Charlie with it.

Maybe he was going to lose him anyway. Maybe he'd already lost him.

He wrapped his aching fingers around the steering wheel and rested his head on his hands. It was as if he could feel again the pipes of the hockey net in his hands, pushing it across the ice.

This turn in life was like that. He had to push. He lifted his head and stared at the wheel in his hands. Then at the stick Charlie'd given him. That healed bit of it, the wound, as he'd seen that day in the candlelit church, came to mind. He did pick it up then, ran fingers over it. He had to go back, go to Grammy Moth's, wake up Charlie, gather him in his arms, take him to

the car. Drive. Park in the underground. Carry him up the elevator, tuck him into his own bed. He had to. The steps, the pieces,
to the days and nights. One followed another. The push had to
be. He wrapped his fingers around the stick, felt the gnarled bits,
rubbed at them.

Maybe someday the feeling of this abyss, this loss that he and
his boy could both fall into if he wasn't terribly careful, would go,
would disappear. He had to build to fill it, to cross it. There was
no walking away for him. He turned the key.

Twelve minutes later, he pulled up outside that gingerbread
house. It was after midnight, and felt later. A parking space,
enough to ease in the car, was right out front. He had to pause
before climbing out of the car. He couldn't recall ever having
seen this parking spot empty. It shook him up — not a rational
thing — and left him feeling as if some curious half act of abso-
lution was in the air.

He needed to get it together. He started to open the door, and
then closed it. Within seconds of stopping, the windshield was
again covered in rain, all was blurred, the shine of lights blended
into each other. He wondered if Grammy Moth might see in his
eyes the thought that had come to his mind.

How it had come, the thought to go, to walk away. He knew,
knew, that his love for his boy was such a part of him that if it
were cut from him there'd not be enough left.

He struggled for breath then until a sob choked out, and he
held onto the steering wheel like a teenager, hands at ten and
two. *Breathe.* But he couldn't. He started to shake so hard, and
his ribs heaved. He moved and moaned and bawled, and held
onto the dash, until the storm passed and left its alarming stillness. Outside, still raining.

He had to clean up the snot, and snapped open the glove
compartment, reached for old napkins there. His face must be
red and blotchy. More time passed. He opened the door a crack,
hoping the cold air would work some sort of miracle. He had to

get Charlie. He finally opened the door and kept his eyes down. He didn't want Grammy to see into him.

He knocked softly, heard stirring. Grammy came to the door, wearing plaid flannel under a heavy robe. If she'd had any doubt that he was going to return, it didn't show. He saw only her pleasure in seeing him. "Would you like a cup of tea? We can sit in the kitchen and let your boy sleep."

He surprised himself by saying yes. He was afraid of being alone right then. And they sat under the heavy glass in the kitchen nook and listened to the rhythm of the rain, slowed, and a little Bill Evans piano leaked through her speakers. He told her about the game, and she told him about the stories she had shared with Charlie and the popcorn they'd made. She said nothing about his face, his reddened eyes. He started to breathe again.

Charlie had shown her how to play chess, she said. "No one has shown me before," she said. "Without a word, he taught me."

27 *"Dance Me to the End of Love"* / *Leonard Cohen*

"Not Yet Dark" / *Bob Dylan*

"Love is All Around" / *Hüsker Dü*

Keith laced boots to head to the Alexander Street studio. He pulled gloves over his hands, still bruised and sore. Snow was beginning to fall. That didn't happen often in this city, white drifting on grey background, clouds thick.

Sam noticed the snowflakes on his shoulders as he came through the doorway. "I had no idea. Been working. Prabh made some coffee. Join us."

"I will." The studio, with the smell of fresh coffee, was cozy.

Sam set an envelope on the desk at his elbow, and Keith fought a sudden sense of finality. It was different to be in this place now, and he wasn't in a rush to see those images. He tucked the envelope into his pack, unopened. "I'll be with you in a minute," said Sam. "I have a quick phone call. But we can talk with coffee."

Prabhjit rounded the corner. "So good to see you." She gave him a warm hug. "Can I show you my new project?"

First though, she introduced him to the photographer who'd taken Raziel's space. The man nodded when introduced, but didn't join them. She left Keith with the images on her pad and went to get mugs of coffee. Third one in was a snap of Raz half-turned away. She never allowed her photo to be taken this way. She couldn't have known a lens was on her. He didn't ask Prabhjit about this. He moved on.

"Do you miss her?" Prabhjit's voice was a whisper. Before he could answer, she rephrased, with a mutter of, "Sorry. You must miss her, of course."

The shadows in the next photograph caught him, taken in brilliant sunlight and black and white, worthy of comment. But words didn't come. He plumbed his own depths. Where was the sense of missing?

"Yes," he said. "Of course." He moved on. Cityscape, at night. *How do you miss someone you didn't know? What part of them do you miss?* Who could he even ask such questions of? What would have been Raziel's answers?

Prabhjit had photographed a piece of card with words scrawled across it: *Photographers need to resist their own knowingness, and to remystify what they do.*

Sontag was under the words. He remembered Raz reading Sontag's photography book.

"Do you remember these words? Raz talked about the knowingness." Prabhjit scrutinized him. But he couldn't fault her the unappealing hunger he felt from her just then.

"Not really," he answered. "I suspect she talked about other things with you here."

"Maybe," she conceded. "What did you talk about?"

"What's for dinner, what did Charlie do today." He read the Sontag words again, and added, "We used to talk about our work. Before I started to write about parenting." That had been a shift. "Do you think about *knowingness?*"

"Every morning I walk to work here, and it takes twenty minutes. Unless I stop to look at things." She laughed. "While I walk, I practise stripping away what I know. I end up stopping often. I try to see everything as if I'm a little child. You're lucky. You have Charlie to discover with. Raziel used to tell us about how curious he was."

Keith didn't say that that wasn't happening so much these days. He missed that curiosity on walks, and tried to see through Charlie's eyes. He'd point out the light or shadow, words on a wall, or the one-legged seagull. Things that Charlie would note, if he were speaking. But Keith hadn't put knowing and unknowing together like this before this moment, and this moment was one of gratitude. What a strange gift to be handed by his boy, not that that had been Charlie's intention.

"So by the time I get here, to work," Prabhjit went on, "I like to think that my eyes are made new, so I can see what the day holds. Sometimes, for several weeks, I'll force myself to take the same route, which I've never liked to do, not from the time I was a kid walking to school every day, and I make myself find something new that I've never noticed before. Look." She reached over the giant book on her working table, a visual journal much like Raz's, and opened it to a collection of black and white photos with one coloured item in each image. "I did this for one hundred days, down three blocks of Cordova Street.

"Do you have time?" she asked, as Keith moved to a closer chair.

"I have time," he said, staring at an image of a dead pigeon at the edge of a sidewalk, gutter filled with winter leaves. One leaf was red. On the next page an ugly white brassiere, utilitarian straps, big enough to nest that pigeon, shapeless and collapsed, white embroidered flowers with pulled and loose threads. "Raziel shared that quote with you. What do you think she thought of the words, the idea?"

Prabhjit paused. "I think she loved to find and share. Ideas would catch her interest, and we'd talk, and a handful of words from her could keep me busy for months, but she'd be onto the next thing. Maybe she knew she was going to have a short life." Her voice drifted off. She looked uncomfortable. "I'll get more coffee."

Keith caught a glimpse of Annika in the open doorway. What was the expression on her face? She moved away quickly as their eyes almost connected.

He turned the pages, three blocks of Cordova, and the unknowing.

That fevered speech of Raz's, and the momentum with which she worked. He'd wondered how she would age. Pixie with high

270

energy. People buzzed on her. She did move from one interest to the next, photography being the one constant. So much could be processed and lived through photography, her life medium, a perfect fit.

He wanted his thoughts not to go further. He turned the pages, absorbed the images, the working cranes of the port, corners of buildings, signs, living pigeon with the dead.

Prabhjit returned, poured, and set down the coffee pot. Sam came in, phone call done. "I've been meaning to go through those, too. Would you mind?"

"Please," said Keith. Sam pulled up a chair.

A series of alternating photos: graffiti one day. Sprayed over the next. Back in place. Gone. Reappeared and angrier. Painted over again. A week's battle. "She's good, isn't she?" Sam said in a low voice. "Detail, and context."

Prabhjit left them with the photographs. She had to take a call. And Keith stayed maybe an hour. "Come by anytime, man," said Sam.

Not long ago, Keith had intended to see this as a lasting connection, a piece of legacy. But legacy had a cloud, and what felt like it might have been his was now blocked. "Thank you for the photos," he did say.

Annika was nowhere in sight when he let himself out of the studio. The scarf he'd given her was hanging on a hook in the new workmate's space. Had she given it away? What did she know?

At home, he took the photos from the envelope after wiping down the bar. How strange to think that after a life of working with a camera, these were the last. Does a photographer think about the last photos they'll ever take? The film had been completed with Charlie's efforts, a beginning.

He held the photographs in his hands. That day of entering the hospice, with the first photo of the care aide coming towards them as they went through the entrance door, and the next of sun streaming through the window, caught probably seconds before the sun had moved on. The beams cut a sharp line, and Keith saw himself crossing that line. Half of what Raziel accomplished with her work was the timing. He was stepping out of the beams, clear and stark, and into the shadowed part of the room. Such a strange photograph. Typical of Raz's work. The wonder in it pulled on people.

Next, Charlie emerging from an explore of the bathroom, his face so strangely aged. Keith had to pull the photo closer. Raz had caught a shadow you're not supposed to catch in a six-year-old's face: how he might look at seventeen. And thirty-five.

Keith set the photo down again but felt himself drawn back to it, and again. Was this what Raziel had wanted to see? Once, when she was sick in those short weeks, he'd mentioned Charlie's looming September birthday. Her eyes had teared at his lack of sensitivity. But surely they both knew she wouldn't be around by the second half of September. He'd been thinking she might put together a gift and card. But he couldn't share the thought.

The next photo made him cry out. She would have taken it when he was napping in that chair across from her bed. He had to get up, move, look out the window. Walk. Breathe. *Breathe.*

Was this him?

Raziel had a reputation: she took photos that caught the way her subjects wanted to appear. Some photographers have the ability to see souls; Raziel recorded what they yearned to be. She could hide brushes with poverty and disappointment and draw the hope that was supposed to be for the young.

But this sleeping person in the photo isn't me. He had no recollection of her taking this. His head rested on his hand, his elbow propped on the armrest of that big chair, Charlie asleep, too, across him. His face was one of lines and worry and care, and something else, broken in him. It left him with an intense sense of not knowing himself, even some pity. He didn't like to think of himself with pity. He could recall another picture she'd taken, shortly after Charlie's birth, in which he was also asleep. He needed to see that photo again and went to the shelf of family albums she'd put together, each marked with a year, and opened it.

Yes, a different man, young, filled with dreams, thinking he'd arrived at the place. He'd felt content, had believed that life had settled as it should. How is it that when life is busy and full, with no time, or little time, for reflection, it seems to be caught in a place that will not change? In the exhaustion of having a small child to care for, it did feel as if the boy would always be small, and life would always be busy. Was there a word for that?

Filled with dreams.

Delusional.

He felt small spirited with that thought. He should have more respect for himself, for who he'd been not long ago.

He set the recent photo next to the one in the album. The older photograph had been taken later in the day, Raziel's blue hour. She'd wait for that time; she knew how that light changed through the seasons, filled with colour, intensity. And more forgiveness.

Or perhaps, with this recent image of him, the difference was just age and sadness. Age and sadness showed.

He'd heard what people said, had read what people said, about Raziel's abilities as a photographer. At times he'd met the subjects of her photos and been shocked to see their faces, their expressions. He'd come to think of her ability as her gift to them. If that was true, then the gift didn't extend to him.

He forced himself to see it from her point of view.

She was dying. She knew she was dying. And he was asleep.

He pushed the album back into its space, and returned to the photos in his hand, the photos taken by Charlie: Grammy Moth. *Heron and Me.* The woman was looking at him and laughing. In the next photo, she was patting his arm as if he was a boy. The angle of a photo taken by a child wasn't flattering, but real.

He had a frame he could put this in. Charlie might like it for his room: his dad and his Free Granny, a photograph of now.

But of the other images in his mind, the memories, some real and some grafted by words, he was weary.

An hour's drive from the city, there was the last regional beach where you could have an open fire. He packed the box of journals and postcards, threw in a section of newspaper, a lighter, a thermos filled with coffee. He would stop at a convenience store for a wrapped bundle of split logs and fire starter.

Everything packed ready to go, and Old Daisy sat alert on the back seat. She whined and licked the back of his ear before settling onto her blanket.

The beach was empty except for a few locals with their dogs. Old Daisy momentarily lost her stateliness and dashed off, but returned in short order. It was a cool and sunny wintry day, a break. If he were here for any other reason, he'd call it a beautiful day. Maybe he should anyway.

He balled up pages of the newspaper, set the starter and the logs over them, and poked in the lighter. The flames ate the edges of paper and then struggled, found the starter and came to life. He felt numb as he placed the first postcard on the logs, and watched it turn colour and curl over on itself. Ash rose upward, sparks, too, as he fed the cards to the flames, piece by piece. One fluttered out of his hands, landed in the fire with the picture face down, and the flames hesitated at the edges. He could read the words, in loopy hand: *Stolen waters are sweet, and bread eaten in secret is . . .* The flames took the words, and he wished he hadn't seen.

He tore pages from the notebooks, the journals, too, and fed the flames. Finally the box. The fire grew, warmed him. He sat on one of the logs, fireside. He opened the thermos and drank. He'd forgotten that he'd stirred in a handful of cocoa chips to the coffee, and was pleasantly surprised.

He sat on the log and watched the flames, watched until they died down, cocoa-coffee gone, too. He was breathing rhythmically, with a sense of something having passed. *You can walk away.*

Snowed and conical, Mount Baker rose to the south. Waves lapped the shore, gentle. Clouds floated. He caught a drift of salty air. An old couple cycled past, some distance away on a gravel path, on matching beach bikes, and he was grateful he could enjoy the sight.

V

•

Holidays

They always put up the artificial tree on the first of December, but this was the night of the twelfth. Charlie stood at the window, looking to the full moon sailing, and the colourful lights in apartments nearby. It was close to bedtime after a late dinner, Keith was about to tell him to get on his pajamas and find a book. Instead he said, "I'm going down to the storage locker."

Charlie nodded, and Keith locked the door behind him. His task wouldn't take long. Raziel had bought a dolly, and four plastic tubs fit perfectly on it. Two held the tree, and two the decorations and lights. He took all four up the elevator.

"All right!" said Keith. "Get your jammies on now, because when we're finished, you'll be so tired you'll just fart and fall into bed."

Charlie giggled and dashed off for pajamas. Timing of that four-letter F word could make things happen if used infrequently, a parenting trick worthy of its own post. He should make note of it. But didn't.

Keith found the string of lights that went across the full length of windows, and tucked them up into the hooks already in place. "Do the honours." He handed the plug to Charlie. He turned off the overhead lights, and could hear Charlie's intake of breath.

They pulled green stuff out of the bins. Might Charlie speak about the tree?

Some of the branches went into funny places, ending up lopsided and top heavy, a clump of more lights in the middle, and a lot of shiny decorations on what must be a favourite branch. Keith knew better than to redistribute even if it dragged to the ground. There was an untouched bin that could be finished tomorrow or put away. Once the tree lights were also plugged in, they sat to feast on the glow. Charlie was silent, but glowing, too.

"I'm going to take the dolly back to the locker," Keith said, no word about the plan growing in his mind. He returned with the air mattress they saved for visitors, the one he'd meant to take along in Hopper back in August.

He showed Charlie how to use the foot pump, and assembled a quilt and sheets. "Go get pillows," and Charlie ran off, eyes shining. Keith did pajamas, too, they brushed teeth together at the sink and spit with gusto, Charlie got Owl, and they climbed under the quilt, Old Daisy's forepaws crossed over Charlie's knees.

Keith told the story of how he and Raziel had found the treetop star, vintage 1950s, at a garage sale. Charlie didn't miss a word, stared at the star through the whole telling, then seemed to fall asleep, but after some long and quiet minutes passed, they must have been minutes of thinking, he got up from the air mattress and padded off to his room, reemerging with something in hand.

For the briefest of moments Charlie invoked Stella as he handed that rock back to Keith. As Keith's fingers closed, once again, around that collection of surfaces, it came to him that he'd actually gone to the garage sale all on his own. Last minute something had come up. His hand tightened around the rock then as if to hang on.

How had he forgotten that? How did he remember the story as being the two of them? He'd picked up that star in its red cutout vintage box, shown it to someone. Maybe another person at the sale? He looked over to Charlie, asleep, and marvelled at how he'd related the story as truth. And it hadn't happened at all. How we tell ourselves stories.

Keith couldn't fall asleep, and he watched the lights go out over the city, except for the few, like theirs, that remained. Others trying to keep monsters away, too.

•

After dropping Charlie at school, last day before the holidays, Keith went to Chinatown with a yen for almond cookies and was walking back, cookies in pockets, when he realized he was a block away from Grammy Moth's. More than once she'd said to come by any time. Now might be any time.

"I have cookies." He held them up, in crinkly cellophane.

Her eyes lit. "Come in for tea."

Nina Simone was singing "Baltimore" in the corners. There was a large pot of tea keeping warm under some puffy fabric thing, as if she'd known. Rain rattled the glass in the eating nook, perfect complement to Simone's *ain't it hard* words about America.

"Honey or brown sugar?" She held up both.

"Honey'd be good." He set the almond cookies on the table.

"Oh, I love those."

"It's like we planned this."

"Everything about this friendship was meant to be."

He handed her the milk. She poured and handed back, a rhythm. "My mother died a long time ago," he said. "Raziel's mother's never cared much for Charlie. We needed a grandma."

Maybe an angel. He'd long suspected that Charlie might believe in angels, and it had scared him. Did it still?

She paused. "Maybe she's afraid to care."

He didn't want to speak about Miriam.

The woman stared back, questions in her eyes. The lying thing. Already, he was tired of this legacy: this was his future, wasn't it? Keeping so much hidden.

A long silence.

"What is it?" she asked.

It had been a relief to tell his story to Stella. But he'd known that Stella would never be in his neighbourhood, never meet his friends. And he had some regret over saying anything to her.

"I can keep secrets. I have many that'll go to the grave with me," she said. "But don't tell me anything. Unless you need to."

What if he told her that sometimes he woke up in the middle of the night, too long before the sun, and all he could feel was the coldness of thoughts of people you've loved, who you thought loved you — in the way you hoped — but not. Of how ugly was the big-people world, how self-centred. How for some, others seemed to be interchangeable, and not one was . . . He stopped himself. Grammy Moth had an expression on her face, anxious and waiting.

"It's hard to tell. And hard not to." This much he blurted. He could stop there. Or proceed slowly, wait to see if anything felt different. Would ears appear in the walls? Would it all go dark? Mostly, would Charlie sense if there were words spoken? Or did he already? Now there was the other secret, the deeper one, and it held its own secret, the one he'd leave untouched.

Finally he said, "Raziel wasn't who I thought she was."

Her face shadowed. "Ah," was all she said.

She removed the cookie from noisy cellophane. The first bite was crunchy, and she had to pick up crumbs, brushing them from tabletop to palm and into a napkin. The act appeared to require focus.

He opened his own packet. He couldn't say anything about Charlie. He and Charlie were still the same people. That's what he'd been telling himself these past days. The strange thing was that he did feel to be the same, and Charlie was the same. Even with the lab report locked into his fireproof lockbox, hidden under his will and other papers. What to do with it beyond that, he couldn't think. Yet.

He took a bite. He wasn't hungry.

"Thank you for the cookie." She dipped it into her tea, had another bite and closed her eyes. "You're a good father." Her eyes opened. "You know that, don't you?"

"I do my best. But have tough moments, times."

"Do you think you will let Charlie know? About his mother?"

"Someday. Maybe. If I feel that the world and I have put enough love into him to let it land okay."

"Why?" she asked. "Why do you think he needs to know?" Her eyes held an ache.

He had to think about words for this. "I think I'm going to be one shit of a widower. It's not going to make sense at some point. Not for those who see me, watch me."

"Maybe it'll shift somehow."

"Maybe." He thought of how he'd invited this woman to join them for Halloween and she'd said no. How she'd insisted on staying home, with the excuse of handing out candy. There were things she denied herself. Pleasures, even little ones. There was some core to her that he couldn't know.

"It's hard to keep secrets, isn't it?" he asked. "Hard to live with them, I've always thought. Maybe I'm wrong. They come with a cost, I think."

"I carry many," she said, musingly, over stirring her tea. "I wasn't making that up. Maybe I take that cost for granted." She went silent.

"Do you think they are like some form of energy if you hold on to them? Maybe they change shape, but they can't go away? That they continue to affect, maybe even generations on?"

She didn't answer. She appeared to be thinking.

He sipped the tea she'd placed in front of him. Some craft project was spread out on the table, glue, fabric, ribbon, browned and brittle edges of a dismembered children's book. He wanted to move on to another subject. "What's all this?"

"A friend of mine," she began. "There was a fire in her home. Most of it burned."

He leafed through the book with care, a 1960s copy of *The Night Before Christmas*, ashes flaking out. "What are you going to do with it?"

She picked up several miniature picture frames with glass. "I painted these red. And cut out bits and put them inside."

She held up an image of Santa Claus stepping out of the fireplace. "I'll attach this velvet ribbon to make new decorations. There was nothing left of the old ones."

He held the book to his nose, but the bitter smell of housefire made him pull away.

"Do they know you're doing this?"

"Not yet. I helped her clean out the house, and she cried when we found this, and threw it in the bin. I retrieved it."

"You have your own decorations up, too," he said, noticing small red lights twined around greenery over what must have been a mantel in the early era of this home, fireplace long filled in. There were photos he'd not noticed before, lined up, of two girls as babies, children, teens. They appeared to be twins. "Are they yours?" he asked, surprised.

"Yes," she said, after the slightest hesitation. "I bring out the photos for the holidays. Maybe that's a strange thing to do." She pointed to the twin on the left. "Katya." She took a breath. "Was killed by a drunk driver on the night of her high school graduation, and my other, Pippa, she disappeared, two years later. I don't know where." Her voice faded away.

Then she straightened and put her shoulders back. He watched this motion, tried to make sense of it. Did she do this every time those words had to come out of her? After the focus on his own self, just moments ago, he felt winded with her words. When he could, he stood to look closer.

"I learned that they're not really ours," she said, so softly that Keith had to listen to the words over in his mind and stop from asking her to repeat. He'd heard correctly.

"No. I should speak for myself, not for anyone else. I'm sorry. I should have said that I came to believe that my children were not really *mine*."

"But you were — you are — their mother."

The moment stretched long. She sipped tea. Maybe she needed motion as much as he did.

How old was she? Her face belonged to someone who'd never cared to protect herself from the sun. No, she'd lifted her face to it as often as she'd been given the opportunity. And she loved to laugh; that all lined up.

He fought his sense of sad when he envisioned her here by herself. A sense of waste, even: human love was a treasure. Perhaps the most seemingly ordinary love was the most treasure. Had he always thought this? Before Charlie? Before now?

He couldn't imagine Charlie being in the world, and he not knowing where, never hearing his voice. No, he knew now what it was not to hear his son's voice.

Dare he ask? "Their father?" he said, tentatively.

She didn't answer. She said, "Forgiveness. People will tell you about forgiveness." A long pause. "Maybe you're all right with that. Maybe you'll work that through."

"Did you?"

There were such gaps in this conversation, between the words. She was struggling.

"No," she said finally. "I didn't want to take the time. I didn't feel I had the time it would take. I needed to put the energy into other things. I thought perhaps time would reveal a path." She gave an odd laugh. "Or someone would come up with a cure." She didn't say whether she was talking about the girls' father or the driver of the vehicle. "You do what you need to." She stood, and reached for his empty mug.

While she rattled dishes, he picked up that book again, and turned its pages, came across an image of the children emptying stockings. "What about this bit?" He held it up for her to see when she neared.

"That's a keeper," she said. "Cut it. Use the glass as a template."

He marked it out, and cut. Couldn't remember the last time he used scissors like this.

The friend whose house had burned: when she saw these pieces on her tree, would she remember the book before the fire?

Or after? Reading with her children? Throwing it away?

Grandma Moth was looking at him curiously. "You're still a hopeful person, aren't you?" She didn't wait for an answer. "Don't let that go."

Nina Simone now singing about how *heaven belongs to you*. If you love right.

Yes, the hopeful person. The one who doesn't poke around. Trusting and loyal. *Simple.*

No, he didn't want to lose that person; that was who he was. But he had to protect him a little better than he had.

He liked the feeling of those scissors in his hand.

29

"Sheep May Safely Graze" | Ron Cooley

"Auld Lang Syne" | Jimi Hendrix

"4am" | Our Lady Peace

Felicity called with the annual Christmas Eve invite. Keith should have known. His instantaneous response was no. He couldn't ask if her husband would be there.

A muddle of plans surged into him, for a big-hearted potluck. With Alphonso and Juliana and this Mrs. Moth they'd met, he told Felicity. Grammy Moth, they called her now. Words came out of his mouth: he had to change it up this year, he added. Norah was around for the holidays. Often Norah and Trev went to stay with her mother, but this year they'd decided they needed to be with Keith and Charlie. Auntie Nele understood.

Both he and Charlie wanted to be at home. Felicity said she understood, too. He wished her voice wasn't quite so wistful.

Of course, when Trev and Norah were in town, they would join in the festivities at Ron's. Felicity didn't bring that up. He wanted nothing to do with Ron, and he was getting better at this lying thing. Though as soon as he was off the phone, he'd make it all true.

What had Ron shared with her of that moment outside the pub? What story did he create about the aftermath of another friendly hockey game that left Felicity with the idea to invite Charlie and him to dinner? How had he explained the black eye, the messed-up nose? Any words about their conversation?

He called Grammy Moth. Could she come? Yes. And Alphonso. Yes for both. Retroactive truth took shape.

Last minute, he invited a neighbour he met in the elevator, with arms full of groceries. Keith asked about his holiday plans, and he said he had none. His name was Nicolas, he said.

"You can call me Nic if you want, though." All his family was in Hamburg.

"Come to apartment 2105, late afternoon-ish," Keith told him. "Bring anything. Or nothing. Or someone, if you want. The more the merrier." Later, he said to Charlie that there was no way he could *not* invite someone named Nicolas.

Keith bought a smallish and round turkey, and worked on his annual stuffing of brown rice with Italian sausage, almonds, and dried cranberries. He and Charlie could have a chill leftover kind of Christmas Day, he'd decided. Lots of doing nothing, with Trev and Norah. Hanging out looking at tree lights seemed just right.

The Eve potluck would be people time, and the turkey would be their contribution. Charlie helped him. His smaller hands pushed stuffing into the cheesecloth bag in the cavity, and no small amount on the floor and counter, which set Old Daisy slurping. By late afternoon the apartment was filled with the sizzle of juice dripping in the roaster, the hiss of the gas fireplace, and the fragrance of pine-scented candles.

Grammy Moth showed up first, an enormous dish of macaroni in her hands, surface crisp with roasted cheese, hot pepper flakes, and bits of potato chips. She'd picked up on Charlie's predilection for crunch.

Charlie had his camera on the table by the entrance door, and he picked it up to take a photo of each guest as they came in. Grammy Moth posed. Alphonso and Juliana, too. Juliana stuck out her tongue and leaned in close. She was carrying a basket of buns.

"She helps me bake," said Alphonso, and he set down his jug of homemade eggnog, rich with bourbon and rum.

"We should do a bakeoff some Saturday," said Keith, as he lifted the cloth on the basket to take in a long draught. Yeast, with sweet richness. He set it on the bar, and found knives and butter. "Here."

He had to remember to feature Alphonso as a grandfather in one of his posts. Should he jot down the idea? Most of the time now, his head felt blank, and an idea had become a gift. He should start to pay attention. He went to find pen and paper. He scribbled, and tucked away the note, an action that had been familiar for so long renewed.

Charlie was getting braver with this photo taking, and climbed onto a chair for a new angle. That positioning, so like his mother, gave Keith a start. It was good, he told himself, even as it sat oddly in his gut. What other pieces of his mother might be around corners? The neighbour was the last to arrive, and after that Charlie set aside the camera.

Neighbour Nicolas poured the wine he'd brought, even a mouthful each for Charlie and Juliana in some tiny glasses he found in the cupboard. Keith was astonished with how this fellow made himself at home, but he liked it. Raz would have done this, invited a stranger-neighbour. Keith was not uncomfortable with having done it.

When Charlie accepted his wine glass, he held it up in the air, and Grammy Moth noticed, and smiled. "Indeed!" she said. "A toast! Yes. To you, Charlie." All toasted. "To friendship, and to friend-family. And Merry Christmas!"

"To friends old and new, and to family." Keith raised his glass. "Merry Christmas."

Grammy Moth sat in the comfy chair, pulled up to the fire. Keith found Charlie's eyes; a memorable holiday was what Keith most wanted to give him. Nicolas — he couldn't call him Nic yet — was laughing at some words of Alphonso's.

Alphonso, Nicolas, Charlie, and Norah sat on stools, and Keith, Grammy Moth, Trev, and Juliana put their plates on the coffee table. Amazing how Grammy, so spry, could take her place on the floor with the younger ones. Nicolas connected an eccentric collection of Christmas tunes with the Bluetooth, and Keith had to ask for the playlist.

Through the meal and the time shared, Keith could hear snippets. Nicolas was getting some sense of what they were about, with some whispered and brief words. Whatever was being shared was with the best of intent.

A year earlier he would have marvelled at this collection of human beings coming together. And in years past, with Raz, eyes would be on her. She loved to tell a story, and everyone in the room would turn her way. Now, the group was in shifts of trios and quartets, sometimes just two with heads together. Laughter would happen, and they'd switch up. Halfway through eating, Trev ended up moving beside Norah, and Juliana shyly sought out the seat next to Charlie.

Three in the kitchen did dishes, and Grammy Moth read with the children, a new *Night Before Christmas* Keith had bought.

There was a knock at the door. Norah said, "Who'd that be?" Keith grabbed a tea towel to dry his hands and made his way to open it, to hear loud and off-key singing. Lucy, belting it out. She appeared to be holding up her mother. Felicity had her drunken spark, and was singing, too. *"Father Christmas, give me the money! Don't muck around. We're gonna beat you up . . ."* But by the end of the third line, the spark had disappeared. Felicity sang even louder, drowning out Lucy. Did she realize her lyrics were wrong?

Keith felt a jolt, then long seconds trying to overcome. He had to look around behind these unexpected guests. Why were they here? They were supposed to be at their own party, at their own house. Was Ron right behind them? No sign of the man.

"You're drunk," Keith said to Felicity.

"Of course she is!" shouted Lucy. "It's Christmas! Can we come in?" She pushed her mother though the doorway, and followed close without waiting for an answer. "We had to come," she said. In a sort of ghastly whisper, head turned away from Charlie's direction, she said, "And a shit Christmas it is."

Keith attempted to put this together in his head.

"You like The Kinks," said Felicity. She was looking to Trev and Norah as she spoke. She really was quite drunk, more so than Keith could recall. "Someone let us in the front door," she said, almost apologetically but too far gone to be.

All Keith heard was the word 'us.' He had to open the door again at that and peer down the hall. Empty. "Ron?" was all he could say, turning back to Felicity.

"Ron," she echoed in a disgusted tone. She made a noise as if she was about to throw up, and Lucy wrapped an arm around her, boots still on, and hustled towards the bathroom. Keith felt like he was going to be sick himself even as he, on some weird level, noted that in Felicity's hair were flakes of snow. *Merry Christmas.* It was, still. Out there, anyway.

The bathroom door closed behind mother and daughter, and Keith turned to his guests, caught Charlie's eyes on him, perturbed. Old Daisy had slunk, arthritically, behind her boy's chair.

When Lucy emerged from the bathroom alone, singing gone and her face anxious, it occurred to Keith that the real adults in the room were Charlie and Lucy. Count Juliana, too, with her curious big eyes. The longer people lived, the more messed up they were. Look at Grammy Moth now, inching away from Alphonso, a person she did not even know, afraid of who-knows-what. The evening had taken a corner.

No doubt Grammy Moth had reasons. But he didn't like how his mind leapt about at this point. He wanted to hold on to the feeling of festivity. He focused on Lucy, now standing at the bar, hands grasping the edges as if she needed them.

"Are you hungry? We have plenty to eat." There was sudden silence in what had moments before been a room filled with mellowed voices, cutlery meeting crockery, a hum. But with the invite, there was a shift. Even though no one else in the room knew what Keith knew, there was a sense of intrusion. Or maybe that corner he was feeling. Or was it all in his mind? That came to him, as he looked face to face. Alphonso held his gaze momentarily.

"Really," Keith said, holding out a plate to Lucy, young Lucy — what did she know about her father? Wherever that man was. What did she know about her mother? Who was some kind of functioning alcoholic. Really, this had been brewing for years. Felicity had always been brighter, shinier, when she'd had a few. Ron had never discouraged that. Had maybe encouraged, really. Now she was too bright and shiny, even for the season.

Then, too, maybe Lucy had a brother. Now there was a thought he hadn't put together before. Charlie. Ron. Lucy.

Felicity emerged from the bathroom, looking as if she'd washed her face. She reknotted the scarf around her neck. "Ron. You asked. He's busy." She patted the scarf. "Lucy and I thought we'd join you. We wanted more than just us." She looked at her feet, still with boots. She bent to pull them off. And muttered, "No. Damn. Ron's not busy. I lied. He . . ."

Lucy stared at her mom.

"He didn't want to come. Is what he said." Felicity wavered ever so slightly, standing in her stockings.

Lucy stepped closer. "Yeah, he said that, and a lot more. You *saw* him packing. You saw as much as I did."

Felicity shrunk. "I'd like a drink."

Lucy put her arms around her mother. The two children were watching, Charlie with his mouth open. Juliana sidled closer. Their elbows touched.

Norah stepped up, a small mug in each hand. "Alphonso has made the best eggnog. I think you need to give it a try." She held out mugs, one with little more than a mouthful.

The women accepted the mugs, and Lucy held hers to her mom's. "Merry Christmas, Momsa," she said, after a breath.

"Merry Christmas," Felicity murmured. She did appear to have sobered some small degree.

Norah filled mugs for others. "Grammy Moth?" she asked.

291

Grammy looked at the mug, gave Alphonso a quick glance, and all of her reservation slipped into place. Keith fought an urge to shake her gently. What was it about Grammy and men? His sadness over this surprised him, made him wonder. Made him think he should set it aside. It had nothing to do with him. What was this in the woman who set out a sign to be Free?

Norah poured a fearless nog for herself and went to sit by Trev, who reached for it, took a sip, handed it back and said, "I'm going to get my guitar and play all six chords I know." He was back in minutes, and the next hour or more was spent singing, laughing, making up lyrics.

Juliana was yawning, and her grandfather suggested they go home. "Santa won't come if we aren't asleep. We need to set out the cookies and a drink." She nodded sleepily.

Charlie looked to his dad, and Keith's eyes slid to Felicity's. No one had given a half thought to this: every Christmas Eve, Ron was the guy with the red, threadbare Hudson's Bay suit. He'd disappear from the festivities, and at some point there'd be a thumping sound on the roof or a smattering at the window, a shout or song, and he'd show up, talk with Charlie and any other child visiting, and rumple his hair to a mess. He'd switch up his usual booming voice to another kind of boom. One year, when they'd had to stay home with Charlie sick, he'd phoned and asked to speak with Charlie. The man had had his moments, Keith had to give him that. Felicity'd always given Charlie a packet of steel-cut oats, mixed with sparkles, to take home and leave out on the balcony. "So Santa can find you, and the reindeer can have a snack." They'd seemed like the right people to spend the Eve with.

Alphonso didn't seem to pick up on the sudden quiet. He was gathering their coats and scarves and gloves and mittens, saying thank you for the evening.

Grammy Moth looked from face to face. Nicolas spoke up. "I should be off, too," he said, though he'd only just opened a cider. He slipped out, in the middle of Alphonso's *Buon Natale*.

"You might want to get your jammies on," Keith said to Charlie as he closed the door. On his way to his bedroom, Charlie paused to go close to the window. The stadium was lit seasonally red and green, with its usual star lights over top. He looked up beyond, higher. What was going on in his head?

Felicity sat close to Lucy, who stood to wrap an afghan around her mother, and then sat beside her again. She whispered, and Felicity shivered.

Maybe she could be topped up with a hot toddy, some comfort. Really, what was she going through, with her spouse? Miserable ass that he was, leaving her, presumably, on December 24, packed and walked out, it sounded like. Keith headed to the kitchen to see if they had honey. He had a lemon.

Charlie was rounding up his bedroom flannels when there was a sharp knock at the door. At the sound of a loud, "Ho ho ho!" Charlie appeared in the doorway, hiking up flannel over his backside.

"Why, it's Father Christmas!" said Grammy Moth. Charlie stared. This was no ordinary Santa Claus. "Come in!" Grammy said. It took a full minute to realize what was happening, and who. Felicity stared, too, as if the man at the door was absolutely real and magical. Lucy was laughing.

Father Christmas's robes were thick, long, all deep crimson velvet, edged in some sort of fur. His hat was trimmed the same. He held a burlap sack over one shoulder, and had long curly hair and beard to match, and the most shining eyes. Which caught on Charlie. "Ho HO!" he cried. "My boy!" He took the sack off his back and reached into it. "Merry Christmas, Merry *Merry* Christmas." He handed an orange to Charlie, who reached for it, but could not take his eyes off the man.

Father Christmas handed out oranges to everyone then, and he looked around the room. "There was another child here, no? The reindeer and I will visit her house now, leave an orange there. But first we'll sing, and you can go to sleep." He reached into his sack and pulled out a tiny wind-chime-looking instrument and a mallet, and sounded out the first four notes of *Silent Night*. Trev strummed his guitar to find a chord that might almost fit. With a baritone, Father Christmas led them through the first verse, then slipped out the door, closing it behind him and shouting out to some invisible reindeer, if Keith was hearing correctly. Lucy kept them going with the second verse. She hugged Charlie goodnight, and he went round the room for hugs from all. Then he knelt at the coffee table with the orange, digging his thumbnail into the top, pulling the peel down and off, breaking the fruit into its segments. He set out all the crescent pieces rocking on their backs on a bright holiday napkin from Grammy. He pushed the napkin into the centre of the table, and created a wall of candles and books around it; he'd remembered his dad's story of orange-the-morning-after. "I'll make sure no one eats it," Keith whispered to him as he followed him to his room. He tucked him in, gave him a hug. In his mind he could see the orange that Charlie'd handed to his Momma last Christmas morning, the crescents all left out in preparation and given, gifted. "This is all dried up!" she'd said, and popped it into her mouth. Charlie watched her, waiting for the response he expected. Even after she chewed and swallowed, he waited. It didn't come.

All the times that was true, the waiting for a response that didn't come, Keith had ignored. He'd said nothing. But felt he had to make up for them in some way. This was a Christmas he didn't feel that.

Grammy Moth worked to remember the words to the third verse. Then Trev created some irreligious fun, still with his wandering chords: *Hockey night! Goalie night! In the net, Keith's a fright! Round yon far end, take the puck . . .*

Keith left the bedroom door ajar so Charlie could listen still as he fell asleep on this surprising Christmas Eve.

Some minutes later the front door opened and in slipped Nic, in jeans and button-down shirt. No one said a word as he picked up his cider, and sat. Grammy Moth stared at him. "You surely have the spirit of Saint Nicholas in you, you do," she said softly.

Nic looked a bit bashful, but not unhappy at her words.

Keith filled a small mug of eggnog and handed it to her. "You really should have some of this, Grammy," he said. "You will like it."

She looked at him sharply, then appeared to make some decision, and took it.

"I promise I won't tell Alphonso that you tried some," he said.

She looked faintly embarrassed. "Oh," she said, as if trying to make light of her uneasiness over the man. But all else she could say was to repeat the monosyllable. "Oh." Then she sipped the rich and seasoned nog. "It is good." She settled back into her chair with another sip, followed by another. "I'm not sure what I'm afraid of, really."

VI

●

Next summer

30

"Children's World" / *Maceo Parker*

"My Way" / *Sex Pistols*

"Three Little Birds" / *Stacey Kent*

Felicity shared Hopper again the next summer, and they made their way across the country, with different roads and discoveries.

As the days passed with Cat and Eryk, and Keith and Charlie spent time with Baby Billie, the right moment for the ashes didn't make itself known. Before they left Gimli, Keith slipped the box from the cabinet and asked Cat if he could leave it with her. Cat understood. She and Eryk would let the ashes go someday that felt right, she said. Or they'd wait until Charlie was older. It would happen when it should, she said. Keith didn't know how relieved he would feel until that moment of passing the box to her; he didn't have to do this.

But the place felt right, even if the timing didn't. The prairies didn't have the shadows of mountains. They were overexposure, quick dips of sunset and dark, and too much light again. Nowhere to hide. Was that why Raziel had left? Mountains were replete with hidden surprise.

Had Raziel cared for peace? She seemed to have wanted something else. Raziel had done the living, and soul building, of her choices.

Soul building. It was new to him to consider that this was what life was about. That moment of striking Ron was not a soul-building moment. Or was it? Soul building wasn't light and happy business. Mostly, it was hard. Because after soul building, there was inter-soul business, the stuff of what happened between people. That night he almost didn't go back to Grammy Moth's was still with him; he'd always be building what was between him and Charlie.

At some point they could return to Cat's lake and let the ashes go into the depths. Or release them in the midst of a prairie thunderstorm. Or Cat would, some morning on a whim, if it felt right. He'd said yes to that possibility. Cat had reassured him that he wasn't alone in this. Eventually, a time would come. Time was a friend who knew when to show up for coffee.

West side of the Rockies they stopped to spend a night in the mountains. They'd left Old Daisy with Norah and Trev. She was getting old, as much as Keith didn't want to think about that.

They organized their packs and tidied the van, closed the curtains, locked, and set off and up, early in the morning. Charlie took care with putting his truth stick in the side pocket of his cargo pants, and silently followed his dad.

The day was one year from the day of taking Charlie's mother to hospice.

Charlie wanted to sign his own name on the hiker logbook at the trailhead. He waved his hand in the air for the pencil. Keith, knowing the purpose of the book, always thought the signing had an ominous feel. But Charlie scratched his name into the logbook, drew a sun with a closed-mouth happy smile and, after looking at it, Keith did the same.

Charlie set a sturdy rhythmic pace. He did occasionally stop to look around. Keith commented on what they were seeing, but the wind tossed off his words, and he'd repeat in a raised tone. But it wasn't at all in keeping with the silence of the cedars and firs, and after a while he stopped.

Charlie didn't need to hear every thought that passed through his mind. Instead, to let a thought pass through in quiet, to examine it before rushing to the next, seemed right. Keith's ideas seemed to work with the pacing of his feet, and even with the rhythm he found when the path took a steep incline, and they began to climb, to catch exposed roots in their hands, to pull themselves up. Thoughts slipped into his mind, and after moments of pondering, slipped away. Charlie was nimble, and Keith was both envious and cheered.

The day had begun overcast, but as they ascended, the sun came out. By the look on Charlie's face, and his drawing of the sun with smile, Keith guessed he'd been hoping for this. They stopped to slurp water from their bottles, and to share the bag of mixed nuts. Charlie pulled a bag with favourite Gordal olives from his pocket, and Keith laughed. He must have gotten them from the camper fridge.

Keith took two and handed the bag back. Charlie held up his olive, large and green, and then took a small bite from it, with a savouring shiver at the saltiness. Then another bite, drawing it out as long as he could. Keith did the same. A silent exchange, no less for lack of words.

They reached the summit with an hour left of sun, and set about putting together the tent, then lighting the stove, a pronged torch screwed atop a tiny can of propane. Keith wrapped a windshield of tinfoil around it, secured with stones, and they listened to the whispering hiss of gas, then the bubbling of water, over the wind in trees, and distant burble of stream. They opened packets of dried dinner, poured in boiling water, resealed the packets, and wrapped a jacket around to cozy while the meals rehydrated. They sat on rocks, waiting and absorbing the home they'd created for the night. Keith couldn't remember when all around him was this quiet. Charlie appeared to be at enviable ease in the silence. There was wind, it wasn't still, but it was at peace.

They ate slowly, even with their hunger from hiking, sharing a smile every once in a while. This quiet was what he'd been feeling from Charlie for months now. And now he'd been invited into its depths, into the voicelessness. Charlie kept looking at the hemlocks, their upright blackness and spires, and he finished spooning the beany lentils out of his dinner pouch, then wrapped it up, placed it with care in the bag they'd established as 'garbage,' and stood to walk.

Keith watched him move to the base of a tree and pause.

Charlie took a close look, running fingers over the bark, examining the ends of low-hanging branches. Then he bent to open that side pocket on his cargo pants and gently pulled out the stick. He made a movement as if to set his stick on the ground, but he hesitated and turned to his dad. His look made Keith go dig in his own pack and pull out the rain jacket. Yes, his part of the stick was there. He'd promised himself not to forget it again. He made his way over to where Charlie waited.

Charlie placed his stick at the foot of the tree, Keith followed his actions. Charlie stood a moment with bowed head. Keith did that, too. Charlie flashed his quick and beautiful smile. He'd remembered Grammy Moth's words about replacing the gift of the cedar.

They sat against a log to watch the sun set. The shadows over the mountains around them stretched, leaving peaks in golden light. So many shades of green, then shadows of grey and memory-green. Minute by minute the light changed over the pass, an outstanding peak illuminated, gold, burning pink, deepening hues in layers of ridges. Blue. Grey. Before it grew completely dark, they zipped into their sleeping bags.

In the middle of the night, Keith awakened Charlie to the moon on the clouds around them, around their summit-island, and they stood, shivering witness, before returning to the tent. In the morning they awoke with the sun. Even with the early morning birds, there was still the mountain silence holding them, deeper than birds and burble. They breakfasted, took down the tent, and set out, packs and hearts lightened.

After a lunch stop and through the afternoon, their steps settled into a slow rhythm. There was a sign for a toilet. Keith pointed to it. Charlie shook his head. But he'd want to see it, mountaintop toilets fascinated him. Two summers ago was all about the enormous metal thing, dumpster sized, a throne overlooking the view. Charlie had spent a good twenty minutes taking in the panorama, and letting it out.

But this was a cedar box set in the trees with the low buzz of a couple of happy flies that Keith would have to batt away. "Stay close," he said. He set the toilet paper roll nearby and settled in. He could hear the parting of branches as Charlie explored the vicinity, the crack of a twig and another, the unsettling of a surprised bird. The afternoon moment smoothed out to forest sounds. He loved to see Charlie's face as he registered these, looking up, looking about, joyful and open.

Keith finished, put down the heavy wooden lid. Replaced the toilet paper in his pack, found the hand sanitizer.

It was the quietest. No snapping. Bit of a wind in pines, and the sound stopped him. If there was one sound in the world that made everything in him go still, this was it. He closed his eyes. Long after he was dead, this sound would still exist. It was a sound that simultaneously connected every era and facet of his life, and filled him with both yearning and the sense that everything would be all right.

He opened his eyes. "Charlie?"

He pulled his pack back on and into place, started to walk. "Charlie? Son?"

Walked farther. Farther again.

What had he been thinking, sending him off, a boy not speaking? He stopped still, hoping to hear snapping twigs, anything, and called out louder. "Charlie!"

The wind through pines sounded high over him, more now, gustier, sun gone behind clouds. If he listened hard enough, he could hear the stream they'd passed, and would have to return to for water. But no footfall, no human sound.

He fought down fear. It had no business with him, wasn't useful.

Instinct said to head to the stream. Charlie loved water.

Keith started to move faster and faster. He called out, re-traced steps.

"Dad!"

Keith stopped, his breathing heavy, hearing from memory.

"*Dad!*" Not memory.

The call came again, not from the water, but from beyond, up an incline, and with wonder in the tone. "Come see this!"

Keith's eyes stung with a sudden strange pressure, inside, pressing in at the sides. He registered that it actually hurt, and was an utterly new sensation. Then his face was washed wet with the tears, pressure gone.

"I'm coming, Charlie—I'm almost there."

He began to climb the path.

Keith's collected playlists can be found at the QR code below.

Acknowledgements

Much gratitude to Daniel and Myrna, and to Janice and Terry—
early readers, generous in time and spirit.

And to Rachel, who shared her photographs of the Icelandic
Punk Museum in Reykjavik.

In these times, when creating books is a subversive act, a
heartfelt thank you to Kelsey, Naomi, Natalie, and all the team
at Freehand Books. You are brave and wonderful.

And to Amy T., who continues to find homes for my strays.

I also wish to acknowledge BC Arts Council's support for the
writing of a short fiction collection, and the one story that grew
and grew and grew again.

Discussion Questions

1. Charlie seems to be naturally predisposed not to question the mystical in life, which is something that Keith resists, even as he appreciates nature. He doesn't link the natural with the mystical. Do you see Keith as becoming more open to the mystical in his own life, through the story? Do you see this as being useful in his life?

2. Keith and Raziel had consciously decided not to live with the idea that marriage is about "two halves." They gave each other room to breathe, and privacy and respect. How did this work for them? Is this something that Keith would do again? Is it possible to truly know someone?

3. In spite of Raziel being a central character in many ways, we only ever encounter her through her written words and photographs, and through the lens and reading of Keith and other characters. Do you think there might be other ways to see her?

4. Journals. Have you ever found someone's journal? What would you do if you stumbled over someone's journal?

5. Statistically, men are more likely to have affairs than are women. But these numbers have changed in the last decades. Can we still think of certain behaviours and choices as gender-specific? How does this story explore these ideas? Does this exploration resonate with you? Can we make assumptions about sex and gender?

6. Other than the foray with the camper van, the story has a very urban setting. Cities are often considered colder and more anonymous places to live. But Keith creates multi-generational community around him and his son. How does he do this? Do you think it's possible to have real "community" in a city?

7. The mini-playlists of several songs at the outset of each chapter connect with Keith's former life as a music reviewer. Music plays a role in his life, and songs and artists are frequently mentioned. Does art—in any form—have a role in grief and mourning?

8. Grief is the private processing of loss, while mourning is more public, ritualistic, and shared. Both need to happen in times of loss. Can you see both of these paths in the story? What shape does each take?

9. Charlie stops talking after Keith goes away. Does this seem like a fitting response to what is happening in his life? How does Keith's response to Charlie's silence compare to the reactions of other adults in Charlie's life (his teacher, Grammy Moth, Ron, etc.)? What role—if any, and in your experience—does silence play in grief?

10. Keith must come to terms—or something like that—with the lack of any real answers to his questions. How does he live with this? Is this a conscious decision on his part? What is the role of acceptance (or time, or love) in dealing with what life has offered up to him?

11. Cat says that, "It's a mistaken belief...that women are natural mothers." And Raz told Keith that he was "the best mother." This speaks to nature and nurture. Do you see Keith's approach to parenting as male or female, or does such classification exist?

Alison Acheson lives in Strathcona, Vancouver, down the street from Keith and Charlie. She has published works for all ages, and *Blue Hours* is her twelfth book. She taught in the Creative Writing School at the University of British Columbia, and now pens a Substack newsletter, The Unschool for Writers.